LENA WOOD

ELIJAH CREEK & THE ARMOR of GOD

VOL. IV

STORM GOD

Cover art and map illustrations by Daniel Armstrong

Printed in the United States of America
Published by Braughler Books LLC., Springboro, OH

First printing, 2019

ISBN: 978-1-970063-23-3

Library of Congress Control Number: 2019911262

Ordering information: Special discounts are available on quantity purchases by bookstores, corporations, associations, and others. For details, contact the publisher at:

sales@braughlerbooks.com
or at 937-58-BOOKS

For questions or comments about this book, please write to:

info@braughlerbooks.com

Braughler™
Books
braughlerbooks.com

All praise and honor to
The Gentleman
Who binds the Pleaides and loosens Orion

GREATEST APPRECIATION

The Fam for support during the long, dark haul
to the brink and back. Love and coffee

Lynn Lusby Pratt for the story concept

Karis Pratt, trip planner, translator,
fellow-adventurer, intercessor

The 100 who prayed

The five who did deliverance:
Dawn, Tammy, Pat, Gail, Francine

Brave ones who serve in high places alone and anonymous

Mountain Singer

Dr. Garland Bare

Editors/readers: Lynn Pratt, Karis Pratt,
Andy Rector, Denise Brelitch, Kim Jackson

David Braughler of Braughler Books

Haruka Otsuka, language advisor

Daniel Armstrong, artist

Casey Overberg for the miraculous photo

Musicians whose songs set the tone:

Andrea Summer, Mae Klingler,
Josh Garrels, Jonathan Maiocco, Matt Kearney, and Plumb.

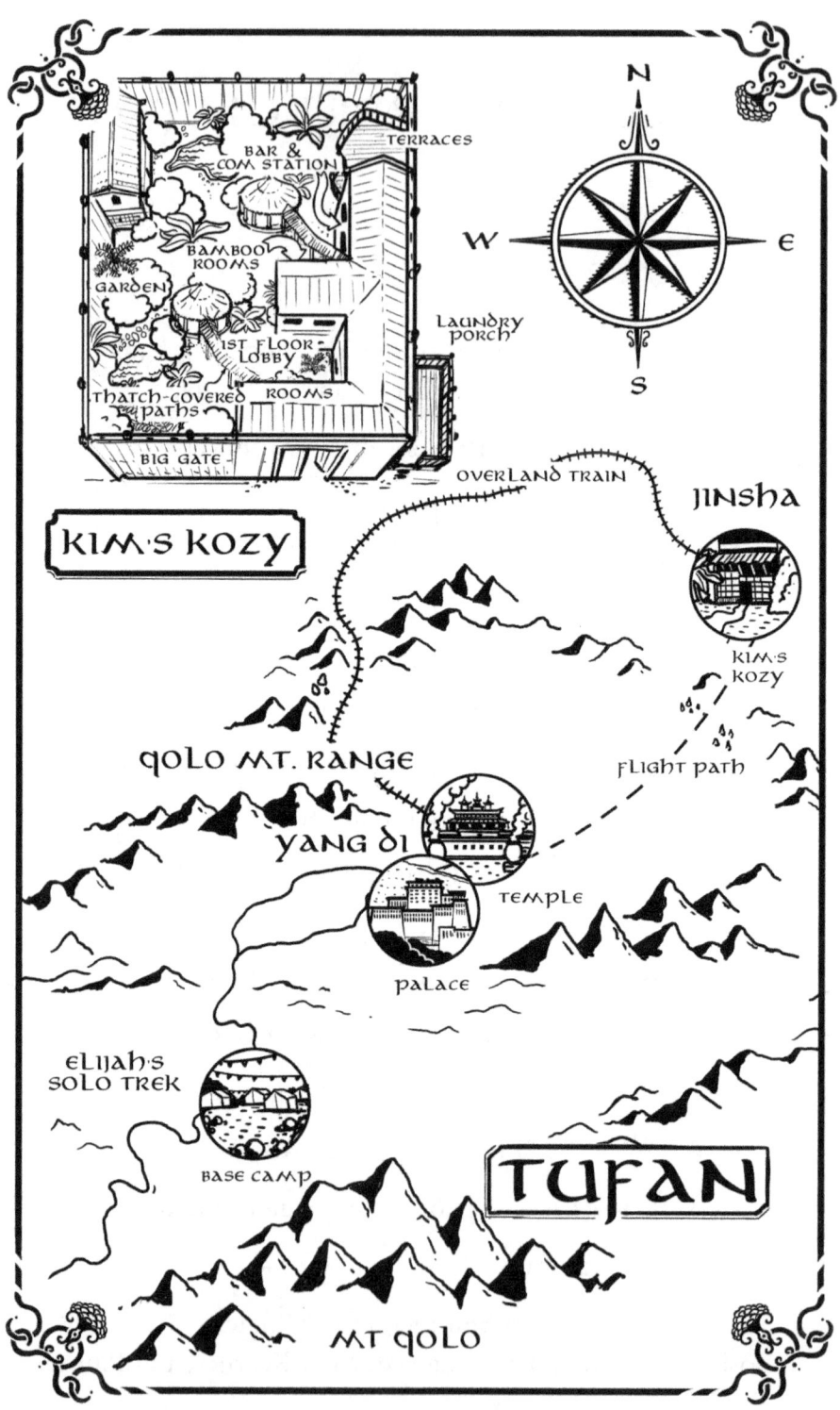

N

W   E

S

TERRACES

BAR &
COM STATION

BAMBOO
ROOMS

GARDEN

1ST FLOOR
LOBBY

LAUNDRY
PORCH

THATCH-COVERED
PATHS

ROOMS

BIG GATE

KIM'S KOZY

OVERLAND TRAIN

JINSHA

KIM'S
KOZY

FLIGHT PATH

QOLO MT. RANGE

YANG DI

TEMPLE

PALACE

ELIJAH'S
SOLO TREK

BASE CAMP

TUFAN

MT QOLO

STORM GOD

a novel of fact
and mystery

*Dark is His path on the
wings of the storm.*

—ROBERT GRANT,
"O WORSHIP THE KING"

CHAPTER 1

Find my thoughts high in the heavens,
Way up the mountainside.
Hesitate before searching,
I will be hard to find.
—Andrea Summer, "Wanderer"

The sun rose on Mt. Qolo, Holy Mother Mountain, a golden glow shearing across her frozen face. She was miles away but appeared much closer. I stood outside the tent at base camp and breathed thin air. Through the cloud of my breath, I spoke to her: *"Tzav latzav, tzav latzav, qav laqav, qav laqav, ze'ir sham, ze'ir sham."* The verse was a rhythm in my head. I pulled the Quella out of my pocket and looked up the translation: "Do and do, do and do, rule on rule, rule on rule, a little here, a little there." Gibberish. I'd figure it out later.

I switched off the Quella and checked the rotating cameras mounted on poles at the pass. The eastern face of the pass was solid, but there was a fissure in the steep west slope to my right. Whether it cut through to the other side, I wasn't sure. But it was my only option to escape. In a few minutes the sun would break over the cliff and briefly blind the camera scanning that fissure. I'd been watching, calculating, half the night.

Inside the dim tent, eight of my team were awake, peeling back their sleeping bags, yawning, shivering. Three were still asleep. One pretended to sleep. Our Tufani host mama had brought out breakfast plates from the other room of the tent. I wolfed down pancakes and nearly frozen honey. Minutes before, I'd announced that I was going solo from here.

Steven was the first to object. "Whoa. No way, Geo."

His brother Ben, scraping a fork across his plate for the last bits of potato and egg, had said, "No one goes alone. It's policy. Two by two."

My team knew me as Geo—George Telanoo. Only Karinna knew my real name: Elijah Creek.

Ben licked the fork front and back. "Threat level is red."

"I know that." Another verse had been whispering for weeks: "For the Lord spoke thus to me with his strong hand upon me, and warned me not to walk in the way of this people, saying: 'Do not call conspiracy all that this people calls conspiracy, and do not fear what they fear, nor be in dread. But the Lord of hosts, him you shall honor as holy. Let him be your fear, and let him be your dread.'"

I gathered my things in the chill of our hotel, a base camp tent with black canvas exterior, lined on the inside with homey-looking, blue-checked cloth. Tufani nomads rigged up these tents in spring and summer to withstand high altitude weather so that untrained pilgrims wouldn't freeze to death. Narrow bunks lined three walls. The fourth wall had shelves of provisions. Kettles simmered on a dung fuel stove in the center of the room.

Silence hung in the cold, smoky air. The team was worried, except for Suzanne, the one faking sleep. She'd be glad to see me go. Roz, a big girl with cranberry-colored hair, sat cross-legged, wrapped in her sleeping bag. She sipped tea and watched me pack. "You won't be crossing one of those rivers with giant water snakes, will you?"

"Bu-rin inhabit tropical rivers, not high mountain streams.

So they say. Bone up on your geography."

Steven, our linguistics intern, was reprogramming his triskele. Technology had come a long way in seven years. What used to be a pendant of coiled wire with information bent and scratched into it was now an electronic dog tag/itinerary/homing device. For security reasons we changed the shape every year, but the name had stuck: triskele. This year it was a jade leaf. Steven asked to see mine, probably for info about where I was going.

I pulled the pendant off my neck and tossed it to him. "Like I said, the tribe is nomadic. Suzanne knows the general direction. I'll start at the abandoned monastery." I kept packing.

"We won't know when you're coming back," Steven said.

"Couple weeks, buddy. Three, tops," I said.

He tossed my triskele back. It hit the floor. "We'll be back at HQ by then, Geo. You're doing everything you taught us not to do."

I flashed my Bowie knife. "Taking this. Taught you that." I didn't mean to be flippant. Something in Steven reminded me of my cousin Rob: the super smarts, the open-faced goodness. Steven was sort of my protégé. I didn't want him worrying. I got the Quella and repeated the gibberish verse in Hebrew. "Am I saying this right?"

He said, "Correct. The 'a's are 'ah' sounds. It's zeh-ear, and *sham* rhymes with Tom."

"You're too smart to live," I joked.

A thick voice mumbled from the corner, "We can' wait on you, Geo. We'll be arres'ed if we don' clear zeh region." It was Edouard, our French negotiator. He always sounded sleepy.

"I'm not asking you to. We'll reconnect at Kim's Kozy," I reassured him, "as always."

Roz nudged my knee with her sock foot. "It's not just giant water snakes. It's bandits. And that shaman…"

Ben said flatly, "They'll kill you in your sleep."

"They're not violent," I lied.

Edouard raised his wobbly head and blinked. "Zeh up-date—'Stoned by Children'—doesn' soun nonviolence to me."

"Kids throwing rocks, guarding their turf from intruders," I defended. "Nobody died."

Ben, darker than his kid brother Steven, grunted. "When I said they'll kill you in your sleep, I wasn't just talking about people." He was speaking of the unseen population in the Qolo range: spirits, gods, demons.

Squatting next to my pack I addressed my eleven team members now awake and the one still faking sleep: "Co-sufferers (I was being sarcastic), it's the last unreached group on our watch. We're running out of time. Jam the hatch before it closes. I taught you that, too."

Suzanne's goose-down sleeping bag was gathered around her pretty face. An Egyptian princess lying in state. *Faker. You're listening.* I grabbed an oxygen canister and stuffed it in my pack.

"We're here as mountain trekkers," said Karinna, stating the obvious. "We have to be trekking." She handed me a cup of steaming tea, leaned her freckled face to mine, and whispered, "Dom won't like this. At all. I'll cover best I can." Karinna knew about my seven years. She could be trusted.

Steven still pressed. "It'll take you a week just to get across the mountains."

"Four or five days," I corrected. "Two if I catch a ride on a cycle. Suzanne makes decisions while I'm gone."

"Got redundancy?" he asked in a tone of concession.

"Double on essentials." I tossed an energy bar at Suzanne, hitting her on the shoulder. She turned her head and opened those copper eyes on me. Yep, she'd heard every word. She'd be more than happy taking over. I went on. "You twelve are registered with the gov. My paperwork is a problem. Do your thing. I'll do mine. Safer."

Steven wouldn't give up. "If I may ask, why do you think no one has been able to reach these people?"

We all knew. Conditions in the Qolo range were brutal. High altitudes and thinning atmosphere made nearly every traveler sick to some degree. The Edifice had mandated an off-limits to the region, reinforcing the order with troops and drones. The tribe I'd be reaching was wild and unpredictable. And the head shaman had threatened death to any foreign believer entering his turf. Our own agency—Peregrini: Central Asia Division—had documented enough freak accidents, illnesses, and mysterious disappearances to blacklist the area. Stories went all the way back to Rijnhart, Shelton, and Dittemore before the World Wars. "Tufan: On Hold" was the word. We so-called fundies weren't to be tromping through their so-called sacred ground. But I'd detected a hint of cowardice from headquarters, compliance with The Edifice, and didn't like it. Wasn't this planet—at least in theory—still a free world, and if not, weren't we under higher orders?

I went on snapping, zipping, and tying my gear. Someone started a friendly argument about whether I could pass as native Tufani: "He's dark enough, but too tall."

"The eyes are wrong."

"He'll pass. He's part Native American."

"The beard's a dead giveaway. Asians don't grow 'em like that."

"Some do."

"His accent stinks. Geo, you have a vocab of maybe forty words total in their dialect. How do you plan to communicate?"

I pulled a phone-shaped gizmo out of my backpack and held it up. "Quella. Solar-powered."

Steven's jaw dropped. "You have it in their dialect?"

I nodded. "Before our translators were shut down. Many Tufanis can't read, so—" I didn't tell them that this prototype actually spoke.

"And," Steven argued last-ditch, "we don't know that they are a separate people group, from DNA studies. Maybe we're done here. Maybe we are done."

Suzanne had peeled off her sleeping bag. She sat up in T-shirt and flannels, tousling her black hair and stretching out her bare arms, as if the cold didn't bother her. Roz handed her some tea.

I hauled the pack onto my back and said to Steven, "You're overanalyzing. This small tribe has never heard. We thought they were coming our way. They didn't. I need a couple of weeks to make a connection. Okay. Break camp. Answer any inquiries about me with blank stares."

Suzanne tapped bare feet on the floor and warmed her fingers around the mug. "Don't be an arrogant jerk. You're not the only one who can take on territorial spirits—"

"I'm not doing that!" I locked eyes with her and lowered my voice. Inside I was boiling. "'From all tribes and peoples and languages.' That's what the prophecy says. People from *all* tribes. And that's the way"—I punctuated my words with blunt nods because this conversation was over—"it. Will. Be. Suzanne."

The others stopped what they were doing and looked at us.

Suzanne half smiled—she loved a good argument—and said in that creamy whisper of hers, "*Que sera, sera.* What will be. Will. Be. Geo."

The way she said my name cut to the quick. I went to the door, saying to the team, "Pray for me." Ducking under the doorway blanket, I paused, letting in a shaft of daylight and a cold draft. "I mean it. Pray. And leave your warmest clothes with the Tufanis when you leave. We won't be back." I stepped again into the stone-gray morning of base camp. Mt. Qolo glowed above her shadowy sisters.

Steven followed me out, putting on his coat, whispering in the silence, "Some people who went up against that religion came out different: suicidal, psychotic."

I emptied my lungs completely before inhaling deeply, a necessary habit for stamina up here. "I'm not going *against* anything. I'm going *for* a reason. Some weren't prepared." I breathed again.

He pleaded quietly so he wouldn't rouse pilgrims in other tents. "How do you know *you* are? You should wait for authorization." He pulled his satellite phone out of its holster and looked at it, puzzled. "I'd contact Peregrini myself if my sat worked. I think you should wait. At least let Dom know. Your honcho's supposed to know where you are. But see, there's no signal. How can there be no signal? We're at 17,000."

Karinna emerged from the tent to see me off. I grabbed the rice paddle stuck in the pot by the campfire, scooped out a glob of sticky rice, and handed it to her. She always got up early to make rice balls for our daypacks. Keeping my voice low I said, "One for the road?"

She whispered back into the tent, "Come on, guys, we need a send-off," then grabbed a strip of seaweed from the food box and wrapped a rice ball. "Take more." She smiled and made another, then another. "There's nothing to live on out there unless you run across nomads and sponge off them. And bandits—you know what they can do to you. And wild mastiffs. And the guards. You can't fly under every radar."

"I know."

She sighed. "You have tea? And here's cinnamon to warm you up along the way." She dug packets out of her vest pocket and pressed them into my hand. We exchanged a long, deep look. Karinna was a jewel. "And your medicine pouch—are the vials full?"

A few more of the team straggled out—Suzanne wasn't among them—and lobbed trail mix packets and jerky sticks at me, the usual going-away shower. I gathered them from the ground and stuffed them in my coat pockets. My mind flashed back to a time when other friends had sent me off to parts unknown. I remembered the looks on their faces, the tears.

There were no tears here.

Keeping an eye on the security cameras, I headed around the corner of the tent, pausing to press a finger to my navel—a morning ritual—to be sure the red diamond stud was still there. I thought of the Magdeline Five, as we'd called ourselves back then: kids on a mission. Warm sentiment welled up. I yanked down my waistband and pulled out the stud with a grunt; it seemed to have grown to my skin in seven years. I pressed it into the center of one of the rice balls, then went back to Steven, gave it to him, and whispered, "Look inside when you're alone. Don't show anyone. Don't tell anyone. Protect it with your life. Understand? Your very life." I grinned. "And don't eat it."

Steven looked at the rice ball, mystified, then at me. His eyes watered. "Give me a minute. I'm going—"

I slapped his shoulder and smiled. "You're not thinking. I may have to cross borders. Now listen, there's a girl in the States. What's in there,"—I nodded at the rice ball—"see that she gets it if something happens. Dom will know who I mean. Don't tell him anything, you hear? Just ask him this question: 'Who'd remember Geo best from when he was a kid?' Then go from there. Still in Ohio, I think."

"If the weather turns ugly—" he shivered hopefully.

"It'll hold. Now promise. See that she gets it. Start praying." I turned and walked away.

"Call if your sat works," Steven whispered. "What code?"

"If we need one, let's go with Caesar Shift Five. And we'll do that thing with the vowels. Keep the vowels."

"Good. I can read outright in CS Five."

"And airport glyphs. Know them." I walked thirty yards, turned. He was still there at the corner of the tent, alone in the mysterious glow of Mt. Qolo. "What about moonrise, Lockhart?"

"Cloudy. New moon, which means no moon. It'll be pitch black. Sunrise at seven hundred hours. But if you're in a valley…"

"You know your stuff."

"Do you have a fire kit?"

"Who are you—my mom?" I tightened the hip straps of my pack. "I'd outpace you two times over. Hate to leave you out there for the wild mastiffs."

He took no offense. "Will you use a code name?" Behind him the campfire was a nugget of gold sending up sparks into the blue, as if a burning chip of Qolo had broken off and fallen to earth. "Um…" I stalled, glancing again at the cameras, six that I could see, on high poles.

In earlier days, loose in the woods behind Dad's nature camp, I'd named my wilderness The Land No One Owns, Telanoo for short. My alias now. I instructed Steven, "Don't do anything you don't feel comfortable with." I was putting off the lie I should have been used to by now, the lie that Geo was my real name. "Even orders from Peregrini. Don't obey if you don't feel right about it. Watch out that no one deceives you. Got it? Think things through."

I backed up, curving my path to miss the camera. *Now or never.* I lied to Steven one last time. "If you have to contact me, use my real name." He looked pretty desolate standing there. I added quickly, "What we talked about last night, the catch phrases. You and me and Karinna. Only."

He nodded. "Pleiades is bound."

I nodded back. "And Orion is loosed."

CHAPTER 2

As the sun goes down
I get one more wear of your golden crown.
Though I am just dust upon the ground,
I glow for a while.
—ANDREA SUMMER, "GLOW"

My boots crunched on the rocky slope. The compass said due east. The altimeter said 15,400. The sky said mid-afternoon. The mountains said nothing. I took it slow, broke out the O2 for a snort, just in case. Crossed over one bare, brown mountain to find a hundred more. Late spring air still had the hard bite of winter. On the high passes, wind came like a tide from a distant deep, like rip currents rolling in and doubling back. I felt the pull.

Then evening winds maneuvered through valleys, some sweeping up the slopes only to dissipate as if they were never there. I stopped and listened for the Lord to speak, for wind as words. Despite my assurances to the team, I half hoped God would flat-out tell me to go back. But I believed the prophecy and knew my responsibility. Who else would go?

No shadows were cast across the landscape, except myself and some standing stones draped in ragged prayer flags. I ripped down a few as Mountain Singer had done. I felt guilty, but she—one of their own—had done it. The natural cone shapes of the mountains received light on all sides except at the extremities of the day or when a cloud crept by. Qolo and her sisters appeared to be bathed in an unsourced glow even after twilight. *"Tzav latzav, tzav latzav,"* I said to the sisters.

Weeks ago, as we flew into Tufan, Karinna had commented, "The mountains, Geo, it seemed as if the mountains themselves are proud. Or maybe the spirits who dwell there."

To the Tufanis certain mountains did have their own spirit gods, or demons-in-residence, but Karinna hadn't known it at the time. Here stood an army of mountain behemoths carved out of time, activated and energized by secret rituals, and I was a flea hopping across their backs. Over the past few years I'd spent way too much time acquainting myself with the dark side—terms and practices of the native religion—so I wouldn't be taken unawares. *Can't unthink it. Can't close that door.*

Night approached. "Having a friend along would be nice," I said aloud to hear a human voice. Steven had volunteered, but his allegiance was more to me than to the mission at this point. "I'm faster alone. Tufani potatoes and eggs a few days ahead. Two hots and a cot: dinner, breakfast, and a sleeping bench; folks hovering around a campfire. It's not the people against us. Our struggle is not with flesh and blood…except when flesh and blood is soulless. But I've done this before. So what if their shaman burned our book and drank the ashes. So what. I'm a servant of the Most High."

I stopped now and then to listen for the hum of a motorcycle, the rattle of a horse cart, the footfall of bandits, the bark of a dog. Not much chance. No roads. I kept an instinctive eye to land and sky as far as I could. Twelve miles: the range of The Edifice's thermal imaging capabilities, last I'd heard. It was a breathtaking view. Literally. The altimeter said 16,200. I took a drag of O2. Yahweh was here, but it wasn't just me and him on this mountainside. Another dry whiff came up the slope and back down, as if the gods were breathing me in. I laughed it off. "I'll huff and I'll puff and I'll blow your house down!"

I shouldn't have said it.

. . . . .

In two days I crossed two streams: one by leaping on stones, the other—a swift glacial stream—I'd swum stripped down and freezing with my pack thrust above my head and a cautious eye upstream, a knife in my teeth. I was safe from *bu-rin*, but there were legends of other creatures in Asian headwaters. Only legends. But legends start somewhere. How far upstream do they start?

Over the years I'd been through hunger, cold, death threats and close calls, centipedes and seasickness, getting lost and left behind. I'd pretty much seen it all.

I reached another high mountain pass littered with prayer flags and said a prayer of my own, one that filled the mind instead of emptying it: a prayer to someone rather than emptiness. I emptied my lungs and filled my mind and praised the maker of mountains tinted with blue, rose, and gold. "Rob would go camera crazy here. He'd be talking weather, air masses and stuff, while he click-click-clicked."

I missed him and the old clan.

You've ruined my life. Words came from nowhere in a tone I hadn't used in a while, especially to God. It kept on. *Nothing growing here. Only thing not dead and flapping in the breeze is me. I could be back in the States, having a life.*

Wait. I'm accusing my Father? I didn't mean it. It's grand. There was a heaviness in my chest. *Really, it's grand. Who gets to see this, the wilds of Telanoo only a million times bigger and three miles higher? I'll find a man of peace who knows a little English, leave the Quella, and get out while the gettin's good, back to someplace warm and secure: Kim's Kozy. Salmon fried rice and palm trees and bunk rooms. Then stateside to crash a while, earn some money.*

I could lead expeditions over here except for the security problems. Or hide out in Canada. Or stay home and work at camp with Dad, take back my name, if possible.

The jagged horizon renewed my confidence. I caught sight of a crystal-blue holy lake off to my right, turning green then bronze as the sun set. I comforted myself with the lake. I didn't want another night like last night, reds dripping from the sky, soaking into the mountains and drying black. Was it a dream, that wail of blood crying from the earth? Or just the wind.

The lake was no doubt full of fish, but it was in the wrong direction and off limits. Holy lakes were receptacles of the Tufani life force, which must be preserved at all costs. "Even if the people are starving, the fish are spared? No mercy," I said, quickly disliking like the sound of my voice. If worse came to worst, I'd zigzag back there and fry up some holy fish.

The mountains went severely black and lost dimension. Steven had said, "New moon, no moon." But I could see it, a faint silvery ring of light around a dark disc. Clouds moved in. I stopped for oxygen, put the tube to my nose, opened the nozzle, and heard that welcome hiss. Air. My spirits lifted. Should I make camp or go on in the dark? Wear my headlamp and risk detection? I picked my way down the slope and thought of home and the Mag Five. I'd been back to Magdeline a few times, but circumstances eventually dictated that I stay on the move, sending postcards to my family from different countries to cover my tracks. I'd met Rob months ago in Cairo, but had lost contact with the rest. The last time Marcus and I met, things were strained. Mei was all over the map living out her dream travel career. I did keep track of her mish work. And Reece had moved on. It seemed best to keep moving on myself. It would have been hard to contact me, even if they'd wanted to.

I gnawed on a beef jerky stick and wondered how far the

smell of meat traveled in thin air, and if the wind might just direct that smell to a creature who'd do me harm.

Hopefully, I'd passed undetected across the disputed border of a region whose name and political leaders shifted with the seasons. It was complicated: the black magic culture had remained unchanged for five hundred years until The Restructuring fifty years ago. People were tortured and oppressed in the head-butting of atheism vs. demon worship. Ironically the region opened up to our Peregrini teams, if under strict controls. Guards with guns patrolled every road and temple. Unnumbered citizens disappeared. On the other hand, there was infrastructure for the first time: schools, hospitals, roads, electricity. In the chaos Tufanis had a slim chance of hearing the truth. *Truth: the best infrastructure of all.*

Now a new campaign was in full swing, installed by The Edifice: promises of global peace and stability using Tufan as a model. Hogwash. Edifice troops, many of whom were devotees of ancient war gods clasped hands with atheism, spawning an inbred belief system that defied description and was set to bring the whole world with it.

I once believed that the dark forces—those war gods—wanted their stronghold left alone. No. What they really wanted was attention on a planetary scale. At long last they had it.

What's that sound? I stopped. A half-alive sound, like flapping wings and chirps of dying birds. I hunkered down, moved silently to the crest of the hill. It was only an abandoned shrine with a thousand shredded prayer flags strung up and whipping in the wind, carrying chants to Lotus. Ropes strained and squeaked under the weight of the blowing flags.

Some of the team members—especially Suzanne—thought it was funny to say a Lotus chant and watch me cringe. "It's meaningless," she'd chide.

"That's enough now," I'd say tolerantly, trying to push it from my mind, trying to close a door that was coming off its hinges.

. . . . .

Dogs barked in the distance today. I didn't eat. Drank only water. Three days down. No, four. I lost a day skirting around a patrolled settlement. I found a stream, loaded up with water, and slept fitfully with a weapon across my chest, a crossbow I'd bought off a shepherd boy on another mission. I hadn't told the team about it. Until last night I'd kept it disassembled and hidden in my clothes and luggage, a trick I'd learned while piecing together The Armor of God.

Dom often stated an old World War II directive: "Know how to assemble your weapons in the dark." Then he'd smile and add, "That's got gospel all over it."

Day five? For breakfast I made tea and added Karinna's cinnamon, savoring the smell. I kept thinking about what I wished I didn't know: that intelligent, hearty people like the Dhebu-Gampa tribe would creep into cemeteries at night with ritual instruments made from human body parts, would empty their minds of thought and fill them with tranced imaginings—then mystically offer their flesh and entrails, their possessions, and their families as food for demons. "No thanks," I spoke to the powers of the air.

It didn't really matter whether the Gampas saw me as a Tufani wanna-be or a fundie intruder. The spirits knew who I was, and they were running this show. Their shaman probably knew I was coming, too, even if Edifice drones didn't.

. . . . .

I woke and sat up, shrouded in a heavy cloud. Visibility zero. *Is it morning? Afternoon?* I looked at my watch. *Two p.m. Okay. I must have drifted off.* I hadn't thought about getting lost, losing track, hadn't thought much past making contact. *Fingers and toes cold. You still there, God? What if my triskele malfunctions? The monastery can't be far.*

According to agency info, a band of Dhebu-Gampas had been moving from more remote regions to other pasture for the summer.

The Gampas were a wildly unpredictable bunch, prone to violence, taller than other tribes, fierce, and never without a weapon. Their shaman: unbelievably cruel. The tale of the Canadian mish, sewn into a fresh animal hide and left to be broiled and squeezed to death in the sun, had been the final straw for Peregrini. Never made the news. The Dhebus had intermarried with a small clan of Gampas, formed a new tribe, and were thought to be less hostile. *I can trade my crossbow for food, say I'm lost. Yeah, of course they're wild. Living by a thread. Appeasing demons to survive. The isolation alone could turn a man into a ghoul.*

A little O2 now. Not sure how much I have left. A full canister weighs the same as an empty, I guess. It's air. I was going to keep track.

I made a stealth fire with sticks and rubbish gathered from stream beds, praying that the fog would shield me beside this rocky spine. A steep incline to my left and white nothing to my right. I sat praising Yahweh. *For creation, Lord, for the power of your Word, which sustained me these years. Thanks for the team. Remind them to pray. Thanks for my mission, for your other mishes out there doing the work.*

There was a verse in the Quella, a mountain passage I read outloud: "He who forms the mountains and creates the wind, and declares to man what is his thought, who makes the morning darkness, and treads on the heights of the earth—the Lord, the God of hosts, is his name!"

Morning darkness? I never noticed that before. He makes the morning darkness? He makes the day dark?

· · · · · ·

Hadn't thought of the Quella all day, maybe two days.

No, yesterday was that one mountain pass, wasn't it? Stay with me now, I said to my mind, and to my heart, *Stay strong.* A verse had pressed upon me to make this trek in the first place: that people from every nation, tribe, and language would be around the throne when he returned. The gibberish verse came, too, that rhythm in my mind. The third verse spurred me on: "Do not fear what they fear."

I was low on water. I sidetracked to a stream.

A sand fox spotted me, meandered closer. His coat was pale and coarse like the mountains. A wolfish face, a half-smile, a side-stare from slanted, black-rimmed eyes. A studied, almost human intelligence. I sat my pack down, readied the cross-bow, aimed. Disinterested and unthreatened, he trotted out of range.

What else do I need to know? What words to address the shaman, if I should be so fortunate as to meet a holy man with a death wish for believers who venture too close? What about his falling into trance to manipulate dark forces? What verse of authority against their gory cemetery rituals, offering their flesh to demons? There's nothing specific in the Word about the situation I'm walking into. There can't be.

I'd bring truth, but was the truth enough? It hadn't worked here since...since forever. A graveyard for missions, it was called. I cursed at the fading green sky. Another night and no monastery or nomads. Qolo caught the last sun rays. "I see why they worship her, their Mother, their light. *Tzav latzav, tzav, qav laqav...*"

In pre-field training, the instructor ends the final session with, "In the event you find yourself in a hopeless situation, one for which you do not foresee escape and do not wish to endanger others with a rescue or recovery attempt, snap the triskele in two and discard it, if possible. This will disable the homing device and prevent an enemy from learning our technology. Your information will be lost. Then go with God."

I'd heard it dozens of times, like pre-flight instructions on planes: "In the event the cabin should lose pressure..."

The next evening—what evening, what day?—uncast shadows came around, pointing fingers toward another night. Snow fell. The old monastery was supposed to be around the next mountain. That was a few mountains ago. *Is this triskele even working? My compass still working?* It bothered me again that there was nothing specific in the Word for this mission.

Look.

It was him. *Father!* I was in a dry stream bed. I skimmed the encircling mountains and purple sky. My heart raced. *Look? For what? There's nothing here.*

Look, he said again, and I understood. I plopped down against the rocky bank, pulled a small Bible from my waist pack, and switched on my headlamp. *Really? You want me to look?* I didn't want to be presumptuous. I'd been through that genie-in-a-bottle phase of my spiritual journey, which had ended badly. *You want me to just...open the book?*

Go ahead.

Okay. In anticipation of an answer, I let it fall open. Isaiah. The book was a mountain range of prophecies and visions. You could look at one truth and see beyond to more and more. His very voice resonated from the page:

I was ready to be sought by those who did not ask for me;
 I was ready to be found by those who did not seek me.

I said, "Here I am, here I am," to a nation
 that was not called by my name.

I spread out my hands all the day to a rebellious
 people, who walk in a way that is not good,

following their own devices; a people who provoke
me to my face continually, sacrificing in gardens

and making offerings on bricks; who sit in
tombs, and spend the night in secret places;

who eat pig's flesh, and broth of tainted
meat is in their vessels;

who say, "Keep to yourself, do not come
near me, for I am too holy for you."

These are a smoke in my nostrils, a fire that burns all the day.

Behold, it is written before me:
"I will not keep silent, but I will repay;

I will indeed repay into their lap both your iniquities

and your fathers' iniquities together, says the Lord;

because they made offerings on the mountains
and insulted me on the hills,

I will measure into their lap payment for their former deeds."

Holy smokes! Sure enough, here it was, words for the ho-
lier-than-thou shaman who said, "Keep away." The disgusting
feasts and sacrifices, the graveyard trance ceremonies. All here.
This was written 2,700 years ago. It was nothing new. Same
old perversions.

I shuddered from the chill and a rumble in the air. Maybe
a distant avalanche, or a tremor. I fixed on the last line. *I will
repay?* I dropped against my backpack and stared up at the sky.
*You called me here for judgment? I thought it was a rescue mission.
These people don't know you!*

Somewhere along the way—a day or two ago—my head
had begun to hurt. Altitude sickness had never been much of a
problem. Occasionally a little loss of appetite or confusion. But I
was ravenous on this trek. A good sign. And my mind was clear,
or seemed to be. I read the passage again.

This isn't what I came for. I drank water, pulled out the last jerky stick and nibbled, forcing calm into my pounding head. I wished for a few more of Karinna's seaweed rice balls. *Like those fancy little rice balls that Mei used to make with bites of salty fish in the middle.* She'd carried them in a lacquered lunch box when the four of us—Rob, Marcus, Mei, and I—built a bridge into my wilderness, into Telanoo, so Reece could go with us, by wheelchair if necessary. *Seven years ago. Who were those silly kids and their dreams of adventure?*

And how'd I get to this? From the best friendships a kid could have to secrets and lies. From there to here. Lost. There, I said it. Lost. I tried to stand. *Get moving. You're not lost. You're almost there.* My vision blurred. *Just the wind. It's dusty. Bad for the eyes.*

You've been set up, said a featureless voice.

I fell back into the stream bed.

Too late...

I have to be close, I argued. *I'll reach the pass and see lights in an old monastery. Or maybe I missed it. Maybe I'm nowhere. Triskele sabotaged? Okay, don't panic.*

Was Suzanne right, that I never should have attempted this? Did I set my head on this damnable mission just because she didn't want me to? Did I ignore the others because of her?

I couldn't get up, couldn't reach the O2 canister in my pack. *This isn't altitude sickness. This is something else.* Immediately when I admitted it—*this is something else*—they came in a single swarm from the heights, swooping, settling around. Black, papery, unseen things.

My backpack weighted me to the stream bed. "The Lord Almighty says this," I yelled aloud into thin air. "'I revealed myself to those who did not ask for me! I was found by those who did not seek me!' The Lord will be found!" I made a fist, pounded my thigh. "To a nation who didn't call on him, he said, 'Here am I!' All day long he held out his hands! Day after day—" I emptied my lungs, growling, gasping, "This is what Sovereign Lord says: 'I revealed myself to those…who sit among the graves.'" Wrenching pressure squeezed my lungs. *Breathe!* "At night keeping. Secret vigils!"

You set me up! No. Don't accuse him.

I turned and threw up dried meat and water. *Wild dogs will smell this. Get away from it. Get to the people.* Black fluttering wings, which I couldn't see or hear, circled above.

Okay, you say judgment. Then, judgment it is. I cried, "The Sovereign Lord says, 'I will pay back in full.' You hear? In full!"

I'm shutting down. No shelter. Triskele. Steven sabotaged it, thought I'd turn back when I found out. Suzanne did it, her fingers on my throat as I slept. Gotta break it. Break it. Fingers on jade… Bandits leave corpses naked and frozen. Mastiffs tear victims apart alive. Not that way, okay? Lord? Let me freeze first. Okay? Okay? Karinna, don't wonder and wander. Don't search. Steven, don't risk prison. It doesn't matter, I'll be saved.

Mag Five will never know. She'll never know.

My life. Make of it what you will. Horror and great peace, deep peace. *No one dies alone. You send angels. Right?*

From the high bank above the dry stream, a crunch or snort.

What's that? Who's there?

A crunch, a snort.

Eyes open not seeing, mouth open not breathing. Shutting down…

A deep, guttural, fluctuating sound from above.

What is that?!

CHAPTER 3

Thunder is good, thunder is impressive,
but it's lightning that does the work.
—Mark Twain

Rapid-fire lightning tore the sky over Cedar Ridge, Ohio.

Reece clapped her free hand over Olivet's tiny ear, but too late. The toddler wailed in her arms. Reece bolted back up the front porch steps, thunder penetrating the planks under her feet. Clouds burst over the town. From her hillside vantage point, Reece looked down the length of Main Street which dissected the village into east and west halves. "It's a deluge."

When the storm didn't let up after a few minutes, Reece motioned to her friend Brooklyn, who'd been sitting in the car in the driveway. "Come on" she called. "Make a run for it."

Brooklyn wiped the steamy windshield, signaled okay, and wrangled her little boy out of the back seat.

Once inside, Olivet wriggled from her mother's arms and toddled to the toy box. Brooklyn changed Desmond into dry clothes and was drying her own black curls with a towel. "It's dangerous out there. Lightning, flash floods..."

Reece headed to the kitchen for sandwich makings. "If we can't shop, we'll eat."

A siren wailed. Brooklyn said, "I bet something got hit by that big bolt a few minutes ago."

Reece brought a platter of meats and cheeses to the table and went to the screen door. The town, charming mid-century bungalows nestled in wooded hillsides around a downtown of old brick, was drenched in gray, except for one brief flare, like the strike of a match. "Oh no…"

"What?"

"I don't see the steeple."

Brooklyn rushed to the door and squinted through the downpour toward the church at the far end of Main. "Is that smoke?"

"I can't tell," Reece said, "but I thought I saw flames. There's Greg!" His silver sedan turned into the driveway and slammed to a stop. He made a run for the porch and leaped the steps. Reece and Brooklyn backed away as he burst in—grim faced, pants dripping, white shirt clinging to his skin.

Reece assumed the worst. "It hit the church."

He gave her a look. "Again. I need dry clothes."

"How bad's the damage? Is it burning? I thought I saw—" She followed him into the bedroom. The door shut.

Brooklyn tended the toddlers at the toy box as heaven pounded and Greg growled behind closed doors. He came out running a hand through his wet brown hair, Reece turning down the collar of his fresh shirt.

Brooklyn asked, "How bad is it?"

His mouth curled in a crooked smile. "It struck an owl on the spire. He's toast. A gust of wind finished off the steeple. Rain is dousing the fire, so there'll be water damage, too."

"And you were inside when it hit?" Brooklyn asked, wide-eyed.

He glanced at the meat platter and said to Reece, "Make me a couple of those. I'll be at the center the rest of the day." He muttered an "uh-huh" in answer to Brooklyn's question, and said good-naturedly, "It's time to get rid of that spire. This is the second hit."

The sandwiches were rushed and ready. The rain let up, gray-green wisps of cloud creeping over the hills. Greg took the sack of food. "More rain's coming. Don't wait up."

"Bye," Reece called after him cheerfully. The screen door slammed.

Brooklyn tousled her damp curls again. "Second time?"

"Even with a lightning rod. I don't know how they're supposed to work, but..." Reece scooped up Olivet and deposited her into the high chair. "It was a year ago. Just before you starting coming to church—I mean, to the center."

Brooklyn joked, "Could be a sign from God."

"Or just an unlucky owl."

"Perched on a metal cross in a lightning storm? Dumb bird."

"Good things are happening at the center. We're growing. You want mustard or mayo? I have some lettuce from the garden. Tomatoes?"

"All of the above." Brooklyn's head tipped. "A lot of those good things are because of you."

Reece dismissed the comment, cutting a sandwich into little triangles for Olivet.

"I'm not saying it because you're my friend, Reece. Once you got back on your feet, the whole atmosphere changed."

"What do you mean?"

"I don't know. It was brighter."

Reece headed into the kitchen, calling back, "That was just the new paint color in the atrium. I will take credit for that. What do you say we risk lightnings and flash floods for rock-bottom prices? We'll stay to the high roads."

"I'm in."

Reece came back with a bowl of fruit. "Let's start at the consignment shop—"

The phone rang. She grabbed it with one hand, placing

strawberries on Olivet's tray with the other. "Hello? Rob? Hey, guy. Wow, it is so good to hear from you!" She pressed the phone to her shoulder and whispered to Brooklyn, "It's an old friend. Excuse me a minute." She sat next to Olivet's high chair. "Hey, what's going on?…I'm good. The last surgery went well. I'm doing therapy, working on that limp…yeah, a metal rod. I'll set off alarms at all future airports…like old times. Call security and all that. So what's up?" She stood and drifted toward the front door, dropping her voice. "No, I haven't. I see his mom sometimes when I'm in Magdeline. They don't hear from him much. He must be busy." She shot a backward glance at Brooklyn, who'd stopped eating to listen. "Tufan? With anyone we know?…Okay. I'll let you know if I hear something. Oh, you too. Are you ever back home? Come see us, please, please. And do something about this weather, will you? Lightning just struck our church steeple. For the second time. Yeah, really. Stay in touch. Okay. Bye."

Reece came back to the dining room and sat down.

Brooklyn asked, "Something wrong?"

"A high school friend, Rob Wingate. One of the old gang." She admitted sheepishly, "We used to call ourselves the Magdeline Five: Rob and his cousin Elijah, my friend Mei from Japan, and another guy, Marcus. What a clique we were. Rob's a meteorologist and storm chaser now. His house was hit by a tornado once when we were kids, and that's how he got into the weather business. The Mag Five…we were going to be friends for life." She fluffed Olivet's blond curls. "But you know how it goes."

"So what's wrong?"

"Nothing, I guess."

"C'mon. You don't have to be "preacher's wife" with me. You and Greg were arguing back there a minute ago, and not just about the fire. And something in that call upset you."

Reece blushed. "Two different things. Greg's stressed, that's all. And Rob just wanted to know if I'd heard from Elijah. The last he knew"—she unconsciously lowered her voice—"Elijah was in Tufan."

"Tufan," Brooklyn said the word soberly. "What's he doing there?"

"Oh, he works for an international agency, in education. I'm not sure," Reece answered vaguely.

"How long since you heard from him?"

"Not since Greg and I got engaged." She paused, laid a hand on a napkin, moved it absently around the table as if wiping a spill. "Elijah and I dated, but then he went to work for that agency. There was a lot of travel."

Brooklyn waited for more.

"He was a good friend. Rob just wanted to know if I'd heard from him." Her hand stopped.

"Why would a guy you haven't seen in years call you?" Brooklyn asked.

She wadded the napkin. "I don't know."

. . . . .

"Where were you?" Greg asked, letting the screen door slam behind him. It was near midnight.

Reece looked up from her Bible study notes scattered on the dining room table. "What do you mean?"

"I drove by at five and you weren't here."

"Brooklyn and I went shopping, remember? The storm delayed us." She went back to the notebook. "What's the latest?"

He stopped and stood behind her until she turned to look up at him.

"Where were you?" he asked again.

"Consignment shop," she stated matter-of-factly, then smiled. "Olivet's outgrowing everything. That's all we had time for, one store."

He moved toward the kitchen. "Why can't you trade baby clothes with women whose kids are in the nursery? Joyce's girls always look nice."

"I have nothing to offer her in return." She got up and followed him into the kitchen. "Want to see what I got? Five pieces for less than twelve dollars. They're adorable."

"Sure. Later."

"What about the building? Is it as bad as you thought?" She rubbed her thigh muscle, having sat too long.

He drank from a pitcher on the counter and looked tiredly out at the backyard. "Why's the security light still on?"

"I keep it on when you're not here."

"The stage is drenched, the equipment's damaged. A gaping hole in the roof, the power's off. Insurance will owe us big time."

"What about Sunday?"

"Can't have it there. We'll split up into small groups for a few weeks. We can still use the children's wing for the kids. Parents can drop them off and go to small groups in homes."

"That's a good idea." She flicked nonexistent crumbs from the counter. "I was thinking earlier today…how nice it might be to have family worship a couple of times. You know, we could get into groups of families with children of the same age, maybe. It's the same as your idea except we'd be including the children, just for a week or two. It would be a little messy," she laughed, "but the children's ministry people could use a break, and families would have a chance to worship together. Just once or twice. An adventure, sort of."

He made a half sound, indicating something between, "I might consider it" and, "That makes no sense." He went to bed.

Reece found herself on the porch. The empty lot across the street sloped down toward the business district, rain-soaked, reflective. She breathed in the smell of saturated earth, propping one foot on the white wooden rail to stretch her leg muscles, deeper each time, counting to thirty, then another thirty, until sweat dampened her forehead. Why was Greg angry at her idea about family worship? He'd been under a lot of pressure. The center, as they were calling it now, was growing and with that, more responsibility. Then the baby, then her surgeries coming within a couple of years. Now the bills. It was a lot for a guy fresh out of seminary.

Sometimes he'd be irritated when she'd show up at church with a nice lunch for the two of them. She offered to work with the drama team or join an outreach group. She wanted him to be proud of her and wanted to help out, but with the tiniest suggestion to be more involved, conversation would dry up. Unless it was his idea.

Cedar Ridge was especially dreamy tonight, street lights glowing in a straight line like an airport runway, the surrounding hills twinkling with lamplit windows of homes like hers: wide porches and cozy yards. Postcard pretty. The safe quiet gave her permission to consider, *Why does it bother him that I want to do things on my own? Should I stay in the background, slow and uninvolved, like before?*

Reece had compensated for her disability with cheerfulness and prayer and encouragement, to balance the burden she'd been. *We've been good lately, haven't we? The problems of the first years are over.*

Recently—and for reasons Reece couldn't remember— Brooklyn had blurted, "He's afraid you'll outshine him."

Defensively, she'd answered, "I'm not trying to."

"You don't have to. You glow. You jump into any job that needs to be done, you help whoever needs help. People love you."

"People love him too," Reece had argued, then changed the

subject. "After years of wheelchairs and crutches, I'm just happy to be walking. I'll never be totally normal, but I want to be everywhere and do everything for as long as I can, that's all."

I just need to explain that to him.

A car passed. She waved absently, not seeing the driver. *Maybe I'm overcompensating for lost time by jumping in too fast. It's not a competition. Should I be sitting on the back pew in a wheelchair, admiring him from afar?* She didn't get it. But she wanted to. Greg's agnostic family didn't have the faith that had kept her and her mom afloat in tough times. His work kept him in the spotlight but isolated him too. And his old friends? She and Greg were only twenty miles west of Magdeline, but he hadn't kept in contact with any of his hometown buddies.

But then, neither have I. She missed Mei more in the last year than ever before. Some things on her mind she could tell no one, not even Brooklyn. *If I could hear her voice...well, why not?*

Mei Aizawa's number—the last one Reece had—was a hotel on Guam. She went inside, looked it up and called, tiptoeing back to the porch, feeling relief as soon as it rang. A man answered: "Grand Reef Hotel. How may I help you?"

According to the desk clerk, Mei had been transferred to Japan.

Reece explained, "I'm Reece Moline, was Reece Elliston. Mei and I were friends years ago and I'm trying to get in touch with her."

"Ah," he said. "She mentioned you before. Yes. I can't give out her private number, but I can transfer you."

"Thank you!" It would be about noon in Japan. The front desk clerk of the Osaka Grand put Mei on. Reece said, *"Moshi, moshi, tomodachi!"*

"Aaaah, Reece!" Mei cried. *"Moshi, moshi!* How are you?"

"Great. And you?"

"I am *genki*. How is your health?" Mei's Japanese accent was less evident than in their last conversation, but her polite warmth was the same.

"It's good. I'm walking much better."

"I prayed for you."

"Thank you. I'm sorry I haven't written or called in so long."

"Me too. We are too busy, I think."

"You must come see me when you're in the U.S."

"I want to come."

Reece mentioned Rob's phone call. "I know what a stretch this is—Asia's a pretty big place." She laughed. "But I was wondering if you'd seen Elijah or heard from him. You're well connected with the…the work there, right?"

Mei answered after a silence, "I have not heard from him recently."

There was hesitation in the silence. Reece tried another tack. "Have you heard anything at all, not necessarily from him but about him, from Dom or anyone?"

"There was news he had gone with a team into Tufan."

"Are they still there?"

Mei's voice went quiet. "With Peregrini. Their trips are only for a few weeks. You know…"

Reece did know. There'd been a brief note years ago from Dr. Eloise Stallard about her continued involvement with Peregrini missions. "Rob seemed to think I might know where he was."

"You haven't heard from him?"

"Not since before the wedding."

"Oh. Reece…" There was great sympathy in those two words.

"It was for the best. He needed to go. I needed to stay."

Encouragingly Mei said, "You will walk perfect, *ne.*"

"Not perfect, but better. I'm a mommy and a minister's wife. There's lots to keep me moving. Olivet is two. She's blonde and blue-eyed like me."

"She will be beautiful and strong like you. And have great faith."

"She has Greg's smile," Reece said proudly. "If you hear from Elijah, let me know, okay?"

"It is difficult to contact him, I think."

"I know. But if you do…"

"What about Marcus?" Mei suggested. "Did you ask him?"

"Last I heard, he was in California. I wrote a couple of times but got no reply."

"I might be in L.A. next month. I will try to contact him."

"Stop over in Ohio anytime. For as long as you want."

"Thank you. Ah, sorry. They need me at the desk."

They said good-byes, and Reece surveyed Cedar Ridge, thinking of Magdeline instead, images of a town once her home. Nowadays she visited there to see her mom and stepdad. The rest was a closed book, a diary sealed. The Mag Five and their search for The Armor of God, the hideaways around Camp Mudjokivi, secret talks in school hallways, the bridge that the others built for her…treasures so precious they were painful. *That's why we lost contact. It was too impossible to keep going. It had to end the way it did. Once-in-a-lifetime things happen only once.*

The surgeries and physical therapy, everyone knew about those struggles. But if she were in Osaka this minute, she'd pour out her heart to Mei about a deeper trial that even her mother didn't know. She couldn't talk to anyone from the center, which had broken off from an older church and was still fragile. The congregation was her entire circle of friends.

Reading the Psalms helped, and recalling her mom's fortitude in a similar hard time. Memories of Mag Five adventures gave her strength, as did Elijah's gift from that time, precious jewelry for each of them, hers a pair of earrings, beautiful, secret, dangerous, dropped shyly into her open hand those years ago.

While Greg slept, she could look at them, an ancient gift full of spiritual meaning. She wanted to hold them in her hand in the light, maybe put them in a new place. She went into the house and tiptoed to Olivet's nightstand in the dark, lifting the lamp base to peel back the felt pad that sealed the bottom. It fell open. The earrings weren't there.

She ran her hand around inside the hollow base, around on the nightstand, thinking they must have fallen out as she lifted the lamp. Down on hands and knees she felt the carpet, fighting panic. Had she moved the lamp while dusting, and dropped them? Had she sucked them up with the vacuum? She padded to the kitchen for a flashlight, thinking, *Did I re-hide them and forget where?*

Back in Olivet's room Reece laid the flashlight on the floor, panning the beam back and forth under the crib, hoping for that deep red glimmer. *I must have moved them. I must have!* She searched the previous hiding places. Under her jewelry box. Behind the living room painting. Behind the tea box. Behind the roasting pan. *Not there! I sealed that lamp base. I know I did. No one knew where they were but me.*

CHAPTER 4

The real war will never get in the books.
—WALT WHITMAN

"I'll get it," Reece called to Greg, who was dressing in the bedroom. An early Sunday phone call had to be a volunteer cancelling. Teacher? Greeter? Nursery worker? She'd offer to fill in. She smiled before answering, "Good morning!"

"Hi." It was Rob.

"Hey," she said lightly, suppressing her excitement. She grabbed her coffee and went to the old church bench in the entry hall. Greg had been so preoccupied with the building, she hadn't told him about Rob's previous call. "How are you?"

"Hi, Reece," said another voice on the line, smokier, deeper. "Marcus?"

"S'me."

"It is so good to hear from you!"

"I'm here too," came a sweet, familiar voice. Mei.

Reece's heart thumped. "Where are you guys?"

"All over the place," Rob said. "Conference call."

Reece eased open the front door with her backside and went to the wicker swing. "How's everyone?" she asked guardedly. Adjusting the pillow to her back, she half expected another voice—Elijah's.

Rob answered, "We're fine." She knew Rob well enough—even with years and miles between them—to know he wasn't fine. He went on, "I got us together here 'cause there's news."

The town swayed before Reece's eyes, moving to the rhythm of the porch swing. Then she was seeing nothing. "Rob…?"

"The mission agency, Elijah's agency, they issued a release. I have it in my hand here. Marcus got one too. From his dad." Rob stalled. "It says here, it says that Elijah—only they use his code name—that he's been listed as missing. MIA." His voice sank to a whisper, "And they're saying presumed dead."

Reece heard Mei's voice catch.

"Presumed?" was all Reece could say. "Presumed!"

"Yeah," came his hoarse whisper.

"Have they searched? You said he was in Tufan. Have they searched there?"

Marcus said darkly, "They searched, Reece. Dad searched. He was Elijah's honcho, his superior."

"What about his team? Where's his team?"

Mei broke in. "Rob, tell us everything."

"That's sort of all I know. Marcus, do you know any more from Dom?"

"Not really." Marcus sounded noncommittal.

"What did his team say?" Reece asked shrilly. "Why don't they know where he is?"

Marcus said flatly, "He left the team, Reece, went out on his own. He broke the rules."

"Don't they have high-tech search equipment? Marcus, I thought your dad had the latest—"

"He searched, sweetheart. Hey, people, Dad swept the Qolo range by himself, with every resource. He defied mission policy, risked his life. Parabolani don't respond to a sudden-end transmission anymore. Elijah's homer just stopped a few days out.

Meaning, it was broken. Had to be blown up, or crushed, or he broke it. Triskeles are designed to take anything but a bullet or bomb. With the exception of a couple of people taken down in land-mine explosions, triskeles have always kept emitting. Even if he fell and broke his neck, the triskele would send signals. Even if he drowned. Where he was, there in the mountains, the most likely option is that he snapped it himself. And that's policy. You're supposed to end transmission if you're in a hopeless situation. Dad found the broken triskele lying on the ground."

"They haven't found—"

Impatiently, Marcus broke in, "The Parabolani no longer recover bodies in a prohibited region, even if the triskele is emitting. Dad couldn't have done it anyway, not by himself—haul a body miles over rough terrain. No safe place to send a copter. Dad broke policy, Reece, he tried everything. He looked everywhere."

Weakly Reece asked, "Elijah broke his homing device? Why would he do that?"

Marcus explained again, "He didn't want to be rescued. He got himself in too deep, took a risk and it didn't pay off. Dad went to the last transmission coordinates and somehow tracked it to a stream bed. There was nothing but the broken triskele. No body."

"So he could be hiding," Reece said desperately.

Marcus said, "The official statement is presumed dead. There are bandits out there. And packs of wild dogs. There was nothing else there at the scene. Nothing to track."

Rob spoke, his voice thick and gentle, "I called you last week, Reece, because when Dom notified me, asking if I'd heard from Elijah, we thought—Dom and I thought—that if Elijah were somewhere, and if he had one call, he…he might have called you."

"Call me? Why?"

"Reece, you gotta know."

She shook her head automatically. "No. That was over."

The painful silence on the line was interrupted by a faint squeak of the screen door and the movement of a shadow, listening in.

· · · · ·

Greg was slamming things in the kitchen. It was Monday, his usual day off, but he'd dressed for work. Reece stayed in Olivet's room, humming over the slams, getting out a storybook. "How 'bout this one, sweetie, you want this story?"

"Wa. Stowee."

Wa meant "yes." Reece smiled. "Momma loves how you repeat everything, trying so hard to learn new words. I'm going to miss it so much when you outgrow saying *wa*. Let's sit out on the swing, okay?" Reece padded on bare feet to avoid Greg as long as possible. He was furious. Her eyes were red.

"Wa. Sweeeeee."

"Okay, we'll swing and read a book."

They were settled in the yellow wicker swing, shaded from the morning. Cedar Ridge was sunny and bright, its shadows deep blues.

Greg came out. He didn't look at her.

"I've lost an old friend," she said, half imploring, half frustrated, trying again to explain her sadness.

He said nothing.

"I don't understand what you're so angry about."

He surveyed the town, eyes darting agitatedly. She admired his clean good looks objectively, distantly. She smelled his aftershave from ten feet away.

"You think he's alive," he practically sneered.

Reece kept the swing going with her toes. She turned the pages of Olivet's book absently, pointing to the pictures, speaking to Greg in a tone as if she were reading A is for Antelope, B is for

Bear. "It's a shock. It's denial," she said, resenting the need to explain her grief. "We knew each other for years."

He stood there tentatively, as if trying to choose between leaving, lashing out at her, or taking a stab at sympathy. She flipped pages slowly and pointed at the pictures: "F is for Frog, G is for Giraffe."

He put his hand in his pants pocket—a strange, slow, threatening gesture—and pulled out something. He opened his hand to her: the red diamond earrings.

She looked at them, her heart thumping in her ears, her face composed but hot. "My earrings."

"You hid them."

She tried joking. "They wouldn't look good on you."

There was a fire in his eyes she'd never seen. "I had them appraised, Reece. They're worth thousands. The appraiser was dumbfounded. Pure red diamonds. He'd never seen anything like them."

"I never knew how much…" she said casually.

His eyes leveled at her. "You had to know."

"I knew they were valuable. But never how much."

"Where'd you get them?" He was seething.

Her face flamed.

"They're from *him*, aren't they?"

"It was years ago, Greg."

His fingers closed around the diamonds. "He was a kid, Reece! You expect me to believe he could buy these with money from running errands at his daddy's camp? Come on! I've been busting my keister to pay your bills, and you had these all along!" His voice echoed down the street.

Reece prayed that no one heard. She couldn't tell him about the promises and secrets tied to diamonds with value beyond money. She only hoped the appraiser wasn't into antiquities.

This could be trouble.

"I'm selling them," he said.

Her toes stopped pushing the swing. Her finger stopped pointing at pictures. She laid the book aside and stood with Olivet in her arms, waiting until his eyes moved from the town to her face. She was calm, firm. "No."

"What other secrets are you keeping from me?" he asked in an ash-dry voice.

"There are no secrets." She was tempted to add, "Except for yours, and you're right, I have kept those." But she bit her tongue. She'd buried the past in forgiveness.

He opened his hand again. "These were in Olivet's room. In the base of a lamp!" He shook his head and clenched his fist and his teeth.

She lowered her voice as a cue for him to do the same. "I didn't want to put them in with my other jewelry. They could be stolen."

He looked over the town, eyes still darting, as if hatching a plan.

She moved into his sight line with Olivet on her hip. She held out her free hand. "I'd like my earrings."

"What else has he sent you?"

"I've had these for seven years. Greg, I love *you*."

He huffed coldly.

She was stunned. What? Did he think she didn't love him? Where was this coming from? "The earrings were a gift from way back when, and no, I didn't check to see how much they were worth. Yes, they're valuable. Is that what this is about? The money? I'll...I'll back off my volunteer work at the center and get a part-time job. I'm feeling stronger...."

Her offer only angered him more. "We're selling them," he said resolutely, putting them into her hand as if to make it more painful when she'd have to surrender them again. He seemed ready to leave, but didn't. She matched silence for silence. Then he sauntered down the steps.

"They should have been insured," he called back. "That's irresponsible."

We were kids, for heaven's sake, she thought. *Anyway, how can you insure a priceless secret?*

. . . . .

Reece had put Olivet in her high chair for early lunch when she heard footsteps on the porch. She leaned across the dining room table and looked through the entry hall. At the screen door stood a trim young man in shadow, a familiar silhouette. Rob.

She ran to the door, threw it open. They hugged long and cried hard.

He backed away, sniffled, and looked her over. "You look great. And you ran. You ran to the door."

"I'm working on it. Come in, let me get you some iced tea. I'm feeding Olivet. Want some lunch? Leftover pasta salad with chicken. You look great too. You must be working out. And your hair's a shade darker." She ruffled his spikey hair and gave him another quick hug.

"Lunch sounds good," he said. "Sorry to just show up. I wasn't sure what time I'd get here. I drove most of the night."

"Why are you here? Are your parents all right—" She stopped. "Or did I miss…Is there a memorial service—?"

He shook his head. Rob's last words on the phone had been, "Keep this quiet for now."

"I'll get lunch," she said.

Reece had allowed herself a good cry last evening while Olivet fell asleep in her arms on the porch swing. She'd slipped into bed, determined to be smiling if Greg should join her. She couldn't talk to anyone about this, not to Brooklyn about Elijah (it might get back to Greg); nor about the earrings (no one should know about them, ever); nor to anyone about Greg's raging suspicions (the center didn't need fodder for gossip). Rob's sudden appearance was fresh air. Even if they discussed nothing, he shared two of her three secrets: Elijah's disappearance and the diamonds.

She hurriedly set out tableware and plates, with an eye on the screen door, should Greg stop by.

"Aunt Jodi and Uncle Russ haven't given up hope," Rob said. "The twins are devastated. They idolized him. But until a body is found…" He sat back heavily and shook his head.

"What?"

"A body won't be found. That's Dom's view."

"Why not?"

"You don't want to know."

Reece put a bib on Olivet. She brought out a pitcher of tea and two glasses of ice.

"I'm going," Rob said solidly as she filled his glass.

"Going?"

"To Tufan. I'm inviting you and the others to go. The Mag Five…Four."

Reece sat down across from him. "You can't be serious."

"The last time I saw Elijah—" He broke off, dropped his head. Reece laid a hand on his arm. She'd been so grieved herself, she'd hardly thought of Rob losing his cousin and lifelong best friend.

"The last time…," she coached.

"Was in Cairo. He'd sent me a note with the time and place in a code he called Caesar Shift and these glyphs they use in the agency. Symbols for airports around the world. They look sort of hieroglyphic, but are really the layouts of international airports. Pretty clever. This was agency insider stuff, but he'd put me in the loop months before, with no explanation. Don't tell anyone. Anyway, we met up. He gave me a hug and whispered,

'Careful.' He was with a woman. Really beautiful. There was some kind of heat between them. I couldn't tell if it was"—he paused, slightly embarrassed—"lust or love or hate. I couldn't tell. Maybe all three. Sorry. I'm being honest here. Anyway, we had dinner in this little outdoor cafe down a narrow back street. There were mirrors on the walls of the cafe on both sides. If you knew where to sit—and he did—you could see reflections of reflections. You could see everyone on the street, coming and going, and who was in the alley behind you. He kept looking into those mirrors, watching. When that girl, Suzanne, left for the powder room, he hinted at trouble in the agency. He started to write stuff down on a napkin and show me, but wadded it up and put it in his pocket when she came back. He was worried. I couldn't say anything about this on the phone. The story Marcus is telling is that his dad risked his life to look for Elijah, that he went out on his own. I did some snooping to see if that was so, but couldn't confirm anything." He poked at his lunch.

"Are you thinking that Marcus lied? Or that Dom lied?"

He moved restlessly in the chair. "What kind of sense does it make that they have his triskele, but there was no trace of him? Not a shred. With all their technology? I can't swallow that."

"What did they post as cause of death?"

"They didn't. The theory is he was attacked by wild dogs, but I don't buy that either. Remember when we were attacked by Salem, that crazed malamute?"

"How could I forget? Elijah saved my life that day."

"Even back then as a kid he was always geared up with bow and arrow. You can't tell me he would have gone out there un-prepared, as well trained as he was. And even if—*even if!*—what they say is true, there would have been something left, you know? There would have been something. A scrap of cloth. A bone." He pressed his elbows on the table, clasped his hands together, and leaned his head against them in grief or exhaustion. Then he looked hard at her. "Captured. That makes the most sense, but they're not saying that. What if it turns out he's trapped somewhere or held captive, and we're all stateside twiddling our thumbs and crying?" Angrily he took a slug of tea. "I gotta know."

"How long has he been gone?" she asked.

"From the time he left? Three weeks, two days. He told the team he'd be gone two weeks at the most. There'd be something left, wouldn't there, if the triskele was right there? Why am I the only one asking that question?"

"Tufan's been in the news. I hardly paid attention, but you can't just go there, can you?"

Impatience hardened his face. "It's a disputed region. You need a permit. The Edifice took over, presenting it as a prototype of quote 'cultural preservation'. They're reintroducing the old religion. That's the new path laid out for all of us, each culture to its own ancient way and place. No interference. Supposed to bring peace and harmony."

Reece tried to sound informed. "It's not working?"

"It only works if you toe the line." Rob dug into lunch again. "I'll go as a meteorologist. It's common knowledge that wind currents over the Qolo range go so high aloft as to affect weather across continents. I'd say I'm a researcher."

Reece grinned. "That's not common knowledge, about the winds."

"Okay. Well, among us weather geeks it is."

Working her leg muscles with one hand, she fed Olivet with the other, thinking.

Rob digressed. "See, it was as if he wanted me to meet that woman for a reason. Like you'd want to introduce a fiancée to the family. But it wasn't like that. He never said anything. Or maybe he wanted to be seen with me, a stranger, in that cafe. I'd changed a flight through Paris to meet him, and all we did was chat. I have to say, looking back, that Suzanne was unpleasantly surprised to see a friend of Elijah's. She called him his other name, Geo. I knew he was using an alias, so I measured everything I said, playing off him, watching his expressions to make sure I didn't step over any lines. Maybe he was testing me. Or preparing me for something." Rob paused to watch Olivet. "She's a doll, Reece. Spitting image. Olivet's a cute name."

"Thanks. From the Mount of Olives."

"Cool. If I ever have a kid, I'm gonna name him Valley of Megiddo."

"Are you making fun of me?"

"Or Merriweather. Good name for a meteorologist's kid."

Reece squeezed his arm again. "I've really missed you, Rob. I've missed the Mag Five." They ate and watched Olivet smear food on the high-chair tray. "I couldn't take her…if I went. Could I?"

"No way. There's no oxygen up there on the heights. Medical care is horrible. We'd be gone a couple weeks. At least. It takes a few days to get there, then you have to acclimate. The altitude can be dangerous. There are pills you can take beforehand that might help, but don't buy 'em on the streets there." He shuddered, made a face of disgust, and went on. "We'd have to go as a group tour, and you're right—you can't get in except by special permit. Tourism is encouraged though. If we had to make a run for it…" He sat back suddenly. "And that's another question. How'd he even get into Tufan? I think he's on a watch list, why he switched names. If he was stuck somewhere, how would he get out? Anyway, if we find him or if we get any hint about his whereabouts and it drags on, I'd stay behind, and the rest of you could come back. Is your passport current?"

"I think so. But I can't leave right now, Rob. I want to help in any way. But it's not a good time."

He put his fork down, sat back again, and crossed his arms for an explanation. He studied her with a caring frown. "You're right about that. It's not a good time. You've heard of the massacre over there."

"Massacre? It was an explosion at a prison, wasn't it?"

"More an internment camp. A thousand people died, whole families hauled in for as little as being tuned in to an underground radio station. It was reported as an accident. Rumor has it The Edifice staged it to stomp out dissenting voices. Things are dicey over there. Real dicey."

"Do you think he was in that camp?"

"Who knows."

"It's not that I don't want to go," Reece tried to explain, "but lightning struck the Spirit Center. For the second time. Greg's the director, and he's working all hours. He couldn't take off to watch Olivet. Mom works. I can't leave Olivet with a babysitter for two weeks. I mean I could, but money's a little tight right now."

Rob leaned forward, intrigued. "Struck a second time? You said that before."

"Yeah. I thought that couldn't happen."

"It happens a lot." He emptied his glass of tea. "Here's my idea: you could go as my assistant. I'd fill you in on the way, teach you some weather lingo, in case we're questioned. Marcus would be our backpacking friend, and Mei would be our travel guide. She has special clearance, I hear."

"You've thought it through," Reece said admiringly. Olivet grunted for more food to be placed on her tray. "Sorry, sweetie. Here you go."

"She sure is a doll," Rob commented again. "I'm engaged, you know."

"I heard. My mom saw your mom somewhere. Her name's Lydia, right, and she's a theatrical design major and she's wonderful and you met while doing community theatre."

Rob beamed. "She's working up in the Boston area this summer at a couple of little theatres."

"When's the wedding?"

"After she graduates. We're thinking next summer. Have you done any more acting?"

Reece wrinkled her nose. "I'm not that good. Nothing like you. It was fun in school, but you know, I've been having babies and surgeries."

He looked at his watch, then wadded up his napkin and dropped it on the plate, signaling a change back to the subject. "It could be dangerous. And we couldn't be in any way connected to the mission agency. The Edifice keeps an eagle eye on them."

"But Marcus's dad is head of their rescue department, the Parabolani. So we're already connected, aren't we?"

"That could be a problem." He stood and gathered his dishes. "If you can't go, I understand. But whoever's going, we've gotta leave soon. A week to get the paperwork, then book a flight. We don't want to be in Tufan when fall comes."

CHAPTER 5

Clear is what I want. Clearly it's not easy to find.
—ANDREA SUMMER, "CLEARLY"

"You think he's still alive." Greg had said it with a genuine sneer when he caught Reece looking sentimental.

His words rolled roughly over her. She went out to the swing, rocking and cozying her Olivet, a bundle of platinum curls, chubby face, fingers and toes poking out of pink pajamas. Reece studied the city, the trees, the housetops fading in twilight. Hair piled on her head, and barefoot in a gypsy skirt and blouse, she wished she could move out here to the porch, sleep in the swing with Olivet, eat on the steps, watch cloud shadows play across the town by day, follow the moon's face by night, and wonder at the stars. It was hard to be indoors.

Did Greg actually want Elijah to be dead? Could he be that jealous? To let Elijah go was the hardest thing she'd ever done, but she'd put it all behind her. When she'd started dating Greg, he was bothered by mentions of Elijah or the Mag Five. So she'd stopped.

Chances had seemed slim that another great guy like Elijah would ever care about a handicapped girl. But she and Greg were in another school play together and their chemistry was great, the director said. Greg went to church with her, gave his life to the Lord, and that was it. With hopes of corrective surgery for Reece and with everyone's encouragement—even though they were young—they married.

I did the right thing, she had told God. *We all knew that Elijah needed to go on mission. The rest of us—Rob and Marcus, Mei and I—we needed to stay home. It's the way things worked out. I didn't want to stop what you had planned for him, Lord.*

First loves run deepest, they say, and Reece had worried that she might never get over Elijah. But her mom was living proof to the contrary. Speaking of her second husband, Darrell, Rachel had whispered to a friend that God saved the best for last. So it wasn't a rule; the first didn't have to be the deepest. Reece's marriage to Greg, her corrective surgery, and having Olivet—all were dreams come true. She could share a life of ministry with her husband and have a family. Mind tripping from subject to subject, Reece gazed down at sleeping Olivet. "I can't leave you, gumdrop, not for two weeks. If I did, though, Grammy could watch you, on weekends and overnight. You have your own room and lots of toys there. Brooklyn could watch you other times. You and Desmond could play together. You love Desmond." How would she explain it all to Brooklyn? to the congregation? A few of them knew her history with Elijah. She kept rocking. "And Daddy'd be here, sweetie, on his day off and every evening to play with you. He would. He'd stay home for you. He loves you so much."

How could I explain it to Greg? No. I can't leave. I can't. But what if I'm the only one who doesn't go? What if they find Elijah, and I'm not there? What would he think? He'd understand. I'm the only married one. I have a child. No one but Rob has committed to going. What if it ended up being just Rob and me: a married woman and a single man...even though we're like brother and sister...I should see what the others decide.

And why was Rob so suspicious of Dom? There were moments during lunch he'd seemed conflicted, as if he had more to say, but couldn't. Hesitant. Like Mei.

What if Elijah's alive and in trouble, and I do nothing? What if my not going changes the outcome? How could I forgive myself? Dr. Eloise was his mentor in the Word and in undercover missions, always in the know. I should call her. Oh, what am I thinking? I don't have any money. It's impossible. If Parabolani couldn't find him with all their military technology and training, what can four civilians hope to do? What if Dr. Eloise doesn't know? Someone should tell her. Elijah was her special project. But she's up in years. Why upset her? I could call Dom and ask if she—no, I shouldn't call Dom.

The rosy sunset turned Olivet's velvety little cheeks to lavender; her chubby hands lay softly curled against her gown. So still. "I won't leave you. Even though you'd be fine and Grammy and Grampy would spoil you as rotten as a rotten apple."

• • • • •

Rob left a phone message on Wednesday. "Sorry. I don't mean to push, Reece, but I need to know in a couple days."

On Thursday she grieved, wrestled, paced the house, played distractedly with Olivet, waited for Greg to soften, found herself outside that evening, the town swaying to the rhythm of the swing again. *I can't leave Greg. He's been out of trouble for over a year. We have a new start, a new place. Things were going better until the storm damaged the church…the Center, and until he found the diamond earrings. What if I left and he relapsed into his old behavior? I couldn't have that on my conscience. But saying no to Rob would be saying I didn't support his search. What if he calls it off because of me? He's not calling it off. He's going.*

Rob was the newest meteorologist at WCW-TV in Tulsa. Reece called him late. He was in a meeting, so she left a message of apology, declining his invitation, thanking him profusely for the offer, promising prayers and blessings for every day of his search. With one more apology she hung up, sick at heart. *I've abandoned Elijah a second time.*

She drifted to the front steps. The moon had risen—a coral moon over a purple town with yellow windows like eyes all around, Main Street lights like a landing strip aimed at the wrecked, steeple-less church. In the time it took to make that call to Rob, Cedar Ridge had changed from small town to what felt like a crash site. *I'm staying,* she said to the patched-over church. *It's the only thing that makes sense. What can I do in a strange, restricted country anyhow? I can't speak the language. I can't walk far or run fast. I can't leave Olivet. I can't leave Greg. I can't. There. Settled.*

Olivet had sensed her tension and was balking at bedtime, so Reece packed her in the car seat and drove to Cedar Ridge Spirit Center. Greg would be home soon, probably, but she wanted to make amends this very moment while the decision was fresh and strong in her heart. Maybe they'd go out for ice cream, come home and make love. She'd apologize and affirm him, find out what his doubts were all about. She'd stay home more if that's what he needed. Be less involved at church. She had other ministries. First, her daughter. Then her prayer map and the new believers meditation group he'd asked her to start. She could keep those, even with a part-time job. She'd send Rob a little money for the trip.

Elijah was in heaven. She thanked God for bringing him out of an unbelieving family to the very work of the Lord in one of the most remote, unreached places of the world. She fought tears of sorrow and joy. And guilt. She'd had a part in his death. She'd pushed him to go into all the world. By ending their relationship she'd practically sealed his fate.

Reece pulled into the front parking lot of the center and

looked heavenward. *Lord Jesus, tell him how much I loved him. I really did love him. Make something great of his sacrifice.*

She wiped her eyes, looked in the backseat. Olivet was sound asleep. Greg's was the only car in the front lot. She pulled up to the door and whispered to Olivet, "I'll be right back, baby. I'm just going to run in and give Daddy a big kiss." Quietly she closed the car door and locked it. Two minutes, no more. She unlocked the front door of the church; the entrance hall was empty and dark. *Electricity still off? How can he be studying?* His office window had been dark as she drove in.

The battery-run exit lights glowed red. She zipped down the hall lightheartedly in quiet sneakers. *He's probably closing up. I'll check around.* The church at night was always a little creepy. Big empty halls. Sounds of settling walls...

...and a woman cooing.

She was a few steps from Greg's office. She slowed, stopped. Heard his deep murmurs, and a woman's soft chuckle.

Not again. She stopped breathing. Her heart turned to iron. *God!* Anguish vaporized into fierce clarity. She moved to the door, put her ear to it, brain and heart hammering. There was music, a medieval chant, and two low voices. Reece turned, moved cat-quiet back down the hall and out the front door. *This time I know what to do. This time I know.*

She pulled the car around—lights off—to a safe distance from the office window. She was too short to reach it. *Find something to stand on. Empty a flowerpot or...crate. There's a plastic milk crate in the trunk.* She popped the trunk, quietly emptied the crate, and carried it to the window. *No more believing the best, no more expecting honest answers.* Filthy rage welled up. *No room for pain or stupid hope this time. Only truth. Olivet must not wake up in the dark and be alone and afraid. This won't take long, baby. They might see the bushes move. Who cares? At least I'll know who it is this time.* She placed the crate between bushes, ignoring the scratches to her arms. She stepped up. They were undressing each other, moving to the rhythm of a worship song. By candlelight. *God help me. God. God help me.* She furiously breathed his name again and again. *Oh Father. Help me.*

This time—unlike the last times—she was more angry for the sake of the church than for herself. The woman was Brooklyn's cousin, Audrey. Reece stepped down, grabbed the crate, ran it back to the car, shoved it into the trunk, and eased out of the lot. She looked back. It had only *seemed* like the office was dark. She'd missed the flickering candlelight.

She drove home, head swimming. Olivet roused and whimpered when Reece transferred her from car to crib, patting her back to sleep, humming an old hymn, "I come to the garden alone, while the dew is still on the roses…" She changed into a long-sleeved top to hide the scratches on her arms. "And He walks with me and He talks with me and He tells me I am his own."

Pacing through the house, she crept into Olivet's room again and again, thinking between waves of anguish how much she loved looking at her. *Like salve on a raw wound. All right, what to do. What to say. Check the paperwork. See if he's up to* all *his old tricks. Hurry.* She staged the scene first, in case Greg came in. Grabbing a stack of medical forms, she tossed them on the dining table. While tea water heated, she rummaged through the garage until she found an unmarked box under the workbench. *Finances. He knew I wouldn't look. He assumed I'd trust. I told him so. Not this time, love. Innocent as a dove now, wise as a serpent now.* She rifled through, searching for the kind of discrepancies she'd found before: back taxes not paid, fake addresses, huge credit card bills. Anything a wife might be culpable for. Fearing she'd lost track of time, she flipped off the light and ran back, checking the water on the stove, glancing at the clock. *Four minutes? Seems like hours. He won't be back yet. He's busy.*

She peeked out the front door, just in case. A car was parked on the other side of the street. In front of the empty lot. *Someone's out there!* She crept to the darkened living room window and looked through the sheers. A man was sitting in the car. *Greg's having me watched? Followed? He's hired someone! Call Mom, tell Darrell to get over here—in uniform.* She grabbed the phone, went to the dining room, and dropped down beside the toy box, out of view of the front door. Why had she wanted a glass door anyway? Any wacko could look right in. Had she locked it while bringing Olivet in? No.

Knock, knock, knock…knock, knock.

Her heart jumped. It was ten o'clock. Who'd be here this late? Was it the man in the car? It was a soft knock—soft to see if she was awake? Soft because the visitor felt bad stopping by so late? Soft so he wouldn't wake the baby, having watched her bring Olivet in? Maybe it had nothing to do with Greg's affair. Maybe it was a church member, someone needing help. Had he seen her walk into the dining room just now?

Okay, stop. Get up and answer the door. She took the phone. *He'll see me coming with something in my hand. I'll put it to my ear. He'll think I have a friend on the line. Get a hold of yourself.* Briskly she opened the door. There stood a nervous young man with a kind face and wavy hair. He was dressed neatly and had a small box in his hand.

"Hello," she said crisply. "Was that you sitting in that car across the street?"

"Yes, ma'am. I hope I didn't scare you. Are you Reece?"

"Yes."

Relief washed over his face, his posture relaxed. "I'm Steven Lockhart. I just flew in. My flight was delayed. I'm sorry to come by this late. I waited to see if anyone was still up. I'm a friend of

Geo's. It's good to meet you." He sort of bowed and said more deliberately, "It's an honor to meet you." He held out the blue velvet box. She considered his shadowed face: gentle, intelligent eyes behind glasses, a small nose, a mouth half opened in uncertainty. For all appearances, this could be prom night. Or a marriage proposal. She almost laughed. He nodded toward the box. "This is from him. He wanted you to have it."

"I beg your pardon?"

He blew out air and withdrew the box. "I'm sorry. Let me start over."

Forgetting her fears and feeling sorry for him, she stepped out on the porch, phone in hand.

"I worked with Geo," he said. "I was on his team in Tufan. He told me that if anything—" His voice broke. He bit his lip. "—happened to him, that you were to have this." He held it out again.

"Geo…"

Steven nodded. "George." An expression of embarrassed horror crossed his face. He withdrew the box a second time. "You didn't hear what happened?"

She stopped short of saying Elijah's name. "I did. I heard. So you're a mish?"

"Yes, ma'am. I'm with Peregrini: Central Asia Division. I'm sorry. I didn't know where to start."

"That's all right. Come in. Please."

He followed her into the dining room.

"The water's hot. I can make coffee or tea," she said. "Would you like some?"

Eagerly taking in the details of the house, from the heavy, old crown molding to the hardwood floors—as if this was someplace special to him—he began to relax. "Yes, either. We drink anything. Got to be adaptable."

In minutes Steven had recounted the details of the last morning he'd spent with George Telanoo. "No one could believe he'd go solo," he said. "It's forbidden. Before he headed out he gave me this. He hid it in a rice ball." He put the ring box on the table. Reece's hand went to her mouth, supposing what might be in the box.

"I guess it meant a lot to him," Steven said reverently. "He made me swear not to lose it—on threat of death practically." He smiled weakly.

She took the velvet box, one probably gotten from a jewelry store, chosen with care by Steven. As if she were someone to impress. What a sweet touch. She lifted the lid. It was Elijah's red diamond stud: his chip of the Tear of Blood extracted from the ancient Armor of God. The only pure red diamond known to exist. Despite its rarity, Elijah had it broken into pieces so he could share it with the Mag Five—provision if they should ever need a large amount of cash. Only to be used for mission purposes, to save a life.

Reece's fury over Greg's affair and her panic over this stranger at the door slipped to the back of her thoughts. She lifted the jewel from the box. "Thank you so much, Steven. You came all the way here to deliver this? Where are you from?"

"Originally Cincinnati. I'm on a month furlough. You...you brought him into the kingdom, didn't you?"

"It was a group of us." She turned the gem in her fingers, holding it to the light, a tiny burning ember flashing gold and red. She smiled at Steven with a twinkle of conspiracy in her eye. Here was another perspective, perhaps an unbiased one, the closest to Elijah's. "Steven, all I heard is that he's MIA and presumed dead. What do you think?"

"If anyone could survive, Geo could. But in Tufan..." He asked cautiously, "What do you know about Tufan?"

"Not much. It's mountainous. The Edifice is in charge."

"It's been called a graveyard for the gospel. For centuries. You won't get that from the mainstream. All you'll hear is the return of the old 'rich culture,' as they call it. Does anyone call a culture disgusting or immoral nowadays? No, they're all *rich*. I'm a linguist, and I pay attention to words. *Rich culture* has no meaning anymore. Any society can live however they want and that makes it worthy of preservation, especially if it's old. If everything is rich, then nothing is. I'm not talking about how people dress or what they eat. It's worldview, all tied in with culture. Sorry, that's my soapbox. Anyway, Geo would never let me look at his research notes. But that stuff, the beliefs of their religion, kept him up at night. He'd get mailings from the agency—histories and updates. Then he'd go deeper on his own. Dom called him on it once, and from hearing only Geo's side of the conversation, I could tell that Dom was telling him to back off. But he didn't. Sometimes I'd see him scribbling stuff as fast as he could go, then he'd stop and stare out into space for a long time. Then shake his head like he couldn't believe what he was thinking. Geo taught me the ropes, you know. He knew the ropes. He wanted to get to that one last tribe in his area that didn't have access to the Word. He was determined." Steven stopped. "So you guys were…friends?"

"Thanks for telling me all this, Steven. Yes, we were very good friends from middle school on. I was a believer, he wasn't. But I prayed that he'd come to know God. Then I enlarged my prayers, that he'd have great influence in the world." She smiled. "And he did."

"He changed *my* life."

"You've been holding on to that gem since the day he disappeared?" What a tiny, heavy burden. She could relate. "We went together for a while," she confessed, "but I had a bone condition, walking was difficult. In the end we both realized he needed to get out into the world and I needed to come back home. We parted on good terms."

Steven took a sip and said confidentially, "He and Suzanne. They went round and round. She made light of him, and he'd go brood somewhere."

Clearly he assumed that Reece knew more than she did. "Make light of him?"

"The dark stuff he was finding out. About the Lotus, about demons."

A chill went through her. "Lotus?"

"Yeah." Steven looked around the dining room again, soaking in details. "He wouldn't talk about it. I'd hear him say things to himself like, 'It's all connected,' and 'It's all the same.' But he wouldn't tell me anything. He might have told Karinna. I don't know."

"From the SOS ship—that Karinna?"

"Right. Karinna Welsch. You know her? They met on a Students of the Seven Seas trip. She's great. We're the only ones he really trusted there at the end, Karinna and me."

It dawned on Reece that Karinna would have known Elijah by his real name. *I have to be careful. Think before speaking.* Grateful that Rob had already warned her about Elijah's alias, she put the diamond stud back in the velvet box. "Thank you so much for this. Tell me, what do *you* think happened out there?"

He mulled over her question, his eyes steady on her, with only a hint of suspicion. "I can't believe he's dead. I can't. But Tufan is a dangerous place on lots of levels. People think it's all exotic and spiritual. Oh, it's spiritual all right—spiritual darkness."

"When he left, which direction did—"

A car pulled in. Startled, Reece stood and glanced out the door. "That's my husband, Greg. Listen, it's complicated, but I have to keep this quiet. For Geo's sake. You know, security. I'm going to shoo you out now, but thank you so much. So much! Call me if you hear anything." She placed the velvet box on the seat of her chair and scooted it in. Light footsteps sounded on the walk outside. "No, wait," she whispered. "I'll call you. I'll call Dom and get your number."

Steven made his way obediently to the door and said hesitantly, "I don't know if you should call Dom."

Greg came in. She made cheerful introductions. "Greg, this is Steven. He's a missionary. Steven, this is my husband, Greg."

Greg leaned smoothly into a handshake. "Good to meet you. Reece has always had an interest in missions."

Reece said, "Thanks for stopping by, Steven. Come back when you can stay longer. Godspeed. Oh, and tell Karinna I said hello. By the way, is there a guy named Li still with the SOS? If so, tell him I said hi too."

Steven was out the door. He turned back. "I don't know much about the SOS. I'm with Pereg—"

"Oh. That's okay. Take care and drive safely." She waved and closed the door.

"Who was that?" Greg dropped a handful of books on the dining room table.

Brittle and calm and hoping to heaven he didn't sit in her chair, she answered, "Someone from the mission agency. Dom Skidmore sent him, I guess. You remember Dom, Marcus's dad? Big military guy, a great heart for training believers. Steven dropped by to be sure all of Elijah's old friends had the news."

"Nice of him."

"A military-type thing, probably Dom's idea, showing up at the door with the bad news."

He gave her a look. "In the military they notify the *spouse* when a person dies."

"Well, military meets ministry, I suppose. But you're right, it was very nice of him."

He looked at the cups and the stack of medical forms on the dining room table. "Who's Karinna?"

Reece had been right to stage the paperwork, and she moved toward it, leaning on the back of her chair. Her hands were steady and cold, her cheeks warm as she gathered and stacked the papers crisply. She couldn't believe her own composure. "We met in Japan seven years ago. She and Steven worked together. Whew, I didn't get half done here. I'm going to be burning the midnight oil."

"Is there iced tea?"

"I'll make some more. I'll bet you're thirsty, working so late," she said generously. "I'll get these put in order."

· · · · ·

Reece cleaned and filed, dusted the living room, scoured the bathroom. It was 4:00 a.m. She needed to find a place for Elijah's diamond—and her earrings; Greg hadn't called for them yet. She ended up in the front yard with a pickle jar, a penlight, and a trowel.

Few things were clear, but the clear things were blazing like midday. First, she had the funds now. She could sell Elijah's diamond for a plane ticket, and with the proper reason: to save a life maybe. Second, Elijah had not stopped caring about her, even though she'd ended their relationship. The jewel illustrated Rob's belief that Elijah would have made one last effort to contact her, if he could have. The jewel said more than, "Here's provision, if you should ever need it." It said, "It's okay between us."

She quickly buried the jar in the flower bed, patting the dirt and arranging the mulch to look undisturbed. *I'll call Mei and tell her where it is. Or I just might dig it back up tomorrow, drive into Columbus and pawn it. Or go to a small-town jeweler, one less likely to know what a treasure this is. Aren't jewels registered, though? I have no paperwork, so maybe I can't sell it. I could claim I found it. Or it was anonymous gift from a guy who called himself George. A river town in another state is a better idea: Maysville or Beckley. I could be there and back in a few hours. Will Greg check the odometer? I found a few dollars loose in the dryer last week. I can buy a little gas. How will I explain, though, if he asks where I've been? Should I lie and say, "Preacher's wife, always on call, you know. Had to make a run for…" I'll think of something.*

If he asked for the earrings in the morning, what would she say? The diamonds were a secret and a promise, both to be kept. She'd felt bad not telling him all this time, hiding things. It felt like lying. Reece went into the house with one new certainty burned into her head: Greg's accusations of hidden passions and lost hours were nothing but the pot calling the kettle black.

CHAPTER 6

You understood me better than most.
I'll love your forever from the other coast.
—ANDREA SUMMER, "TUNNELS TO CHINA"

Wired from lack of sleep, Reece slammed the file drawer shut and went downstairs to the entry hall, passport in hand. Dressed in celery-colored blouse, jeans, and running shoes, Reece stared at the passport, listening for Greg's car. Sometimes he'd drop in mid-afternoon. Like the passport photo, her blonde hair was pulled into a ponytail and fringed around her face. But she'd lost weight. No appetite this week.

I don't like the layout of this house. The first thing you see when you come in is the dining table, like there should be a fancy dinner ready. Olivet's toys are always scattered around. The kitchen's in the back, closed off. It faces north, it's dark, I'm by myself when I cook. The front porch… She turned to the porch. *Unlike the kitchen in every way: facing south, bright and open, a place to camp out in all kinds of weather, to rock Olivet, to pray over Cedar Ridge.*

The lot across the street brimmed with summer wildflowers: black-eyed Susans and daisies and those tall purple ones. She grabbed a pair of scissors, ran outside, and cut handfuls of tall-stemmed blossoms, taking them back to make a bouquet.

"There!" She sat the vase on the dining table, then peeked in on her sleeping baby. *I have to get out of here.* She tiptoed to the entry and surveyed the house again. *What a blessing it is, old and comfortable, with touches of elegance: a transom of stained glass above the door, a vintage chandelier. But I have to get out.*

She called Brooklyn. "Hi, it's me. Sorry to bother you, but it's been a hectic week. I need to step out for a couple of hours, and Olivet is in the middle of her nap."

"Are you okay? You sound out of breath."

"I just picked a bouquet of wildflowers across the street. They're so pretty! What a gorgeous day!"

"I'll be right there. Desmond's up. I owe you a couple of hours anyway."

"Thanks so much. Help yourself to leftovers."

· · · · ·

Reece pulled under the wooden arch of Camp Mudjokivi and stopped on the rise overlooking the campus. Camp Mudj like a shallow bowl, Silver Lake at its center, its edges scalloped with cabins, tree houses, the lodge, a nature center, and to the left Elijah's house. Children were everywhere—in paddle boats and kayaks on the lake, loitering around cabins. Behind the lodge and out of sight was the pool, obviously busy, given the squeals of campers and twangs of the diving board. Nostalgia swept in from all points. *This feels like home.*

She'd been on crutches for her last official visit years ago, returning to Elijah's parents the things he'd taken to Japan but which weren't allowed at SOS boot camp in the Pacific Islands. His was a blunt decision, delivered in an international call to his parents from a youth hostel in Shimabara. Russ and Jodi Creek agreed only after a half hour of fruitless arguing. Elijah, still a teen, wasn't backing down.

Reece had struggled up those steps to Elijah's house with his bag of clothes and souvenirs for the family, determined to present it personally to his mother. They had both cried. Jodi

Creek wanted an explanation about Elijah's call to missions and was irritated when Reece tried to explain. Why would Elijah—so attuned to nature and the camp, so close to his family—go a million miles away with perfect strangers? Jodi had even used the word *senseless*.

Passing the Creek house now to avoid a chance meeting, Reece pulled right, toward the wide-open maintenance building. She parked, and with airiness in her step, walked in. "Hi, Bo."

A rugged man in greasy jeans and green camp shirt paused from working on a golf cart. He beamed with recognition. "Doggies, if it isn't little Reece Elliston."

She smiled back. "It's Moline now."

"That's right. An old married lady. Haven't seen you in years. How've you been?"

"I'm good."

Bo wiped his tanned hands and face with a bandana. His hair was cut close, receding, his neck thick and muscular. He reached out to shake her hand, glancing uncertainly at her leg. She was used to the look of puzzlement by now, and anxious to get past it.

Reece smiled. "I had surgery. They put a rod in."

"Well, good for you!"

"Thanks. I guess you heard about Elijah."

Bo chose one of the tools spread out on the golf cart seat. "Terrible. Just terrible. His dad's holding out hope, but…" Light from the open door caught tears welling up in his eyes. "I knew that boy since first day of camp." He glanced up expectantly. "You got news?"

"No. I'm sorry." Rob's plan was not to be shared, not even with Elijah's parents, in case things went terribly wrong. And it had already occurred to Reece—though she hadn't mentioned it to Rob—that Elijah could be alive but didn't want to be found.

All the more reason to keep quiet. "Would it be okay if I took a short hike into Owl Woods—for old time's sake?"

He half smiled, a wrinkle of sadness over his damp brow. "Help yourself."

"Thanks. I might go all the way to Great Oak."

"Stop by on your way back. Just so we'll know."

"I will."

"Glad about that surgery," he said.

"Thanks."

The sunny path curved around the lake and into the dappled shade of Owl Woods. Children's voices skimmed the water. Birds chirped, insects hummed...echoes of innocent, joy-filled summers. Reece had never been an official camper, always with Elijah who, as his dad's right-hand man, had the run of the place. The Mag Five, usually steering clear of campers and in pursuit of The Armor of God, had dug into mysteries and soared into adventures. Starting at Camp Mudj, they'd found it all. *It's beautiful, Lord God. I'm in Owl Woods for the first time on my own two legs. Thank you! Thank you so much!*

A long path lay ahead, white clouds drifting above, questions pursuing: *Can I sell the diamond? I have to tell Mom what's going on. Will she keep Olivet for a couple of weeks? How could Greg do this to me—to us—again? Can Elijah really be gone? Lord, you have all power. You could bring him back. You could fix it all.*

She soldiered on down the path, the sweet surroundings at odds with her troubles—until there it was ahead: Great Oak, on a rise to the right of the path, a watchtower at the far corner of Camp Mudj. Reverently she dropped down on a root and leaned against the rough bark. Breezes ruffled the top branches, swirling leaves and clouds together, dizzy and wonderful.

"What can you see from up there?" she'd asked Elijah once. She asked again aloud, echoing his answer. "Everything." She had climbed with him to the top, one foothold at a time, ignoring the pain, because she wanted to see the world as he saw it. And up where branches swayed under their weight, Elijah had kissed her. Right in the middle of an argument.

She stood and studied the trunk, measuring the distance to the first branch. *Six feet. From up there I could see what I should do next. All I need is a heave to the first branch or a log leaned against the trunk.* It was a bad idea, even with therapy and with stronger arms from carrying Olivet. She argued with herself: *If I get stuck, Bo will come looking. He wouldn't forget me.* Caution argued back: *Your answer isn't in a treetop. There's no right or wrong. It's simply up to you. Make a list of pros and cons.* "Okay, why stay?" She paced before Great Oak, grimacing; she'd walked too far too fast. "Stay because of Olivet. Because of the danger in Tufan. Stay because of Greg." *Huh! He should be on the Reasons-to-Go list. I'd have to avoid people's questions about where I'm going, and why. I could slip away quietly, but either way will arouse suspicion. It'll look like I'm running, hiding something. Rumors will start and I won't be here to answer. They'll press Mom and Darrell for the truth. If Greg's answer is different than theirs, it'll look like someone's lying.*

Someone would have to lie. So staying is less complicated.

Thirsty and wishing she'd brought a canteen, Reece plowed ahead into Telanoo where the path was rougher, trees dry and sparse. *Reasons to Go. One: Greg should handle his problems himself this time. Let him answer the awkward questions. Let him lie his way out of it. Two: Whatever the outcome in Tufan I'd come back satisfied that I did my best, that I helped my friends, that I gave Greg space to come to his senses. Three birds with one stone.*

The path narrowed and dipped through a rocky hollow. Sun and wind moved shadows around in a lonely, unsettling way. *Olivet's probably up from her nap. Was she afraid because I wasn't there? What will Greg do if I go? Margie or Gayle could fill in at church. It's a few weeks, that's all. I was out with surgery longer than that, and things went fine. What will Mei think if I don't go? Brooklyn would help with Olivet, even without a full explanation. She can bank some hours. I'll pay her back. Is the diamond a sign from God to go? What if Elijah doesn't want to be found, and our search draws attention to him? What if we make things worse? No no, we'd go as tourists. But how do we find him without asking questions about him? Maybe Rob's got that figured out.*

Another reason to go: to see firsthand what Elijah was up against. To meet the Tufanis, the people he gave his life for. I could encourage the others and pray. But I could pray here at home. Okay, prayer counts for going and staying.

Pausing to catch her breath, that other reason came to mind again: that Elijah's disappearance was a little bit her fault. He'd lived on this hundred acres of paradise and worked side by side with his father, had more freedom and responsibility than guys twice his age. More stability than most. "Nature Boy," the Brill brothers called him in school, poking fun. Jealous.

Reece had liked his back-woodsy shyness, had admired his integrity. She'd prayed. In the end, Elijah abandoned everything to follow a God he scarcely knew. Her prayers had propelled him from the comforts of Camp Mudj. Asia had swallowed him up. *Maybe he'd still be alive if I hadn't prayed.*

On their searches into Telanoo for armor pieces—and later across oceans—Elijah had always told her, "If I'm going, you're going." He wasn't going to leave her behind, back then. But where he wanted to go with the SOS she'd have only held him back. He'd been friend, boyfriend, co-conspirator, hero. Even a world away and years apart, just knowing he was on mission adventures had given her soul an anchor of purpose. Whatever happened in the future, she always had the Mag Five. Elijah's clan.

On the far side of Telanoo—beyond where the path ends, in those hidden places he'd talk about, in Gilead where only he could get to—Elijah had found strength to go solo, to be strong alone.

I'm not strong alone.

The place carried an atmosphere of twilight in it, even in midday. Reece imagined she was him, stashed in a cave and hearing a still, small voice from the one he'd first called the Master of Breath. She listened for a call to go or stay. A twig snapped. She whirled around with a stab of fear, then a bolt of hope that it was him: Elijah hiding out in Telanoo, safe after all. Nothing moved or skittered in the underbrush. Was Elijah's spirit here? She huffed at the idea. *He's no earthbound soul. Why would I think such a thing? He's alive in a prison or alive in Paradise.*

At that fresh realization, she threw her hands heavenward and let them come to rest on her head. *There are only two conditions you can be in, Elijah: alive or Alive.* Her hands went heavenward again. *Look, Elijah! I'm here. On my own power! If you could see me now! And you're okay, wherever you are! We're both okay, because we're in him!*

From her jeans pocket, Reece took out the red diamonds, wrapped in a square of paper. Too beautiful to be kept buried, she'd exhumed them after one night, ready for a standoff with Greg if it should come to that. She opened the paper and moved into a spot of sunlight. Chips of the Tear of Blood, deep and dazzling. Elijah's was the smallest of the three red stones but—aside from The Armor itself—his most precious possession. Maybe his only treasure. His instructions to the Mag Five about the gems had been, "Only for an emergency, to save a life." And here it was, hand delivered from the other side of the world. For an emergency. Maybe to save his life. She didn't need the thousands her earrings would bring. This one chip, this spark, would buy a round-trip ticket. It glimmered in her tired hand like the drop of wine from her Communion cup a few Sundays ago, when Greg stood before the congregation, praying about the blood of Christ while Audrey smiled at him from the second row. Reece's cup had trembled and spilled a drop in her palm. She'd licked it up, keeping that hand to her mouth, glancing at Audrey while most eyes were closed in prayer. *I knew. I knew something was going on. Weeks ago I knew. I just didn't want to face it again.*

Decisions had to be made. *What about Olivet? What about Greg? What about the church?* "I don't know!" Her voice echoed through Telanoo—"Don't know, know, know…" as if she herself were hiding in Elijah's place, calling back to a solitary girl in a celery blouse and jeans.

Shadow Bridge spanned a deep gully, well beyond Owl Woods and probably farther than Bo had ever come. Why would he? This was Elijah's domain. Telanoo. The Land No One Owns. The bridge, primitive to begin with, had weathered and was half consumed by overgrowth now. Elijah, Rob, Mei, and Marcus had built it wide enough for a golf cart so Reece could reach the far places with them.

She crossed the bridge, felt it sway. Shrunken planks creaked under her feet. She leaned on the railing and looked down. A puddle in the gully below caught a patch of sky and sparkled, sending sunny shimmers across her blouse and face and arms. Elijah whispered from her memories, *If I'm going, you're going.*

· · · · ·

Reece heard his car pull in. Greg had come home early. As if he knew. As if Reece had been wearing the secret preparations on her face, along with the worry when Mei got suddenly ill, and it seemed like Rob might have to go on his own. The agonizing days of delay wearied her mind and muscles, so surely they must show on her face.

Reece slid her rucksack under the bed and ran to the kitchen, pulling food out of the fridge. Then back to the dining room. "You're home early."

Greg dropped his briefcase on the dining table. "I have to mow the yard."

"Okay. I was going to have peanut butter sandwiches and fruit for Olivet and me. But there's chicken in the freezer. I could thaw it. For a casserole."

"What kind?"

"With noodles. And peas and carrots. A cream sauce."

"Okay. Your face is red."

"Oh?" She touched her burning cheek. "Oh, I was cleaning under the sink. Standing on my head practically."

While Greg mowed, she quick-thawed the meat and threw the casserole together. She moved the rucksack to Olivet's closet, always listening for the buzz of the mower engine as it circled the house, watching to make sure he was actually mowing, not idling in order to come back in for some reason. She dug in her pocket for the checklist. *Not out where he might see it.*

"We'll be gone two weeks or more. I'm glad you're going," Rob had said without questioning her change of heart. "And Mei, too. Take clothes for tropical and wintry weather. Pack light enough to carry your gear the whole time, if we should have to be on the run."

She'd packed and repacked, each time watching the clock, watching the door, hiding her bag—as she'd hidden the earrings—in different places each time, always looking for a better one. She'd forgotten once and had gone to the previous hiding place. The pack wasn't there, of course, and for a second she was terrified, certain that Greg had found it and was playing a horrible trick on her.

Dinner conversation dawdled. She'd argued with herself over and over about telling him, but he was gone every evening—except this one—and the right words never came. And too, her paper-thin resolve couldn't take any push-back. She kept Olivet in the dining room to play so he'd have no reason to go into the nursery. He spent the evening puttering in the yard. She wondered if it was over between him and Audrey. Reece told her husband she'd be up late working on a Sunday school lesson.

· · · · ·

Eleven thirty. She'd planned to take her car, but since he'd blocked her in before she could park on the street, she'd have to take his. One quick, quiet call to Darrell, and yes, her stepdad would be glad to return the car by daybreak.

Reece loaded the rucksack into the car, all lights off, still in her nightgown in case Greg woke. She had spread out a lesson plan on the dining room table next to a fresh wildflower bouquet. She coached herself through each move, whispering. "Shoes in the car with Olivet's bag. There. Look at the checklist. Outfits: check; toiletries: check. Jacket still damp from laundry. Put it on a hanger. It'll have thirteen hours to dry in the back window. Check." She smiled. "Thirteen hours." Rob and Mei were thrilled that she was going. They hadn't heard from Marcus. *We'll have a day in L.A. to look him up. If I forgot anything, I'll get it there. Passport and voucher: check. I'm going: check. I'm going.*

When it was midnight and Greg's car was packed, she quickly threw on a skirt and top in the kitchen. Nauseated, heart pounding, she tossed the gown in the laundry and put a note on the dining table, leaning it against the vase, taking a minute to prop it up with the saltshaker so it wouldn't slip. Her hand was now strangely steady, nails polished, wedding ring shining. *A note on the table. How cliché.*

She crept barefoot into the nursery and with quiet shushes lifted Olivet from her crib, "Shhh…Momma's gotcha, momma's gotcha. Shhh." *If Greg wakes, I'll say I needed to run out for an ingredient for a cake I'm making for tomorrow—for a shut-in—and that Olivet cried out in her sleep. I'll grab the note before he can spot it. A few more seconds, that's all I need.*

Olivet roused and murmured, "Mommgoshhh."

Reece crept out of the house, easing the front door closed. She buckled Olivet in the car seat, focusing on each movement to steady her mind. "It's okay, baby, gonna see Grammy. We're good to go. There. Shhh." The car doors didn't fully latch; she'd wait to slam them farther down the street. *Back up, headlights off. Foot on brake. Check.* She watched the darkened house, its outline blurred by a balmy midnight fog.

Driving toward Magdeline through empty streets with one hand on the wheel, she reached back with the other to touch Olivet's toes. "Momma's going on a trip with her friends. Not too long. We have to see if we can find our friend. He'd do it for me, so I have to do it for him. If Momma were missing or lost, he'd come. He would. He built me a bridge once, so I could go into the woods with my friends. They all helped, but it was his idea. So I have to go, baby. We all have to go. Until I see you again, you'll be safe with Grammy and Grampy. And Daddy too. See the pretty fog, Vetty, it makes the town look like a sweet dream. Like a fairyland. All the houses are castles and you're Sleeping Beauty. Whatever happens, you'll be safe. You'll be safe, baby, and we'll all know what's true. And that's the best thing in the whole wide world, isn't it: safe and true."

She'd been down this country road a thousand times, but the fog—or a lapse in concentration, or a new perspective on the town she was evacuating—gave things the wrong shape. *Where am I?* Images from the past moved into the here-and-now: bustling train stations in Osaka, back roads of Ireland…and new pictures: the harsh majesty of Tufan in a travel book she'd flipped through at the library. She slowed down until a familiar street name established her bearings. *I won't have my bearings there either. Nothing will be familiar. Get used to it.*

Reece saw herself remotely, a bird's-eye view of a young woman in a car on a dark road, not to Magdeline but to an unknown place. It was a worrisome image, as if she were far away, separated from her body, like the subtle soul journeys Greg had spoken of in one of his messages.

She pulled down the rearview mirror and fixed it on Olivet's velvet face. "I'd take you if I could, Vetty, you know that, don't you?" She almost sideswiped a parked car, unable to keep her eyes from that precious face. One more look, then one more, while speeding through a tunnel of trees silvered by headlights and softened by fog. Old times lay ahead, the past was in the future, the Mag Five together again. *Four,* she corrected herself. *There may only be four.*

The Taylor house was a small, crisp, gray cottage with hanging pots of ferns on a porch bordered in petunias, pansies, and herbs. Reece got out of the car, lifted the baby's dead weight, closed the door with her hip, and leaned back against it for one last cuddle. She lifted her face to the night sky. "Lord, only you know what lies ahead. If something goes wrong…I'm giving her up for adoption. To you. She's yours. Be father and mother, Lord, be all she needs. Keep her safe. And thank you for her. Thank you, thank you. You've blessed me beyond measure." Olivet roused. Her head turned and flopped heavily on Reece's shoulder. Her fingers clutched her mommy's sleeve before going limp.

"Mommy loves you. I will always love you. You're in God's hands now, like Dr. Eloise always said. Until I come back." She climbed the steps to the porch, her throat tight, her voice cheery. "And Grammy will play with you. All those games and toys. And Daddy will be here to play with you. And wherever we are, you and me—you remember the storm with the thunder?—even in times like that when it's scary, you're safe in God's arms."

The porch light was off, Rachel Taylor a petite silhouette framed in the doorway. Without a word they went to the guest room, a nursery of white and turquoise, gray now in the glow of a single night light. Reece gentled Olivet into the crib and patted her with one hand, covering her own mouth with the other, breathing shakily.

Rachel whispered, "I bought enough ice cream to last a month, Reece. She'll be a porker when you get back. Come on now. Be on your way."

In the living room, small, blonde Rachel Taylor faced her daughter. "I am so sorry! What you're going through. You deserve much better. But you're strong, Reece, stronger than you know. We weather the tough times—and we do it with grace, don't we? Trial and error, maybe."

Reece folded herself into her mom's arms. "I have to do this."

"I know you do. But guard your heart. You know what I mean. Guard it. Pray and be safe." She brightened. "Darrell bought passes to the zoo, and we have everything she needs here. Don't worry."

Darrell had come into the room in a T-shirt, sweatpants, and sock feet. "We got this," he said, handing her a thermos of coffee.

"Thank you so much." Still clinging to her mom, curling the thermos in her arm, Reece pulled back, wide-eyed. "What if Greg won't let you? What if he takes her and won't let—"

Rachel took her daughter's face in her hands. "Listen. We have that paperwork you found. Darrell's looking at it. I'm not past ratting to the church if he gets difficult. Granted, it's a little like blackmail. We'll call it leverage. You're talking about my grandbaby here. My one and only. And you, my one—" She choked. "My only. We love Greg, but he's been digging this grave for years. I wish you'd told me."

"I kept thinking—"

"—that things would change. Don't apologize for being hopeful. And there is hope. Don't second-guess God now. Two weeks of think time will do that boy good. If he wants to talk, we're here."

"Okay."

Mom and Darrell exchanged glances.

"What?" Reece asked.

"Nothing. You kids go and do what you need to do." Rachel took a sack from Darrell. "Sandwiches. If you get sleepy, pull over. And call when you get to California. Night or day. We're praying for everyone and everything. The Creeks are torn up with grief, so you come back with Elijah if you can. Or news. We all need closure."

Reece's mouth dropped open. "You didn't tell the Creeks, did you, 'cause no one's supposed to know. That's one reason I'm driving—not just the weather on the Plains, but so I can't be tracked, at least until I'm out of the country."

Rachel said soothingly, "And no one *does* know except for my prayer cell. You have money?"

"Yes."

"I mean cash, in case Greg stops the credit card."

Reece gave her a look.

"Oh, honey, he could say it was stolen and cut you off."

Darrell butted in. "Or follow the paper trail, catch a plane, and be in Los Angeles before you are. You didn't tell him where you're going."

"No. Just that I had to get away."

Rachel said, "Then he'll probably think you've gone to a cabin somewhere close. But honey, you can't be naive. No one's untraceable nowadays. Has he…ever hit you?"

"No."

Darrell put a steadying hand on his wife's shoulder. "Tomorrow's west-bound flights out of Columbus are full as of an hour ago. He'd have to drive to Cincinnati or Cleveland. He has a passport?"

"Yes," Reece answered. "You think he might follow me?" She'd had no time to consider all consequences. Preparing for a secret trip while in the public eye strained every nerve. The whole town was still talking about the storm, the fire, calling to see how they could help. Reece was flooded with goodwill and support, but terrified of letting her plan slip.

Greg's passport, acquired for the honeymoon, was current. So he could get to Asia. But special permits into Tufan can take weeks. Mei had pulled strings to get theirs.

Darrell handed her an envelope. "A little cash. Not much. I'm sorry we didn't have time to talk more, but here it is: you want to be as untraceable as possible. If you have to use the credit card, use it every few days and only as you're leaving a place, not when you first arrive. That gives you a head start."

Reece tried to joke. "I can borrow from Rob. And Mei can find us deals. And Marcus is probably rolling in dough."

"No doubt," Rachel said unconvincingly. She handed Reece a car key. "The rental is a one-way, as you asked. We'll get Greg's car back to him before dawn, but he has keys to your car, correct?" She took Reece's face in her hands once more and smiled fiercely, her eyes swimming, smiling. "My baby. My one and only. Take care. We'll meet you at the airport when you get back. Or if you drive back, call first. Don't be anywhere by yourself. I'll come get you. Anywhere."

"Am I doing the right thing, Mom? Should I have told Greg? Should I hav—"

"Too late now, sweetie," Rachel said bluntly. "You're doing the best you know how. Go with it."

Reece pulled into the waiting silence, the smell of coffee and meatloaf sandwiches along for the ride, ghost-like fog slipping away through the countryside. She headed back through Cedar Ridge to pick up 23 North, pulling over after a few blocks to check once more for her flight voucher and passport, peeking into Darrell's envelope of cash. There were several hundred dollars and a heart-shaped note that read "Psalm 27:1-3." She began quoting the familiar passage as she pulled the Quella out of her bag and looked it up:

The Lord is my light and my salvation; whom shall I fear?

The Lord is the stronghold of my life;
of whom shall I be afraid?

When evildoers assail me to eat up my
flesh, my adversaries and foes,

it is they who stumble and fall.

Though an army encamp against me, my heart shall not fear;

though war arise against me, yet I will be confident.

God's hands. Reece tucked the Quella away and drove on, passing her house. The light was on. He was standing in the doorway, looking into the foggy darkness, his posture rigid, a piece of paper in his hand.

CHAPTER 7

Just like a sunrise, open eyes and go.
Where it will take us nobody knows.
—ANDREA SUMMER, "THE BEGINNING"

"Hi, Rob. I'm in Joplin." It was noon the next day. Determined to be alert—if not refreshed—by the time she met him, Reece had found a drive-through coffee shop at an exit on I-64.

"We're tracking right now, but I'll leave with you as soon as you get here."

"Tracking?" she asked.

"A tornado."

She smiled as she pulled out into traffic. "You want me to drive into the path of a tornado to pick you up."

"Not much happening…" He trailed off, mumbling to another person something about location, then back to her. "Right now we're at the intersection of 33 and 177 and heading toward Stillwater. Call me from Tulsa. Did you drive all night?"

"Yeah."

"Reece—"

"I've got coffee. Almost there."

"Those straight stretches are hypnotic. Be careful, girl."

"We can take turns driving the rest of the way."

"I'll go first."

The sun had risen at Reece's back and was beaming down through the windshield onto her lap. Fresh steam rose from the thermos. Olivet would be napping at her mom's. Greg would be…

A ridiculously straight stretch lay ahead. She put an arm out the window and stepped on the gas.

Her thoughts rambled, but with a touch more focus than in the dark hours across Indiana and Illinois where one radio station had crackled into another. *Keep a single-minded goal: get into Tufan and find Elijah. Or his remains. Or an eyewitness account of what happened. Or evidence of a mission cover-up. Something. Anything. Eyes open, wits about you, pray hard. That's all. Okay, cry. Come on, get it out before you meet up with Rob.*

She set the cruise control and took her foot off the pedal to stretch her throbbing muscles, with miles of ribbon-smooth road ahead. *Greg's not even hiding it well this time. Anyone could have come in the church that night and found them, anyone with a key: the pianist, the janitor, a group leader. Is he* trying *to get caught? Is this his way of asking for help…or dropping a hint that he never loved me? But he did. I know he did. Does. Did.*

Blind hope—even with exhaustion, even with Olivet on her mind every moment—wouldn't let her cry. *I'm leaving my child, my husband, and ministries for pure insanity. Why does this feel right? Is it the thrill? Nostalgia? Is it pride? Revenge? Too late to question motives. You made the decision at Shadow Bridge. Like Mom said, go with it.*

She thanked God that her mom would drop everything to keep Olivet for what seemed like a wild-goose chase. And for Darrell's generous gift; for Rob, who'd planned it all and had been willing to go alone; for Mei who'd covered the high-se-curity paperwork. *I only had to buy a ticket and pack and drive. Simplicity. Freedom—this time without crutches. That's why it feels right. Impossible steps are possible.*

Rob had been flat-voiced and uninterested when asked about Marcus: "He's in Laguna Beach, Reece. That's all I got. We have a day in California before our flight. We're going, with or without him. Fine by me either way. See you soon."

Reece reached the crest of the hill. Another straight strip of highway narrowed to a hair's breadth at the horizon where a bank of blue-black clouds hovered. Reece had always been told that she could handle tough times. And she had. The surgery to put a rod in her thigh required weeks of recovery. She found ways to adapt. The arrival of Olivet and more weeks in bed had strained the marriage. But she'd stayed cheerful; things would improve. The start of the trouble, though, had come early on— two months after the wedding when he spent the afternoon with an old girlfriend. *Did I push him into ministry? Is he trying to get himself fired? Is he looking for a way to end it? Am I leaving to give him what he wants or to help Rob? To see Mei again and reconnect with Marcus? Or simply, purely to find Elijah?* She put the straight stretch on auto-pilot and continued the loop of self-examination.

At a rest stop, she pulled off and walked around, clearing her head. *There's nothing you can do about Greg. You're not helping the Mag Five or Elijah by dwelling on it. Pray about the trip instead. Prepare for that!* She stretched her legs at a park bench, got the Quella out of her bag, and looked up *peace*, with a side glance at the darkening western horizon. *I wonder what Greg told Audrey—wait, stop it. In a few days you'll be in Tufan. Prepare for that battle. Fight that one.*

Reece buckled herself in and backed out of the parking space. Pulling in behind her was a silver sedan. She gasped, slammed on the brake.

It wasn't him.

She barreled onto the interstate. *He doesn't know which*

highway I'm on, nor where I'm going. I'm not meeting Rob at his house. I'm meeting him under a tornado. She smiled. *Like old times.*

. . . . .

"Hi, Rob. I'm just west of Tulsa on 51."

"And we're east of Stillwater now, same road, tracking a cell. Big one forming as we speak."

"I think I can see it. You want me to come there?"

"Yeah."

"Is it heading east?"

"They usually do. Until recently. Come on."

"All right. I'm driving a blue—"

"You can't miss us. See ya." And he was gone.

In an hour she'd pulled off the road behind a weird, gadgety, armored car. Rob and his fellow trackers were beside the vehicle, eyes glued to the southwest horizon—a strip of white sky separating bulging black clouds from brown prairie.

Rob motioned her to come. He was in navy T-shirt, jeans, and work boots. Eyes on the skies, he reached back and gathered her to his side, pointing with the binoculars in his other hand. He gave her a squeeze. "Glad you're here. If it's gonna show, it'll probably be there. Guys, this is Reece."

The "guys" were three men and two women, ages twenty to fifty and all in jeans and T-shirts. A few flashed obligatory smiles but couldn't have cared less.

"No basement to run to this time, *ne,*" she said, trying to include herself.

He said to the others, "Reece here was with me for my first close encounter." Then to her, "Are you okay to wait here a few? This could be a good one. It's a big system."

"Sure. Should I wait in my car?"

"Yeah. Take a nap if you want, but pull up close to the Peeler." He nodded toward the vehicle. "She's built to withstand an EF-2 direct hit. If one comes, you can jump in."

"Peeler?"

"Yeah," he said with no explanation.

"You should have named it Rob's Attic."

She couldn't nap, but laid the seat back and kept her eye on the sky, the door swung open to a prairie breeze. Banter between the chasers was light, redundant. Every car that roared past sounded like a silver sedan. But she had Rob now, and his buddies.

"What do we do if a tornado comes?" she asked lazily.

Rob was leaning against the front fender of her car, arms crossed. "We watch it. Take footage, readings." He added dryly, "Or run like the dickens. Depends."

After a while he kicked gravel and sighed. "We should probably go." But he lingered, and something caught his eye to the southwest. "Guys, watch that bulge. See it there. Rotation. Straight on there."

Reece got out of the car and stood by him. Green clouds eased almost imperceptibly downward and into a wide circle.

"Rotation," he repeated.

"I see it," she said.

The team fixed every nerve on that section of sky. Rob glanced at his interactive map, then back at the sky, then overhead uneasily, then down the road. He checked traffic. He looked worried. A moment later he was pointing, his voice rising. "Rotation within, guys, looks like a multiple!"

Everyone sprang to life, each charged with a specific task.

One of the guys cursed. "It's two! Touching down!"

Rob grabbed his camera. "Okay okay okay!" He scanned the heavens, yelling while instructing Reece, "It's multiples. We've had a rash of them, one tornado with several vortices rotating inside the main. Can mean big destruction. Sometimes they dissipate. I've seen one go horizontal. The doggone thing started leaning and you could see inside the vortex. Incredible." He snapped pictures frantically, then switched to video, glancing at the weather clip hooked to his belt loop, glancing up. Others kept up a banter of technical terms. A curtain of rain approached.

A white, writhing twister dropped down several miles away, its delicate tentacle stirring up a bowl of dust where it touched earth. The next one came faster, closer. The storm chasers swore and yelled and groaned in awe.

"Are you seeing this, Reece?" Rob asked, continuing to film.

"I'm seeing it."

A third twister manifested, a chain of them dropping in a straight line in the direction of the chasers. Reece glanced at Rob for a hint of whether to jump into the car or the Peeler. "I have my passport on me, and the tickets, but my bag's in the car."

He nodded, transfixed by the twisters moving liquidly in his direction. "Wrong way…wrong way…"

She said, "If we're going in the Peeler, I'll need a few seconds to get my bag. Should I get it out now? And what about the rental car? Abandon it?"

"I'll let you know. Are you insured?" He kept recording.

"Heavily," she said casually, with no earthly reason to be casual. "If we get stranded in Tufan, the insurance company is supposed to send in a military helicopter. But Parabolani would get there first."

He switched from filming back to photos, kept shooting. "Don't count on either." One of the girls yelled from inside the Peeler, jumped out, and looked straight up. "Fourth rotation!"

Rob looked up. "Go! Go!" He ran to the Peeler and hauled out a rucksack, yelling at one of the guys, "Bug out! I'm going with her!"

Reece buckled in and cranked the engine. "Which way?!"

Rob jumped in on the passenger side and slammed the door,

stepping on the seat, hoisting himself up into the open window, the camera in one hand. "Go!" Rain swept over them in a fury.

"Which way?!" Reece screamed.

From above the car his voice barked, "West! Step on it!"

"Follow the Peeler?!"

He ducked down into the window, dripping, made eye contact, and said steadily, "No. They're going in. You turn right up ahead. I'll tell you."

She tore out into the westbound lane. Tires screeched behind her, a horn blared. She hadn't signaled or looked back. A car careened around her, driver cursing, horn fading as he sped off.

"Sorry!" she yelled out the window, squinting against the downpour. "Rob, get in!"

He kept yelling, "Go! Go!" So she went. Fifty miles an hour, sixty, seventy…with Rob in the window, taking the cloudburst full force. To the southwest three tornados writhed. If another was dropping on their heads, Rob wasn't saying. Her skirt whipped and lifted. Her ears popped.

The Peeler sped toward the twisters.

"I can't see the road!" Reece cried.

Rob jumped into the seat, soaked. He rolled up the window. "Take a right up there. See it? Right there!"

She slammed brakes, turned, slammed gas.

Rob scanned all directions—backward, forward, and skyward through the windshield—listening over the engine and pulse of the wipers, over the slaps of the storm on the rental car. "We're good, I think. Take the next left you see, half mile, and then another left, and we'll be back on the main road." He grabbed a bandana from his jeans pocket and wiped his face, wiped his camera, wiped the steamy windshield. "You did good." In apology and defense he added, "We know a lot more than we did a few years ago. We can get closer and stay longer. I was watching. I was."

"I believe you." She glanced over and found him studying her, smiling.

"You okay?" he asked.

"I'm awake, that's for sure. You can drive after we stop for dinner."

When they'd cleared the storm and the twisters had fizzled in the east, he rolled down the window to dry his clothes. "I've got friends in Oklahoma City, Amarillo, Tucumcari, and Phoenix. We have places to stay and I allowed plenty of time. We'll be in L.A. by Sunday easy. Are you sure you're okay? I'm sorry if I scared you. It was a little close."

"I'm fine." She shot him a smile. "Gotta be ready for anything, *ne*. So catch me up on your life. Anything new in Tulsa?"

Still watching the sky and checking his weather clip, Rob said tentatively, "I have a new…hobby, I guess you'd call it."

"Yeah?"

"I've been doing research." He hesitated. "I coined a name for it: escha-meteorology."

"*Eska?*"

"You know. End-times. Like eschatology. It means end-times weather. But, hold on. I'm going to save it for when we're all together."

Reece went through a kind of time warp: crossing states and states of mind, falling asleep in one state, waking in another; changing landscapes, physical and emotional; from prairie to seemingly endless desert to ocean beach; riding the highway up and down, from 700 to 7000 feet to sea level; from an identity as a married woman with a child, to a girl on a mission with a different man taking charge of her life.

CHAPTER 8

*I don't know how else to tell you, don't know how else to say
I need you so far from me. I need space.*
—Andrea Summer, "I Need Space"

Reece and I made it. Laguna Beach, California. Sunday. Sunny, 80° F/26° C, wind steady at 5mph. Perfect. I ordered avocado burgers for us at an oceanside bistro. The sun was waning, the sky clear, the breeze balmy, the hiss of waves coming in on sand. My mind went back years to Farr Island and us three guys playing wild men in the jungle. My heart got heavy. Elijah...

It was easier for Reece to talk seriously when she wasn't looking me in the eye across a table. In the car was fine, but meals were chitchat. I'd been schooling her on weather terms, since she'd be posing as an assistant if the situation got dicey. She was hiding something and thought I didn't know.

I asked the waiter for a refill of iced tea, and told Reece, "Marcus said anytime after seven. We have a couple hours to kill." The smell of salt sea and mesquite-grilled burgers put us far from home. Bicyclers rolled past. Across the highway, oily volleyball players sprang around on the beach. Restaurant goers murmured, waves broke.

"Perfect breeze," Reece said, closing her eyes.

"You're beat. And that humongous snarl of traffic..."

"I'll sleep on the plane."

"We can't get there exhausted. You ever had altitude sickness?"

"No."

I pulled out a bottle of pills. "Take one of these."

She complied, gulping down a pill without question. "Are we staying at a hotel or with Marcus?"

"He didn't offer. I just told him we'd stop by the day before the flight." Golden sand stretched out under the lowering sun. "Reminds me of Farr Island a little bit." I couldn't help mentioning it, the memories were so strong. "With Elijah, you know, when Marcus's dad took us guys there to toughen me up, then scared the living snot out of us with his all-night jungle maneuvers. Best week of my life."

"Rob…the storm chasing. How much do you do that? I mean, how dangerous is it?"

"They're on the increase, and we're trying to figure out why. To hopefully save lives."

"That's not an answer."

"We go out more than we used to, sometimes starting in February. I went three times in May. Five times this month. It's no more dangerous than, say, deep-sea fishing or high-rise construction. Safer actually. You're on the ground, on land."

"The end-times weather? I know you want to save it for later. But can you give me a hint?"

"All the talk about global warming and cooling. It doesn't explain why other planets are warming. And cooling. We couldn't measure these things accurately until the last century. So it's hard to gauge normal parameters. Global models keep shifting, ours are not the most accurate. We blame it on pollution, but that doesn't explain the seven years of drought in Egypt during Joseph's time 3,500 years ago. And woolly mammoths suddenly frozen in Siberia with half-chewed vegetation in their mouths. Weather cataclysms are going to happen, but why? Everyday weather is predictable. When a rain system moves through, we can tell when it'll hit your street. The extreme stuff is defiant. When you said that your church got struck by lightning—there's a lot of that happening, an unusual number of sacred places being hit. I started keeping track a few years back. It's peculiar. There's the science, you know, but something else is working. There's a piece missing."

We ate silently for a while. Reece said, "I guess we pretty much talked out our whole lives through New Mexico and Arizona, didn't we?"

"How much are you going to tell Mei and Marcus?" I asked.

"About what?"

"You and Greg."

Reece couldn't hide her surprise. "What?"

"Your mom ratted on you. She called and asked me to look out for you, in case…"

Her shoulders drooped, probably in relief. "In case he showed up?"

"Or called."

"I'm not taking his calls."

Reece was so pretty…face, figure, hair, eyes, smile. The whole package. Personality. Smarts. Faith. I wondered what that jerk was thinking. "He didn't know you were leaving?"

"He does now. I left a note, but I didn't tell him where. He'll probably think I found a cabin in Amish country. I said I had to get away—and that he needed to search his soul."

"Are you sure he doesn't know? Maybe we should check your purse and rucksack for a tracking device?"

"I kept my purse with me all the time."

"Even when you slept?"

"Are you serious? He didn't know I was leaving. I'm sure."

"Your mom's worried. She went through things in her previous marriage that she never told you."

"She told *you*?"

"No. But she's had experiences. I'd listen to her advice if I were you."

"This trip is not about my troubles."

"Mei will pick up on it. You won't have to say a thing. She knows you." My comment seemed to comfort her.

"It's like you said a couple hundred miles ago—where were we, New Mexico—when you were talking about missing Lydia. 'The problems of this world...' How'd that go?"

I corrected her with my best Bogart impression. "The problems of two little people don't amount to a hill of beans in this crazy world."

The sun went behind a bank of western clouds, cumulonimbus piled high, purple and rimmed in gold. She asked if I'd been praying.

With more conviction than I felt, I said, "Yep. I learned my lesson from our days as the Mag Five." I dropped a couple of bills to cover the meal. "You want anything else?"

She stood slowly, stretched. "Stuffed. Thanks. You didn't have to pay."

"Let's see what's up with Marcus."

Reece drove, the ocean beach at our left and a mixed bag of architectural styles on our right: Spanish villa-style apartments, a run-down gas station, beach shops, modern offices. I navigated, glancing at a map I'd scrawled on a piece of paper. "His apartment is on this block...oh, there he is!"

Leaning coolly against a bus-stop sign, in yellow T-shirt, black jeans, and mirror sunglasses, was Marcus Skidmore.

Reece pulled left onto the sandy parking lot, jumped out, ran to him, and hugged him hard. He hugged her too, then set her at arm's length and said, "You're running now, Elliston."

"It's Moline, remember. I'm still doing therapy, but it's a smaller limp, *ne?*"

He and I exchanged a brief embrace with fists in each other's backs and a couple of grunts.

Reece said, "Thanks for letting us come."

Marcus said, "Eh, you're the ones who drove 1,500 miles."

"Over 2,000 for Reece," I corrected.

"Why didn't you fly?"

"Turbulence across the whole Midwest," I said. "It's unstable. With a backlog of flights, we could have been delayed for days. Couldn't risk it." That's all I said.

She nodded to the ocean. "I'm jumping in there."

Marcus warned, "Surf's rough. Red flags are up. Let's kick back first. I'll rent some beach chairs."

The sun drizzled gold flame on a red ocean, quivering toward some invisible place in the sea where the West becomes the East.

Marcus paid a guy in a Hawaiian shirt, pulled three Adirondack chairs into a circle, and sat. Dark and lean, he folded the mirror sunglasses and hooked the earpiece into the neck of his T-shirt, his green eyes unreadable. He asked a few questions about the trip and listened to our tornado story without offering any info about himself or an invitation to stay the night.

He pulled a little bag out of his pocket, laid it in Reece's hand, and nodded for her to open it. A chain slid out into her palm, then two chips of green stone.

"Is this jade?" she asked.

"It's Elijah's triskele," Marcus began. "His tracking device. He broke it on purpose. Dad found it in a ravine. It wasn't crushed by a landslide, and he didn't fall off a cliff or get blown up. He broke it." As Reece frowned over it, he concluded, "In a hopeless situation, if you don't want to put others at risk trying to find you, you break the device."

Reece fit the two jade fragments together, as if trying to make the crack disappear. "Was there information on it?"

"A triskele isn't like the black box on a plane. You break it and the information is gone so no one can trace it. But Dad defied policy, like I said. He went there and found it."

"He didn't find anything else?" Reece asked again. She watched his face closely. We'd been through this over the phone. Reece seemed as skeptical as me, but in a gentler way.

"Hold on," I asked. "How could your dad track it to the middle of nowhere if there was no tracking information? That doesn't make sense."

"Dunno," Marcus said simply. "They knew the general direction and destination. Dad mapped it out like the crow flies and followed the nearest path. I guess. He didn't elaborate."

"What do you think happened?" Reece asked.

"Dad gave two options: either Elijah was attacked by bandits who stripped him of all his gear, and a pack of wild dogs took the rest; or he was attacked by the dogs first, and the bandits took the rest."

Reece shuddered, put the triskele back in the little bag. "What if he met someone, like The Edifice or the local police, and they arrested him? He was out there illegally, right? What if he located that tribe he was looking for and went with them?"

Marcus answered, "If he went with the tribe—even under duress—he'd have kept the triskele. Least, I think so. We have a person on the ground in YangDi—"

"We?" I questioned his use of the word.

"They," Marcus corrected. "The agency. Dad asked around. There was no news of nomads taking a guy in or of a foreigner being arrested. We're talking remote, people. Not that either the tribe or The Edifice would come clean."

Reece asked, "Elijah's whole reason for going was to reach

this tribe. How close was he to their camp?"

With an edgy expression, Marcus sat back in his chair and pointed a long, steady finger at the pendant. "That's all we have. You don't understand about these people and subsistence living. They make use of every scrap. Every day's a struggle to survive. You find a coat, a pack of provisions, you take it. You find a body with said provisions, no need to report it. You find a hunk of jade on a chain, it's yours. Simple as that. People are disappeared there. Lots of ways they do it, but they can wipe your slate clean—your flight reservations deleted, credit card expenses erased, social security number reassigned. As if you were never there. The whole region was on hold, and Elijah went anyway."

I said, "Well. I'm going. You going?"

"Dad's not keen on it," Marcus said.

"I bet not," I said. We locked eyes, and Marcus seemed perplexed by my cynical tone.

I half-expected Reece to break in and flush out the tension in her usual girlish way. She didn't, easing the lull in the conversation with a fake yawn and a sleepy-eyed smile toward the sun. "I need sleep really bad, guys. Two thousand miles, you know, and several tornadoes. Where do you recommend we stay, Marcus? Someplace close and cheap is fine. The flight leaves tomorrow noon, pending the weather as always." She stood and looked out over the ocean. "This is so beautiful. What a great place to live! I'm happy for you. Will you be joining us tomorrow? I hope so because it really, really wouldn't be the same without you. And if you want to come and don't have time to get to the bank by flight time, I have some extra cash."

Marcus stood abruptly, as if her comment about needing cash offended him. "No sweat." He returned the rental chairs, then led us across the street to a ground-level apartment.

The exterior was nice, gardeny. A cheap metal lounge chair

on the stoop was chained to a big hook cemented into the wall. He opened the door and motioned us inside. The one room studio had a crumpled sofa, a dinette with two chairs, a bare kitchenette along one wall, a tiny bathroom with shower, and a sliver of ocean view from the one window. There were blinds but no curtains. On the dining table was a basket as if to hold fruit, but it was empty.

When Reece got ice from the fridge, I saw that it was bare except for a jar of spaghetti sauce and a door rack of salad dressings, olives, and peanut butter. I got a glass from the cupboard and whispered to her, "Subsistence living."

"I'll bring the chair in for you, Reece," Marcus said. "You're small enough to sleep on that. Rob, you get the couch. I'll sleep on the floor."

Reece said cheerily, "We don't want to put you out."

"Not at all."

"Thanks so much, Marcus," she said graciously. "It's nice that you live close to the beach! I'll be out like a light in no time. If you guys wanna stay up and play cards or anything, that's fine. But we have to leave early," she added informatively, "nine o'clock at the latest, with traffic and all."

As we got our beds ready, Marcus dragged a duffel bag and some clothes out of his closet, threw it open on the floor, and started tossing things in. Reece glanced hopefully at me. In spite of the tension between Marcus and me, I was relieved. He had height, muscle, and threat in those unusual green eyes, all of which might come in handy in Tufan. Not as scary as his dad by any measure, but not the kind of guy you'd want as an enemy either.

Reece adjusted the lounge chair to flat position, and was even brighter and cheerier now that Marcus appeared to be going with us. "So, guys, I'll drive us to the airport and turn the car in, if you guys navigate. I can't wait to see Mei. She'll meet us at Umeda Station in Osaka. We'll take that big shuttle bus like we did before. She gave me the necessary names and numbers in case we get lost. Just think, in one day we'll all be together again!"

Marcus paused. "Not all." Then he went back to packing.

Settled in on the couch, I repeated Reece's offer. "If you didn't get a chance to get cash, I can shoot you some."

"Thanks," he said.

"Will you…did you have trouble getting off work?" Reece asked.

"Nah."

"Well, that's good." She fluffed the thin pillow. "Tomorrow morning should I get us some snacks to take on the flight? Any preferences?"

I looked around for a blanket for Marcus and said. "I don't care. How 'bout you, Skidmore? Nice breeze from the window there. It'll be like Farr Island again. You have linens for yourself?"

"I have a sleeping bag."

I asked Reece, "You going to be okay?"

"Sure. I brought a wool shawl that doubles as a blanket. I won't need it tonight though. Be sure to pack warm, Marcus. Is it okay if I pray?"

"Have at it."

Reece scooted the lounge chair parallel to the couch, with Marcus between us still packing. I didn't see a coat go into that bag, but didn't mention it, figuring if he wanted to freeze his butt off on the heights, it was his business. If he didn't own a coat, we could pitch in later and buy him one. Better to wound his pride after we were on the ground.

Reece said, "If I fall asleep two minutes in, someone take over with the prayer, all right? Oh, and here's a snack bag from the car. Anybody want some? Marcus, will you need to get a ticket?

I'm just asking because standby was packed when Mei checked. You may have trouble—"

"It's covered."

"Oh, good. Good. I've missed you, Marcus."

CHAPTER 9

Take me to the edge of the world and back.
You have my whole heart, no turning back.
—ANDREA SUMMER, "THE BEGINNING"

Osaka, Japan. 4 p.m. Somewhere above the ocean in the ether we lost that mysterious day we'd get back in a few weeks, God willing. Breezy afternoon. 85° F/25°C. After a break-neck ride through downtown, our bus came to a crawl in a loop surrounded by a fortress of high-rise buildings. A dozen other buses were loading and unloading at Umeda Station, the huge hub of a huge city. Mei was surprisingly easy to spot in a sea of mostly dark-haired, dark-suited business folk and city dwellers. She was in a bright turquoise dress. Her hair was below her shoulders. She beamed when she saw Reece waving at her through the bus window.

Reece got off first and ran stiffly, throwing her arms around Mei, drawing the four of us into a group hug, with Mei repeating, "You're here! I cannot believe it! You're here!" All of us were, in varying degrees, laughing and crying.

I said, "Hey, someone should be stifling their emotions. This is a reserved culture."

Marcus became a different man when that certain little Japanese girl stepped into view. From peevish to pleasant. "It's good to see you, Mei. It's great."

"Are you hungry?" she asked us.

Reece said, "No! They stuffed us all the way here."

"I could use some sushi," I said. "I didn't care for that stuff on the plane. It was chewy roast beef with some potato-y thing."

Marcus smiled smoothly. "That was squash, my friend. Mei, you look wonderful."

She flashed him a shy smile.

Reece bubbled, "You're so gorgeous! And Rob is as fit as a fiddle, isn't he? And Marc—"

Marcus broke in. "Ladies, ladies, let's get our baggage and haul ourselves to the nearest sushi emporium."

Deja-vu. We squeezed into an orange-upholstered and chrome-trimmed booth. There were no windows in the subterranean restaurant, but the bright globes over each table—and a sea of humanity rushing past the open door—helped the slight claustrophobia I felt being underground in a quake-prone country. Japanese pop music and the clatter of little plates competed with conversation.

Marcus commented on the aroma of frying tempura. "Mei, how about you order for us."

Reece sighed. "*Natsukashii, ne*? It's so nostalgic!"

Marcus and Mei pored over the menu while Reece smiled across the table at me and mouthed, "We made it."

I stopped myself from saying, "We ain't there yet." No need to ruin the moment. I turned to Mei. "How are things in your neck of the bamboo forest?"

"Good." She ordered tea and sampler plates, then said, "We don't need to exchange the money here. I will take care of this meal."

"No—" Marcus began.

She cut in, "—and everyone will stay at my apartment tonight. I'm sorry it's so small."

Reese said, "Oh, thank you. All we need is a little floor space.

I'm excited to see it."

"Mei, listen," Marcus objected again.

She said tersely, "I am your host, and I will provide for my guests. We have early departure tomorrow. Let's have a pleasant meal. It is very noisy here. When we get to my apartment, we have important things to discuss."

Marcus let Mei's gentle snub roll off, but the mood shifted. He changed the subject. "Hey, anyone know where The Armor of God is?"

Mei was startled at the mention of it.

"If we don't find Elijah, it could be lost," he added.

Mei bristled again.

Reece said, "He would have left a clue with the agency, probably."

"He didn't trust everyone there," I added.

Marcus shot me a half-angry, half-confused look.

Reece jumped in. "We're out to find *him*, not the…relic."

Mei leaned in quietly. "We will discuss these things later. Not here. We got what we needed from it. Remember, the power was never in the metal. It was in the message."

"Sure," I complied, figuring she must have a reason for shushing us. "Anybody been overseas since our Mag Five days? Mei, for sure. You've been everywhere."

Mei said, "Mostly Asia. And you?"

"Canada for a camping trip with my dad. And once to Paris, then Cairo. I met Elijah there."

Mei nodded correctively. "Please do not mention his name. Marcus, how about you?"

"Hawaii. And California's Big Sur. Tea, anyone?"

Reece said, "We went to Belize for the honeymoon. Nowhere else big. I'm a wife and mommy now. Here's the family." She passed around a picture of herself with Greg and Olivet. "It's been a busy few years. We moved a couple of times. This is my first getaway in a while. Mom's watching Olivet while Greg's at work." She reached across the table and squeezed my arm. "And this guy's engaged!" The gesture was friendly, but also a solid signal. The others didn't need to know any more.

"No date set yet. But yeah," I said with a grin. "Thanks for the help on the travel arrangements, Mei. Are we cleared for passage into Tufan?"

Briskly Mei whispered, "Please. Do not talk of these things."

"Oh. Sorry. Um, should we"—I weighed my words—"get take-home for breakfast?" Her leadership skills had certainly blossomed over the years.

"I will have breakfast," Mei said, relaxing a little. "The 7-Eleven is in my building."

I made a fist of victory. "Yes! 7-Eleven, the fount of all abundance of fast food!"

· · · · ·

Mei unlocked her narrow apartment door with another apology. "It is very, very small. I am not here so much."

The motel-like room on the sixteenth floor had a short set of kitchen cabinets on the left and a bathroom not much larger than an airplane toilet on the right. The *ofuro* bath was next to it, a separate room as immaculate and compact as the rest of the apartment. Mei had a foldout couch and two futon mattresses ready, with a narrow aisle of floor space between them. A couple of framed kanji symbols hung on the wall. A small desk, bookshelf, and bistro table with four chairs filled the rest. All spotless. We took off our shoes.

"It's adorable, Mei. Everything you need, and look at the view!" Reece opened the door to the balcony where laundry dried in a warm breeze. There was a small table a foot square with one chair, and a sea of city lights beyond. "I could sleep out here."

"Oh, but my clothes would drip on you. Everyone, please use the *ofuro* if you like. And the laundry." She gestured to a tiny washer beside the kitchen cabinets. "Your things will dry outside by morning. It's a good night. Not too humid."

"That would be lovely," Reece said. "I have a small load. Anyone else need some done?"

Mei presented a crisply folded stack of *yukatas*. "Wear these after the bath. We'll talk."

I whooped. "Robes, like we had in Nikko. Girl, you thought of everything." We got settled for the night by waltzing around luggage, furniture, and each other—without complaint.

Marcus was the last to bathe. Steaming and wrapped in his navy and white print robe, he emerged from the *ofuro*. The rest of us were having tea on our pallets. He plopped down and said, "All right. Let's talk."

Mei took over. "Have your bags packed and ready to go, except for traveling clothes. We should know details of each other's lives before we get to Tufan, more than we talked about at the restaurant. We will have time to talk in Jinsha City, during the layover. But we must prepare our minds for a different way of speaking. Rob, you can begin. Tell us about yourself."

Going with Japanese formality, I said, "I'm a meteorologist and storm chaser and I do community theatre."

"Community theatre. What is that?" she asked.

I thought she'd know. "Well, ours is new and small, with volunteer actors, by the community and for the community. We've done shows like *Our Town* and a couple of Agatha Christies, *Casablanca,* two musicals. A little Shakespeare. Traditional stuff. I usually play the comic roles, and I've done a romantic lead. That's where I met Lydia."

Marcus raised one eyebrow. "All the world's a stage."

Reece nodded at me encouragingly, hinting that I should share my new interest. "And okay. Now don't laugh, but I'm dabbling in a new hobby. We were in Bible study at church, going through the book of Luke. We got to the verse where Jesus was giving signs of the end of time. He said that the nations would—how'd it go—'distress of nations in perplexity because of the roaring of the sea and the waves, people fainting with fear and with foreboding of what is coming on the world.' And it hit me. What's going to cause that? It won't be the usual tsunami or occasional storm surge. That wouldn't be a sign. It has to be far worse than normal for people worldwide to faint in terror. I'd been hearing at the station about the 80 percent increase in Category 4 and 5 hurricanes in the last forty years. That may be hype. But I got curious and started looking up storm, waves, lighting, hail, flood—any weather-related term that I could find in the Bible. I had no idea there were so many references to weather phenomenon in prophecy. I haven't mentioned any of this to the people at work. A few months ago, I got bumped up to a semi-regular spot on the news, and I don't want to screw it up. Lydia knows, but that's it."

Reece spoke up. "Tell them some of the things you told me on the way out here about your research so far."

Mei looked at the clock. "I think it will have to wait until Jinsha. Reece, why don't you give us the latest on you and your family?"

Reece shrugged lightly. "It's obvious, I guess, that the last surgery worked and I'm almost limp-free. There are no guarantees. It's new technology. I already told you about Greg and Olivet. She takes most of my time, and I love her like crazy. I squeeze ministry in between my highest calling of being a preacher's wife and a proud momma. Pretty simple. Your turn, Mei. Tell us about you."

"I love my work," Mei said humbly. "I meet people all over the world. I help them to enjoy themselves and have adventures"—she looked warmly at each of us—"like we did. Knowing you has changed everything for me. Elijah…he saved my life. I will always be indebted. Reece, you led me to God. All of you did. And Marcus, you gave me confidence in myself. Rob, you always made me laugh. If I have a hard time, I think of a funny thing you did, and I always feel better."

"Like when I ripped my nightgown on the mean streets of Nikko?"

Marcus nodded, a reminiscent twinkle in his eye. Or more like a twinkle of gratitude. I'd gotten us together again.

Reece said to Mei, "And knowing you has changed me. You'll always be my best friend. But tell us about your mission work, the secret church."

"This is why we could not talk at the restaurant. In this country it is generally safe. But changes are happening quickly, and we are going to Tufan. The Edifice knows we're coming." She spoke softly, as if talking in her own home carried some risk. "I have clearance in my job. And if I pass the security review each year, I have Class Three status."

"What's that?"

"Class One is military, and Class Two is disaster aid. In Asia I am permitted to move about freely as Class Three: travel host executive status. As Haplo D-A—the DNA from my Ainu ancestors—I am one of the endangered people groups. My Ainu ancestors were persecuted and killed like your First People. We are the First People of Japan and very low in population now. So we are protected status."

"Like the African cheetah," Marcus said in a silky tone. "Rare and beautiful."

She sort of ignored him. "Haplo D-A don't have to go to war or work in high-risk jobs like plague medicine research. God put me in a very good situation." She bowed unconsciously. "I can go to more places and be safer than most civilians."

It would have been a boast if anyone but Mei had said it.

"This is great!" I said. "Plumb lucky."

She nodded. "We will travel through Tufan with a guide, no problems, I think. My clearance is good. But I must protect my status. I am thankful to go to the secret churches in other countries, to deliver goods, to bring news and encouragement." Mei informed Marcus, "I am a free agent and not connected to your father's mission agency or to anyone but my church in Osaka. I want to stay unconnected. You understand?"

"You mean I shouldn't say anything about you to Dad?"

"When I'm working, I answer to my employer; I go where I am sent, without question or complication. On my own time, I help secret churches. I don't think the agency knows about some of them. This is good."

Marcus was taken aback. "Um, but Dad already knows we're going. He's the one who told me about Elijah."

"Yes," Mei allowed. "But no more information, okay? And we shouldn't say the word *church* once we leave. Okay, your turn."

Marcus adjusted the sash around his robe. "I'm not connected to Dad's work either. We talk some, but not a lot. He's not crazy about this trip because of the instability over there, and the recent disaster. The explosion. As for jobs, I've worked in advertising, but it's not steady. I'm backup airport security at LAX and at a local business. If you don't have a forty-hour work week—if it's twenty here and ten there—you're expendable. Know what I mean? You can drop out for a week or two and nobody cares. I like the freedom."

Freedom or subsistence living?

Mei said, "We talked as friends. Now I will question you as Edifice would. I have seen this done many times. We could have trouble if you answer questions in the friendly way." She turned to Marcus again. "Maybe you can coach us to act more relaxed. Please tell us if we show fear or worry."

"Sure," he said uneasily.

I jumped in. "Let me say something first. Tomorrow we officially begin our search for Elijah. All I know is what he told me when I saw him last. In Cairo. Which wasn't much. I was in Paris for a climate convention and took a side jaunt to see him. We met at a tea shop. He was trying to fade into the woodwork, I could tell. He was always glancing around. There was this beautiful woman with him named Suzanne. I think she may have been Egyptian, but I don't know. She had only a slight accent, as if she'd studied in the States. It was all light conversation through dinner, but when she left to go to the girls' room, Elijah ran his fingers under the table—to check for bugging devices, I guess. He kept an eye on her hands when she came back. Was he watching to see if she was planting something? I don't know. He wrote half a message to me on a napkin while she was gone. Otherwise it was light conversation."

Marcus asked, "What'd he write on the napkin?"

"I don't know if I should say."

Mei said crisply, "You should not say."

"Okay." I went on, "Every move he made was strategic, and he'd look at me in a way he never did before. Like he was analyzing me. He kept his eyes on my face except when he was watching Suzanne's hands or glancing in the mirrors that hung on the walls. A couple of times he took her hand. I couldn't tell if he was holding it 'cause he liked her or if it was a very subtle way of letting her know she couldn't put anything past him. Sometimes, it seemed they were"—I glanced awkwardly at Reece, "a couple. But he didn't trust her. I could tell that. All we know now, Mei, is what Marcus said, that Elijah disappeared and Dom went to look for him, even though it was against mission policy.

He found his triskele in a dry stream bed. It was deliberately broken. Whatever happened, he didn't want to be tracked."

Reece showed the triskele to Mei and said, "We don't know that he broke it, do we? Someone else could have broken it."

Marcus said, "Only someone who knew what it was would have done that. It's jade. Anyone else would have stolen it and sold it as jewelry. Whoever broke it knew what they were doing. It's snapped clean in half."

"Someone from the agency could have been following him," Reece said. "Did they check it for fingerprints?"

"Dad would've, if it had been important," Marcus answered. "Once you see the terrain, you'll know why he wasn't followed. It's wide open for miles and miles. Nothing can sneak up on you."

Mei said, "We need to sleep. But each one should have an identity answer, an IA, in case of security interrogation. Here is mine: I am Mei Aizawa from Osaka. I am a tour guide with Pacific Rim Travel. I am here as a tourist to help my friends in Tufan because I speak enough Mikan to get around." She concluded with a polite bow. "See? Your IA must be very simple, and we must know each other's IA, but not say it word for word. That would be suspicious."

Rob said, "I have mine. I'm Rob Wingate from Tulsa, Oklahoma. I'm a weather intern for Channel 2 News and I'm researching the effects of the Qolo range on global weather changes. Reece is my assistant."

Mei said, "You said nothing of the theatre."

"Oh yeah, and I'm involved with a little theatre in town. But that's a hobby. Okay, I got paid a couple of times when I helped with the set."

Mei said sharply, "An actor? You are very good at pretending to be someone that you are not."

"Yeah, I guess," I said, glancing at the others to see if they picked up on the icy change in her tone.

"Do you learn languages and accents for your theatre?"

"I've done a few accents, but—"

"Which ones?"

As I realized what she was doing, Mei said to Reece in her regular voice, "You should know a lot of weather terms, in case you're isolated and interrogated."

Reece said, "I've been studying. Rob gave me a book."

Mei looked unconvinced. "You must answer calmly and honestly. They are trained to spot liars." She became cold and detached again. "Mrs. Moline, what weather problems are you studying in Tufan?"

Reece said haltingly, "Um, we're looking at how the system works as a whole. And how the high-altitude currents over the Qolo range affect rainfall globally. We're especially looking at projected models of humidity and temperature, should the highest glaciers melt."

I gave her a thumbs-up.

"And what do those models tell you?" Mei asked officially.

"We're not sure. We want to observe the increased rain north of the Qolo range."

Mei went on. "I see you are a married woman. Where is your husband?"

Reece looked uncomfortable. "Uh, he's at home with our daugh—" She broke off.

Mei pressed. "You have a daughter? What is her name?"

Reece stalled. Her voice lowered, she leaned in confidentially. "Should I tell them that?"

Mei didn't flinch. "What's the problem, Mrs. Moline? Why will you not answer the questions? They are simple questions."

Reece swallowed and sat up. "My husband is at home. My daughter's name is Olivet."

"What is your address and phone number?"

Again Reece stalled. Her face flushed.

"Address and phone number," Mei demanded, then went out of character. "I'm sorry, but it's like this. If you hesitate, they push and push. They look for weakness and they jump. Tell them the address. They can find it anyway. It is your hesitation they are looking for. But they do respect courage over fear."

Reece began again. "I am Reece Moline. I'm from Cedar Ridge, Ohio. I'm here as friend and assistant to Rob Wingate, to help him collect data—"

Mei broke in. "Don't say 'collect data.' It's too much like 'information gathering.' Don't say research unless you explain it clearly. Journalists used to say that when they went to expose the political situation. It's good to say 'global weather research.' Many are doing this. I believe it's still a good thing to say, but not 'collecting data.' Okay, Mrs. Moline, you say your husband is at home. Why are you with these two men that are not your husband?"

Reece stalled. "They're friends."

"No, you're working for Rob, remember." Mei corrected, "Now, Mrs. Moline, does your husband know you're here? Did he give you permission to come?"

Reece went pale. She shot me a look, as if I'd ratted on her.

"Why do you hesitate?" Mei demanded.

Reece wilted. "Did Mom call you?"

Mei slipped out of character.

Marcus asked, "What's going on, people?"

Reece straightened and answered crisply, "No, ma'am, my husband doesn't know I'm here."

Mei froze.

Marcus sat up. "What *is* this?"

I insisted, "Let's move on, Mei."

Mei gathered herself quickly. "We must all be ready to answer any question confidently and—if we can—it must be the truth. If they ask if you're a Christian, say yes. If they ask to see any books you have, show them. One Bible is allowed, but it must not be left behind. Take no tracts to give away. It's illegal. Now you, Marcus."

"I'm Marcus Skidmore. I'm from Laguna Beach, California. I'm friends with these three and going along for the ride."

Mei instructed, "At this point they will see that we are all friends. But you, Reece, are also Rob's assistant. Have your relationship clear between the two of you. Are you being paid? How are you his assistant if you have no education in weather and you live in Ohio? Know these things." She turned back to Marcus. "Where do you work, Mr. Skidmore?"

"I do security at LAX."

"Be specific."

He squirmed. "Night watchman."

"Do you carry a weapon?"

"A nightstick."

"Do you have any other weapons?"

He paused. "Yes…"

Mei coached him. "Be specific. Any hesitation is viewed with suspicion."

"I don't own it, but yes. I have access to a Glock. It's the weapon of the L.A. police. I don't usually carry a gun at work, but it is on hand in the office."

"Do you own any other weapons?"

He paused. "No."

She held up an invisible piece of paper. "I see here that you do, registered in your name."

He looked stunned. "What?"

She gave him a hard look. I couldn't tell if Mei was playing interrogator or being herself.

Marcus admitted, "I did…I owned a .38 revolver and a vintage Bowie knife. But I sold them a few weeks ago." His frown betrayed puzzlement and anger. Just what did Mei know about him and how did she come to know it?

Mei nodded coolly. "And what work did you do before the security job?"

Marcus squirmed again. "I did some modeling for mail-order magazines. I still—"

"And before that?" Mei seemed to be prying.

"Sports club maintenance. I was a janitor." His dark face flushed with embarrassment.

Mei sat back, strained. "Do you see? When we share as friends, you are very different than when I question you as The Edifice would. The way you answer might cause us trouble." She patted her damp forehead with a handkerchief and managed to smile at Marcus. "Later you can coach us on how to act more relaxed."

I jumped in. "This is good, Mei. We all need to work on this and get our IAs down by morning. I'm getting it, how they'll start in on you if they see weakness. Let's work on it."

Her old self again, if a little flustered, she turned to Marcus. "We must be relaxed, but not too much. We'll review in the morning and again in Jinsha. But not on the plane."

When Marcus excused himself to the toilet I whispered to the girls, "I'm gonna make this quick. I'm not 100 percent sure Marcus can be trusted. If we have time later, I'll explain. Elijah had reservations about the agency, even Dom. He told me that much. He was worried and lonely. So use discretion. Okay. Now teach us a few words in Mikan, Mei."

We exchanged good-nights and Mei turned off the lights. The glow of the city through sheer curtains gave enough wattage for us four shadows to see each other. On a floor pallet foot-to-foot with mine, Marcus folded his hands behind his head, thinking.

I checked my weather clip, which cast an eerie blue glow on my hands. Reece sat up on the sleep sofa. "Before we sleep, let's pray."

"Go for it," I said.

She took a deep breath. "Lord, Most High God, we have gathered in your name and in the name of your Son, Jesus, at whose feet every knee will bow. We pray first and foremost for Elijah. Only you know where he is. If he is with you now, then help us to settle things in our hearts and find purpose in his last mission. Lead us to the truth. His family and friends would want to know that his mission was not in vain and that the gospel penetrated into that hard place. If he's alive, Lord, you know we want to find him. Guide us, because we don't know the way. Please protect us where we are going. And if we may be of service to the people, open our eyes and open the doors. If Elijah is in prison or lost or sick, keep him alive until we find him. May we be prepared, cleansed of our many sins, filled with your Spirit, emptied of fear and doubt, and protected against the enemies waiting for us. Not flesh and blood enemies. Remind us of that. In the name of our Lord Jesus, amen. Oh, and give us good rest and thank you so much for Mei to host us, and for Rob to get this project going, and to Marcus for coming to help in ways that you will reveal as we go. And bless Olivet. And Greg. Your word is a lamp to my feet and a light to my path. Amen."

"*To kakaretearu*," added Mei, translating, "'So it is written.' We will sleep with Reece's prayer in our hearts." She paused. "And when we get to Tufan, you must not speak of The Armor or the church, unless asked. Do not speak the name aloud, unless he himself tells you so."

I closed my weather clip. "What name? Elijah's or God's?"

Mei said oh-so-quietly, "Ah. Both. What is the weather for tomorrow?"

"Calm the whole way."

CHAPTER 10

One foot in front of the other, I've got you covered.
—Mae Klingler, "Dragons"

Day One of the official search. Noon. A mix of sun and clouds. Light wind from the west at 5 mph. A monsoon was veering to take a swipe at us midday. But we, the Mag Four, were descending toward Jinsha—thank God—and would land momentarily.

Mei squinted out the plane window. "You were right about the weather, Rob. It was calm the whole way."

"Yep." I was wary of starting a conversation. Mei seemed to have mastered the interrogation techniques of The Edifice, easing into a subject, asking shadowy questions in different ways so you wouldn't notice they were the same question, tripping you up if your answers showed the least inconsistency. So I gathered up the bits of trash around my seat, took a slug of water to deal with cotton mouth from sleeping on the plane, and hoped she didn't sense my uneasiness.

Looking a little worse for wear, we four made it through customs, retrieved our luggage, settled ourselves into the shuttle on seats facing each other, and were soon plowing through the crowded streets of Jinsha. As Asian cities go, it was sort of opposite of Osaka. Sure, it was big and bustling, but it lacked the polish of Mei's home city. Jinsha was trying to spiff up though. Their shiny new international airport put most U.S.

ports to shame.

Jostling along with his duffel between his knees, Marcus commented to Mei, "Bet you've done your homework and Kim's Kozy is the best place in town." He was warming up to her, if not to Reece and me. Maybe he was just trying to get on her good side. My guess is we were all a little afraid of Mei by now.

"The best in all of Asia," she corrected him cheerfully, her voice a bare whisper above the roar of the shuttle engine. "It is clean, safe, and very cheap, as you say 'a well-kept secret?'" She leaned in. "We should not tell anyone or we won't be able to get reservations in the future."

Buildings of semi-sophistication lined Jinsha's main drag, a few stories of glass and tile and brick. Store signs were mostly in Mikan, a few in English. Tree-lined side streets whizzed past with their open-air mom-and-pop businesses: machine repair shops, street kitchens, food markets. Then out of the blue we were beside a set of wooden doors as big as a castle entrance and opening on gigantic hinges. Our shuttle made a sharp right, out of chaos and into a little paradise.

Marcus said, "Whoa…"

Reece cooed with delight.

"Kim's Kozy Tropic Inn," announced Mei, her dark eyes sparkling. A nice-sized tropical garden opened up to our left—maybe a quarter acre—with a pond, bamboo park benches, an arched footbridge, and palm trees. To the right was a plain, three-story building stretching back to the rear of the property. It was joined to another wing in front of us with a tunnel through which you could see more gardens. I'd snoop around later but could already tell that Kim's Kozy was shaped like an upside-down F with gardens on either side of the center crossbar.

Mei nodded toward glass sliding doors to our right. "We check in there."

We piled out of the shuttle exhaling city fumes, inhaling rain forest. Above the lobby at an upstairs window, an old man of Asian descent looked down on us, smoking a cigarette. He made eye contact for a few seconds, then disappeared. We lugged our gear into the low-ceilinged lobby. Bland couches, dated coffee tables, and a concrete floor gave it the feel of a basement rec room (or Marcus's apartment, but nicer). From behind the plywood reception desk, Asian girls briskly tended to travelers, checking them in, explaining maps and tickets. Adventurers of different stripes came and went: four guys with rucksacks; a shaggy, middle-aged man; girls in long skirts and hiking boots; an older couple, sun-dried and fit, wearing safari hats and drinking from water bottles.

Reece eyed the couple. "They're like the Stallards, aren't they? Has anyone heard from Dr. Eloise?"

Taking charge as she approached the desk, Mei warned, "We can talk about her later. You need to show passports and permits. Keep me updated on weather, Rob. We may have to rebook the flight to YangDi if the weather changes. We can stay here a day or two longer, without reservations." She smiled at Marcus. "Because it's secret, *ne.*"

Marcus took stock of the bustling lobby. "Not too secret."

She spoke a few words in Mikan to the desk clerk, then switched to English. Soon we had keys and instructions about the laundry porch and curfews and such. A nice-looking Asian lady with two children came in from the garden. Mei greeted her in Japanese and dug into her bag for treats for the little girl, about five, and her toddler brother. "Sachiko, these are my friends from the States: Marcus, Rob, and Reece. I told them this is the best place!" She said to us, "Sachiko and her husband own Kim's Kozy. She is from Japan, so everything will be clean and very good."

"*Domo. Domo,*" the innkeeper nodded twice. "*Heya wa dō?*"

"We're going to our room now, but it will be excellent. Thank you. *Mata ne.*"

We lugged our bags upstairs and back a narrow, windowed hallway overlooking the garden. From the very spot where the Asian man had looked down on me, I peeked down on a taxi letting out a tall trekker with a brimmed hat and huge backpack. *It's him! It's Elijah!*

The brimmed hat tipped up. Pale blue eyes nervously cased the place before glancing up at me. A squared-jawed, Nordic type in his forties handed the driver some bills.

Not him.

Our room: three sturdy, homemade wooden bunks with silky, orange curtains drawn around each bed for privacy; padlocked storage lockers under the bottom bunks; each bed with its own rotating fan mounted above, which kept the orange curtains flowing, giving a person the feeling that people were already in the bunks, moving around. But we were the only ones there. Between the toilet room and the shower room sat a little table with a hot water pot and three chairs. A single open window looked out on the laundry porch. I dropped my pack and stuck my head out. Clotheslines were strung the length of a long deck with a few coin-operated washing machines at the end. A roof of corrugated plastic kept the weather off. *Homey,* I thought, and ducked back in.

"Festive," Marcus commented ambiguously about the room.

"We stay together, as you see," Mei said. "Two other guests will come later. It is safe, but I recommend to keep your money and passport with you. A waist belt is good. You should also have a card with travel information and contacts"—her voice lowered—"like the Stallards taught us. But memorize the information. Also there is no schedule here. Rest and shower and eat when you like. People sleep day and night. If you see the curtain closed, please be quiet."

"Jet lag recovery room," I joked.

Mei went on with the crucial info: "The cafe is on the ground floor beside the second garden. We order food there. The dining terrace is on the top floor and is very nice and peaceful. The cooked food is safe here, but don't eat any raw food from the street markets. Drink only boiled water and tea. Use bottled water to brush your teeth. Don't let the shower water go into your mouth. You will get sick. People steal the toilet paper, so keep your own. A store down the street has supplies. I'll take you there. The entry gate closes at 11:00 every night. You do not want to be left on the street." Mei chucked her rucksack to a top bunk. "Reece, please take the bottom bunk. It will be easier." In a lowered voice under the whir of fans, she added, "You may have conversation with other guests, but remember your Identity Answers. Don't bring up the name unless they say it first. Even then, be careful."

Complying, Reece slung her pack on the bottom bunk. "Kim's is great, Mei. Thank you so much for arranging this. It reminds me of our times at Camp Mudj, you know, the overnighters in the lodge together."

"I think so too," Mei said with a soft, sad smile. "I have the best memories."

We got settled and milled around in the first garden, then went down the street for necessaries. Bikes and parked cars jammed the sidewalks, wedging in at odd angles with pedestrians weaving around them. A group of men sat on the corner playing mah-jongg. I held up my camera and asked, "Okay?" One of the men nodded. They all struck poses with studied frowns, rubbing their chins, as if deep in the game and oblivious to being photographed. Hams. As we moved on, I drawled in a syrupy

Virginia accent, "Nehvah, in awl my ye-ahs on the stage, have ah seen mah-jongg played with such dipth of feelin'!"

Marcus elbowed me, Reece snickered, Mei had trouble understanding.

We meandered through a couple of stores—my refound best buddies and I—buying up supplies and cheap souvenirs. The urgency that had gripped my gut in past weeks subsided. *You did it, Wingate: got Mei and Reece and Marcus here, all three. Made it to LA, Osaka, now Jinsha. Next YangDi and Qolo. Three of five points on the map. Four out of five people. So far, so good.* I hankered to get to the heights where Elijah had disappeared, but to reach YangDi jet-lagged and dodging storms could compromise the mission. Marcus and I followed the girls down the street while they shopped—until my body, still on Tulsa time, demanded food.

The cafe at Kim's Kozy, a dim little downstairs bar off the second garden, had a few tables—all occupied—and neon signs advertising beer. Tucked behind a wall of glass along the rear was a narrow, windowless communications room, a place for guests to check messages, get news. The long desk facing the wall had several com stations, all occupied by young men and one older guy: the man with the cigarette. I watched him for a minute, but he was glued to his station, typing like mad.

We ordered meals at the bar and went upstairs to a multilevel bamboo terrace that wrapped the rear of the building. I checked my weather clip and reported, "Rain moving in."

Reece ran to the rail and oohed over the garden with its gazebo and winding, thatch-roofed walkways. "Look! You could stroll through the garden in a downpour and stay perfectly dry!"

The terrace itself had been put together piecemeal, with step-ups and add-ons that gave it a sort of Tarzan-tree-house effect. In bad weather or for privacy, we could dine in one of the side rooms with sliding glass doors and walls of bamboo. Around the garden's perimeter high walls and higher apartment buildings blocked out the city. We found a table, sat, and just looked at each other for a minute. "I owe you one, Mei," I said. "This tropical tree-house-fortress-garden-jungle thingy is the best! It sure is nice having friends in far places."

At the Osaka sushi bar, Mei had shushed us; at her apartment she'd grilled us. Now in the open air she let us catch up. We listened intently to details of each other's lives, in case of interrogation. Mei said chances were slim we'd have to use our Identity Answers, but made us whittle them to perfection anyway. She reminded us that Marcus had worked airport security and that I was in the field of news journalism. Both were liabilities. Reece fit the typical tourist profile except for the metal rod in her leg that required stamped clearance on her passport. Mei had double privilege as a tour guide and as a member of the endangered Ainu tribe. It struck me that world governments had joined forces to preserve nearly extinct people groups the same way they'd recovered the bald eagle and black-footed ferret: tagged and catalogued.

Reece hardly spoke about her marriage or the fact that Greg didn't know where she was, sticking instead to Olivet and the church. Marcus kept mum about his private life. I had nothing to hide. Well, actually I did. But Mei did too: her stuff about the secret church. So there we were, the Mag Four with heavy stuff to hide on a secret mission that a few months ago would have been the furthest thing from our minds.

Mei had taken on the logistics of the mission, hopefully getting us *gaijins* in and out of Tufan in as few pieces as possible. But I couldn't shake the feeling that the final consequences of the trip, tragedy or triumph, would fall on me. For the first time in Mag Five history, Elijah wasn't in the lead. I was.

Our meals were served. Mei warned, "We should not speak of any connection to our friend or of Dr. E. Their names are connected."

"Recently?" I asked.

"Maybe," she answered.

Even in a little pocket of paradise, we'd best not forget that we were days from facing the great unknown right in its beady little eyes.

Partway through our meal of rice, grilled vegetables, and fish, I caught Marcus staring at someone on the terrace at the back of the building. He said, "That girl over there…she looks like one of the SOS."

A slim young woman with long, wavy red hair was obviously looking for someone. When her eyes fell on us, she came over smiling. "I think we know each other."

Marcus stood. "Karinna, right?"

"SOS. Seven years ago in Nikko." She was tall, freckled, pretty—tougher looking than before—in a denim jacket and flowy cotton skirt, not barefoot like I remembered her, but booted up like the girls we'd seen in the lobby. She looked us over. "How is everyone?"

Reece stood and hugged her. "We're doing well. How are you?"

Marcus said, "Are you meeting someone? If not, come join us."

"As a matter of fact, I'm here to meet you."

"Us?!" I asked. The unintended snap in my voice startled even me.

Unflustered, she said, "I'll order a meal and come back up."

When she left, I turned to Marcus. "Did you ask her to come?"

Marcus put up a hand. "Nothing to do with it."

Mei said, "Remember your IAs."

In a minute Karinna was back. She pulled up a chair at the end of the table, between Marcus and Mei. "It's good to see everyone again. My deepest sympathies about your friend. And mine. I worked with him often and respected him deeply." She didn't say his name.

"Do you know anything?" Reece asked.

Karinna broke apart her chopsticks and rubbed them together to clean off the splinters, anticipating the meal to be brought up. "No. But I was part of his Qolo team. We're all having a hard time about this. It's more difficult because he wasn't recovered. I understand why you want to search. A few of us wanted to…" She changed the subject. "Tell me about yourselves, each of you."

I was having none of this casual crap. "How did you know we were here?"

"Dom asked me to come."

Marcus seemed as surprised as me. Rain swept across the garden. I never tire of the smell of it, even if there's a twister tearing up the countryside around it. We moved into the bamboo room with sliding doors, set our plates down on the picnic table, and pulled up the benches. The sky darkened. I checked the path of the rains on my weather clip and as predicted, a wide hook of the storm system had veered over Jinsha. Karinna turned on the wall lamps. Her meal was delivered. She closed the doors.

Despite the pelting on the roof, Karinna kept her voice down, like Mei had. "Dom admires what you're doing," she said as we resumed eating, "but he's concerned for your safety. He asked if I'd be willing to escort you into Tufan. It's not an easy place to negotiate. I know a little of the language." She paused. "You do understand that everything was done that could be done to find him. Our friend's last signals were reviewed. Dom was able to find the triskele after it had been disabled. It was a chance miracle, a needle in a haystack! And a great comfort that our friend chose in the end to protect us from the dangers of a search. And that he"—she pointed heavenward—"guided Dom to find the proof."

"We know this," I said shortly. "We have the triskele in our possession." I glanced at Marcus who'd told us that his dad had used "some method" to find the triskele. "Unbelievable luck," I said to Karinna. "How in the world does a person find a pendant no bigger than a silver dollar in the Qolo mountains?"

"I know!" She beamed. "All he had was the general direction. It was a miracle!"

It was no haystack miracle. It was "some method." Marcus returned my puzzled look. I glanced at Mei. If her steel-trap mind had picked up the discrepancy she didn't show it.

Karinna poured herself a cup of tea in an authoritative way. "Dom would have accompanied you himself, but Tufan is off limits to him right now."

Firmly I said, "Thanks, but I think we can handle it."

The others were stunned. Karinna offered the little white pot. "Are you all in agreement about this?" Only Marcus held out his cup to her.

Reece gave me a stricken look, but in answer to my tight lips she said, "Well…it was Rob who organized the trip, so…um…"

Karinna stood, smiling. "Tell you what, I'll refresh our teapot while you talk it over. I can check the flights to YangDi." She slid open the glass door and looked back at us. "But if you decide to go through with it alone, I ask that you not mention the agency. And should there be a problem, Parabolani would not be able to come to your aid. The Edifice knows something's up."

"Aren't you part of the agency?" I asked.

"Not officially."

"A couple of questions. How can we *not* be associated with the agency if you're a former employee and if Dom's son is with us?"

She glanced out at the terrace, checking for people within earshot. "Marcus works at a market and has had few communications with his father in the past year. His airport security position might have been a problem if he were still working there. Security staff have weapons permits."

Just as I was thinking that something didn't jive, Marcus said, "I still do work at the airport, as backup, not regular. I carry a taze rod. Work at the market is off and on." He feigned nonchalance but had to be thinking back to Mei's interrogation and thinking, *Is everybody in the whole stinkin' world nosing into my life?*

Here was another detail of misinformation. Karinna said Marcus didn't work at the airport. He said he did, though not regularly. She didn't mention the advertising job. He hadn't mentioned the market to us. Karinna must have gotten her intel from Dom, and Marcus hadn't updated his dad on his ever-changing employment.

Karinna said, "I'll get the tea. Please know that I'm prepared to go along, to show you the places he went."

"Wouldn't your connection to the agency still be a problem— for us?" I said, keeping her in the doorway with rain at her back. "After all, he disappeared from *your* team."

"They didn't know he was with us," she answered a tad testily and resumed her spiel. "I would be your guide, a guide from Germany not the States, which looks better to The Edifice for a number of reasons."

I argued, "I thought you were from the States."

"My parents live in Germany now."

Mei reacted with the slightest stiffening of the neck.

I said, "Mei can guide us and she's Asian, which is even better, right?"

Karinna stepped back in and shut the glass door. Her voice went tender. "Rob, this is difficult for me too. On that day, I could have insisted he not go. I could have followed him or drawn attention to him. He might have been deported or arrested, but still alive. Once he made up his mind, he couldn't be dissuaded.

Dom wants to make this as easy as possible on you. That's the only reason I'm here."

Marcus picked at his food. "Why didn't Dad tell us he didn't want us going?"

Karinna answered, "When Dom got word that you had a ticket, he asked if I could delay going home for a couple of weeks in order to accompany you."

I persisted and tried to sound friendly. "We appreciate it, Karinna, you coming all this way. But we don't need anyone's help. People go to Qolo all the time. It's a pilgrimage place. Mei speaks several languages and is a tourism professional."

Reece added, "And if anyone suspects us, Rob is doing a study on weather—"

I jumped in. "That's just if we get stopped and our map gets confiscated or anything." I wished Reece hadn't mentioned it.

Karinna advised, "Go as pilgrims. Posing as a scientist has been overused by mishes and conspirators in Tufan recently. So-called scientists are pulled for questioning and jailed if their story proves false. Go as pilgrims unless your employer has actually sent you. The Edifice can check out your story."

"I *am* a scientist," I said.

Mei quietly pressed, "I believe the weather story is acceptable, Karinna. Many enter Tufan for that very reason."

Reece added, "And I don't want to give the impression that we're paying homage to their gods on pilgrimage. I like the weather research idea."

Karinna nodded. "You understand that your tour tickets fund the temples."

Reece sat back. "What?"

"Sadly, yes. To get into the region, one must book a tour. And the tours fund temples and monasteries, indirectly, through souvenirs, offerings, and the like. It's a match made in Hell. The evil one has a nearly perfect system there."

"Nearly perfect?" Marcus asked.

She said mysteriously, "Two wrongs can make a right. Romans 8:28." She left to refill the pot.

"I need to think," I muttered. We sat listening to the rain patter on palm leaves. I felt bad that she'd come all this way, but I didn't like Dom imposing his messenger girl on us.

Karinna returned and served tea all around. Very hospitable.

I said, "We appreciate you coming all the way from—from where?"

"H.Q. East."

Why was she coming from agency headquarters if she no longer worked for them—officially? I asked again, "And how'd you know we were here?"

"As I said, Dom sent me." Smiling she added, "He knows where his son is."

I asked Marcus, "Does he have our whole itinerary, bud?"

Marcus had been tapping his fingers nervously on the table. He looked to Mei. "Did you book the Qolo tour already?"

"Yes. But tours are contingent on political situations, weather, and road conditions." She added rigidly to Karinna, "I report to no one."

"I would like to go back to Tufan one last time," Karinna admitted, still nudging us. "It's possible we missed something in the investigation."

Playing a sympathy card now? Well delivered, Karinna. Just in case she considered secretly tailing us, I said, "A woman shouldn't go there alone, I guess. And if you get in a fix, no one would come, even for you?"

"Correct."

"And we're not to be associated with Parabolani, right, your own department—formerly?"

Karinna saw she was getting nowhere. "I was Peregrini. Our friend was working toward being 'bolani." She paused to smile. "He often blurred the lines. We also have the third branch." She tapped her index finger to her lips.

Mei mouthed to Reece, "Seraphs. Secret church," before asking Karinna, "Where?"

"On the move."

I declined her offer for the last time. "We'll be going by ourselves. Thank you for your time."

"All right." She nodded resignedly, taking a seat. "If you don't mind, though, I'll fill you in."

"We'd love to hear," Reece said.

Karinna paused to get her thoughts in order and—I suspected—to give it one more shot. "He joined us seven years ago and kept a low profile so the trail on The Armor would fade. We don't know exactly how she did it, but Dr. Eloise disappeared him. If you haven't heard about this in the States, The Edifice is known for disappearing people. One day a person is just gone—no record of flight tickets or hotel reservations, no ID numbers…as if he never existed."

"We know," said Marcus, one hand spread on the table, the other resting on his thigh, his green eyes dark and rather unfriendly.

"Dr. E provided paperwork for him, of a person who never existed. At the same time there were leaked reports of rare antiquities being discovered, not just The Armor. Most were later exposed as hoaxes. That, we believe, was to throw people off his trail. When one relic after another was found to be a fraud, the legendary armor was also put in a bad light, as if it too was a hoax. The timing could not have been a coincidence. This went on for a few years. His new family name, Telanoo, now shows up in the State Department's genealogical records as Native American."

Marcus mused, "Wiping out one guy, inventing another,

creating fake relics. All to throw people off his track. A pretty important guy, our friend."

"Who knew about the hoaxes?" I asked.

"We suspected Dr. E, but who could we ask without arousing suspicion? I did overhear Song, a girl from China, and Steven from the States discussing fake bronzes made to look like they came from the Shang period. The discoveries were convincing enough to get the press involved but not fool the scientific elite. We suspected that she did it to manipulate the press. But if Song and Steven knew more than that—The Armor's whereabouts— they didn't say." Karina looked at Reece. "Do you know?"

Reece blushed. "No."

"We don't know." It was my warning for the others to keep quiet. "None of us knows."

Karinna went on. "You remember that he trained in the Pacific and served two tours of duty with us in the SOS. He was grooming for 'bolani. Everyone saw his natural talent. His weaknesses were language and cultural protocols: how to blend in. But Dom invested in him like no other. His team suffered terrible setbacks his first year as leader, more than their share. We're trained to manage troubles, but it was bad. They lost a team member in a climbing accident. In addition, Suzanne and he had a volatile relationship. They would be close, then split up to different teams, then get back together…" Her voice trailed off.

Did that pause carry a touch of longing? Doggone if this wasn't complicated.

"Geo told me—you know he goes by George Telanoo…"

Reece jumped in. "We know. Someone told—" *Oops* was written all over her face. The girl can't lie worth a hoot. "Someone told us. Maybe it was Dom. I think."

Karinna was playing the trust card, sharing his alias with us, building camaraderie. I asked, "Was anyone jealous of him?

Would anyone wish him harm?"

She studied me a moment. "Are you suggesting that the accident on Geo's team was not an accident? That someone intended to discredit or harm him?"

I stammered, "N-no."

"We train in conflict resolution," she said professionally. "Feelings are worked through openly. Geo's teams were tough, and people admired him. He was the first to teach the North Games, if you've heard of them."

"Nope," Marcus admitted.

"I have," I said. "Crazy feats of strength and agility. Balancing your body weight on your fingertips. High-kicking way over your head."

Karinna was strolling us around from one subject to another, like a walk through the garden. "The North Games are stamina games of the Inuit," she said, "survival skills for their world: scissors broad jump to go over ice floes, walking on bent toes to prevent frostbite."

I checked my clip. The worst of the storm was yet to come. I added, "The four-man carry and the one-arm reach…he could do those?"

"Yes," Karinna grinned proudly. "Extreme exercises strengthen a person's will to endure when he reaches the end of his body's limitations. Geo would give anyone a chance to qualify. The sickly or overweight…if they wanted to try, he'd work with them. If anyone was jealous of that, they should be ashamed. He wanted his teams—all the teams—to be excellent." Her head dropped, her chin puckered. "He wanted them excellent. He had such a natural way about him."

Marcus put his elbow on the table, his fist covering his mouth, and stared off into space. Reece got teary-eyed, then Mei. A rainy quiet came over us.

Our freckle-faced friend sniffled. "I don't know if this is important to your search. But Geo told me about an encounter with an entity he called Lotus while he was with you in Japan. He wanted to understand what it meant, to 'get to the bottom of it,' he'd say. At the agency we keep only one or two specialists in the occult; people get sucked in and lose their way. He became obsessed with his studies, refused to back off and was put on leave. For a time no one knew where he was; he used our own security techniques against us and vanished. Dom found him and sent him here for recovery."

"Here to Kim's?" Reece asked.

"Yes."

"Did he tell you about all this?"

"He did. See, my parents are trance channelers, believers in dark powers. They devoted me as a child. He knew I'd believe him, whatever he'd experienced." She got up as if to leave, scanning the terrace. "As far as I know, it's safe here. But be careful what you say. If you intercede together (she didn't say *pray*), a good place is by one of the garden fountains where it's noisy—and keep your eyes open so it looks like you're having conversation." Leaning against the door frame, she said finally, "Be safe. Be wise. Be calm. In Tufan it's easy to forget who is ever-present and in control."

"The Edifice," I answered.

Practically glaring, Karinna waited for me to correct myself.

"Oh," I muttered, casting my eyes heavenward. "You mean *him*."

As if to save me embarrassment, she turned the subject back to Elijah. "Geo would not open up about his darkest period, not even to our counselors. The advisory team considered dismissing him, but he was so valuable to us. He got through it, or seemed to, and requested high-risk missions, even with a team of new recruits."

"He trained for that at Camp Mudj," I threw in. "Since middle school, his dad would call on him to get kids out of trouble, rescue the ones who got lost or broke an arm—"

Reece raised her hand sheepishly. "Or collapsed in a park at sundown."

"So I heard," Karinna said warmly. "The recruits who endured his boot camp were among the most rugged, the most adaptable for resistant missions. The ones who passed muster adored him. Even those who didn't…" She smiled at each of us, spending a second longer on Reece. "You may be surprised at what I know about each of you. During his first weeks with the SOS, you were everything he talked about. But," she concluded, "though he worked with discipline and great patience to teach the protocols of teamwork, he himself defied them at the end. Dom's concern was Geo's recklessness."

Eyes open, Karinna prayed over us, never addressing God by name, but in a nearly inaudible whisper at the end saying, "in the holy and precious name, Yeshua." She folded her arms. "To what extent his last mission was a relapse into his dark period, no one knows. He broke critical rules on that day. Dom was beside himself. Be very careful. You cannot be too careful."

She left. Questioning eyes turned on me. I defended my decision. "You all didn't see his face when he and I sat in that tea shop in Cairo—how he kept watch on people's reflections in all the mirrors on the walls, watching up and down the aisles, up and down the alleyways, how he hardly made eye contact with that Suzanne girl. He was more on edge than I'd ever seen. And when I almost said his real name once…that kick under the table and the deadly look he shot me—" I shook my head with finality and even gave Mei a half-threatening glance on the outside chance she had other ideas. "I know my cousin, and I say we go alone."

CHAPTER 11

So here we are, at home on the edge of things.
—Andrea Summer, "Know It When I See It"

Day Two. I was awakened at 3:20 by a strip of bright light from the opened door. Two unknown roommates were creeping in for the night, but for a second—in my half-dream state—I thought we were being abducted by aliens. The unbuckling of backpacks and rustling of sleeping bags was followed by the flush of the toilet, a few whispers, then the squeak of bunks and all quiet. When we got up, their curtains were closed. We four got ready with hardly a word.

We met in the garden, sat on park benches, and watched the goldfish swimming lazily around the pond. I did have misgivings about sending Karinna away; it might be easier with her along. "When I met him in Cairo," I said to the others, shoring up my decision, "there was someone in the ranks he didn't trust. Maybe more than one. He didn't mention names, so I'm not taking any chances."

"I don't think it could be Karinna," said Reece.

"Me neither, but she's been trained how to act under pressure. Actors can spot an act. I say she wasn't telling us everything."

"You can spot an act every time?" Reece asked in a tone of irritation.

"I work with people who can take on a persona nothing like themselves, from Jekyll to Hyde. It's what actors do." Tears sprang to my eyes. "That was insulting, Reece."

Her mouth fell open. "Rob, I didn't mean—"

I shut the tears off like a faucet and smiled. "See? See how an actor manipulates people?"

Off their stunned expressions—Mei's being more of suspicion than surprise—I said, "As guides go, Mei is all we need. We're going on our own, or I'm out."

We prayed in the garden with eyes open, then ordered breakfast at the bar downstairs and went up to the terrace to drink tea and wait for eggs and muffins, rice and miso soup. Karinna joined us for a few minutes before her taxi was due. She checked the table and chairs for bugging devices before sitting.

More tersely than the night before, she told us, "Follow the advice from your tour guide in YangDi. Mei might have told you: don't point a camera at the troops. Don't mention the name unless you're in wide-open spaces. Even then, remember that long-range mics could be anywhere. It's best to talk in code. Have water, oxygen, a little extra food, and toilet tissue with you at all times. Do you have Hi-moxx?

"I have a few doses if we need them," I said.

She reached into her waist pouch and brought out a pill bottle. "This is all I have left. You should have started taking these sooner. Get more in YangDi—this brand only—if you feel symptoms of altitude sickness coming on: headache, loss of appetite, loss of sleep. It's a dreadful condition and can kill you. The air is dangerously thin, and only gets worse as you ascend. Don't push or exert. It will be crowded with the holiday coming. Stay together and support each other. Your tour may change at any moment without your approval or knowledge. Retracing his last steps through the mountains will be impossible. You'd die of starvation or exposure if you tried. You'll see that. And there are wild dogs and bandits."

I countered her scare tactics. "Exposure? It's twenty to sixty degrees at base camp. We're taking a tour. In a car."

She corrected me. "Chill factors from high winds turn a mild day deadly. Don't go off by yourself, especially to higher altitudes. In forty-five mph winds and with a sudden drop to zero degrees you have a windchill of thirty below. Flesh can freeze in ten to thirty minutes. There's more than climate at work up there. The political situation can change, too. If a skirmish breaks out, don't cause trouble. We won't know for certain where you are, even if we had your itinerary. If you attempt to leave the tour, The Edifice will know. If you communicate with anyone stateside, do not use the name or mention—" She tapped a finger to her lips. Meaning the secret church. "And don't expect even sat phones to work at base camp, if you get that far. Ours malfunctioned more than once. Better to leave phones here. They have lockers for your valuables."

She hugged each of us around the table. "We'll keep you covered," meaning prayed for.

I felt guilty when she left, even though I'd seen in her last glance a look of utter detachment. We'd been let go. A couple of things didn't wash. She'd said "we" as if she were still part of the agency…or some new team Dom had formed. She talked about conflict resolution within the agency as if it were a done deal every time, but also about Elijah's volatile relationship with Suzanne. And his near dismissal when he wouldn't back off delving into the occult stuff. It can't work both ways. Either the agency had its members under control, or they didn't. Then there was the miraculous retrieval of Elijah's triskele. Dom had said he'd used "some method." Which was it—miracle or method?

All of which brought to mind another nagging trust issue:

what the Mag Three didn't know about me.

Most of the day I wandered the gardens in the rain, pushed my body to recover from jetlag, and did what we call back home "stewin' the bones," what you do to a chicken carcass to get all the nutrients and minerals into a nice broth. Good for what ails you. For me, stewin' the bones is a big chunk of quiet time, thinking deep on a subject to extract all the truth from it.

Weather issues were causing turmoil around the planet. The sun had been in an unusually long heating cycle, so some of Earth's changes were coming from old Sol himself. The problem of industrial and domestic CO_2 emissions was a dog fight, nation blaming nation, one scientist at odds with another. Strong, deep cold snaps were another surprise. But an issue had come to my attention that could trump them all. In recent months I'd caught snippets about weather-control experiments in the upper regions of the atmosphere in Canada, Siberia, New Guinea, and the latest one perhaps in Tufan. Climate change in Asia or anywhere else hadn't been connected to (or blamed on) the ION Task because The Edifice was trying to keep it off the radar—literally—using satellite maps with large areas blurred out, like people's faces in witness protection photos.

And here's where it got a little creepy. The Inter-Operational Nimbus fields, ION for short, were more than research outposts and acres of high-powered towers located in remote areas around the world. Experiments were being done that no one at my weather station seemed aware of or was willing to discuss: weather as warfare, as weaponry. I'd done prelims and it appeared that the ION fields themselves could be the source, at least in part, of aberrant weather. And why not? When you beam mega-zillions of energy waves into the firmament, things happen. No surprise there. But the long-term effect on the symbiotic relationship between high heavens and deep earth?

A few papers had been written, the faintest rumblings from the scientific community on the subject, but nothing published in popular journals. Weather warfare made perfect sense. He who controls the weather controls the world. I'd thought long and hard about that after I'd found so many end-times prophecies in Scripture associated with weather phenomenon.

Equally disturbing was information-fudging in areas of government, communication, health, and science. It went something like this: First, there's a secret project. Information leaks. Its existence is denied. Anyone asking questions is branded a marginalized wacko: "Nothing's going on! What are you talking about?" When proof becomes undeniable, the story changes: "Well, of course it exists," they'd say, as if you're an idiot, "but not as you understand it." When the next layer of truth peels off, usually by a silenced conspiracy theorist or by the surviving friends of such a person, the story changes again: "Yes, it is as you say, but it's for everyone's good, the lesser of two evils. We must act now." Between first discovery and final disclosure a few investigators and watchdogs die mysterious deaths. Most of us world citizens are too sheep-like and distracted to notice.

There was another aspect to the ION Task I'd found in an unpublished document that supposedly didn't exist, but which I'd acquired from one said "conspiracy nut." It was 400 pages long and technical, but a few paragraphs buried three-fourths of the way through got me thinking about Elijah. Similar wave experiments were being done on animals to see how their brain functions might be affected. The research was ongoing, the results disturbing: stupor, blindness, death. What if Elijah had spent days on the heights with ION-induced waves bouncing around in the upper atmosphere? He was at anywhere from 14,000 to 17,000 feet or higher where he could be exposed. What might be the effect on him?

I'd checked the maps for lakes in the area, sources of food and water. Elijah knew how to catch fish, make shelter with rocks, and build a cooking fire with a few sticks. Had he gotten disoriented? Karinna said their sat phones had failed. At three miles in the air? Nonsense…unless ION rays had interrupted phone signals in the lower troposphere where those rays had no business being. What if he wandered around out there, having broken his triskele because he was either half-crazed or knew something was terribly wrong and didn't want to put anyone else in jeopardy?

I ate by myself mid-afternoon, brushed my teeth with bottled water, took a cold hard look in the mirror, into the hollowness behind my own blue eyes, and faced a fact I hadn't admitted even to myself: that if we found Elijah a walking zombie, I might not want to bring him back. Another consideration: that my prime directive for coming here and bringing the Mag Four along might deep down have almost as much to do with scientific curiosity and intellectual heroism as it did with rescue. Was I being dishonest with the others? I really, really wanted firsthand hard evidence about the ION Task. If there was a cover to be blown on weather manipulation, I wanted to be the one to blow it. I confessed to the face in the mirror: *Sure, I want to find my cousin. We had a bond like brothers. But what can I do that Dom hadn't already done? Nothing. Less than nothing.*

. . . . .

Day Three. Mild, drizzly. Our two anonymous roomies had moved on. We'd heard them snoring, whispering, showering, dressing in the dark, but had never seen them. We were hidden in our own bunks behind orange silky curtains. "We pack tonight," I told the others. "The weather's winding down. Flights are catching up from the delays. I've hung out in the lobby and had a few conversations. I'm going back down."

"I'll join you," Reece said.

"I'll be on the laundry porch," Mei said. "Reece, I'll do your clothes."

Marcus gathered up an armful. "Wingate, you got anything to wash? I'll do it."

I handed him my wad of laundry. "Thanks."

The lobby's old couches, cement floor, and wide-open doorway to the garden had the feel of a downstairs family room with the garage door up: nothing you could hurt, everyone welcome. You smelly, rough-hewn vagabonds? Come on in, set a spell. One such person was picking through a giveaway closet of clothes and gear that people had left behind. The sign said, "Help Yourself." I found a warm scarf, sniffed it and checked it for bugs.

Rain came steady and straight down. I hung the scarf over a park bench to wash in nature's laundry. Reece and I got hot drinks and kicked back near the open door, reading and watching people dash in and out. I could see why people loved this place. Forget crowded airports and jammed flights. Time slowed to a sleepy crawl here. Food was great. Rooms were clean. Beds were comfy. Everyone looked interesting. An oasis in the middle of an urban jungle.

Two hikers wearing heavy-duty backpacks stood at the front desk for a long time, rain dripping from their straps. The young clerks made calls and frowned and talked and made more calls. After a while the couple came over. The girl undid her pack and collapsed on the couch opposite us. She was muscular and too thin, with damp, sandy hair. He was of the same ilk, and tall with rimless glasses. The girl rubbed her forehead tiredly.

Reece asked the girl, "Are you all right?"

"Yes, thanks."

"Where ya heading?" I asked.

"We just came from Tufan and are trying to change our flight to go back." She pulled out an energy bar. "But they won't let us."

"Go back?" Reece asked.

"Yeah." She breathed hard, closed her eyes, chewed her bar.

The guy headed for the men's room.

Reece said, "That's where we're heading, soon as the storm passes."

"Ah, good luck."

"What're the best sights to see?" Reece asked innocently.

"Qolo, of course. And the temples."

"You've been there, to Qolo?"

"Many times. We hiked the sixty miles to base camp and back. Training for the ascent."

"Wow," Reece said.

"You doing pilgrimage or trek?" the young woman asked disinterestedly, throwing in a question just to be polite while focusing on breathing and eating. Her accent said she was from the States.

"Seeing the sights, that's all," I said. "We're not trekkers. Tell us about Qolo. Any travel tips?"

"You won't be going the way we went."

"Oh? Where did you go?" Reece asked.

"We stayed with locals all the way to base camp."

I asked, "But you still have to stay on the main road and check in with the military, don't you?"

"Of course."

We were boring her. I went on anyway. "Can you just set out and hike across the mountains? We'd thought of doing that—if we felt like it."

Her eyes opened at me as if I'd made the world's stupidest statement. "Mmm…no. And you won't feel like it. You climb in the States?"

"Not really," I said.

She smiled smugly. "You have to acclimate."

"Staying with the locals. How was that?" Reece asked.

"A rich experience if you can embrace their culture. We do," she said proudly.

So I'm a subhuman, uncultured species of non-trekker? I went with it. "You have to be pretty hardy, I guess. We're not very hardy. Are you guys on your own or with a group?"

"On our own."

"You speak the language?"

"A little."

"Super!" I went to the hot water machine a few feet away and stooped to refill my cup, glancing back. "You spent time in the back country around Qolo?"

"A month. Our permit expired. We're trying to get back."

"That's impressive. Did you meet any other long-distance trekkers like yourselves?"

She took a slug of water from a high-tech bottle. "Lots of people, especially here."

"No, I mean in Tufan. At Qolo. While you were staying with locals. You know, off the beaten track."

"Not many," she said proudly.

Reece pressed, "But you have met a few?"

I added a twinge of Tennessee to my voice. Elijah had done the same years ago, pretending to be a bumpkin to get to truth. "We're wimps but we're hopin' to be doin' whatcher doin,' you know, get out there amongst the mountain people. We heard of one guy doin' that kind of thing, and we wanted to get some tips. But the other tourists we talked to, they hadn't been out there like you guys. Supposedly there's an expert trekker who's all by himself."

"A hiker going solo!" Reece jumped in on my act. "Can you imagine? Do people even do that?"

The guy came back, plopped down beside his girl and gave us a greeting, hands pressed together and a nod. "*Namaste.*"

"Glad to meet you," I said. "We hear you guys were hiking Qolo and wondered if people ever go solo up there."

She said, "We did hear about one guy. I doubt if it was the same person you're talking about. Thousands of pilgrims go every season."

"Oh yeah, the seven shadows guy," he said. "Going solo's a bad idea. No guide book would recommend that." He surveyed us doubtfully.

"Seven shadows?" Reece repeated.

"Probably from Tufani spiritual practices, which are centuries old. The great masters hid scrolls of secret doctrines in caves. Thousands of scrolls. There's much wisdom yet to be discovered for the coming age. We want to go back to join an archaeological team. To be part of the awakening."

"That's cool," I complimented. But from what I knew, the ancient texts were little more than crusty old black magic. "We're going with a package tour. We're first timers, but we'd like to be trekkers like you guys."

His grin said "Good luck with that." He went on with this and that for several more minutes. Neither offered their names, so we didn't either. She handed him an energy bar from her pack.

"The seven shadows…" Reece reminded him.

"It was Tsering, wasn't it," the trekker asked his girlfriend, "talking about the seven shadows man while we were sitting around the fire that night?"

The girl swung her leg up onto his lap, telling her saga in a painfully slow second-hand way, repeating obvious details to her partner that were actually meant to impress us. A quarter inch of rain fell before she gave the faintest hint of circling back toward the subject of seven shadows. "You know, love, Tsering might be a great guide to get us to the caves. We'll need a translator. The Tufani researchers and those Italian archaeologists…their English was abysmal. We should see if we can find Tsering again." She wadded up the energy bar wrapper and looked at my shoes critically. "Will you be hiking in those?"

"Yeah." It was time to impale them with my rapier-sharp intellect. "It's cool that you're doing science. I'm a scientist too, a meteorologist. I hope to study the effects of the Qolo range on high-level global currents. The collected data could improve understanding of atmospheric circulation, particularly regarding the exchange of air masses between the troposphere and stratosphere and the thermal gradient. Meteorological services would then use my information to improve weather forecasting for mountaineering expeditions—for people like yourselves. I'm also studying noctilucent clouds." I slapped my knee happily and went all Tennessee. "But right now were jes' tourists."

Neither was impressed.

She said to him, "Remember when we ran out of food and Tsering got those farmers to give us a ride if we helped load their grain. We could work our way back with the help of the villagers."

He patted her leg sympathetically. "We have to have enough in the account to make it home."

Reece edged back into the conversation. "Um, the seven shadows thing? Sorry, but it sounds so mysterious. I like tales and myths. Anything along that line is just fascinating."

The guy said correctively, "I don't know that you'd call it myth. The Tufanis spoke of a foreign traveler passing through and that he cast seven shadows."

"What's that mean?" I asked.

"I've no idea," said the trekker.

CHAPTER 12

Sheol beneath is stirred up to meet you when you come;
it rouses the shades to greet you, all who were leaders of the earth.
—ISAIAH 14:9

Day Four. 9:00 a.m. Clear and cool. Skies opening to allow our departure.

Nice smooth flight. Then, on the monitors at our seats, a camera mounted on the plane's belly showed us the approaching landing strip. A few prayers and we descended safely to YangDi, a small, well-laid-out city surrounded by enormous mountains. The airport was compact and plain. Edifice guards, crisply uniformed and with Botoxed expressions of authority, herded us through customs. We acted all natural and honest and happy-clappy to be there.

A white sport vehicle waited for us in the parking lot. Our tour guide introduced herself as Tashi. She was a tiny woman most likely in her thirties, with very small eyes, a short ponytail, and a shy smile. She wore jeans, T-shirt, and a jacket. Mei spoke to her in Mikan and greeted the driver. We'd been taught how to say ten words in Mikan: *hello, good-bye, please, thank you, yes, no, help, cost, sleep, eat,* and how to say *Jesus* in Tufani: *Yeshu.* But we weren't to use his name openly. Mei said to use Y. We could say, "I told him about Y" or "She knows Y," and it sounds like *why.* We used half our Mikan words in the first few minutes.

Tashi wrapped silky gold scarves around our necks in greeting, like they do in Hawaii with flowers.

The driver helped with our luggage but said very little, nothing in English. We never did know his name. Tashi did the talking with a thick but understandable accent and great vocabulary.

A drive across a wide, clear river took us into YangDi. I was taking in the busy downtown and fresh new buildings when I caught Mei's surprised look.

"What?" I asked.

"This is not what I expected," she said quietly. "I didn't think it would be so modern."

She leaned forward to Tashi in the front seat. "The downtown is very nice!"

Our guide nodded agreeably.

There were clothes stores and ice cream shops, nicer and cleaner than in Jinsha. In some ways it wasn't all that different from Tulsa. But this was the new section of town. As we drove on to the old town, YangDi took on a distinctly Tufani look: chunky hewn-stone buildings with black trim. The occasional horse cart and rickshaw. And in store windows, giant posters of what I'd call monsters, ghouls, ogres, demons. Here they called them gods.

Our driver pulled into a small paved courtyard flanked on three sides by the hotel. The central facade was fresh and classy with the sign "Ascent Hotel," but the extensions on either side were shabby. First impression, great. Second impression, not so much.

Big white couches, long drapes, and shiny floors decked the lobby. A table—like an altar—sat at the entry with a ceramic sheep or goat head smiling at you, and dragon carvings all around it. We dumped our gear while Mei checked us in at the front desk.

Reece said, "This is very, very nice! Thank you, Mei!"

Mei handed us keys. "Tashi said we can walk to the market-place, but not to leave the city. She offered to guide us, and I accepted. We will listen and look."

"Good call," Marcus said. "Info gathering starts now, *ne.*"

She said bluntly, "It began weeks ago." Then to all of us, "We will stay here two days to acclimate to the altitude."

Marcus didn't have much to say for the next hour.

In a corner near the elevator stood a golden idol, arrayed in jewels and positioned to greet every traveler. Canned music emanated from it—a chant playing over and over. We jammed onto the elevator. I pushed the button to the fourth floor, glad to get out of range of the tinny, robotic one-line song. When the doors closed I turned to Mei. "You seemed surprised by the town."

She glanced up at the corners of the elevator. Sure enough a camera had its one big glassy eye trained on us. Tipping her head down, she spoke quietly. "We hear about the oppressed culture because of The Restructuring fifty years ago. I expected run-down buildings and poverty. But there are cars and buses and shops and many people working and looking very well. Even the old town, it's very busy."

I said, "Let's unpack and take a walk, check things out. Keep conversation light."

Tashi had cautioned us to take it slow. YangDi's two-mile high elevation meant you get about 50 percent of the oxygen your lungs are accustomed to.

Between the long flight, thin air, and everyone on alert for signs of a tall stranger, it was slow going. Whitewashed stone buildings lined YangDi's old market streets. Thick trim on barred windows and closed wooden doors added to the heaviness of the place. Maybe it was just the strain to breathe.

Every other souvenir shop was selling those posters of grue-some-looking beings: blood red and blue creatures with bulging eyes and long, claw-like fingernails and toenails. Some were dressed in shawls of human corpses, some had flames behind their heads. Others were squashing people under their feet. I'd done a pile of research beforehand and had warned Reece about it while we were driving across the Great Plains, but there's no preparing yourself when you've grown up in the Midwest. Of course, things were changing back home too—and not in a good way. I leaned over to Reece. "Brace for culture shock."

Casual strolling took effort. We stopped often at little shops to catch our breath and peruse the souvenirs: boxed cookies and snacks, leather goods and umbrellas. Tashi suggested we buy hats for protection against the sun. The air was crisp, but we were warm. The farther we walked, the smaller the stores. Then the main shopping district opened up to a bazaar-type atmosphere with booths set up around a wide courtyard. There were tons of souvenirs, and pretty cheap too. I'd get a few nice things for Lydia. Maybe one of those lacy umbrellas.

Tashi pointed to an elaborate building at the end of the promenade. "There is the temple. We will go on another day."

The style of the temple was similar to the rest of Tufani's Old Town district: boxy, with whitewashed stone, broad and sort of grand. Two open furnace-looking things stood on either side of the entrance, smoke rising from them, people throwing something into the fires. Also in front were two big poles, like totem poles.

Tashi commented here and there, warning us about all the things Karinna had mentioned: don't take pictures of the military, walk slow, buy bottled water. She seemed to appreciate it when we admired something, and at first the girls were oohing and aahing over everything. I couldn't take my eyes from the gruesome art posters. And in a minute neither could Reece. She was walking slower and taking deeper breaths.

"It's the altitude, Reece," I said comfortingly.

"Those…what are they…gods?" she whispered.

"What you're feeling, it's just the altitude." I moved behind her and gave her a quick shoulder massage. "We're not looking for posters."

Mei glanced at Reece. "The mountains are beautiful, aren't they? We'll be going higher and higher in a few days."

Reece took our cues and admired the mountains and the people's handsome faces, saying hello and smiling.

I had worried about Reece as we finished up the first day, but it was Mei who fainted.

We were heading up to a rooftop eatery that overlooked the market street and temple. I took the lead to the top of the steps and happened to look back just as Mei toppled backwards, eyes rolling back in her head. I grabbed her arm and yelled at Marcus, a few steps down. A young waiter ran over to help us get her to a bench. He brought bottled water.

"I'm okay," she said weakly to an attentive Marcus. "I climbed too fast, that's all."

We ordered meals. Mei assured us she was all right.

Tashi wasn't the least bit shaken. "She be okay. It happen a lot with tourists."

"Take it easy for a while, Mei," I said. "We've all been living near sea level."

Edifice troops had stationed themselves across the street on a rooftop with an outpost tent, a satellite dish, and machine guns. Their heads moved side to side like automatons. They were here in great numbers because—we were told by the travel brochures— Tufan was a prototype of things to come, The Edifice serving as peacekeepers, guardians of threatened cultures around the world. Once lasting peace and native culture was reestablished—travel writers assured their readers—the troops would withdraw. Sure, but point your camera at them now and you could lose your camera along with the hand that held it.

After the meal, which was really good and a lot like an open-air picnic (except for the rooftop forces, armed and ready to kill us), we headed back to the hotel. We kept eagle eyes out for tall foreigners. Whenever one of us would spot one in the crowd, we'd freeze like pointer dogs. Not very subtle. We'd have to work on that. We thanked Tashi for the tour and headed up to our rooms. Marcus and I unpacked and met again with the girls in their room.

"How's everyone feeling?" I asked.

Reece had propped herself up on her bed with pillows. "I'll be fine. Mei, how are you?"

"I'm better. It was my fault, climbing steps too fast. I'm so happy to be here. I wanted to come to Tufan last year, but it was closed because of riots."

Reece looked out the window and muttered with a weak smile, "I won't be jogging up that mountain, that's for sure."

"It wouldn't be allowed in the States!" Marcus blurted. "Religion crammed down your throat like this. Try to do the same in our country, you'd be sued."

"What are you talking about?" I asked.

"You don't walk down the streets of every town and see Mary and Joseph Hotel and River Jordan Outfitters and...and Baptism Bakery and Twelve Disciples Deli. You see what I mean? But here it's Holy Mountain Motel and Pilgrimage Pizza. Gods and amulets and posters in every shop. If this is the new model for the rest of the planet..."

I shrugged. "Centuries ago, according to their legends, a great spiritual master corralled all the local demons and converted them to—(I wasn't sure if I should say the name of the religion out loud, or even the word *demons*, but too late for that)—well, it's the native belief and they're sticking to it."

Without saying the word *Edifice,* Mei added, "They control the belief. They suppress it with violence and promote it for profit at the same time. 'It's quaint,' they will say. 'Come see people living the old ways,' like a pioneer town in the American West or an Ainu village in my country. We saw the new, secular city as we came into town, then the traditional part. They would insist that one can choose secular or sacred. But it is not so."

Reece said, "We're not allowed to teach people about Y here. So it's not free."

"Free but closed. A protected culture," Marcus corrected.

"Contradiction of terms," I said, "free but closed."

Marcus sat up, hands on knees and said to Mei, "Back up. Are you telling me that they *promote* the religion here? I heard stateside that they crushed it."

She answered, "They tried to crush it, but refugees spread outside the country and others learned about the oppression. They stopped crushing and started to promote pilgrimage to sacred places. They have concentrated on infrastructure, and really, I think they did an excellent job. The people have roads and airports. We will ride their overnight train. People have schools for all children, and hospitals. Before, this region was primitive and dangerous. You should read the mish stories about the culture before."

"So now it's progressive and dangerous," Marcus grumbled.

"For money." I was back at the other subject. "They promote religion for money."

Mei said, "Millions and millions. Does anyone want to walk to the palace? We'll go inside tomorrow, but I want to show you what I saw as we drove by."

The sun had set, but the desk clerk assured us that a walk to the palace was safe. Units of soldiers patrolled, marching in small formations, guns on their shoulders.

The palace was like no other, an architectural mountain rising out of the earth. Looking down over the city, it conveyed the root name of the reigning oracle king: "He who looks down." You couldn't help but feel small in its massive shadow. From a gold-trimmed, dark red stone section at the top, the Palace of YangDi angled out in whitewashed splendor three or four city blocks wide. It had size and grandeur, an ancient statement of indestructibility. From the side, though, it was quite narrow. The front view gave the impression of much greater size, not unlike a stage set, where the illusion is three-dimensional but the reality is a painted flat, propped up with two-by-fours.

Dozens of worshippers prostrated themselves on the sidewalk, bowing toward the palace. We took pictures of ourselves in front of a nine-foot stone guardian lion, noticing afterwards that his chin was slimy and he appeared to be drooling. Even Mei couldn't explain it.

In the open air and with the noise of night life around us, Mei shared her distress in full voice. "Their god-king has not lived here for years, but they chant and prostrate. Some go around the whole palace bowing and bowing. Some go around holy mountains or holy lakes to earn blessings. Some die along the way." She turned once more to the palace. "It sees every corner of the city. Nothing is hidden. But across the street, this is what I want to show you."

We crossed four lanes of traffic to a courtyard with great fountains and nice landscaping where people could stroll and have picnics and admire the palace. At the edge stood a giant screen. Tourist ads ran in a loop, welcoming people to Tufan, showing maps of the tours and train routes. A picture of the inside of one of the temples came up: a giant golden god in the background looking down on its worshippers, then another shot, a closeup of the candles and altars. And around the burning candles lay hundreds in bills of Western currency.

We watched the ads loop again. Mei said, "Their religion is not done in secret here, like ours must be."

Marcus said it like a headline: "New gov crushes old religion but keeps it afloat for their own benefit?"

Mei said, "They are opposites, but together they have total control of the people."

Reece huffed. "And the money we're spending here—"

Mei nodded. "—supports both. How many tourists from our countries have come to admire old gods and new ones, gods that have recently appeared, and have not understood this? How many people take horrible images home, into their houses where children sleep at night?"

Marcus quoted Scripture: "'What pagans sacrifice they offer to demons and not to God. I do not want you to be participants with demons.'"

"Is that what we're doing?" Reece asked, horrified. "Participating?"

Mei said, "These people are between, as you say, the rock and the hard place. Between the dark religion and the no-religion. Two powers against each other, but together in persecution." She turned back toward the hotel, then whirled and faced us fiercely. "Who can resist? Who can escape? He was trying to do something about this! He was trying to let the light in. I am happy we came. It's good to see this. Thank you, Rob!"

We escorted the girls back to their room. Exhausted and pale, Reece sat down on the edge of her bed and burst into tears.

"What's wrong?" I asked, as if it wasn't obvious.

She weakly threw pillows against the headboard, climbed into bed, and curled herself into a ball. "For a second it was as if…as if I could see these people like Y sees them." She pointed heavenward, sobbing quietly. Marcus sat in a chair and propped his feet on her bed. He looked as helpless as I felt, hoping Mei would do the hugging-comfort thing for her best friend.

Reece sank deeper into the pillows. "Y sees how trapped they are. This place is full of his grief."

Mei sat next to Reece. "This is hard. It's not like this in my country."

Reece took her hand. "I know."

Marcus said, "I think it is, Mei, just in a different way."

Mei started to answer, then stopped and thought. "Maybe… in some way. What do you mean?"

"You've got freedom to choose, but the consequences can be harsh."

She reluctantly nodded. "I would not be arrested or killed for making my choice, but I am excluded at social events and business opportunities. My father pressures me to marry someone I don't like."

Reece sat up and gasped. "Mei, you never told me! How awful!"

I muttered something similar. Marcus got up and stared out the window at the mountains, their snowy tops lit by a full moon.

"My mother is on my side." Mei's faint smile showed strength. "In Japan the women handle the family finances. My mother has gold in a secret account. If my father tries to force me, she will give me money and he will not know. She told him I would run away to the States if he forced me." She held her head high. "My mother is stronger now. Maybe too pushy. I think she got it from living in America."

Marcus turned from the window and said suavely, "We *gaijins* like our women tough."

Though I wasn't a fan of his Mr. Irresistible act, Marcus did manage to melt our friend with one line. She went sort of fluttery. I gave him a secret thumbs-up.

Reece said to her, "Your father will stop pressuring you, I hope!"

"I think he will stop. It is changing in my country, but we decide as a group, because ours is a small, ancient country, and we live best in harmony as groups. To lose the respect of the group feels the same as dying. Your country is opposite. You decide things as individuals, because yours is a young country of wide spaces."

· · · · ·

Day Five. We met the girls for a complimentary breakfast in a tiny upstairs hotel cafeteria. It had a few tables and a few booths, with a mounted yak head and a couple of framed photos of mountains as decoration. There were windows along one wall with a great view of real mountains, jagged and dusted with snow at the peaks. The breakfast choices were eggs and meat, fruit and pancakes, juice, milk, tea, and coffee. Mei hadn't slept and couldn't eat breakfast. She said, "This is altitude sickness. I should go to a doctor. I'll tell the front desk to call Tashi."

Tashi escorted us to a storefront clinic. There was one nurse and one doctor, a big old guy sitting behind a desk and wearing a dirty white smock. He asked her a few questions in Mikan. I could tell the difference in the languages already, Mikan being kind of sing-songy, Tufani being more guttural. The doctor picked a thermometer off his desk and rubbed his fingers over the end. I thought, *Mei, don't put that in your mouth!* He stuck it in her armpit. The nurse brought out two bottles of pills, Mei paid cash, and we were on our way. She looked warily at the bottles, but took one of the pills right away. Tashi led us to a store for canisters of oxygen.

Marcus and I went on the palace tour with Tashi while the girls went back to bed. It was an amazing building, dark and eerie in places, and more "gods" than you could shake a stick at.

We were only allowed to see twenty of the hundreds of rooms. The windowless hallways that I would have liked to snoop out were off limits.

We brought in food to the girls' room and took the rest of the day easy. Confident that we'd be heading out tomorrow, Mei coached us from her bed, about talking code to avoid suspicion and about contingency plans should we get separated. My brain got tired. I went back to the room to turn in early. Marcus stayed with them for a while. I heard him come in later and take a shower. But before I drifted off for the night, I had to remind myself why we were here. So strong was the hope of finding a morsel of truth about the ION Task—and so close—that every now and then my missing cousin slipped from my mind.

CHAPTER 13

If there be dragons beyond this,
Daggers upon us,
I'll keep my eyes upon us,
You'll keep me honest.
—Mae Klingler, "Dragons"

Day Six of the search for Elijah. 7:30 a.m. Data from Qolo at 4 p.m. previous day: air temp -10 °C/-4 °F (the heat of the day), relative humidity 41%, wind speed 18 ms/40 mph. Brutal. But that was the summit, two miles higher than where we'd be, the Qolo Plateau, called the biggest scar on the planet.

Before departing, we met in the little cafeteria. Reece apparently didn't sleep. I heard her tell Mei in the breakfast line how she missed her little girl. She sat down between Mei and me with a plate of toast and a few bites of egg. She glanced at her wedding band and sighed, then spread jam on her toast.

Marcus sat down across from her with his back to the window. "You doing okay?"

"Just jet lag and altitude." She stared out the window. "I miss Olivet."

Marcus sympathized, "Sure you do. And Greg too. I saw you look at your wedding ring." He was playing it. We'd talked the night before about Greg not knowing where his wife had taken off to, but I'd kept it brief and vague.

She nibbled while the rest of us ate and talked, then sat her fork down and said, "I think I made a mistake in coming."

We all stopped eating.

"I won't be any help. I mean, what can I do?" She defended herself from our stricken expressions. "I'm trying to be honest, that's all. I'm sorry, but last night…I couldn't sleep. I sat there in the dark, and I've never wanted to *not* be somewhere so badly in my life." She leaned forward and whispered, "It's not you. It's the tours. They're pilgrimages to *you know*, and we're paying for it! I don't feel right about that. I don't want to leave you guys"—her breathing was shallow—"but…what was I thinking? To leave Olivet for weeks? I don't know how Greg is doing and—"

Marcus reached across the table and took her hand. "Listen, Reece. I get it. You need to call him, see what's cooking on the home front. Do it."

Mei's face had set like stone. My heart sank.

Marcus didn't let go of Reece's hand. "What brought you here in the first place?"

"I…wanted to help. If you all found him, I wanted to be there, with everyone. I didn't want him to think I didn't care."

Marcus removed his hand, leaned back, and said bluntly, "Well, maybe you should leave then."

I couldn't believe it. How was her answer wrong? What was this, reverse psychology? I started to object.

He put up a hand and drilled me with those acid green eyes. "I got this."

Mei excused herself to get a spoon. I followed. Once we were out of range, Marcus leaned in to Reece, pulled her by the arms until the two were nose-to-nose, and whispered furiously at her. I stayed in the food line getting a refill and taking my time, wondering if I should go punch him in the face and get myself murdered. Mei lingered at the tea station. We waited to see when the coast was clear. Reece left the breakfast room, left her plate and everything.

I was afraid to ask but did anyway, taking a cautious seat, making a fist under the table as if I could face off with Skidmore if he got nasty. "What's going on?"

"Who knows?" he growled.

Was he trying to talk her into leaving or staying? For someone who had to be convinced himself into coming, Marcus's short fuse had certainly been lit by Reece backing out.

In a few minutes she came back and sat down. She'd been crying. She took a bite and apologized with a couple of sniffles. "I'm sorry. I'm sorry." That was it.

Marcus said, "Okay gang, we stock up on O2 and bottled water. And extra food." He smiled broadly. "Did you girls see the empty bottles lined up on our window sill? Rob and I've slugged a dozen bottles. We'll buy our meals on the way, but on the train ride back we should have extra food, isn't that right, Mei? Train food's expensive, and if there's a road washout or landslide, we could be stranded for days." He wadded his napkin and tossed it playfully on his plate. "I saw a coat at a shop down the street a few blocks. I'm gonna need it. Who wants to go with me? A few minutes."

"I'll go," I said.

Reece brightened. "I will too. Mei, you want to come with us?"

With the same reserve she'd had all morning, Mei said, "Yes."

Marcus turned to me. "D'you bring long underwear?"

"I'm not your size."

"I didn't mean—" He shook his head. "Wingate…"

Bad mood shoved under the rug. Reece finished off her breakfast like nothing had happened. She'd done a complete 180, leaving the Mag Three in her wake, bobbing around in a sea of uncertainty, and I guess you could say, feeling as empty as those

water bottles lined up in our hotel room. I hadn't expected anyone—least of all Reece—to bail. Not tough-as-nails little Reece.

. . . . . .

In the hotel's tiny paved courtyard, Tashi and the driver loaded
us up for the trip to Qolo. Reece hadn't come down, which
worried me. Mei was so brisk and businesslike, I couldn't bring
myself to ask. Marcus, tight-lipped about what he'd told Reece
at breakfast, shrugged and said, "I'm done." We were officially
an un-group.

Then Reece appeared all decked out in jeans, long-sleeved
shirt, and wool vest, with a white bandana for a headband. Tashi
sat in the front. I gave the girls the window seats and sat in the
middle, Marcus in the back with the luggage and a pillow.

"This will do us all good, trippin' through the countryside," I
said. "Like Japan. Like Ireland."

That brought smiles. I wanted to hug everyone but thought
it might be weird in Tufani culture. And we couldn't start off
with open prayer. So I leaned up to Tashi. "We're ready."

I was no longer the top camera-snapper of the Mag Five, like
in high school. This time we were all leaning over each other
to get good window shots. We switched places often so that
everyone could have time on the "best side," which changed
every other mile. I'm rusty on my geology, but the landforms
were spectacular: bare, brown mountains and wide river plains,
strangely angled outcroppings like old lava floes. We were com-
menting on it when Tashi turned to us from the front seat. "This
land was once all under water."

We knew about the global flood, of course, but was pretty
sure she didn't. And I didn't want to get into a big debate on
continental drift or religion.

Tufani beliefs were a mix of three religions with lots of demons and gods, who were supposedly nothing more than an

illusory part of a person's psyche, but greatly feared nonetheless. Human origins—according to their own scholars—went back to a monkey mating with a crazed ogress. Actual historical data: slim pickins.

Marcus raised an eyebrow at the flood comment. "Aren't we at 13,000 feet?"

Tashi gave a commentary about the area. She was helpful and friendly, dedicated to her profession. While we were asking random questions, though, the darker side of Tufani culture showed up in her spiel. White ladders had been painted on rocks along the highway. Reece asked what they were for.

Tashi said, "We have four kinds of buries." (She meant burials.) "When child dies we paint a ladder so they get to Heaven."

I refrained from a tacky comeback like, "You might need an extension ladder."

"Tomb buries are only for monks," she continued. "Someone dies in a car wreck, they get water bury. Everyone else gets a sky bury." She pointed to a rocky knob several hundred yards off the highway, maybe 100 feet high, with prayer flags draped over the whole knob. "For sky buries."

"I've read about them," I said brightly and tried to communicate with a subtle head shake to the others, *You don't want to know, not this close to breakfast.*

In the next few hours, Tashi also introduced us to the unique horrors of death by altitude sickness and wild mastiff attack. One man, Tashi told us, recently died from edema while on pilgrimage. Soberly she added, "A terrible way to die."

I explained quickly to the others, to end the story, "Swell up and explode."

Reece asked where the man was from, was relieved when Tashi answered, "Spain." About mastiff attacks, she said, "Never travel alone or without a guide. Wild mastiffs eat from sky buries what birds don't eat. They have taste for human, and they are very strong from eating meat." When she said "strong" her little fists clenched, her arms tensed.

Maybe some folks would find this culturally fascinating, but in light of our real reason for being in Tufan, all of us—even Marcus—slunk in our seats and went back to looking out the windows. Reece switched to the center seat. Like a lot of Japanese people, Mei wasn't the touchy-feely type, but she put her arm around her best friend, pressed her face into Reece's hair, and whispered. Tashi chatted with the driver. He turned on music, a mix of local pop, folk, and instrumental.

Marcus said, "Let me take a stab at travel writing, like old times." We welcomed the idea. He cleared his throat. "Okay… Accommodations in YangDi's popular Ascent Hotel will be amenable to your needs. A cozy breakfast room on the second floor will satisfy the appetite of hearty trekker or casual shopper. Tourists of every stripe should carry ample bottled water, and it is advisable to carry along an O2 canister as well. Under normal conditions, one canister should last a week. Hikers and bikers, take note: While basic necessaries are available along the way, towns are many miles apart. It's advisable to carry extra essentials, if possible. Shops are notorious for unloading expired food and other time-sensitive goods on the unwary. The package tours, besides being the only prescribed way to see the landscape, afford ample opportunity to capture the jaw-dropping panoramas that await." He sat back, pleased with himself.

Mei and Reece clapped like little girls. I called his use of the word *ample* twice in one paragraph "weak journalism." Just what we needed, humor and nostalgia.

Everyone drifted off into their own little worlds, the driver's music getting mellower the higher we went. I switched places with Marcus, shoved my jacket under my head, faced the window, and watched the mountains grow and change color, thinking back to when we were the Mag Five, not Four. I replayed Marcus's travel spiel in my head because it was the best thing to think about. Reece turned around and looked at me. I winked at her. She mouthed the words "Thank you." Her trusting, grateful eyes caused a twang of guilt about the other reason I'd come to Tufan. They were my companions for our search for Elijah—and a cover for my personal mission.

We stopped at a little concrete block eatery in a village as rustic and dusty as the Old West: horse carts and guys in cowboy-type hats against a backdrop of rugged mountains. Tashi and the driver didn't sit with us while we ate. Most travelers want their privacy, I guess.

After Mei talked with the waiter, she informed us that in Tufan one doesn't specifically order from the menu. You use it to see what's available and then order what you want and how you want it cooked. "Very different from Japan. You order from the menu. No changes or you will scare the waitress. When I first saw this done in Ohio, when people substitute one thing and complain about another thing, I was nervous for the waitress!"

The meals came. I leaned over and sniffed mine. "Mmm, big bowls of steaming whatzit." It was hot and delicious.

The owner talked to Tashi a long time. I got it that she and the driver probably stop at the same restaurants on their tours and get kickbacks.

"I wonder if he ate here," Reece thought out loud.

Marcus said, "Good point. People, we gotta connect the dots we have."

"What do you mean?" I asked.

"I mean everyone should tell everything they know, all the dots, so we can connect them."

"Like what?"

"Like, is this the road he would have come in on? Is this the only way in?"

I started to answer, but Mei jumped in. "Two highways. This is the main one. With a cart and horse there are other ways, but his team would come this way. Tomorrow, after the next town, the other highway joins to this. Then only one road in."

Reece said to Marcus, "I think we've shared everything we know. I told you guys about Steven."

Marcus asked, "Did he spill any information?"

"I didn't have time to ask."

I said, "Let's do this on a need-to-know basis. Unless we're in open air, we talk about mountains and weather, culture, stuff like that."

Marcus speculated, "If we find Elijah, he might not be the one we knew."

Mei shushed him. "We call him E, remember?"

"My mistake," he said. "Dad said that people who go in sometimes don't come out the same. The black magic works. Remember how I got interested in voodoo after being on Farr Island? The boo hag story, Wingate. I wanted to know about my roots in West Africa. With all the talk about preserving culture, I wondered which one was the most, you know, occult. Dad didn't know, though he had some ideas. I looked into it and Tufan kept coming up, over and over. Whenever of our kind of work gets started here, it's squelched, buildings destroyed, people go missing. It's always been that way."

"Our struggle is not against flesh and blood," Mei reminded us.

"We have to be ready. If he's alive and weird, or if we find him, or if we don't."

I said, "Mei has prepared us for that."

Marcus's half-lidded green eyes settled on me. "Nothing could prepare us for that. Have we ruled out suicide? He had a lot to be despondent about: he didn't trust the agency, was alone, a failed relationship, a failed mission, his fixation on the occult, no way out..."

Why he was bringing up this stuff now?

Reece dug in her purse for her billfold. Mei studied him disapprovingly.

"Sky buries," Marcus said as a change of subject. "What's with it?"

"Not at mealtime," I said.

"We're adults," he countered.

I answered quickly, "Okay, bodies of the commoners are left to birds and wild animals. Vultures can embody gods and goddesses, so you earn merit in the spirit world by opting to have them pick your bones clean. Some bones are taken by monks to be used for their rituals."

Reece shuddered like she couldn't bear one more thing.

But since Marcus's tough-guy method had worked on her before, I didn't go soft. "What about dead tourists, Mei, like that guy who died of altitude sickness?"

Mei said, "I think his body would be shipped back to his country."

No one asked more questions: what if a person was found on the side of a mountain frozen to death? Any cosmic merit in feeding a stranger to vultures? Probably. Bandits might sell his passport on the black market. I wanted out of this topic, but my mind kept cranking out grim possibilities.

Then our Mag Five clan verse from years ago came to mind: *A cord of five strands is not quickly broken.*

Frayed cords, holding for now. I stood. "Show on the road, travelers. Marcus, how about a commentary on savoring Asian cuisine in an Old West town at 13,000 feet?"

CHAPTER 14

Thy system, dark as witcheries of the night,
was formed to harden hearts, and shock the sight.
—William Cowper

Day Seven. We had a nice breakfast in the nearly empty banquet room of a good-sized hotel. There were two businessmen at the next table; that was it. They could be spies or who knows what, so we talked useless trivialities. It was starting to dawn on me, the difficulty of doing anything other than a planned itinerary, especially venturing out on a missing persons search. How would we pursue clues, should we find any? We were a week into it, getting higher in the Qolo Range but being kept on a short leash, so…getting nowhere really. And every few miles, Edifice checkpoints. If we found him, how would we get him out? We couldn't run a hundred yards at these heights without passing out.

Back on the road, Marcus asked Tashi more culture questions to ease his way into real information gathering. How far do hikers go on a trek? Can they stay in the mountains for days or weeks? How does one survive out there? She kind of smiled and said nicely that Tufani families have lived in the mountains for centuries. In other words, we're wimps.

Do you need a permit, I asked, and must you have a guide, and are the villages scattered pretty evenly so you could hike from one to the next…because we'd like to be trekkers someday.

Reece brought up the lone trekker and wondered, now that she saw how big and lonely the area was, how someone could do that. Supposedly this trekker cast seven shadows.

Tashi's interest was piqued. "Where is this man?"

We didn't know. The hikers hadn't said. Our guide glanced at the driver, as if wondering whether she should say more on the subject. I'd begun to suspect that he had Edifice connections, that every tour was monitored. Reverently Tashi described that such a person would have great beauty and purity, one who is seven times reborn. She turned around excitedly to us. "His radiance, it cast seven shadows. With clear eyes and gentle speech he sacrifice himself and bring great power to who receive his remains."

I hadn't told the others that I'd already checked it out at a Kim's Kozy com station, holed away behind the downstairs bar while the others took naps. I said that was all very interesting, then redirected the conversation.

We made a pit stop at an outhouse: four stone walls and no roof.

I went first, came back to the parking lot, and announced, "Okay, brace yourselves. It's a hole in the floor that drops an individual's ka-ka down the mountainside, say, 100 feet. And the place is full of mulch. A big pile of mulch all over the floor! Why would that be?"

Mei explained that it all made perfect sense when you have no toilet paper, no flush, and no janitor.

The wind picked up. While Reece took her turn, I gathered the rest in. "Guys, I have to explain something. Tashi didn't give us the whole scoop on the seven shadows. I did some research at Kim's."

Marcus gave me a dry look. "And you're telling us this on a need-to-know basis." As if I'd kept an important secret.

"Don't give me any lip," I shot back. "Culture trivia. But it could be significant. The so-called self-sacrifice would likely be a staged suicide and 'receiving' means consuming. The victim's blood and bones would be put into pill form, distributed, and consumed."

Mei dug into her bag, pulled out her altitude sickness pills, and tried to read the fine print. "Some of this is in Tufani." She emptied the bottle over the hill with a look of disgust.

"Hey, you might need those," I said too late.

Her meds were probably okay, but I felt bad that I hadn't mentioned it before. The Japanese tend to be very, very clean, particularly about what they eat.

Before Reece came back, I told Marcus and Mei, "Reece isn't handling stuff all that well. The last thing she needs to hear is about a nice-looking guy who stuck out in the crowd and cast long shadows and got sacrificed."

We had a hearty lunch at an old-style restaurant: dark wood construction with heavy tables, padded benches, and big windows from which to see the mountains. It was a good-sized town. Mei ordered for us again, while we watched the door and down the street for tall passersby. When the waitress left, Mei said reassuringly about our meal, "Everything will be boiled or steamed." She ordered tea, which came quickly. She drank lots and made Reece do the same.

We drove a few more hours and stopped at Pajuu Temple. A kind of Great Wall of China (teeny tiny compared to the real thing, but sort of like it) encircled the monastery in a wide sweep, up one hill and down another, a good half a mile around, I'd guess. With gates closed, it would be near impossible to get in or out. We parked, left our jackets in the car and weaved through the crowded lot. To be over two miles above sea level, the day was surprisingly warm.

Tashi hurried on ahead and came back soon and with more spirit than I'd seen so far. "You get to see the mask dance! You must be good people." She'd said the same thing the day before when we stopped to see a sacred lake. The sky was unusually clear that day too, with widely scattered cumulus clouds giving a rare view of a holy mountain. "You must be good people," she'd said then. "You get to see the holy mountain."

The crowd at Pajuu funneled through a sort of gauntlet of prayer wheels, dozens of them about two feet tall and mounted in rows along the way, some still spinning from pilgrims gone ahead. Tashi, already a ways ahead with Marcus, turned as if to encourage us to hurry on.

Mei said, "It is the belief that one million spins of the prayer wheel will deliver beings from Hell. It has great karma."

"Karma," Reece said thoughtfully. "Greg talked about karma in one of his teachings."

Mei's expression hardened. "My old belief was in karma. Now I see that karma is the opposite of Y's grace."

Reece stopped, the karma wheels slowing beside her. "What do you mean?"

"Karma says that you get what you deserve. That sounds right. If you are bad, bad things will happen to you, and they *should* happen to you, *ne?* But what about a baby who is hurt or dies? Did he deserve it? Karma says yes, he was bad in a past life. Ah, Tashi is waiting. We must keep going. But with karma you must pay and pay and pay. You can never know if you have paid enough. If you have been a good person, karma is always saying, 'Maybe not enough!' I did not understand the fear in my life until I learned about grace." She shook her head, her blue-black hair shimmering in the sun. "It is so wonderful how grace says, 'You can never do enough, but it is okay. Y paid for the whole world!' This is still difficult for me to accept. Grace to me is the most beautiful thing."

We reached the outer fringes of the crowd where people were sitting around on pavement greasy with scraps of food, spilled drinks, and spit. Tashi nodded excitedly to the center of the circle. "It will begin soon."

Only Marcus was tall enough to see over the crowd. Us three shorties were peeking between heads and shoulders. In the center of the circle stood a dozen monks in ornate robes of dark blue and red, wearing bestial masks: bulgy-eyed animals with fanged, gaping mouths or giant bird heads with long, open beaks through which the monks could see. On the other side of the court, overhanging one wing of the temple was a kind of awning, with a woven image of a round-faced, monstrous looking thing, as if he were overseeing the event.

Cymbals clanged and deep trumpets bleated. The people all stood, forming a wall around the ritual area, pushing us to the periphery. We three wouldn't be able to see. I handed Marcus my camera. "You shoot. Use video. We'll see it later."

Reece said, "Travelogue it for us, okay?"

He began haltingly. "Okay. Um, the traditional dancers form a circle now and move slowly, swaying in a...not in a meditative fashion or like they're celebrating. In a...I don't know, a slow prancing way. In the middle of the circle is what appears to be the head monk, and he's...there's this thing that looks like a dummy of a small person. Like a rag doll made of black cloth. And it's lying on a mat and..." Marcus had lost his travel guy voice. "The dummy...it looks like they're tying it up. It's lying on a mat...a painted mat, and there's an image on the mat...I can't tell. And the guy's putting something on the belly of the dummy. It looks like—" His mouth fell open. "Oh, creeps. Okay, the dancers are closing in around it. I can't really see."

"Keep the camera up," I said.

"Keep talking," Reece said.

Marcus went stiff, turned to me, and whispered, "It looks like guts."

"What?"

The whole crowed aahed as if something great was happening. Some chuckled. A few clapped.

"The dancers are dancing in a circle," Marcus said, "and the guy in the middle is throwing the—" Words caught in his throat. He looked at me again, his dark face drained of color, his voice shaky. "It's guts. The guy in the middle is taking the stuff from the belly of the dummy and hurling it at the monks. It looks like human intestines. One masked dancer just caught a hunk of it on his fangs."

Marcus craned his neck. His voice dropped to a whisper. "The monk caught it on his fangs and started swinging the stuff around. That's when they laughed and clapped."

I glanced at Mei and Reece. They'd stopped trying to peek around heads, and just listened.

"Keep shooting," I whispered. We waited for more commentary.

"That's all they're doing," Marcus said. "That's all I see. Dancing and—" He lowered the camera. "I think it's over."

No sooner had he spoken than an Edifice guard appeared and started pushing the crowd near us. We backed up. "What's going on?" Reece asked. "Where's Tashi?"

Marcus looked around. "I don't see her."

All of a sudden I remembered Tashi saying we were "good people." *Does she think one of us can cast seven shadows? Was that a human sacrifice we just witnessed?*

All of us pilgrims were pressed backward to form an aisle so the monks in their creature costumes could exit the courtyard. Marcus raised the camera—subtly this time—and said softly, "The people are trying to touch the garments of the monks with a hand or a cap or a hanky…touching the hems of their robes. To get a blessing or give one. Can't tell."

The shadowed faces passed, monks sweating inside the mouths of their monster masks. The crowd dispersed. That was it. Tashi reappeared. I didn't know what to say. Mei thanked her and asked polite questions: how often is the dance performed, who makes the beautiful robes, that kind of thing.

In the middle of the courtyard, a man was rolling up the ritual mat.

"Get it," I whispered to Marcus, who raised the camera and took a shot or two.

The courtyard emptied out, except for a few children who'd come to the center and were squatting down, poking at a small, bloody-looking blob that had been left behind.

Reece stared in disgust.

I asked, "You're not gonna hurl, are you?"

She whispered, "Elijah…"

"No," I said with certainty. Not that the thought hadn't occurred to me, that something like that could have happened. Because whatever that blob on the ground was, whatever that pile of guts was—fake or real—the meaning of the ritual was clear: it was a reenactment of sacrificing a human being and feeding it to demons. Marcus walked beside me and tipped his camera so I could see that final image of the mat on which the dummy was placed. It was a garish, cartoony painting of a human with its arms, legs, and bowels slit open.

Marcus handed the camera to me. "A formidable religion, *ne*."

There are moments when a new evil breaks on your familiar horizon, beyond what seems real or reasonable. In those moments, that void tells you to accept as truth an awful lie, that God's arm reaches only so far, to a brink beyond which you are no longer retrievable. Curled fingernails of things wanting to get in and things wanting to get out tear at the fabric of the universe. God averts his holy eye and bids humanity do the same. But you want just one peek.

We walked back to the car and, for Tashi's sake, acted pleased. A young girl, maybe ten, came out of the crowd and approached us, smiling. She was dirty and very pretty, with a half-empty bottle of pop in her grimy hand. She smiled at Reece and said something. Mei translated, "She wants money."

Tashi had already told us not to give money to children. "Their parents are lazy," she had said. "If you want to give money, give to old people. They will be grateful."

We moved toward the car. Reece stayed. The little girl smiled sweetly at her and held out her hand. "She's so precious." Reece opened her purse. "I'll give her a coin from the States, a shiny souvenir. That's okay, isn't it?" Without waiting for an answer from Tashi, she fished out a quarter, gave it to the girl, and smiled.

The girl accepted it demurely, looked it over, tipping her head this way and that to examine it, and put it in her mouth.

Mei spoke sternly in Mikan, then said in English, "It's money!"

The girl looked at us coyly and swallowed the quarter.

Reece gasped.

Tashi chided the girl while Mei translated, "That was money!"

The girl shrugged, said something, then went on her way.

Mei turned to us. "She said, 'I know. It doesn't matter.'"

Tashi called angrily after the girl. Reece cried, "I'm so sorry, Tashi! I thought she would like a coin, a souvenir." Expressionless, Tashi said it was fine. I got in the car. Reece stood there in the sunshine, her hand to her mouth, staring back in the direction of the little girl as the crowd passed. I'd just buckled myself in when she whirled into the car and came nose to nose with me, whispering, "I saw him…I saw him!"

"Who?"

She mouthed "Elijah," then grabbed Marcus's arm and pulled him around toward the temple. "That way." She jumped up onto the runner of the van; Marcus jumped up beside her. I was stuck in the van, Marcus and Reece blocking my door. He dropped down, gave me a doubtful head shake, but said, "Let's go look." He turned to Tashi. "Reece thought she saw a friend. We're going to go look."

I unbuckled my seatbelt. Reece moved out of my way.

Horrified, Tashi yelled, "You cannot leave!"

"Once around the block," Marcus said with an easy smile. "We'll be right back. Promise. We can't go far. You're our ride outta here!"

He and I took off. (Mei told me later that Tashi said something urgent to the driver, who jumped out angrily and followed us.)

We sprinted in the direction Reece pointed, back through the gauntlet of prayer wheels and against the flow, trying not to draw attention. I was the only white boy except for a tall photographer who had stood at the edge of the crowd, taking shots over people's heads like Marcus had. We jumped up on a half wall around the courtyard. The driver was at our side saying something and motioning for us to come back. I smiled and held up a finger. "Yes. One minute. Yes, okay."

There was no Elijah.

Back at the car, Marcus said to Reece in an understanding way, "It was that photographer."

Reece's head tipped eerily sideways, not unlike the little girl who'd just swallowed the quarter. "No. I saw."

Marcus apologized to Tashi, saying that we'd met a few adventurers in Jinsha and thought we'd seen one we knew. He jumped in, slammed the car door, and said happily, "To Mt. Qolo!"

Reece whispered to Mei, "And *he* saw *me*."

CHAPTER 15

I said to them, "What is the high place to which you go?"
—Ezekiel 20:29

The great Pajuu Temple wall disappeared from view, and we headed across more brown mountains, with sunlight sifting through high cirrus clouds. The atmosphere inside the vehicle was quiet, tense, confused. Who was oxygen-deprived? Who was traumatized by the ritual of symbolic human sacrifice? Who was worried about the little girl? Who had Reece really locked eyes with?

I made a note in my journal: "Reece saw photographer at Pajuu." Elijah would have made himself known. If he'd seen Reece and had an ounce of sense, he would have.

Our silent driver tackled a dozen hairpin turns leading up to the first high pass of the actual Qolo Range. All those other mountains had been foothills? Kidding me. We stopped at a panoramic overlook of sharp-edged, snowy peaks. "Makes the Rockies look meager," I admitted reverently. There was no sound up there. None. And no wind at what my altimeter said was 16,890 feet. Commuter plane altitude. I scuffed the grit and gravel under my feet as if to reassure myself of solid ground. Tashi pointed out Mt. Qolo and a few of the other highest peaks, a day away but so massive they looked close. And between us and our destination, a zigzag ribbon of dirt road on smooth sepia "foothills".

We took pictures of the mountains and each other. We breathed.

Mei said, "This is the purest air in the world!"

I had my doubts. Smelled like cold bones to me.

Several yards away, Tashi and the driver waited by the car until we got our fill of mountain gazing. Reece said, "Let's pray. Face the mountains, eyes open. I'll start. Lord, you know why we're here." She stopped. A wisp of cloud floated below us.

Mei took over. "We don't know what to ask except we want to find him."

I jumped in casually. "Hey, Mighty One, we happened to be in your neighborhood up here and thought we'd stop by and say hi. You do good work, I must say. But guidance would be useful."

Marcus preached. "Moses needed signs and wonders. The children of Israel needed the pillar of fire by day and cloud by night in the desert. We need something as obvious as Qolo, higher than all the others. You brought us here for a reason. Let that reason stick out. In the Name. Amen," adding a whisper into thin air, "Holy Jesus…"

As we jumped into the car, I said to Tashi, "Thanks. The sky is so clear, we can see the whole range."

"It is very unusual."

I expected her to add, "You must be good people." When we all got buckled in, she looked at us curiously through the rearview mirror and asked, "How are you feeling?"

· · · · ·

We had a late dinner and turned in early. Reece kept insisting that she'd seen Elijah, that he was dressed in a white shirt and dark jacket and had a red braid or scarf in his hair and that he for certain had seen her. "He went rigid and stared."

Marcus said, "Could have been any guy. You're blonde. You're beautiful. We're in remotest Asia."

"No, I mean he stopped dead in his tracks."

Marcus grinned. "What I'm saying…"

Reece fiddled with her food. "That guy knew me. He looked different, but it was *him*."

Hallucination is a symptom of altitude sickness. Add a touch of wishful thinking after that grisly ritual. Even Mei, who has seen more culture than the rest of us combined, came away from Pajuu Temple shaken. "I have never seen this," she had said. "It is a different from my old religion. Very dark."

It seemed that she didn't want us associating her—even her past—with such goings-on.

Reece said warmly, "I know."

I made a note to research the ritual at first chance.

Maybe we were being tracked by a mission agency spy because I wouldn't let Karinna come along. If that were the case, he wouldn't have been shocked to see Reece. Unless he hadn't planned on being spotted. My guess: Dom had posted watchmen along the way, either for our safety or in hopes we'd lead him to Elijah.

I'm not a huge prayer person—being one to think things through on my own before bothering God—but I silently repeated Mei's prayer from her little Osaka apartment: *God, we're completely on our own out here. You can protect us or…not. You can help us or not. But I'm asking.*

No sooner had we got settled in our next hotel than Tashi switched us out to another, saying this one "wasn't clean." We smiled and complied.

Marcus said under his breath, "What's with sudden changes to the no-change policy?"

Nightmare scenarios creep into a body's head at such times: being shipped off in a bus to nowhere; herded into an abandoned monastery, finding Elijah's remains there; dying a slow, prison camp death. Or disemboweled and sacrificed to demons. Or disappeared, never to be seen again. *C'mon, Wingate, we're paying American tourists. State Department and all that. Which is worth diddly-squat. But we do have a Haplo D-A with us. Golden ticket.*

That night we gathered in the girls' room for intercession. I made sure they were loaded up with O2. I got a couple more canisters in case we should decide to separate, to take off for a search. If Tashi questioned us about so much oxygen, I'd say that one of us stupid foreigners had let the nozzle leak overnight and we were afraid of doing it again.

If we found Elijah he might need oxygen. Or food. Or medicine. *Where are you, buddy?*

I'd been to the rim of the Grand Canyon and to Pikes Peak and had felt a tinge of altitude sickness before. But this Qolo range was a whole nother animal. The four of us sat on the edge of the beds facing each other, eyes open, whispering prayers in code. We were getting pretty good at it, talking to God as if he were sitting right there in the middle of us. Which he was. I'd just never thought of him being so *here* and not *up there*.

Reece had her game on. "Yah," she called him by name, "we're glad to know you're near. Thank you for the day." She went on praising for a while, peace and joy on her face. Another good thing about praying with your eyes open: you get to see people's expressions. Mei was reverent when she prayed, her voice humble and heartbroken. Marcus was sort of blank-eyed with a tinge of cocky. But full of honesty and grit. I was glad he came.

After the amens, I told everyone to take a good snort of O2 before they slept. "We're getting half the oxygen our bodies are used to. Don't skimp for the sake of saving a canister. We can get more."

Day Eight. Over breakfast—just us again in a big lonely

dining room (If this was a pilgrimage route, where *was* every-one?)—we talked plans. The hostess stood folding napkins be-hind a counter, in earshot. I dropped a fork and crawled under the linen tablecloth to check for bugging devices. It could have been fun, playing spy games under the noses of The Edifice, and sometime I let the sport of it carry me along. But when reality hit, that my best friend in the world might be dying alone from exposure or sacrificed in some gruesome way like disemboweling, or rotting in an Edifice prison—and since I wasn't sure who to trust, except Mei and Reece, and since they didn't know about my second mission and probably wouldn't—all that lay heavy and constant in my mind. I ate heartily and kept up the fake conversation. "I'll want to ask everything about life in a base camp: where they get their food, do they ever hunt up there, what kind of animals live up there—"

"And the weather." Reece winked at me. "I'm interested in the weather. Haven't we had amazing weather! I wonder if we can go on a hike when we get there, if the weather's good."

"Short one, maybe, around base camp," I answered.

This jabber was all to let anyone listening in know that we were curious pilgrims. And to secretly reaffirm with each other that we intended to question Tufani tent keepers about Elijah, then split up and slip away to search if the chance presented itself. Marcus drank coffee sullenly. My guess: he (like me) had grasped how unprepared we were. You don't know a place until you get there, travel brochures aside; endless miles of uninhab-itable mountains, few water sources. I knew about wild mastiffs and black magic and symbolic human sacrifice and could have guessed about the guides' and drivers' watchful eyes. And Edifice checkpoints. But sheesh, dump all that in the Qolo Range. Vast. Beautiful. Hostile.

With put-on cheerfulness Reece said, "I wish we could go

back to Pajuu Temple. I wanted to see more." Code for, "Elijah was there, guys. He was."

"Unfortunately we can't," I said reasonably and with eyebrows raised sarcastically. "We have to follow the itinerary exactly as it's written. It's all planned out."

"And what of the skies, Mr. Weatherman?" Marcus asked, pouring himself another cup.

"A hundred percent chance of maybe," I announced. "We must be good people."

He grinned in spite of himself. "The tour agency knows the best itineraries. They come highly recommended."

Horse hockey. It was the cheapest tour Mei could find. I'd hoped our guide was slipshod enough that we could blame him or her if we got caught wandering off. But all tours were strictly monitored by the Edifice—no exceptions. And Tashi, as it turned out, was a great guide.

In the middle of all the fake chat—or maybe because of it—our years apart melted and hope welled up again. We were playing off one another with new ease. If Elijah really was gone, I still had them. I wanted Lydia to meet them more than ever. She and I might move back home to Magdeline once we were married. Mei could fly in a couple times a year. Marcus could make a new start close by. We'd rent a treehouse at Camp Mudj. Old times. Sweet old times.

I'd gone to Oklahoma to work in tornado alley, but in the last few years that alley had become a freaking twister boulevard, starting east of the Rockies, raking a wide swath from Chicago to Atlanta and all the way to D.C. At the extremities of the country, such as Beverly Hills or the Berkshires, tornadoes were still rare, but seemingly more violent. My country, 'tis of thee, sweet land of supercells, of thee I sing.

Day Eight. Day Nine. Our lives were a predictable cycle. Eat.

Ride. Sleep. Eat. Ride. Sleep. More arduous miles of gravel road. Almost to Qolo. We stopped at another open-air, steep-holed, mulch-filled outhouse, and to stretch our legs. It was sunny with a crisp, light wind, darned pleasant for three miles high. I was beginning to agree with Tashi that we *were* favored.

Reece gathered us in a circle, adamant. Apparently she'd been stewing. "Finding him is our purpose for coming, trouble or no trouble, right?"

"No drawing attention," Marcus said firmly.

She snipped at him, "We can't go home without the truth. I saw him back there, I'm telling you."

"I wish you had, Reece," he answered in a demeaning tone.

Reece held back a full-blown tantrum with clenched fists, eyes blazing blue sparks, teeth gritted. "You think I'm crazy. I'm not! I'm NOT!"

Mei came to a swift rescue. "Everyone, we must keep friendly for Tashi and the driver. He could be Edifice. We can talk tonight—"

Marcus glanced over Mei's head and whispered, "She's coming."

Tashi let us know it was time to go. "We started late today. I think we will stay at base camp tonight."

Reece switched gears, eyes as big as saucers. "Really? Wow!"

She didn't get it. Another sudden change in the itinerary. We'd been scheduled for a three-hour photo op and a meal at base camp, then a four-hour drive back down to a hotel in a nearby town.

Granted, an overnight stay and cover of darkness appealed to me too, but...

Mei asked Tashi uneasily, "What about the altitude?"

"Same," Tashi said thinly. "Same altitude, base camp and town. Same."

Mei explained to us. "Climbers who ascend 600 meters in a

day must come back down 300 to sleep. The next day, 600 up and 300 down. Even professionals don't climb all day and sleep. They must backtrack to let their bodies adjust to the altitude. It is dangerous." She made a level, horizontal gesture with her hand for emphasis and said to Tashi, "The town we would stay at tonight and base camp, same?"

"Same," Tashi repeated. "Base camp and town. Same."

"Pile in," said Marcus.

We passed an abandoned monastery. I asked about it, because Elijah had been heading toward one when he disappeared. This was on the main road though. I asked to stop, take a few pictures.

Tashi explained, "It is highest monastery in the world."

"Why was it abandoned?"

She gave the driver a sideways glance and said with forced pleasantness, "The Edifice restores our culture. This one was not needed."

The dynamics between Tashi and the driver became clearer, the way she went all cautious over certain questions, especially religious ones. Were all tour drivers Edifice, or had we been specially blessed because of Marcus's and my occupations?

I trudged to the ruin of stones, looked inside with camera in hand. Marcus checked the far end and around back. He reported in. "Empty."

"Sky buries?" I asked.

"No sign."

We pulled out. Reece leaned up to Tashi. "Are there other monasteries up here?"

Tashi said no.

"But there must be," she insisted.

I covered for her. "Yeah with all this territory, one little monastery seems like it's not enough. I guess they're way spread out? You know, it doesn't look like anything grows up here. Where do the tent keepers get their food? Is it trucked in?"

Reece had changed since high school. Once strong and level-headed, she was hesitant one minute, stubborn the next, having a nervestorm the next. Maybe she needed a snort of O2. I handed her the canister and smiled. "Good for what ails you."

She gave me a suffocating look, as dark as I'd ever seen.

Marcus leaned to me. "Food trucks come in full, leave empty."

Possible escape. Noted.

The gravel road rose steeply into a high canyon, tall crags on either side. A milky glacial rivulet ran beside the road, rushing past us down the mountain. Ahead lay base camp, an open rectangle of boxy, black tents, a few cars parked in a center area. The sun had sunk behind the cliffs, leaving us in cold blue shadows. But ahead snowy Mt. Qolo glowed, broad and majestic. The girls oohed. I grabbed my camera.

Tufanis appeared from a few of the tents and made a beeline for Tashi, obviously to get us four paying lodgers for the night. We got out, stretched our legs.

Spread out on blankets here and there in the rocky parking area were souvenir bones and stones and handmade jewelry. I strolled past, scanning for anything familiar. But the only thing I knew Elijah would still have was his gem. He'd never give that up. If Tufanis up here knew jewels, a rare red diamond stud sure wouldn't be laid alongside bones and stones.

We took pictures of each other with Qolo in the background, all of us a little overwhelmed to be standing on solid ground at airplane height: 17,000 feet. We'd arrived at our final destination: where Elijah was last seen alive. *Five places out of five. Four people out of five. Okay, Wingate. do something.*

While Tashi went tent-hopping to negotiate our night's lodging, Marcus went to studying the canyon cliffs on the right side of camp.

I felt sick to my stomach and drank some water.

Shoving his hands in his pockets, he said angrily, "Impossible."

"Yeah." The one cleft in vertical stone looked like it might break all the way through. "Maybe that's where he went."

"Maybe. But that doesn't help. He disappeared days from here," Marcus commented, adding skeptically, "according to Dad. He was wanting to go southwest."

"So, ahead and to our right. Toward that cleft."

"They have security cameras." He kept shaking his head. "Did you ask anybody which way he went?"

I answered defensively, "Who could I ask?"

"Dad. Or Karinna, who *saw him leave*."

"Why didn't *you* ask?" I shot back.

He laughed darkly. "Wouldn't matter." He hissed, "Fool," and walked off. The impersonal tone in his last word told me he meant Elijah, not me. Or maybe he was ticked at his dad risking life and limb up here. A chill went through me.

I didn't know who was the bigger fool: Elijah for wandering off, or me for thinking we could find him when no one else could—not even Parabolani, an elite special forces unit of believers. The best of the best.

But Elijah would do what he would do. He'd build a fire from wet wood, or love a handicapped girl. He'd change the course of his life, not on a whim, but on a conviction deeper than most guys his age could understand. Maybe that's why God had used him. He was grounded. He was rootless.

I broke down and called out weakly, "Elijah, buddy. Where'd you go? Oh, hang the ION Task! Where'd YOU go?" Was he scared that day he set off, terrified all those days alone, freezing to death or dying of thirst, or attacked by wild dogs as the report suggested? Years ago he'd killed ole devil-dog Salem with an arrow to the throat. Survived and saved us all. He'd gotten himself trapped under a slab of rock back in his woods, stuck for days with no food or shelter. He'd survived that too, but only because Dom had flown a Parabolani chopper over the woods and only because Elijah had burned a piece of paper to signal him in the very nick of time.

He knew all the tricks, Elijah did. He'd have been outfitted to the teeth. He knew the North Games. He had a triskele. He could have signaled. But he didn't. Arrested? Attacked in his sleep with just enough time to break the triskele? Did Dom start searching as soon as his signal died, or did he wait? *Why didn't I ask?!*

Maybe it was the lack of oxygen, but something shut down in me, and all I wanted now was to take some atmospheric readings—alone. *I'll make this cursed trip count for something.*

I went over to the girls and gave a cheerful spiel. "Okay, we're at 17,000 feet. A little more than three miles up. But that baby"—I pointed to Qolo—"is over two miles higher. And you'd never guess, we're still thirteen miles from the actual ascent, where the pros start their climbs."

Reece and Mei said things like, "It looks like we're just a couple miles away. Wow, it's huge! It's beautiful! I never thought I'd be here…"

As quickly as I'd shut down about Elijah, I boiled up again, this time in anger. Had they forgotten why we were here? This wasn't a silly tourist trip of 9,000 miles to admire a big rock! *Fools!* I stuffed it.

Marcus had wandered off by himself, fading with the light in the canyon.

I followed, with a cautionary glance at our driver, who was distracted and fiddling under the hood of the car. "What do you think, Skidmore?"

Marcus nodded again to that one pencil-thin cleft between

two stony verticals. "Ridiculous."

"I studied photos of base camp weeks ago, but they didn't do it justice. There are two ways out, the open valley toward Qolo ahead and that gap."

"But cameras cover the whole area."

"Do they?"

"I think so," he said. "Edifice wouldn't leave a chink in its armor. That gap is the right direction, but does it go all the way through? On this side it's a gradual rise to the break. But on the other, who knows? Dead end? Sheer drop? You might need ropes and crampons, a climbing partner."

"He did solo ascents. It's not that different than the canyon at Hermit's Cave back home, just a whole lot bigger. And he had the best trainer in the world: your dad."

Marcus didn't respond to the compliment. He looked around for another option. "He could have headed toward Qolo out in the wide open there, then cut right at some point, but see the cameras?" He nodded in three directions toward miniscule cameras mounted on strategically placed poles. "There are two more. I can't find them."

"Five? How'd you know?"

"Dad sent me a communication at Kim's. The cameras, their fields overlap. All bases covered."

"He was making a case for us not making the trip," I concluded. Should I be reassured that Dom had checked things out for us? Or worried that he was tracking us? "Wait a minute. If the triskele signal was cutting in and out, maybe E gave up, broke the triskele, and headed back here." These were questions I should have asked.

"Dad said the signal stopped five days out and he found it in a dry stream bed. He wasn't specific."

"Convenient," I said cryptically, not sure what I meant. I

stared at the cleft, at the cameras, back at the cleft. "There's no way…what if he…what if they gunned him down in the cleft before he even made it through to the other side? Maybe your dad just *told* us the triskele was found far away so we wouldn't set out across the mountains and get lost or caught. What if he's…still in there?" *Wait another minute.* "Did your dad start his search from here?"

"He didn't say." Marcus squinted at the closest pole. "The cameras move." He slapped my arm with the back of his hand. "See? They rotate."

I watched a minute. "Not exactly in sync. That means…every once in a while, possibly some places might not be covered." We followed their movements for a few moments. "It would take some calculating. But if Elijah watched their rotation—"

"He might have zig-zagged outa here. Dad was speaking truth. He wouldn't lie to me."

Tashi made a decision about our lodging and motioned us in for the evening. We got our gear and went under a heavy flap of dark canvas with a big decorative symbol sewn on it. My eyes adjusted slowly to the interior, like an old-time cabin without windows. There were benches for sitting and sleeping on three sides. The wall on our right had shelves with supplies: food and dishes and things. A narrow cast iron stove in the middle had two burners with big, steaming kettles on both. A chubby lady with a big smile and a bubbling voice greeted us in Tufani and got some tea ready. It was all cozy and rustic and exotic. A young woman and a tiny baby came out from behind another canvas curtain, which meant there was another room to this tent. Quiet voices came from that room, their whole family, I figured, holed away in a kitchen and sleeping area that we weren't invited to see.

Reece and Mei took the center bench. They'd be sleeping head to head. I took the bench adjoining Reece's at right angles. We'd be sleeping feet to feet, our gear taking the rest of my bench. Marcus would sleep head-to-head with the driver. A very small bench was brought out from the back. Tashi set up her bed along the wall with the shelves.

We sat and had tea. Tashi spoke to Mei in Mikan with a strangely apologetic smile on her face. The driver came in, said something to Tashi, and left. Probably car trouble.

Marcus whispered, "Outhouse," and left, too. Maybe he was going to scope out that cliff.

Clearly upset, Mei busied herself with her rucksack until Tashi also left. She said stonily, "Tashi has not told us the truth. Base camp is 600 meters higher than where we stayed last night. She decided to have us stay here because we handled the first high pass very well. You remember our first view of Qolo—that overlook where we prayed? A lot of people get out there and vomit or faint from the altitude. But we handled it well." She looked inside her rucksack absently. "They're having trouble with the car. That's what the driver said. We can't leave, even if we get sick." She looked at Reece and me with calm resignation. "We have oxygen. Take some before you sleep. But we will not sleep."

"You threw away your pills," I said with concern. "Will you be okay?"

"Yes." Her hands dropped tiredly. "It's good business for a guide if she can say that her customers slept at the base camp."

Neither Mei nor Reece were in good shape. I didn't have much strength, my chest felt constricted, but I vowed to be positive. "It gives us more time here. That's good."

Mei said, "These people speak very little Mikan. I can try to ask questions. I know a few words in Tufani, but what can we find? You've seen it out there. He couldn't have escaped, but he did."

"There's that one cleft, one possible way. We could check tonight."

"I'm sorry, Rob. I can't help. They wouldn't harm me. But you…" She looked at Reece, then me. "You are at risk."

Because we were white American Christians.

When Tashi and the driver came back in, our hostess passed menus around. The girls thought it was cute—menus in a base camp tent. Marcus came back moody. He was always a proud sort, but I had an inkling that he often wrestled with issues he didn't bother the rest of us with.

"See anything?" I asked.

"Didn't try. The outhouse is behind the next tent. Don't breathe in there."

We ordered meals, and the host lady disappeared behind the curtain to the other room. In a few minutes the smell of onions cooking filled the tent. In no time we had dinner. Maybe I was just starving, but that was the best meal: a big potato stew with vegetables in a savory broth. We thanked the host lady and went on about how good it was. She beamed.

An older lady, gray-haired and frail-looking with crinkly eyes, came in to help us bed down. We didn't bother changing clothes. There was no place to undress except in front of every-one or outside or in the outhouse. You'd have to be crazy. The tent was cold and promised to be colder as the night wore on and the stove fires died down. The old lady, not as frail as she looked, piled several heavy blankets on each of us, tucking us in one-by-one. I could hardly move.

"When will we get to talk to the people?" Reece asked.

"I don't know. I'm going to make an outhouse run sometime tonight."

"It's awful," she whispered.

"Got that right," said Marcus. "I have menthol cream. Smear it under your nose. Helps. By the way, don't drink any of the glacier stream, the water beyond the outhouse. Tashi said it's contaminated."

"Where does our water come from?" Reece asked.

"You know that big ditch by the side of the road on the way up? That."

"You're joking," I said. "That milky trickle?"

"We've had our shots, *ne.*" was his reply.

"Are you going to other tents?" Reece whispered to me.

"I'm hoping to see somebody out and about."

"I don't think they speak English."

"Right."

As my breathing labored under the weight of blankets and lack of oxygen, Marcus's words rang in my thoughts—*Impossible. Ridiculous. Fool.* The other half of my brain—the half that refused to admit I'd been ill-prepared and uninformed—determined when I might sneak out and take the readings; and whether I should do it overtly to show I was a scientist, or covertly so no one would ask questions; and if I should 'fess up to the others that Tufan wasn't in vain—at least for me—no matter what else happened.

But Elijah was gone. I said the word *dead* to myself as I lay under pounds of blankets, with a full belly, and chilled to the bone. No one could survive out there for weeks, evading dogs and Edifice fly-overs and scanners. And wild tribes. Deep down I'd known it. I just couldn't accept it.

I was mulling this over when out of the blue, Reece asked, "Tashi, would it be possible to go back by way of Pajuu Temple? I'd like to see it again."

Mei, receiving a final cup of tea from the hostess lady before being tucked in, shot a worried glance at the driver, but he was in a conversation with the young man who'd passed out menus.

Tashi looked as if she hadn't understood correctly, so Reece repeated herself. Mei said something quickly in Mikan and turned to Reece. "I know you enjoyed it, but we don't want to miss the Yarlung River drive and the incense factory and the temples on the way back."

I'd planned to ask if there'd be a clear sky, that I wanted to take pictures of Qolo throughout the night. But Tashi was looking at Reece so suspiciously I kept my mouth shut. Chances of getting readings while the others slept might be nixed. And the niggling feeling that there could be evidence in the cleft of the rock, that I might have gotten closure for everyone—the Mag Four, Elijah's parents, and Karinna, if Reece hadn't gotten us all put on notice—I was more ticked at her than I'd ever been. How dare she raise suspicions by asking to go back to the very place where Tashi and the driver had freaked out?

I took my chance an hour later. The baby wailed from the next room. I sat up, turned on a penlight, and made it obvious to anyone watching in the dark that I needed water and O2. Rubbing my stomach like it hurt, I swung my feet into my shoes. When no one stirred, I got my coat, camera, and my instruments,—still rubbing my stomach for effect—and slipped under the canvas door flap.

It was like standing in a crater on the dark side of the moon, a cold, lifeless planet with only the ghostly glow from Qolo as light. I felt a sudden, strange need for it, the mountain they worshiped. I strained to fill my lungs with what tasted like the last of the atmosphere. I didn't have much time, but couldn't help pausing to squint at that gaping crack in the canyon wall. Would the cameras detect me in moonlight?

A sudden crazy hope welled up: that Elijah had broken his triskele five days out, had tossed it aside, had made it back to the cleft, and was living there. He'd steal food from the tents in the night, build a small dung fire undetected by radar, sleep sheltered from the weather and unseen by cameras. He could be right there! Of course! That's why no one had seen him. He had nowhere to go and no one to trust. He was waiting for the right time, still hoping to contact that tribe. Or catch a food truck out. He could mill around with the other tourists, search for a familiar face.

I took a few photos of Qolo by moonlight, then—when would I ever get the chance again—I slipped my instruments out of my pocket and checked for trace metals and residual ION heat in the troposphere. I aimed the sensor in all four directions. There wasn't much east or west sky available because of the cliffs, but I got a good southwest reading in the general direction of the ION station. Sure enough, the upper atmosphere was warmer, and not because of residual heat from the setting sun. That I'd factored in.

I was recording the readout and pondering that old song, "He hideth my soul in the cleft of the rock," when a voice whispered my name. I nearly jumped out of my skin.

Mei said. "It's beautiful, isn't it?"

I slipped the instrument in my pocket. We admired the summit, pale and shimmering, rising above every other thing on earth.

Before I could explain myself, she said, "I spoke with the hostess. I asked if anyone ever got lost up here. She said no and something about the cameras. Then I asked if a man can have seven shadows? She gave me a strange look. I think she'd never heard of it. Then Tashi was listening, and I had to stop. I'm sorry. In the morning we might ask another tent keeper, but after Reece asked to go back to Pajuu, Tashi changed. When you and Marcus took off at the Pajuu temple, she was very nervous. She is responsible to The Edifice if we go missing."

I pulled out my camera and aimed it at the mountain. "I kind of thought the Almighty might help us. We still have morning and the ride back."

"Do you think Reece saw Elijah?"

"If it was him, why didn't he come over? He'd have to know we were there looking for him. We're not on vacation." In the quiet, my voice was thin, piercing. "I'm his cousin. We were best friends. He wouldn't put us through this on purpose."

"What if he is hiding from both sides—The Edifice and the agency?" she asked, mirroring my own thoughts. "Would finding him puts him in danger?"

"I thought about that, him stuck in a country but unable to get out because the people who could rescue you won't. Your friends are now your enemies. I've thought of a hundred scenarios. I can't get any one of them to fit or to work out in a way that we'd find him."

"He is gone…"

I wanted to believe he was sleeping in that cleft of the rock. That we'd get up in the morning, wander in that direction, and he'd come out to steal food or firewood or look for an empty food truck to catch a ride in, and he'd see us. That he'd been just waiting for us to come all this time.

"Rob, even if he came to us, how could we get him out of the country? The Edifice may not know he's here." She stood quietly beside me, looking at the mountain.

I nodded to the canyon wall. "He probably went through that cleft, dodging the cameras. Probably. Maybe. Could he have trekked for a few days, then made it back to here?"

"Are you going to look?"

A stranger came out of the next tent. Another followed. Both Asian. They looked at the mountain, talking in hushed tones, unaware that we were behind them. Mei went to them, talked, but came back with nothing.

We went back in together. I worked my bone-tired body back under the heavy covers thinking I'd try again in an hour.

CHAPTER 16

There are gains for all our losses,
There are balms for all our pain.
But when youth, the dream, departs
It takes something from our hearts,
And it never comes again.
—Richard Henry Stoddard

Day Ten. I woke up sluggish, cold, and heaving for breath. Breakfast smells came from the other room of base camp tent. Reece said she'd gotten five minutes of sleep for every hour of the night. Mei was silently tending to her hair.

Marcus sat up, rubbed his eyes, gasped, blinked, and pitched sideways, struggling out of the mound of heavy blankets. He groaned and grimaced.

"You okay?" I asked.

"Yeah. Why?" he rasped, reaching for the O2 canister.

"I dunno. You kinda look like a pizza that never got delivered. Anything go down last night?" I was hoping he'd tried. Because I'd passed out.

"The baby," he said groggily. "They were up half the night. How 'bout you?"

Meaning either he was exhausted by lack of sleep, or that he couldn't have snuck out because the whole family was up.

I'd missed the advantage of darkness but was almost too

exhausted to care. I snorted a little O2, pulled on my coat, and tried circling the tent, that compelling cleft in the rock only a few hundred yards away, calling me. The sun was rising, pilgrims with prayer wheels worshipping the mountain, cameras rotating. I was more certain than ever that Elijah or his remains were there. *I'm sorry, Elijah. I'm sorry for us all. I missed my one opportunity. All this time and expense. I failed. Failed you, the others, your family.*

Eggs and toast awaited us. And pancakes with cold, slow honey. We ate every last bite. Reece left the tent with hardly a word.

"Should we follow her?" I asked Marcus.

He weakly shook his head.

I was glad we'd stayed at base camp. Who else back home had done it? I had the readings and would take a few more. And if nothing else, I'd satisfied my need to get answers about the desolation of the place, the barren loneliness, the futility of attempting any kind of singular rescue. When we emerged from the tent, an even bigger gathering of pilgrims, bussed in for a couple hours, was facing the mountain with cameras and prayer wheels. Reece stood with them, asking a white guy dressed in native garb about a friend who'd gone hiking up here a few months back and had gotten lost, and had he heard anything.

Mei was mortified. She joined Reece and smiled at the guy, who seemed annoyed to have his wheel-spinning interrupted. Mei spoke to him in Mikan, bowed, and put her arm around Reece as if she were a mental patient. We gathered in a circle. Mei asked, "What are we doing here?"

Not sure what kind of answer she was looking for—and hoping she hadn't figured my second agenda of getting atmospheric readings, which somewhere along the way may have become my first agenda (I was ashamed to even think it)—I said, "Guys… guys, I'm sorry. I thought—"

Reece broke in boldly, "We're here, Lord God, creator of

Heaven and earth. We came because we thought you wanted us to come. So we're here. Now what? You've been silent. But so have we. We've failed to say your name aloud, out of fear. We've hidden you away from people who need you desperately. We lacked the courage that he had. We see now what he was up against…the weather and the fear and the people who would stop him. We see it now, standing in his final place." She began to cry. "We're sorry, Father. If we missed something, help us see it. If we've come here by mistake, presumptuously thinking we're some kind of super-servants who could do the impossible, well…" she chuckled through her sniffles, "well, that's all your fault. You made us a little lower than the angels and crowned us with glory and honor. You said we could do all things through Christ who gives us strength. So there. I thank you for Rob's initiative, for Mei's confidence, for Marcus's willingness to come even though he wasn't totally on board with the whole idea. But now what?" she cried. "In Jesus' holy name, now what?!"

She covered her face and bawled. Mei wrapped her arms around her and cried too, saying, "It's okay, it's okay." I glanced around to see if anyone had heard that stream of forbidden words. I pretended to scratch at my grizzled chin but was covering my mouth, because what had been pent up was trying to break loose. Karinna was right. Parabolani was right. What little pip-squeak from Oklahoma could outdo the special forces of the Son of God?

Marcus kicked the rocky ground. "Dad risked his life for Elijah's dumb stunt…"

Tashi stood at the door of the tent, looking in our direction. Time to pack up.

We brought out our gear and took one last look at Mt. Qolo. Beautiful but boring now. A big hunk of rock on which people die. What point was there to reach the top, take a look around, whoop and holler, and barely survive the descent. Or end up a perpetually frozen corpse. Made no sense to me. Me, the stormchaser. No sense at all.

Mei thanked Tashi for letting us stay at base camp.

Tashi said, "It is rare, no clouds at night and no clouds in morning. You get to see both. You must be good people. The car doesn't work. We will go in the bus." She pointed across base camp to a small, Asian-style shuttle bus.

My options in those last moments at Qolo base camp were: a) make a run for it and try to sneak through the cleft—I was more and more convinced that some clue was there—and risk getting all four of us disappeared; b) own up to a failed mission and throw in the towel; c) get back to YangDi and ask Dom to send a spy to Pajuu. And who was I kidding? Without Elijah, we weren't the Mag Five. We weren't even the Mag Four. We weren't anything…four people going our separate ways, scattered across the planet.

We milled around outside the tent. At the far end of base camp, looking small and lost, Reece stared up at Mt. Qolo. I sent Mei to fetch her. "Don't let her make a run for it. I have an idea: I'll get Dom to send someone to Pajuu. Maybe Karinna could go. It seems like a dead end, but we're not out of options. Or when we get back to YangDi, we could book another tour there. Or I could go myself."

Mei and Reece talked with their foreheads touching, a sad double silhouette beneath the Holy Mother Mountain, as people around here called it. I snapped a picture and lowered the camera, watching two brokenhearted girls standing as high as airplanes fly, in a valley of the shadow of death. I pulled the sensor out and took a few more readings. Couldn't help myself. Sure enough, the sky above that blurred-out place on satellite maps was much warmer than the surrounding space. Massive radio waves heating the upper atmosphere, changing the weather maybe, scrambling signals, and maybe melting brain waves.

I stared at that rift in the canyon wall one last time. *You were a great cousin. More like a brother…best friend.* A lump formed in my throat. *I'm sorry I couldn't bring you back for your parents and your sisters. I'll never…*

Gravel crunched behind me, and for a second I thought with wild hope—

"What's next, boss?" Marcus asked, but not in a smug way.

"Load up."

He threw an arm over my shoulder and looked resignedly at the cleft in the rock. "Fool," he said sadly. "Dumb kid…" He whispered "dumb" once more, gave my shoulder a squeeze, then turned away. He walked off by himself and went behind the bus. I wiped my eyes with my sleeve.

We stashed our gear in the compartment under the tour bus for the return trip. Reece and I were about the only white passengers, Marcus the only black one (or Hispanic or a third white or a percentage, or whatever he calls himself nowadays). Mei fit right in with the other Asian pilgrims. There were a few native Tufanis hitching a ride, probably to pick up supplies for the next herd of tourists.

Reece asked to see my map. "How far is it from YangDi to Pajuu?" She still hadn't lost hope, a touch more of the feisty, positive Reece I remembered. But why prolong the agony?

I handed over the map. "Once we descend the mountain by this"—I pointed to the only northern access to Mt. Qolo—"the itinerary has us veering off to the west and taking that second road back to YangDi along a river gorge. There's no highway cutting laterally across the Qolo Range to hook us up with Pajuu, no way, nohow. At least not on any paper or satellite map I saw." I lowered my voice. "The Edifice isn't past airbrushing the facts, but we would have seen a junction, I think."

Last night's atmospheric readings confirmed my nasty suspicions about a connection between The Edifice and our own government regarding weather manipulation. Take the whole global ecosystem, give it a big poke with a hot iron and see what it might do. Insane. It just might be that finding Elijah wasn't the real reason I'd been compelled to come. Could be I had bigger fish to fry. Or maybe I was glossing over one failure with one achievement.

Mei told us to leave behind any scarves or gloves or sweaters we could spare. These people were always in need, and back in YangDi a jacket would suffice. Then a two-day train ride back to Kim's Kozy. Break out the T-shirt, jeans, and flips. Bunks with curtains where I could hide from the world. I checked the weather clip, hoping another typhoon would stall our return to the real world, a world with a big gaping hole where my cousin/brother should be.

The cheery hostess lady came out of the tent, rosy cheeked in the brisk morning air, wearing a long dark dress and a fancy wide belt of some kind—a big medallion on it like champion world wrestlers wear, only different. We thanked her. She shook Mei's hand and kept holding it with both hands a long time, smiling intently at her. They exchanged a few words, after which Tashi shot them a wary look.

At first chance, I asked Mei what that was about.

"When Tufanis hold on to you, it is a sign they accept you. And I think she said, 'I keep the secret,' but I can't be sure."

"What's that mean? What secret?" *Oh no. Did one of the tent keepers see me out last night taking readings? Did they know what I was doing? Well, of course! These people are nomads. They follow the warm weather up and down the mountains. They know the whole range. They've surely heard about the ION towers, maybe seen them. People from all over the world stay in these tents sharing conversations they think can't be understood. But maybe the tent-keepers do understand!*

Mei answered, "I don't know, but Tashi heard her say it to me." I saw the worry on Mei's face, even though she's a top-notch feelings hider.

I had to go back into the tent, to say "ION Task," and watch for a response. I could leave my business card, offer to pay for information. So I patted my pocket as if I'd left something. "Oops. I'll be right back, Mei. If they start loading, save me a seat."

I ducked back under the tent flap. The cheery woman had the curtain to the other room held open and was talking to someone. She turned, let the curtain drop. I went over, shook her hand, and said, "Thank you. Um. Um. ION Task. Do you know? ION? Task?" I made hand gestures that resembled twinkle twinkle little star and nodded hopefully. "Do you know?"

She said something about Qolo and made a similar twinkle gesture in its direction, most likely telling me I was a good person to see the Holy Mother last night.

I nodded thanks, left, and squeezed in the front of the line with Mei. There were more people than we had seats for, it looked to me. I was debating whether I should offer to stay behind, when the bus doors opened. Hoggishly I flung my butt and my rucksack into the front seat, saving a place for Tashi so she wouldn't have to stand the whole way. Marcus slid into the second seat behind me. He'd said he wanted to sit with a stranger for more info gathering. I appreciated the gesture, glad he hadn't abandoned all hope. Mei sat with Reece a few seats back on the other side.

A new man was in the driver's seat, our driver nowhere to be seen. More change of plans. The word Auschwitz floated through my thoughts. World governments were heating the atmosphere, conducting experiments on controlling the weather. *Who else knows that I know? Who'd want me silenced?* I was on a fast track to paranoid.

The bus made a slow U-turn in the parking lot. I got one last meaningless look at Mt. Qolo, still in disbelief that we, the Mag Four, had half-circled the globe in search of the Fifth. *This close and we leave empty handed. Elijah Creek, you set out alone in broad daylight on a suicide mission for the souls of total strangers. And I didn't have the courage to walk a few hundred yards in the dark for the sake of finding you or your remains. Your triskele quit working and so you broke it and left no trace and came back to base camp. I know it. I just know it. The perfect place to hide. Food and strangers and comings and goings. But winter's coming and you have to find a way home. Now's the time.* I turned behind me and mouthed the words to the others, "Thanks for coming." The girls smiled sadly. Something welled up in me. *I'm gonna do it. I'm gonna jump off the bus and make a bee line for that cliff. I have to have a look. I have to!*

The bus stopped. My heart stopped. Tashi jumped on and counted heads one last time. She looked at me. "You have place for one more?"

"Have a seat." I patted the vinyl beside me. *Now? I should push her aside and go now?*

"A man has altitude sickness very bad. Vomiting. His tour left without."

"Vomit?"

She said apologetically, "Other car left."

No one was out my window except a couple of Tufanis warming themselves around a fire. I remembered Tashi's story of the old guy dying of edema. *I might make it to the cleft. Might be shot. Might hide. Might die horribly, alone, next to Elijah's bones. The cameras. Can't dodge the cameras.* I glanced around. One empty seat in the back, not good for a puking tourist on a hairpin road. *Perfect opportunity. I'll stand. When he gets on, I bolt. Now or never. Okay, go.*

Before I could make myself move, the tourist hopped up on the step behind her, slightly tipping the little Asian bus. His dark head of matted hair, woven with red yarn, barely cleared the door. A grungy-jacketed, puking native was blocking my way.

It was Elijah.

We locked eyes. There was no surprise in the scruffy, confrontational face. He brought a finger thoughtfully to his lips and tapped them. I got his signal: shut your mouth. My heart thudded in my chest, eyes watering like I'd been punched in the nose. He scanned the bus as if looking for a seat.

Tashi pointed out both seating options. He stood there as if deciding, in order to make eye contact with Mei, Reece, and Marcus. I could tell by the direction of his glance and his expression, who he was looking at. He gave Marcus a crisp nod. His jaw tensed when he made eye contact with Reece. I heard a slight gasp-turned-fake-cough from her direction. His eyes touched on Mei with the flicker of a smile, and a kind of secrecy that would register with me again later. Then back at Reece for a long second. Then back at me. Then back at Reece once more despite himself.

He's alive! I didn't need to see the others to know they—like me—were bursting at the seams. He muttered something to Tashi in Tufani. She stepped out of his way. He moved to the back of the bus.

I threw an arm over the seat and tossed a look to Marcus, with a side glance at the girls to see if they were holding it together. "How you doin', Skidmore?"

His mouth was stuck half open. "Fine."

"Those pancakes were good, weren't they?"

"Yeah…"

"I can't believe the weather. It's been great. No clouds to block the view."

"Yeah."

"And we survived the night. So mission accomplished, *ne*."

He blinked. "*Ne*."

"We must be good people."

"Yeah."

I raised questioning eyebrows to Reece and Mei. "D'you guys get all your luggage?"

"We did," Reece said, with the fakest, most pasted-on look of calm I'd ever seen. Her cheeks were flushed, her eyes wide. Mei was dumbfounded too, but you had to look close to see it.

"We got everything then," I said, putting on an easy, breezy face. *He's alive!* Being a part-time actor, I could project that nothing had just happened. But in that blessed blink of an eye, everything in the world was okay. We settled in, staring out windows. *He's alive.* I felt redeemed, vindicated. *My cuz, my best buddy. What the Parabolani couldn't do, I did. I found him!*

Truth was, he'd found us. Minor detail, but who cared.

CHAPTER 17

I found that going out was really going in.
—John Muir

Rob sees me first. We lock eyes. He's ready to stand, to bolt off the bus, but he stays put. I tap a finger to my lips, as if thinking about where to sit. He gets the signal: mum's the word. I make sure they all recognize me before I move to the back of the bus. Unreal. They're here. We pull out from base camp and head down the mountain. I watch the backs of their heads, their necks stiff and uncertain. They don't turn around. They won't give me away. Rob plays it especially cool.

My sudden change in strategy shocked even me, but Rob and Marcus staring at the cleft in the canyon wall, pacing, planning…I couldn't let them do something stupid. I wanted more time, to check things out. To get right in the head. Now they know I followed them.

We ride, my thoughts running wild. I have no control…I'm in the creek bed again and all goes black. Emptiness, smoke, voices. All the same thing. Empty, smoky, voices. Head stabbing pain. Sick. The stirring of a pot. They hover, the people and the shadows. I smell my own vomit. I'm alive, flat on my back, my body in a tent, covered by blankets, soul exposed like raw meat.

Liquidy shadows skim the ground, circling their prey. "There's nothing you can do," they tell me. "We have you. Not even He can stop us." They don't speak it, but I hear it in the smoke. It's not true. Is it? They can drag me under?

That other thing, the grotesque, upright one who'd been after me for a year, he thinks my thoughts for me. "He will eat thy flesh and gnaw thy bones. But thou wilt be incapable of dying." In my mind's eye he's outside of me, a few feet to my right, horned, scrawny, salivating for my next false move. So he can get in.

Hours pass. Or days. Someone gives me drink. Why? I choke. Drug? Murmuring over me. It's not him, is it? Not the shaman killing me with chants? Will he usher me to oblivion, shove me in and slam the door?

I grasp at day and night. This is good. The passing of time is good. I'm alive. They take shifts and keep watch, those beings do…the day watcher—scrawny thing at my side—and the earth-skimmers at night. "You know so much," they flatter me. "Know us! Our names. Get to the bottom of it." They don't speak it, but I think it. We read each other's minds.

Words from the Spirit come. He doesn't invade like they do. He politely takes his turn. "God chooses the weak things of the world to shame the strong." His voice is steady. Different from the others. No rasps, no wheezing. Quiet and strong. He loves me. I feel it. Thank you. Thank you. Forgive me. Thank you. They think they have me. Do they?

The people bring me soup and tea, day and night. The scrawny thing has burrowed into my brain. Can't unthink his thoughts. "Although thy body be hacked into pieces, it will revive again. But thou wilt be incapable of dying," says the lord of death.

"Hello?"

It's an English speaker?! I rouse from the bed a little. "Hello."

I'm still on the bus, still with the Mag Four, still leaving base camp. But it's all downhill in my head, too, and I'm back there, helpless in the dark tent. The English speaker says over me, "You will live."

"Who are you?"

"A trader. And you?"

"Uh…Creek." Did I switch out my passport to that name?

"You're lost." His voice smiles. "They found you in a creek. Sure okay, Creek. We go with that name. From the States?"

It's good English he speaks, not a thick accent. In the dimness of the tent he looks Tufani—brimmed hat, dark skin, rugged jacket.

I breathe deeply again and again, guessing we're at 14,000 feet, maybe 12,000. "Where are we?"

"At the border or across it. I don't know…*Bardo*," he concludes with an unpleasant chuckle.

"*Bardo*." I attempt a chuckle, too. "Got that right." A journey through netherworlds where gods invite and horrify the dying— or the dead—while a shaman narrates the journey into his ear, "Then the lord of death will place round thy neck a rope and drag thee along." Did it happen or did I read about it? Who's thinking this? I'm sitting on a bus, aren't I? The Mag Four are here.

"Accept the visions," the shaman will say to the corpse, "The gods are only figments of your imagination. Receive them or others much worse will come." Did they do this, try to send me into their beyond?

With an exhausted groan I rise from my pallet and ask the trader, "The men, are they Debbu?" Waves of nausea. "What's wrong with me?"

"They don't know your sickness. Yes, they are Debbu-Gampa."

Good. I made it. I reach for the triskele at my neck. It's gone. Oh yeah, I broke it. The trader helps me swing my legs around. He has clean hands. He gives me an O2 canister and gets the tube to my nose. Not sure I'll need it, but I don't know our altitude, and I'm wasted, on a raised pallet in a corner, with a dirt floor under my sock feet. My head. My gut. "Not edema?"

"Not here." He pokes me in the chest. "Not in lungs. Here maybe." He taps my head.

I understand him clearly, a good sign that I don't have the cerebral edema he refers to. I'm sitting up. I can think in words. If I'd been out more than forty-eight hours with a swelling brain, I'd be dead.

"Lost from your group?" he asks, but the answer is obvious. "Who knows you are here?"

The peculiar undertone to his question agitates me. It hurts to keep my eyes open, to see his expression. Dry eyes. Dehydrated. "One knows I'm here," I answer with more confidence than I have. "One by the name of Yah. Yahweh." I'm not afraid to say it. No one knows his name anymore. "Do you speak the dialect?"

"Some. I trade around here," he says. "Will your friend Yah Weh come get you?"

"Maybe. What do you trade?" I act interested.

"Metal. For knives, tools, spoons, machines. You have a knife?"

"I don't know." Is he buying or selling? Or stealing?

A man smelling of livestock sticks his head in the tent, glad to see me up; then another, both in worn work clothes and braids of red yarn circling their heads. I thank them for saving me, and ask their names. Pasang is about forty. Rhabten, a son or nephew, looks to be in his twenties. An older man of fifty or so, Yonten, comes in when tea's ready. They offer me goat cheese and barley bread. I take a few bites. It's good. They're curious about me. The trader translates. My answers are mostly, "I don't know." I ask questions about the unnumbered days I was out. Have I been here a day, a week? Two? And where are we? The place is not a name I recognize.

It takes a while to work up the courage to state my purpose, "I wanted to meet men like you." I point to the braids in their hair. Trader translates. Do I still have the Quella, the one in their language? My rucksack, where...there it is, open. They've gone through it. My crossbow. Gone. Don't panic. The Quella is gone, too. No, Pasang is looking at it. I motion with my fingers for him to hand it over and he does. "I'll show you." I pretend not to understand any Tufani or Gampa dialect. I'll learn more by playing dumb and keeping my ears open.

I say to the Trader, "Tell them it's a book. They can have it. I'll show them how to use it. I have batteries in my rucksack. They go here. Like this, in the back. See, it lights up. It can run on solar, too. This little panel. Put it in the sun. This book is the story of the Creator." Trader hesitates. I press, "It's my gift to them. Tell them thanks for saving my life. Here is a gift. It's a book." I black out.

The tent flap is open. We're on a slope of scrub grass with maybe a hundred sheep and goats. There's a horse-drawn cart. Must have hauled me out of the creek bed in that. The nomads watch livestock all day. I fade in and out. At day's end we sit around the fire and I eat a few more bites. Potatoes and a sort of vegetable soup. Appetite coming back. I change clothes at last and find my body crusted with salt, like when we did desert training in the Middle East. No wonder I'm itching.

Bringing good news to shepherds on a cold night, I read from Luke chapter two and tell them how the Creator of the world sent angels. Trader doesn't know that word. We struggle over it and come up with, "Good spirits of light who bring messages from the Creator to people." I go on, telling how angels came to shepherds 2000 years ago to bring this news. I understand just enough of Trader's words—a mix of Tufani and dialect—to believe he's telling it straight.

The two younger nomads can read a little. I go to the beginning of the book, tell them about the creation of the universe
and the fall of mankind. Trader translates, young Rhabten takes
the Quella and reads for himself. I don't tell them about the
Quella's speaking feature yet. I want them to read the words
for themselves. I'm exhausted and have to lie down by the fire.
I motion for the Quella again. "I'll show you more tomorrow.
This book has sixty-six small books in it. Many stories to read.
May I tell you a poem?"

Trader asks, "What is poem?"

"Song." I punch in Psalm 23, hand over the Quella to Rhabtan,
and quote the psalm, pausing after every line for Trader to trans-
late to the other men so they'll see that I have it by heart, that
it's very important.

> The Lord is my shepherd.
> I shall not want.
> He makes me lie down in green pastures.
> He leads me beside still waters.
> He restores my soul.

Rhabtan reads along, repeating each line in his dialect. The
fire crackles. "The shepherd is the Creator," I say. "He takes care
of us. This book is his story from the beginning of the world to
the end of the world. The song is 3,000 years old."

I show Rhabten how to turn on the speaking feature. Now
they hear the psalm in their own dialect. They're amazed. My
head drops in weakness to the ground. They have the book. They
know what it's about. They can read a little. They can hear it all.
Mission accomplished.

They talk farming and metal and weather worries and failing
grasslands while I lay grasping new words here and there in half-
dreams, which have the texture of reality.

I know that I'm on a bus, that I'm remembering the days with the nomads. I'm aware of the nightmares veiling my thinking here and there, then and now, in and out of focus. At least I realize it.

I ask the nomads about their families, their wives. Many men here on the heights make their women do the work while they sit around drinking and gambling. Pasang's wife is sick, Trader says. Rhabten's woman is expecting. Yonten doesn't answer. Maybe his wife is gone. After a drink of goat's milk fresh from the udder, I fall asleep by the fire recalling how Rhabten guided the flock that day, singing a yodel-y song and slicing the air with a sling and stone.

Sun's up. A blanket covers me. They've kept the fire going all night outside for my sake. I take too much pleasure in the blanket and fire. Two best things in the universe. Blanket and fire. Trader is gone. I stand up, take tea, walk around in the warm sunshine. Pasang watches me, then brings me a clump of flowers from the bank of the stream. A curious gesture. Get-well bouquet? I thank him and look for a can of water to put them in. His nod is honorific and deep, his gaze hollow and unsettling. The nomads whisper about me, heads together, faces unreadable. There's a thin crust of earth between me and the abyss. I could fall through. The agency tried to pull me off this mission. They didn't prepare me because they didn't believe me. If the team thinks I'm dead, they've quit praying.

Trader stops by. He's moving on, having come back to help me communicate one last time. Before he leaves, I ask him to tell the nomads, "This book is the only one like it in your language. The only one. Take care of it." I bless him and nod to the Quella. "Much can be said in a few words in the Quella. It's in your language, too. Thanks for your help."

We break camp. To help out, I carry a share of the gear. Have I overstayed my welcome? I'm eating their rations every day, costing them. We lead the herd to an actual road along the stream. Uh oh. Civilization. I follow like one of the sheep until we reach a settlement. We parade the flock through the main street and into a stone pen. They're selling off some of the herd.

The settlement is nestled in a dusty mountainside. We go up a lane and get a bunk room. Is this where they drop me off? I ask, "YangDi...where?"

They gesture that it's a long way and shake their heads and glance at each other. A wave of terror passes through my body, pauses, has a look around, then exits. These men own me now. I pray to live, to not be turned over to The Edifice or reported to the shaman. I address the throne of heaven aloud, quietly, "I want to live. I want. To live."

Night. Rhabten goes to check on the flock. Pasang and the elder Yonten take me to a dingy, cramped tavern. We belly up to the bar and they buy me a drink. I take a sip and ponder how I might dump most of it without their knowing. Can't get foggy. Can't go down again. Cigarette smoke curls through the air...like jellyfish tendrils through a sunless sea, encircling the heads of drowning people, and like them, and anyone entering Bardo, I can't breathe. He will cut off thy head, extract thy heart, pull out thy intestines, lick up thy brain...but thou wilt be incapable of dying.

Glasses full, smiles empty. One drinker with tiny eyes and a long, angular jaw (a woman, I think) sits at the far end of the bar. She tips her head from behind a disinterested drinker at my right, and peeks at me, smiles with white teeth. An invitation for me to join her? I rub my head wearily, making a statement: Not well. Not interested.

Pasang and Yonten get rowdy. At least they're happy drunks. That lone drinker on my right, I could't tell the gender initially. Long matted hair, high cheekbones, heavy jewelry. A man's hands.

Lifting the glass robotically, he sips, stares ahead. Cold, sterile light from the ceiling reflects off the surface of his drink and catches the lower white crescents of his eyes, like dead moons in eclipse. The methodical sipping, the smoke curling around his head, light curving under his empty eyes…If he turns those dead moon eyes on me, it won't be him, but a thing inside him. They're waiting. They're around me, inside and outside of people.

Unfamiliar songs blare from cheap speakers. The bartender offers to refill my glass. I'd leave this minute, claiming a sick stomach, but it's night, mastiffs will be in the streets, and I don't have a weapon. Outer darkness in the street or inner darkness in this bar, My two choices. They own me. I'd withdraw into my own self, but it's dark in there, too. Oh, to be alone in the glow of Qolo, the Holy Mother Mountain with her ever-present light. I see why they worship her. It makes perfect sense now.

I expect the pale smoke to take shape as a new species of spirit, not the scaly one with horns on its shoulders and elbows; not the shifty ones adrift above the floor. These won't speak, but I'll hear them, and their lies will feel true: "In reality, thy body is of the nature of voidness."

CHAPTER 18

Like fire or the sea, he was too simple to be trusted.
—G. K CHESTERTON, "A PARADISE OF THIEVES"

"I need to stretch my legs," Marcus said. "You coming, Wingate?"

After two hours of bumps and hairpin turns, the bus made a stop near what Tashi called a "sky bury" hill. People got out, stood in line for the open-air outhouse, which stunk even at a distance. There was a drink machine and hucksters with their wares. Tourists took pictures of the sky bury hill, though there was nothing to see: a rocky knob with a clutter of prayer flags at the top. Elijah disembarked from the bus last, bought a drink, and stood apart, drinking it. We Mag Four gathered in a cluster and wondered what to do. Would we look like snobs not speaking to the other sort of white guy? Who should make the first move? Was he standing apart to protect us, or himself? The usual souvenir vultures approached and made things worse. Who can focus when a stranger slips his hand like a vice grip under your armpit and banters, "Lookie, lookie. Cheapie, cheapie," and won't let go?

Marcus edged them out with a mean elbow, made a sound of frustration, and said to us, "You guys keep talking." He caught Elijah's eye and held up two fingers in a peace sign; he drew an index finger across his wrist, then crossed his fingers. Whatever Marcus's signals meant, Elijah understood.

"Stay here." Marcus drifted toward Elijah. We occupied

ourselves with nonsense conversation, of which I was getting
pretty sick. Marcus sauntered back in a few. "A guy over there,
name's Geo. He's the one that got sick."

"Is he better?" I asked.

Marcus grinned. "He drank ipecac."

"Ipecac?" Mei asked.

Reece said, "It's a medicine they used to use if you ate something poison."

Marcus added, "If you drink half an old bottle, you throw
up real bad."

I added, "After which you get left behind." The dude had
arranged to get kicked off his tour so he could end up on ours.
Risky and disgusting, but it worked.

Reece whispered, "So he did know. He did see us!"

I apologized. "A million *gomens,* girl. You were right." Then
to Marcus. "So we await further instructions? What did the
sign mean?"

"Peace. Blood brothers. Cross. From back in the day. He knows
where we'll be tonight, if they don't change it on us."

Reece whispered, "Oh, he's coming."

Expressionless, he strolled over and commented toward the
sky bury hill, "Ultimate homage to the mountain gods," and
walked away.

At lunch break, Marcus invited the Westerner-dressed-as-
Tufani to join our table. We got a corner booth, hoping for
privacy, but the little place was crowded and Tashi was at the
next table.

Elijah bowed deeply to me Japanese style, which was odd.
"I'm Geo."

"I'm Rob. Nice to meet you. Where you from?" Wrong question.

Mei insructed quietly, "Use your IA," then said brightly to
Elijah, "Hi, I'm Mei from Osaka. This is Reece from Ohio.

We're old friends doing the tour. We spent the night up there. A wonderful experience."

He smiled at Mei with that secret look again. "I'm a hiker, culture watcher," he said.

Not sure how to relate to our new travel companion, we were pretty good at fake chatter by now, filling up a half hour with conversation at right angles to what we were actually feeling. Months of planning, and we could only celebrate on the inside with our long lost Fifth. Tan but pale. Skinny but strong. Eyes the same brown but with a darkness and depth, and a strong gleam like that of a spent athlete, or an addict. Scraggly hair, scruffy beard. How Reece had recognized him from a few hundred yards was doggone amazing.

Mei's hands were shaking. His were rough and steady, one curled in a loose fist on the table, the other under the table as if it might hold a weapon.

Reece could hardly look at him and mostly observed how we three responded to him, perplexity clouding her face as she watched Mei watching Elijah. He, on the other hand, kept a roving eye on the door and parking lot, with only an occasional protective glance to his bowl of rice.

Marcus was reserved to the point of unfriendliness, but it was a front; he kept sighing as if with relief or to get his breath. Elijah's chest hardly moved, his body unnervingly still, un-animated except for the hand that fed him and the eyes that roamed. There are tales of the living dead up here. It did cross my mind once or twice, because neither Parabolani nor The Edifice had found him and yet here he sat eating with us, just like old times. Well, not exactly old times.

"What's with the red yarn?" I asked about the hair decoration while restaurant clatter was at a peak.

"Tribal." He guided the conversation by what he didn't say

and by his expressions. If his head turned to one of us, it was permission to speak. He ignored Reece except for a few glances. When she addressed him, it was with a fake casualness so obvious that I hoped Tashi didn't see it. I was worn out by the end of the meal.

Tashi stood.

Marcus wiped his mouth. "That's it. Back on the bus."

I picked up the tab, in case Elijah had no money.

In a genius move, Marcus said to me, "Thanks, Shinobu."

Shinobu—the Japanese nickname Mei had given me years ago, meaning "a person doing something secret."

"No prob…Ryo." His Japanese nickname meant "cool." I addressed Reece as Mayu, meaning "true and kind," then Elijah as Takumi, "sea pioneer." Mei had named us all right before Elijah had decided to join the SOS and leave us four to fend for ourselves back in Magdeline, Ohio, while he took off for the adventures of a lifetime. If I was jealous back then, time had healed it. Who'd want to put himself through such paces and hardships?

Those nicknames might move us forward. It was a little daring under the circumstances to put my palm down in the middle of the table and say, "A cord of five strands is not quickly broken." But I did. It was our kid clan code, a gesture of deep meaning and our last parting words as the Mag Five back then.

Mei followed. "A cord of five strands."

Reece followed, then Marcus.

Elijah looked at our hands. "True."

Tashi and the other travelers went to pay their bills. No one would suspect a few hands piled in friendly fashion between bowls and cups. But he wouldn't touch us.

Karinna had said that if we did find Elijah he might not be the same.

CHAPTER 19

If you don't really exist, that unfolds in all kinds of nasty ways.
—AN UNDERCOVER MISH

Okay, Creek, back on the bus, to the back of the bus. I can't talk to them much. They're afraid of me. Did I say something I shouldn't, a word salad that made no sense? I did speak English, I think.

Sit down and breathe and be alone and ride and remember....

It's morning in the village lodge with the shepherds, and I'm a little bit drunk from the night before. Too strong a drink and too empty a belly. Gotta think it all through one more time, rearrange what's real and what's spiritual...which is also real. Or not. What is the nature of voidness? Outside our bunk room there's a stir. Yonten and Pasang talk quickly. The elder of the two men peers out the door and down the hall. I sit up, reach for my rucksack. They've reported me? Sure, why not. They'll get a reward for a worthless drifter spreading a forbidden religion. My arrest in exchange for a few bills and some good karma. Pasang motions for me to stay inside. He's clearly wondering what to do. They talk, they look at me. Dread sweeps through again, whirling like a madman escaping his own terrors. It checks me out and is gone. What's happening? The men argue in whispers. Pasang presses, the elder shepherd finally agrees but issues an order. Pasang nods and quickly passes the Quella back to me. He doesn't want it in his possession.

"We go?" I ask in a whisper.

They gesture for me to wait.

I want to live, Lord. I want to live.

Within the hour we've left the hillside lodge, hauling our gear down to the stream and behind a few shanties among sparse trees. Like we're hiding. They're hiding me. From The Edifice?

No sooner have we set up camp and I stretch out in the tent...Someone's coming. I peek out through the slit. A man in robes, with attendant monks, makes his way down the hill. With expressions of uneasy determination, my friends motion me to keep quiet. They step out to meet the entourage.

I sit inside the tent and pray, remembering Dr. Eloise's warning a while back. "A few of our archaeologists were digging in the north. A shaman came a long distance to request an ancient skull they'd found. You see, my boy, the skull from a victim who dies violently has more power, they believe, since the spirit attached to it is restless."

I don't want to be used that way, Lord. You know that. You know.

"I was ready to be sought by those who did not ask for me." The verse shown to me comes back, firm and powerful. The Lord says,

"I was ready to be found by those who did not seek me.

I said, "Here I am, here I am," to a nation
that was not called by my name.

I spread out my hands all the day to a rebellious
people, who walk in a way that is not good,

following their own devices; a people who provoke
me to my face continually, sacrificing in gardens

and making offerings on bricks; who sit in
tombs, and spend the night in secret places;

who eat pig's flesh, and broth of tainted
meat is in their vessels;

who say, "Keep to yourself, do not come
near me, for I am too holy for you."

It's the shaman out there, I bet, the very one who threatened
death to believers. Town chatter must have gotten around, or his
spirit advisors whispered into his brain. Either way, he knows
I'm here, that they're hiding me. It sounds like they're telling him
that the stranger has moved on. They're afraid of the shaman,
but they protect me anyway.

When he leaves, I fall into exhaustion, unable to sleep or stay
awake. Or eat. I'm in that middle place of the undead. *Bardo.*
The men are worried. When I sit up hours later they fix a meal
and retrieve the Quella. I'm amazed that they'd hide me from
their high authority, knowing what he could do to them.

I've been AWOL too long. I ask again which way to YangDi.
They don't want to tell me. Do I dare show my face in the village and ask directions or try to catch a ride? Is it ungrateful to
leave? Dangerous to stay? Is the agency looking for me? No, I
broke the triskele.

We go to the bar again to celebrate a good livestock trade. I
offer to stay at the stone pen and watch the remaining sheep, but
they won't hear of it. They think I'll slip away. As we walk along,
skirting the main street, I show them a story in the Quella from
the book of Mark: how Yeshu controlled an army of demons.
Pasang thanks me, holds the Quella to his chest like a treasure.
He's a family man with children. He seems to think more deeply
about life than the others.

Today I will leave. They have my crossbow for certain, though

I haven't seen it. I offer them what little money I have left to pay for the food I've eaten. They refuse it and pack me a meal. They want me to stay. I don't know why. I'm eating up their rations. I think they're going to let me go. I build a fire as if in no hurry to leave them, and tell the story of Yeshu again, how he came and paid off all our bad karma.

Most Tufanis are not impressed by the resurrection. Their shamans often visit the land of the dead, they claim. But the Debbu-Gampa nomads are moved by the story of the cross. They understand human sacrifice.

They mention a town. It's the wrong direction from YangDi, but I understand it to be the closest town, two days walk to a main road. They draw a map in the dirt. I half-believe they're steering me the right direction. I need to go northeast to reach YangDi. But I have no choice than to take their advice and go a little further west first.

I ask if it's okay to weave some of their red yarn into my hair. Presumptuous on my part, but they're okay with it. They help me, and take pride in working the threads into a braid around my head.

We shake hands. I thank God for the pure luxury of having met four men of peace: an English-speaking trader and three Debbu-Gampa nomads. Pasang holds on to my hand a long time. It's a gesture of affection. It says, "You're our brother." I bless them in the name of Yeshu. Mixed emotions. They've been selfless and brave, protecting me at great spiritual risk to themselves. I still don't get why, so I ask. Pasang tries to tell me about tall men around the campfire that one night, the night they kept a fire going. He uses their word for spirit-beings, which can mean demons. But I wonder if he means angels. The walls between the worlds is thin here. It's thin everywhere.

Alone, I head toward the next town, my pack lighter. How

will I eat and where will I sleep, with no weapon and so little money? I pass horse-drawn carts and a few cars. Wearing red yarn may give me safer passage, since the tribe is feared. But I don't know. Maybe it just draws attention. I mind my own business but still get stares due a foreigner.

I'm rattled back to the present. Our bus is stopping. Edifice roadblock? I check the back door in case I have to make a run for it. Documents. I have them here somewhere. Tashi gathers up our permits. Rob shoots me a deer-in-the headlights look. He and the others came half way around the world to find me. Who helped them, who backed them—Dr. E? The agency? The Edifice? Whatever their motives, I can't have them close. Not with spirit predators and watchers circling me, not with me perched on a wafer-thin crust of earth. Too many people too close and I'll fall through.

CHAPTER 20

You've been my light of day, but darkness here has joined us.
—ANDREA SUMMER, "WAITING ON GLORY"

For a few hours our bus had ambled up and down zigzag roads through stony steeps, the massive Qolo Range receding behind us, and Elijah—in the flesh in the backseat—looking less like himself every time I glanced back. As if he too was receding. Tashi gathered all our permits for a checkpoint along the way. I was on pins and needles, half expecting police to board and take him off in handcuffs. But it didn't happen. *Hold it, buddy. You're a free and clear tourist? With legit paperwork? Whoa, you got some explaining to do.*

The hotel was nice. Elijah spoke to Tashi briefly and disappeared without so much as a good-bye. We checked into our rooms, took showers, and on Tashi's recommendation went to a restaurant across the street. Troops were fewer and farther between than in YangDi, but they never let you forget. We topped off our meal with dessert while a regiment marched past the window in lockstep. The mission wouldn't be complete—in my mind anyway—until we were all safely out of Tufan and tucked away in one of Kim's Kozy rooms. The girls talked about curling up with a good book and a pot of tea in their rooms. Mei said of Elijah, "He spoke roughly to Tashi and loudly, so that I could hear. He said he knew a cheaper hotel, but he'd stop back at the desk around 8:00 and leave a message to let her know he had a place. She was very nervous about his going off on his own, but she didn't do anything to stop him.

"She's in charge of the whole busload?" Reece asked.

"Apparently," Marcus said.

"Was she worried for him?"

"Scared of him, I think. Worried for herself."

"Why?"

"He's a risk, Reece."

"He said 'tribal' when I asked about the headgear."

Mei agreed. "It is Gampa. They are known for wildness and violence. If you mix American reputation for boldness with Gampa lawlessness, you see why Tashi is worried. Even The Edifice fear them."

Marcus considered, "A man like that latching on to your tour group…"

Mei said, "She may know he faked the sickness. He looks well now. You don't recover from altitude sickness in a few hours."

"Would she turn him in?"

"She could," Mei answered.

"We're not out of the woods yet," I said.

Reece asked, "Could Tashi be…one of us?" She meant a believer.

"No," Mei answered. "She's been teaching me Tufani religion the whole time. Our friend told Tashi he'd be back by 8:00. That message was for us."

We hung around the lobby until after 9:00, but Elijah never came.

CHAPTER 21

Don't know where I'll lay my head tonight…travel on.
But whatever ground it finds beneath it will be mine.
—Andrea Summer, "Travel On (Somewhere I Belong)"

Day Eleven. Pleasant skies, high clouds. Return trip from Qolo toward YangDi. My numbering of search days wasn't over because our old driver showed up, switched us back to the car, and we took off as the Mag Four again. I was afraid to ask Tashi where the sick passenger—and all the other passengers—had gone, but worked up the nerve because not showing curiosity would be more suspicious than asking skittish questions. "Did the others go in the bus?"

"Yes. Our car is fixed," she said obviously.

"Oh, that's good."

"Stay the course!" Marcus announced brightly, his demeanor anything but.

We rode on pins and needles along a beautiful, thrashing river through spectacularly steep valleys. In normal circumstances we'd be oohing and aahing. We stopped at the incense factory as stated on the itinerary. Conversation hovered around mountains and weather. And base camp. And rivers. Incense. Rocks. Clouds. Tashi used one opportunity at a small temple to try and convert us. The power of this religion—she said eagerly—could be ours.

(It didn't help her cause to point out, high above us, the old dead head and torso of a shaman, encrusted in gold.)

Reece gently spoke of her belief in Yeshu. We didn't try to stop her.

Day Twelve. Tashi showed up wearing a jeans jacket with a sequined skull on the back and the embroidered words: "Love Kills Slowly." We rode, ate, rode, ate, napped and arrived back at the Ascent Hotel late evening. Tashi left us for the night.

Reece practically jumped on me. "What do we do now?!"

"We stay the course, like Marcus said. Back to Kim's. We know he's alive."

"Do we?" she asked with a sharp voice.

I cautioned the others to say nothing about him in messages home.

Day Thirteen. I went alone to the hotel's familiar upstairs breakfast room to plan our next move. I sat at a table next to the window, drinking tea and overlooking the entry to watch for Elijah. All the thinking in the world couldn't change the obvious: we four had to leave Tufan according to itinerary, and Elijah would have to make his own way. He had multiple identities, no doubt. A few extra personalities maybe. But he was alive. Alive.

When I got back down to the lobby, Mei was coming in from the street.

"Anything?" I asked.

"No. And you?"

"Not yet." She didn't say where she'd been.

I tucked myself into the com room—that glassed-in closet next to the front desk—to check messages. Mei crossed the length of the lobby and stood uncertainly at the elevator in front of the ever-chanting golden idol. I called her back over to the com station and pointed to the screen. "It's all in Mikan today."

She got me into my account and whispered, "You are monitored."

"I'm telling Lydia we made it off the mountain and the food is good, that's all."

While I zipped off the message, Mei touched my shoulder and whispered, "He's here."

Elijah strolled coolly into the hotel lobby and past the front desk, which was vacated for the moment. Wearing the same scruffy beard, he was otherwise cleaned up in cargo pants, light jacket, and heavy-duty hiker boots, with his rucksack slung over his shoulder. He went to the elevator door, glanced with disinterest at the chanting idol, then across the lobby at Mei and me.

"You go," I told her. "I'll come in a sec."

Apparently he'd been watching for the front desk to empty out, or for a trace of us. Maybe he'd followed Mei back from wherever she'd been. I closed out my account and sauntered toward the elevator so as not to arouse suspicion should the desk clerk be watching from a back room.

Every move required careful thought. Back home I, Rob Wingate, small-time news celeb, made myself as obvious as possible whether on stage, reporting weather on camera, or hosting a local gig for media exposure. All to say, "Here I am, world!" But in Tufan any old set of eyes settling on a person seemed menacing. Who needs a prison of chains and bars where there's the threat of it in every glance?

Elijah held the elevator door until I got there. He positioned himself with his back to the security camera. We rode up in silence and gathered in the girls' room. He went to the window and stood stiffly. Marcus, in his signature black jeans and jacket, kicked back in the one chair, his feet propped on the foot of Mei's bed. Mei and Reece sat on their beds, near the nightstand and facing each other uncertainly. I leaned casually against the wall near the door. Once again, no joyful reunion, no high fives and jubilation. How much could be blamed on fear of spy cameras was anyone's guess. With appropriately vague gestures I asked him, "Are we…can we…?" Meaning, "Is it safe to talk?"

He mumbled, "Don't know. Keep it light."

"Have a seat," I told him, wondering why he'd plastered himself against the window wall as far from the rest of us as he could. Reluctantly he propped Mei's bed pillow against the headboard and sat. Prying off dusty boots, he stretched out one leg with a mild grimace, unaware that the heel of his sock was pink with blood.

Mei noticed and said calmly, "You're hurt."

He turned the heel to see what she was talking about and dropped his foot off the bed. "It's all right."

She got a towel and her daypack. Digging out a little first-aid kit, Mei gracefully stepped over Marcus's legs, spread the towel over the foot of the bed, unrolled the kit, and stood there waiting stubbornly without making eye contact.

"It's fine," he insisted.

She refused to look at him, her mouth firm, her eyes fixed on the spot where his foot should be. "No…"

How had Mei gotten so assertive? She was on home turf in Asia, of course, and knew the languages, knew the ropes, could melt in. The rest of us—even Elijah, I'd bet—were dancing in the dark compared to our delicate little Mei Aizawa.

What's the big deal? I said in my head to Elijah. *Get a bandaid!*

He brought his leg back up on the bed as if it weighed a ton.

Mei removed the bloody sock to reveal a raw, fresh blister. He'd obviously been running hard or walking far.

"Does that old frostbite injury bother you?" I was referring to when he'd gone off like a hermit years ago and gotten himself stuck under a huge rock in the dead of winter. His foot had suffered severe frostbite.

"You remember that?"

"You disappeared for days. We thought you were dead."

"History repeats," said Marcus dryly. A corner of his mouth curled. "Caught between a rock and a hard pl—"

"Enough!" Mei samurai-swiped the conversation. The others looked as stunned as I felt. Was that a swipe at Elijah for making the same dumb mistake of going solo, or at Marcus for taking a jab at him, or at me for bringing it up in the first place? She went on bandaging the blister.

I veered the conversation toward another subject. "How goes it now, then, when you're out in the cold for long periods of time?"

"Let's move on," Elijah said flatly.

Ah. Maybe us talking about our Mag Five history—if this conversation were being tapped, and Elijah's wound a telling sign that he'd been on the run—was not the direction we should take. When the scene's not going well in rehearsal, the director barks, "Cut! This isn't working!" So we kept our mouths shut and waited for a cue from Elijah while Mei patched his foot. He watched her with an intensity that made me edgy. Reece seemed confused. Mei happened to glance at her, and the exchange of expressions told the tale. Mei had captured Elijah's attention, however eerie that attention was. And well, why not? Old friends, both on mission in Asia; all the fond memories and adventures; both unattached. Who knows when he'd been touched by a girl last? Reece had no claim on him, but she stiffened. It was understandable, given their history. A tiny sound of concern came from Mei's throat. Marcus slumped in the chair, brooding.

Tension was so thick in that room you could've yanked off a piece and gnawed on it. *Criminy!* I thought. *It's a four-sided love triangle! Marcus is jealous of Elijah's attention to Mei, and Reece is jealous of Mei's attention to Elijah, and Mei's upset about Reece's reaction…but Reece is married to Greg. Five-sided love triangle. And Greg probably off with some other…Six-sided!* I was the only one not tangled up in this crazy hexagon.

"There. You must not neglect it," Mei quietly scolded, handing him a few sterile pads. "Change the bandage to prevent infection. I hope you will wash that." She gestured to the bloody sock he'd wrapped in a ball and dropped on the floor. He kept staring at her. She went on. "Does anyone else need first aid?" We all said no. She closed the first-aid kit, went to wash her hands, came back with a bottle of water, and handed it to Elijah. "Drink."

I said jovially, "My tummy is a little queasy, Mei. You got an ipecac cocktail?"

Elijah chuckled once, and I can't describe the relief that washed over me. I grabbed a canister of O2 like it was a bottle of fine wine and offered it. "Oxygen anyone? A good vintage. A good vintage indeed, sucked from the finest elevation. A full-bodied bouquet with tentative notes of gravel and glacier."

Marcus roused, slightly amused. "I'll have a snort. Reece, you look a little pale. Let's make a party of it."

Over the next little while of passing the O2 around, I caught Elijah snatching tiny glances at Reece. He'd finally picked up on the swirling emotions, a result of the foot-touching. If he was sad or perplexed or embarrassed, it didn't show, closed off as he was to everyone—except maybe Mei. An air of uneasiness and hostility worked its way around the hotel room.

I moved toward the window to see how Elijah would react to my approach. He pressed himself back a bit. *What's the deal? You think I'm armed? Have cooties?* I flung my hand toward the mountain view and took a stab at humor again, a line from *King Henry IV,* which we'd performed at our Shakespeare Sampler in Little Theatre: "'How bloodily the sun begins to peer above yon busky hill! The southern wind doth play the trumpet and by his hollow whistling foretells a blustering day. Then," I turned with a flourish, "with the losers let it sympathize, for nothing can seem foul to those who win!" I flung my other hand toward the door and said in the same lofty tone, "Hi ho, let us brunch! I be famished." Sure, I'd eaten half a breakfast, but we had to ditch these close quarters.

Mei agreed. "Diamond Lake Restaurant is recommended by the front desk. They have yak cheese *momos*."

"Yak?" I asked, still in character and with an arched, suspicious brow. "Cheese?...*Momos*?!"

"It's delicious. The restaurant is two blocks away." She got her daypack. We grabbed ours.

I crossed the room, opened the door, and turned dramatically to Mei. "And if thou gettest us lost, wench, thou art a soused gurnet!"

Doggone, why hadn't I thought of Shakespeare before? I should have taught them some of the lingo. We could've had long conversations right out in the open and no one would have made heads or tails of us.

. . . . .

Marcus opened the heavily carved door to Diamond Lake eatery. A hostess led us down a wood-paneled hall lined with art objects: oriental paintings, statues, and such. We passed through the fancy but empty restaurant and were led out to a fenced back yard. Plastic tables and chairs sat empty. Prayer flags fluttered between trees. A rocky little water fountain gurgled in the shade. An unmanned teahouse—a tiny, ornately carved, cabana-type building—sat in the corner. The weather was fair, the sky bright. We were the only patrons.

I was beginning to feel like every place had been staged just for us, nicely appointed and with a few costumed extras hired for ambiance, with minimal lines to speak, but ears to listen.

The hostess seated us, clearly cautious of our tall friend with the red yarn in his hair. Elijah took the chair facing the door, and evaluated the surrounding high wooden fence. He had a plan of escape in mind.

If troops come, I thought, *are we supposed to run or heave you over first and take bullets?*

Instead of asking important questions, we commented on the menu and pleasant garden. Then I mustered some nerve, set my elbow on the table, leaned my cheek against my fist, and looked my cousin straight in the eye. "You and me, we use to brain-wave each other without saying a word. I've lost the gift. Help me out here."

"Small talk," he said unhelpfully, "is hard."

Marcus turned on the charm, taking a cue from my humor tactics. "You mean weather and such? When Rob's around, pilgrim, the weather is not small talk. Au contraire, it's all barometric pressures and every other thing: from A is for altitude to…to what's a Z word, Wingate?"

"Zephyr," I answered. "A wind from the west."

"See what I mean? Informative. Stimulating!" Marcus turned to me, squinting philosophically. "I'd like your professional opinion. If I should get struck by lightning while here on the heights, could you determine whether it's a meteorological event or a theological one?"

I frowned knowledgeably and scratched my chin. "Hmm…it depends. Are you standing *under* a tree *during* a thunderstorm *while* breaking several of the Ten Commandments?" Pure stupidity, but Elijah warmed up a degree, and I returned to the real issue. "See (I still didn't say his name), we don't know what we can talk about, or when or where. Small talk is all we got until we get to another open-air, mulch-filled outhouse with no one around for miles. We're *gaijins* here, and they had us pretty scared about coming—"

"They?" he interrupted.

I lowered my voice. "Dom sent Karinna."

He perked up. "Karinna?"

Marcus said, "She met us at Kim's Kozy and planned to come along, but Rob didn't trust her."

"She thought we'd need help," I huffed, tipping my hand in Elijah's direction, indicating that we'd found him on our own. The food came and we dug in. I observed, "Hey, this is the Eastern version of that old American fave, grilled cheese and tomato soup."

Marcus said, "Hardly, but if it helps you get it down."

"It's delicious, Mei," said Reece, still not quite herself, being the type to use cute, bubbly words like *yummy* or *scrumptious*. "The yak cheese tastes like a blend of feta and cheddar." And they went off on a food discussion.

Trickling water, clear skies, great meal. Elijah warmed another degree.

Reece asked him politely, "Have you had these before?"

"A few times."

I repeated, "Help us out here, cuz."

He gazed long into his teacup, turning it with his thumb and forefinger. "It's happening so fast. The more believers ignore the message and accept the lie…more doors are opened…the wrong doors. And the more they come." It sounded like a summation, not an introduction. He waved his hand as if shooing a fly.

Marcus smiled smoothly with a half-chuckle. "You mean principalities and powers."

A withering glance in Marcus's direction and a critical, "Not funny," sent Elijah back to pondering his teacup, the rest of us weighing words.

Elijah's silences, that bleeding foot…What had he been

running from and why? Would sharing info put us in danger, or were we the danger—to him? Quietly I suggested, "You don't know where to start."

"That's part of it." He ran his hand along the edge of the table, fingers underneath, glanced at the strings of prayer flags. Perfect place for a bugging device.

"I can't leave. I'm not finished," he said. "One thing I need to do."

"What thing?"

"I don't know."

A hint of friendliness, of loneliness, showed in his otherwise hollow-sparkly eyes.

"That red yarn makes you stick out," I mentioned. "I'd think you'd want to not stick out."

"They're trained to spot incognito. You can be too discreet. And," he added, "even *they* don't like to mess with this group. They'd exterminate them all if it were feasible. A thousand people were killed in the spring. It was staged to weed out a few dozen of the tribe." He said of the red yarn, "It's a statement. Solidarity."

"That explosion was reported as an accident. Or an uprising," I said.

"Hogwash. If a people group were to be exterminated before they heard the truth, then the prophecy about all peoples, tribes, and tongues would not be fulfilled." He shook his head resolutely. "That can't happen. Prophecy will be fulfilled."

"It was around the time you disappeared."

Marcus said almost under his breath, "You're a one-man protest march? That could go either way." He blew out air and closed his eyes as one does realizing he may have made a terrible mistake.

Water trickled, prayer flags flapped. Otherwise dead silence.

Comic relief time. "Well," I chirped, nodding to each person in turn. "More *momos*, anyone?" "More *momos*? More *momos*? More *momos*?"

Mei giggled. "Yes, please. And we're out of drinks." She signaled the waitress.

Reece joined in encouragingly, "Rob, this reminds me of those teas your mom hosted when she opened the bed-and-breakfast. That was so fun."

"For you maybe," I said. "Us guys hated it."

Grins from Marcus and Elijah fueled me on. "Remember Mom dressing like a fugitive from Colonial Williamsburg? And did you know she made Dad get into the act? Him in those— what do they call them—*lederhosen*? You know, those britches with stockings where your leg hairs poke through and look ridiculous? After a couple of tea parties when he got laughed out of the dining room, he finally put his foot down...his big-buckled, gnarly, pilgrim foot!"

Elijah laughed out loud, another landmark moment.

A flash of anger shot through me. Everything—not just our collective mood but our very lives—hung precariously on this closed-mouth rogue missionary in worn cargoes and tribal tiara. I'd have to play court jester to keep the group from imploding. What little control I'd had over this trip vamoosed. Our alpha male was back, perhaps not for long...primed for arrest or quick escape or turning on us. But we'd keep adjusting for his sake. I took a deep breath and was unpleasantly reminded that we were at 50 percent of our usual oxygen intake, not unlike having a mastiff sitting on your chest. That fact alone messes with a person's mind. In an emergency, we couldn't run. We'd be winded in half a block. He, on the other hand, could go long distances, and had a bloody heel to prove it.

On the way back to the hotel, we stopped at a clothes shop. Reece went to the back of the store looking at scarves for her mom. Marcus bought a leather wallet. Elijah hung nearby. I caught Mei by herself at the front. "The first aid, that was good. It broke the ice."

She looked troubled. "I think I hurt Reece."

"Don't beat yourself up."

I sort of stood guard on the street and ruminated. Elijah knew about Reece and Greg being married. He'd known about the baby when we met in Cairo. Mei had probably kept him informed. I imagined a few things about the two of *them* that I shouldn't have.

We got to the entrance of the hotel. Elijah stopped. "I won't go in."

"We'll probably stroll to the square later," I said. "There's a big fountain synced to lights and music in the evening."

"Can't," he said.

"Tomorrow?" I asked. "We were going to circle the palace late morning. Intercede. Reece's idea."

"We'll see." Still no thanks for our coming, no jubilation. But when he walked off with a faint limp and turned back to the four of us standing there, I got the feeling that he wanted to come back.

Nonchalantly, I craned my neck and waved like the Queen of England. "How now, yon witty fellow, many good morrows. You must away!"

· · · · ·

It would have been Day Fourteen of the search. I kept tabs, just in case we lost him again. That morning he was already at the corner of Palace Street and Palace Avenue when we arrived, the girls dressed for comfort and style in jeans, sweaters, and brimmed hats, me in khakis, Marcus in black. Elijah just stepped out of nowhere while we were deciding which way to circle the monstrous building.

"Clockwise is an act of worship," he said without so much as a good morning.

"Then we should walk the opposite way," Reece said strongly. "And pray."

"Stroll, don't march," he suggested kindly. "Be a silly tourist who doesn't know better than to go counterclockwise."

She grinned self-consciously. "Okay. But it's empty, isn't it? There's no king to worship?"

"Correct."

Reece grieved over the stream of devotees prostrating themselves toward the empty palace. "And yet they keep praying and bowing, praying and bowing, on and on, doing and doing."

Elijah jolted as if she'd struck him, a strange and sudden move followed by a whisper. "*Tzav latzav…*"

"What?" she asked.

"*Tzav latzav, qav laqav, ze'ir sham.*"

I looked to Mei for translation. She frowned at him worriedly.

He said, "Do and do, rule on rule, a little here, a little there." I thought he was going to yank Reece into his arms. "That's it. That is it!" A frightening intensity of joy came over him. He pulled a Quella out of his pocket and punched in a reference. "You remember this passage:

'Woe to that wreath, the pride of Ephraim's
drunkards, to the fading flower,

his glorious beauty, set on the head of a fertile valley—
to that city, the pride of those laid low by wine! See,
the Lord has one who is powerful and strong.

Like a hailstorm and a destructive wind, like
a driving rain and a flooding downpour,

he will throw it forcefully to the ground.'"

"How could we forget?" I answered. It was tied to our summer in Japan, a mystery explained in Scripture, just minutes before we found the final piece of the armor, the sword of the Lord. A high point of my life.

Elijah said, "The passage goes on. Down a few verses it says:

'Priests and prophets stagger from beer
and are befuddled with wine;

they reel from beer, they stagger when seeing
visions, they stumble when rendering decisions.

All the tables are covered with vomit and
there is not a spot without filth.

'Who is it he is trying to teach? To whom
is he explaining his message?

To children weaned from their milk, to
those just taken from the breast?

For it is: Do and do, do and do, rule on rule,
rule on rule, a little here, a little there.

Very well then, with foreign lips and strange tongues
God will speak to this people to whom he said,

"This is the resting place, let the weary rest;"
and "This is the place of repose"—

but they would not listen. So then, the word
of the Lord to them will become:

Do and do, do and do, rule on rule, rule
on rule; a little here, a little there—

so that they will go and fall backward, be
injured and snared and captured.'"

In a teacherly way he said to Reece, "It's full of emptiness." Then, eyes threateningly fixed on the massive building, he added, "The palace is empty, their minds are emptied by their chants. The religion's very purpose is to empty a person of his soul. And on they go, knowing no other way, ritual after ritual, rule upon rule, doing and doing."

"No grace," said Mei simply.

I was still trying to grasp what he meant about the scripture.

He snorted. "So pray for emptiness. That the palace will remain empty. That the rituals will be emptied of power. That people see the emptiness for what it is. That Edifice insiders—" He faltered, shooting a glance at Mei. She gave him the tiniest nod, indicating that we already knew there were good guys in the bad empire's hierarchy. He finished: "That they'll be free to work." He went back to reading as we strolled, with an occasional dark look to the palace, speaking to it:

"You boast, 'We have entered into a covenant with death,

with the grave we have made an agreement.

When an overwhelming scourge sweeps by, it cannot touch us

for we have made a lie our refuge and

falsehood our hiding place.'"

An old woman who'd been praying at a niche in the palace foundation wall came over to Reece, her hands cupped and empty.

Without hesitating, Reece dug into her purse. "Tashi said we could give to old people. Some of them are hungry." She pulled out a few coins and dug deeper. "Oh no. I should have gone to the bank."

"Give her what you have," Elijah said.

The little woman received the change, fervently repeating thank-yous, edging closer to Reece—too close, in my thinking—until her head leaned on Reece's shoulder.

"Bless her," Elijah whispered. "Like Jesus did the children."

Reece patted the woman's shoulder and looked to Elijah, "I can say his name?"

"It's Yeshu."

Tenderly she said, "In the name of Yeshu, be blessed. May you hear his good news and never have to do and do, ever again.

May you have the peace of Yeshu."

The frail woman backed away with the little treasure in her cupped hands and twinkling tears of gratitude in her eyes.

"It was only twenty-three cents' worth," Reece said broken-heartedly.

"You gave her much more. Let's keep moving," he said, continuing. "All is emptiness. There is no inherent existence. And this bowing and chanting. A little here and a little there. To achieve what? The void." He smirked at the gargantuan palace. "It tells them to be content with futility, as if their lives aren't difficult enough. They go hungry and struggle and cling to perverse superstitions. The shaman overlords threaten them with demons, keeping them from knowing any other way."

We strolled and prayed, and it was powerful. We passed the big screen of rolling advertisements selling religion, past the drooling lion statue, past the worshippers, their foreheads gray from pressing into the dust of the ground. And me, walking beside my cousin who prayed under his breath with holy ferocity.

Around the back of the palace were picnic grounds, a playground, and beautiful rambling gardens. While we were taking photos of monks reading scrolls under a tree, Elijah left.

When I asked where he went, Mei said simply, "He had to."

"When will he be back?"

"I don't know."

In that hour I caught a glimpse of how Elijah must have trained his teams: with a confidence I envied, with intensity and emotional distance. And a mystique that draws a person. They had stayed devoted to him, Karinna said. Even after he'd lost one of his team. Same reason Dr. Watson stayed with Sherlock Holmes, I guess, why Little John stayed with Robin Hood and Samwise stuck with Frodo...Hoping some of it would rub off.

CHAPTER 22

Do not draw me without reason. Do not sheath me without honor.
—Spanish proverb inscribed on swords

A day with no number. It would have been Day Fifteen if we'd still been searching—our last full day in YangDi, according to an itinerary which was as reliable as a weather vane in a hurricane. We were looking at partly sunny, a chance of rain later. Exhausted from circling the palace the day before—more from the spiritual intensity than the mileage—we got a late start.

Could a whole culture make a covenant with death? What did that look like in practice and ritual, that agreement with the grave? The question had kept me awake for hours. Pushing morbid images from my mind, I went up to the second-floor breakfast room, choked down a little toast and fruit, then dumped my plate and shook off the guilt of wasting food in a country where people were starving.

The girls came in together and went through the cafeteria line.

I sat back down with Mei while Reece was still in line. "How's it going?" I asked.

"Good. Where's Marcus?"

"He made a quick bank run for more cash." Not that I wanted in on girl secrets, but to get to the bottom of the Mei-Elijah connection, I asked, "So what'd you two girls talk about last night?"

She saw right through me and answered forthrightly, "Rob, I love God first, my family and the Mag Five second. I owe Elijah my life…"

I waited.

Her hands folding softly in her lap, my pretty Asian buddy looked down at her plate. "There will be someone for me when the Father decides."

That's all I was going to get, not an admission of feelings either way, but simple diplomacy, signifying nothing. I'd been stupid to think we could all be fifteen years old again, life as simple as school plays and a quest for mysterious armor. Another sad commentary on my inability to foresee ruts in the road.

Marcus joined us. We hung out for one more round of hot drinks, glancing down at the hotel entry. Tashi had strongly recommended that we tour the main temple. After all, YangDi Temple, historically known as The House of Mysteries, was the top tourist destination. Mei had agreed, but resisted Tashi's offer to accompany us. We had the printed tour, Mei had told her the night before, and we might decide to sleep in. We'd be glad to meet her in the afternoon for coffee after the tour if we had questions. Tashi didn't like letting us go on our own, and Mei explained to us privately, "Circumambulating—walking around the temple—earns merit for Tashi and for us too, she believes. I no longer believe in those things and don't want to participate. I told her that we were indebted to her and that she was a wonderful guide."

Reece said to us guys, "She told Mei about her life. Tashi never knew her father. Her mother died recently, and her only sister moved away. She described her life as, 'I work hard and travel all the time.'"

Marcus commented, "Her whole life consists of taking whiny, puking tourists on the same long journey over and over? Sounds lonely."

"I know," Reece said, stirring sugar in her tea, "but I think she has friends along the way. The business people probably treat her well to keep her coming back, since she decides where tourists eat and sleep."

"Better than yak herding," Marcus concluded half-convincingly, then voiced an afterthought. "You think she gave her mom one of those...those sky buries?"

"Of course," said Mei. "What choice would she have?"

I added, "They hack up the body so the spirit can't come back in and become a zombie. And that whole vulture/karma thing I told you about. That too."

"Serious?" Marcus said, cringing.

"Yep. In the states we'd call it abuse of a corpse. Here it's religion. Black magic."

Shaking off the cringe to regain his cool demeanor, Marcus got up and led the way back down the narrow stairway and into the lobby. I checked messages at the com station. Lydia had written that she missed me, and asked about news. I hadn't told her much about this mission before I left, just that my cousin had gone MIA, and I had to go back to the place he was last seen to settle it in my mind. I replied, "Right back at you," about missing her, and said nothing about the news. I couldn't lie that there was no news. If things went all complicated when we got back—and why wouldn't they?—I'd say that discussing news was risky, then give her a big kiss and say, "Thanks for understanding," and hope that was enough. Visions of "Welcome Home, Mag Five" banners, of streets lined with admiring folks, and the five of us waving from a convertible—all that evaporated before it got much traction in my head.

The idol by the elevator was silent for a change and I wondered if Elijah had pulled its plug.

We, the Mag Four, lingered around the parking area in case the Fifth happened by, then we took off for the temple.

A little more groomed and clean-shaven, wearing a second set of clothes—clearly Western—except for that blatant red yard still in his hair, Elijah was at the corner buying bottled water.

"We're going to the main temple," I told him. "Last thing on the tour."

"Oh." He hesitated, then nodded, "…'kay."

"You coming?" I asked.

"Yeah." He set off. We followed.

"We leave tomorrow," I said.

He only nodded.

"How 'bout you?"

"Possibly," he said, not bothering to clarify whether or not yesterday's prayer around the palace had accomplished that one thing he still needed to do. I asked if he was done. "I don't know…"

To keep our energy up, we took plenty of time getting to the marketplace square, enjoying the friendly bustle of the city here in the valley and the ring of rugged mountains above. Gorgeous country. Strong, handsome people, but isolated and poor, superstitious and therefore easily controlled. The Edifice had chosen its first victims well.

Rustic souvenir booths crammed with trinkets, leather wares, and bright clothing lined either side of the temple courtyard and blocked easy access to the buildings behind them, those three- and four-story businesses whose upper floors looked mostly empty. The lower windows were plastered with posters. Bulgy-eyed gods seemed to peek at us between the booths.

I muttered, "I guess the locals are used to these images, but they make my skin crawl." Still, I raised my camera to get off one shot. Elijah stayed my hand and shook his head.

"Why?" I asked.

"Are their gods created in their imagination or manifested in reality?"

"I don't know."

"What's a picture of a picture?"

I had nary a clue of the answer he was looking for. Making an idol of an idol perhaps?

The marketplace funneled tourists toward the temple.

Marcus said, "Stock up on souvenirs, ladies."

"After the tour," Mei corrected him. "The temple will be crowded on this holy day. We shouldn't carry packages in."

Elijah slowed. "Holy day..."

"The Day of Appearances," she explained, "when their gods appear in the sky."

"That's today?" He stopped.

"This weekend. But Diamond Lake, where the gods manifest, is many days journey," she reassured him. "In there, we'll see usual offerings and rituals, I think."

A change came over him, wheels spinning in that crimson-crowned head of his.

I was gradually grasping the weird wisdom of him continuing to wear the yarn. Elijah was clearly a foreigner, therefore harder to arrest or punish than a native. He was also a human reminder about the slaughter of the thousand in that explosion, a walking statement that at least one outsider knew the inside story—that The Edifice was trying to rid itself of perhaps the only people group that still posed a threat in this region. And, I now realized, the only one in this region that hadn't heard the gospel. All of which made Elijah a menace and a liability to this emerging global system. *Pretty crazy, buddy, trying to hold that fort all by yourself.*

Having heard my comment about the posters and seeing Elijah's sudden trepidation, Marcus stepped in front of us and turned his back on the temple, his expression cloudy, his smile weak. "We don't have to go. I saw an ice cream parlor not far from our hotel. A tasty option. We could say our prayers from there. And souvenirs. Hey. Last day. Gotta get those mementos."

I had steered Reece away from the creepy stuff, not concerned about Marcus. Things sure were different now. Back in the day it was Reece and Marcus who had the strong faith. Now it was Mei. And not that I'm any tower of power, but yeah, things were different. Elijah eyed the temple, his head tipped back, his eyelids drooping. As if calculating. Or gathering steam. He didn't budge.

Marcus feigned confidence. "Okay. Forget souvenirs and ice cream. Let's stock up on the Word, my people."

Tufanis crowded the outer courtyard, dressed in rich colors, women wearing scarves or flat-brimmed hats and long skirts, men in sweaters or rustic coats. If the towns along the way to Qolo had a flavor of the Old West, the temple grounds echoed old Peru. Hardy people, mahogany-skinned, nice-looking, and in festive spirit. I could see why Elijah cared about them.

The temple wasn't all that impressive considering it was the Grand Central Station of an upsurging world religion. It wasn't huge and high like the Vatican, not over-the-top ornate like Nikko, and couldn't hold a candle to the Oneness Temple in D.C. The entrance to The House of Mysteries was crowned with golden statues of animals facing each other, a shining disc hovering between them. The Ark of the Covenant came to mind, with its two seraphs, their wings meeting above the ark. According to Mei, the disc was the Circle of Sacred Law. The comparison wasn't a coincidence.

Same as last week, people were milling around the two totem poles and throwing stuff into the flames of the white-washed conical ovens. Smoke rose.

Reece asked, "What are they doing?"

"Grain offerings," Elijah answered.

"Why?"

He answered in depth, talking Old Testament stuff. Elijah and Reece were actually having a friendly conversation. Mei smiled at me, relieved. Our one-time star couple paused to take in the goings-on outside the temple. I snapped a few shots of the ovens and totems, looking to Elijah for permission. Here we were again, the Mag Five in a strange land, at a temple stronghold to other gods, and from the sudden spark in Reece's attitude—unless I was way wrong—we were about to rattle the gates of Hell.

Elijah was explaining to her, "...three big idols in there, hundreds of gods on shelves along the maze of halls and inner rooms, and thousands painted on every wall."

"And people worshipping them," Reece added sadly.

"Participating with demons," he said.

Marcus shot him a look of fierce disapproval.

Elijah misunderstood it to be a scowl. "Look it up, brother," he barked matter-of-factly and went off on a mini-lecture: "Deuteronomy 18, 1 Corinthians 10:20, Revelation 9:20. Their gods are no-gods. Their own scholars admit as much. There's no inherent existence, so there can be no distinct spirits. You and I do not exist. Neither do the deities, being only manifestations of the teachings. Release of the soul comes when you understand you don't *have* one. Understand that. Still, they worship and appease and do rituals. Spirit possession is their power base. The oracles become possessed and bring new revelation."

Marcus clarified, "Hey, I'm on your side, Creek. I...I mean Geo."

I was confused. "Possessed by what, if there are no distinct spirits?"

"Indeed," was all Elijah said.

A cloud of toasty-smelling smoke drifted past. We gathered

near the entrance where people prostrated on hard stone, or wandered back and forth chanting and spinning prayer wheels.

Reece asked, "What should we expect?"

We gathered in a circle. "What is your weakness?" Elijah asked. "'Demons leave no stone unturned when trying to gain control over a person. One must put his thought processes under the control of the Holy Spirit.' I'm quoting Thompson on the subject. What's your weakness?"

When no one answered, he qualified, "What is your weakness…*here*? Think."

Breaking the silence, Mei sheepishly admitted, "Sometimes…I miss my old religion. My family goes to shrines and temples, and I can't. If I do, they want me to worship. And sometimes…I want to. It was my life before I met you." Her head dropped in shame. "I love God, but sometimes I miss the gods."

Elijah's brows twitched with concern.

Reece grabbed Mei's wrist earnestly. "It's what you knew your whole life, Mei. That's understandable. It takes time."

I went next. "I guess I'm naive, but I don't see a whole lot to be afraid of. It's just a building with a lot of people trying to earn karma points, right?"

Elijah said, "Right. That's all it is." I wasn't sure if he was agreeing or making fun. But he added in the way of warning, "I opened a door that no man can shut." Before we could ask what the dickens *that* meant, he asked Marcus, "What's your weakness?"

"I'm sort of disconnected from the rest of you."

"That's not it," Elijah said precisely.

Marcus didn't snap back as I expected. He thought some more. "I don't know then. I really don't."

Elijah looked to Reece for her answer. "I…didn't prepare," she said. "I didn't have time. I feel unprepared."

"Break up and pray," Elijah said, curling off toward the market. "Keep in sight."

I should have been thinking about my weakness, but morbid curiosity took over about that opened door that no man could shut.

While the others prayed, I took in the surroundings. The heart of the city was the temple, surrounded by an open square crammed with people. That square, in turn, was surrounded by market booths, which were surrounded by stone buildings with big dark windows. All surrounded by the rest of the city and a circle of rugged mountains spreading out in barren isolation, with only one road in and out, a decent highway but with a high likelihood of washing out in a storm. YangDi was the center of a labyrinth, like the kind they use in the new religions, but on a grand scale. We were very near the center of the center.

Tall and rangy and right at home, Elijah sauntered off past souvenir booths on the other side of the marketplace. He was clearly not tribal, but not a tourist either. An anomaly. He drew a few stares of concern, an alien decked out like a Dhebu-Gampa, the most feared of the Tufani tribes. I'd stolen a few uneasy seconds to research it at the com station and felt the strangest mix of admiration and pity for the guy. Surrounded by nature in all its deadly glory and by a dark religion in all its gloom, he'd been utterly alone. *We're at the center of the center of it, and only Elijah—and maybe Mei—know what IT is.*

The sound of rhythmic locksteps disrupted my thoughts. A block of troops cut into the square. I casually moved behind a crowd of Tufanis and prayed for protection for us all. Elijah didn't reappear until they were gone.

We regrouped in the middle of the courtyard, with Reece smiling a genuine, sparkly smile. "I'm going to praise his name in there, where these beautiful people don't even know he exists—all his names that I can think of in a place where he is never praised."

Mei opened her mouth to object.

"I'll say them quietly," Reece assured her. "*Yahweh, Elohim Adonai, Yeshua ha Mashiach…*"

Mei nodded. "We call him *kamisama*. Honorable God. And *chichi*, which means 'father.'"

Marcus said, "In the Gullah language he's *Jee-dus*. With a long e."

I jumped in, "Some Oklahoma Cherokees call him *Ye ho waah*."

"With this tribe," Elijah pointed to the yarn in his hair, "it's *Yeshu*. But most would not recognize the name. In other regions, he is *Y'wa*."

Marcus added, "You want Greek? *Logos. Kurios.*"

"Thank you, that's plenty." Reece clasped her hands at her chin, all smiles. "I'm ready."

The others headed between the two ovens to enter the temple, but I hung back, hesitant. "Guys, honestly, can't I go as a plain old tourist? I'll take pictures—"

"You can't take pictures. It's their sacred space," Elijah said, adding dryly, "and it would ruin their postcard business."

I went into a big, fake slump and trudged ahead. "Awright. Can I borrow some of those names then? And if anything goes wrong in there, go toward the light, people, go toward the light…"

Reece said, "Got your swords? We need all five swords."

Elijah dared a long look at her, smiling almost like his old self. "Got mine." He showed a corner of the Quella from his pocket.

We headed into that big boxy temple devoted to demon worship, with Elijah once again in the lead. He didn't seem at all worried now. I'm his cousin, and even with a big gap of time and life experiences dividing us, I'd know if he was worried. In a culture where you have to watch your every move, and even though he'd been hit with the bad news that this was a big special day—maybe with all kinds of "doors" opening—he was as cool as a cuke. Cautious, yes, but cool. *Why?* I caught him glancing at the four of us, squaring his shoulders. *Ah. That's why. A leader must have someone to lead.*

We followed the flow of worshippers into a big windowless room. Like Elijah had said, the walls were covered with hundreds of golden god paintings. Rich tapestries of maroon and blue and gold wrapped the support pillars and embellished the altars. A trinity of gigantic idol heads was mounted high across the back of the room. One was especially creepy, its eyes glaring down at us passersby, as if he had a really bad surprise in store.

"Surreal," I muttered under my breath.

"Let me take you back 2,600 years, to the prophet Ezekiel." Elijah narrated Scripture, "'Go in, and see the vile abominations that they are committing here. So I went in and saw. And there, engraved on the wall all around was every form of creeping things and loathsome beasts, and all the idols of the house of Israel.'" He gave me a minute to absorb our surroundings. There were no loathsome beasts here, but I was reminded of the monastery at Pajuu, the scrap of what looked like human intestines dangling from the gaping mouth of the dancer's mask. He continued, "'Son of man, have you seen what the elders of the house of Israel are doing in the dark, each in his room of pictures? For they say, 'The Lord does not see us, the Lord has forsaken the land.'"

Padded benches ran the length of the room toward the idols. Mei commented, "This is where they meditate."

Deeply curious, Marcus asked Mei a ton of questions. Reece went into watch-and-pray maneuvers, softly saying the names, walking along like a typical tourist, but with a sweet beauty that drew male eyes. The crowd, with us in the mix, was herded to the left of the big heads and back into a narrow hallway, smoky with incense, past shelf after shelf of gods, and acres of golden god wallpaper.

The hallway turned right, wrapping around and behind the big idol heads. Branching off that hallway were other short halls to our left, dim and low-ceilinged. Each ended in a shrine room, glowing with candles, crowded with more little gods stacked around and tended by monks. Big chain-link curtains had been pulled back from the doorways to let in the sea of pilgrims, one wave at a time, for some special ritual. I lost my already-weak urge to pray, numbed by smoke and chains and crowds, and tried to ignore the steady, disinterested stares of thousands of deities. And the droning—the monotone chants and half-hushed murmurs of worshippers. The low-pitched num-num-num-num-num-num went on and on like some big, dull, hungry creature wanting to be fed—num-num-num-num-num. All peaceful and powerful to these folks, I guess. Heavy and gloomy to me.

"It feels like a haunted house," Reece whispered.

We were inching past a short hallway when suddenly Reece lurched forward and barely caught herself from stumbling. A worshipper had shoved her aside to get to the shrine room. Obviously without thinking, Elijah shoved him back. The older man, dazed and milky-eyed, fell back against another man who barked a few words at both of them.

"Reece, are you all right?" Elijah asked, putting an arm around her shoulder.

"I'm fine. He just pushed me. He's trying to get to that room. It's okay."

A monk appeared beside us. "Okay?" he asked kindly. "Everyone okay?" He was small, in his twenties maybe, wearing a dark red robe.

Elijah answered politely. The monk seemed surprised at the Western foreigner wearing tribal yarn and speaking Mikan. While they exchanged a few words, the monk's eyes drifted to the girls. He gave them a once-over, a twice-over, a thrice-over. No mistaking that lusty leer. He edged toward Mei, let his hand drop, skimming her thigh.

Marcus was scanning the crowd far and wide for trouble and missed this, but Elijah didn't. The leering went on a for a good blatant minute, the monk edging ever closer to the girls. Without warning Elijah grabbed the monk by his crimson shoulder and growled a few words, throwing him backwards. People gasped at the abuse of their holy ascetic.

Elijah opened his mouth to deliver another verbal thrashing when something in the candle-lit shrine room stopped him cold. A few yards away a special ritual was in session. I'd caught snippets of the odd commotion back there, but now noticed two monks closely attending a muttering shaman wearing ornate robes and headgear, his eyes rolled back in his head. A third monk had an ear tipped to the shaman, obviously scribbling the mystic messages that came from his mouth. The tranced shaman thrashed and grimaced like he was in great pain. An indescribable sound erupted from deep in his chest—an inhuman ripple. Reptilian. Like the purr of a lizard. The hairs on my neck and arms stood up. The color drained from Elijah's face. The eyes of the shaman rolled back into place and drilled Elijah. A flash of insight struck me: that utterance was not the shaman but something *in* him. "*What is that?!*"

Elijah breathed to us, "Step back," then yelled, "Step back!"

His arms swept the crowd away until he was alone in a circle of stunned Tufanis and in clear view of the shaman. Candle flames shuddered. Unwavering glares passed between them, the shaman's face a mask of painful human grimaces, with eyes of another sort. Straightened to full height, Elijah smiled coldly, commandingly, and began to chant the words, "*Tzav latzav, tzav latzav, qav laqav, qav laqav, ze'ir sham, ze'ir sham.*"

We were dumbstruck, the crowd frightened. This stranger, an American crowned as a fearsome Gampa, shoving people, chanting in a strange tongue, and not at all threatened by the shaman who was clearly the flesh vessel of a powerful spirit. An uncontrollable shiver rolled through me.

Elijah drilled an arrow-like finger at the holy man. "Who says there is no room for a creator God? You who keep vigil in cemeteries and make a covenant with death. You want emptiness? You have it! Drought to this place! *Than pa* to this place!" He turned to the crowd and barked the foreign word, "*Than pa!*"

A few people gasped.

He turned back to the shaman. "'We are too holy for God,' you say. No room for *Yah*, for *Yeshu*, you say!" His finger moved with smooth, dance-like precision toward the floor. "He's already here and not like your no-gods, those needy slugs, those rampaging goats, scrawny things without bodies who would possess children of the Most High. Drought to this place! *Than pa* to this place!"

Tears of shock and shame sprang to Mei's eyes. Reece and Marcus were ashen-faced. Chills raced up and down my body and wouldn't stop.

Elijah was on fire. "The Word of Yah is monotony to you?! Listen to your own philosophies: '*Tzav latzav, tzav latzav, qav laqav, qav laqav.*' Do and do, rule on rule. It's empty! *Stong pa nyid!* Your emptiness is empty!"

The crowd broke into clusters of panic and offense. What Elijah was doing was not to be done *anywhere*, much less in the ancient, holy epicenter of the approved culture of The Edifice. And on the Day of Appearances, no less. But he wasn't done....

After one more lizard-like purr, the shaman's angry phantasm left him, and the poor human vessel collapsed. His attendants urgently removed the heavy ceremonial robes, swabbing sweat from his slack face. Over the horrified crowd, the grind of a huge golden cylinder—a prayer wheel behind us—was winding down. Elijah tore over to the wheel, wrapped his arms around it, braced his feet, and held on tight until it ground to a stop. A collective gasp went up. No one stepped in to stop him. He bellowed those words again and again until they echoed through the temple and reverberated the metal of the hollow cylinder. "*Tsav latsav! Qav laqav! Stong pa nyid!*"

With a heave he began rotating the giant cylinder in the opposite direction. People cried out objections. Like a man possessed, like Samson in the Philistines' temple, he pushed the cylinder, grunting and chanting with each heave. The collapsed holy man and his attendants were otherwise occupied, but a few monks ran out into the open space motioning for Elijah to stop. He paid no attention, with each heave flashing a withering glare at anyone who approached, throwing a fierce arm out to keep them back, tears of fury pouring out of his eyes. "*Than pa! Stong pa nyid! Tsav latsav! Qav laqav! Ze'ir sham!*"

An old woman at the edge of the crowd clutched her fists to her chin in terror.

Marcus spun toward a sudden commotion at the far end of hall. "Troops!"

They came, not in lockstep, but boiling through the crowd, guns and gear rattling.

Elijah came to himself and let go of the wheel. "Split up!" he shouted. Then to me, "Kim's!"

How he disappeared, tall as he is, I'll never know. But he was just gone.

I turned to the girls, "Go to the hotel!"

"No!" Mei barked fearlessly. The crowd parted. She stepped toward the stern-faced, armed soldiers bearing down on us. Reece,

Mei, and I were surrounded. Marcus had disappeared into the incense and outcries.

We three were briskly escorted through the hallway of the temple, the soldier in charge snapping at the crowd, motioning for them to resume. I understood Mei to say "Delaney" as she made a flighty gesture with her hand. She translated snippets so we could corroborate her story if questioned separately. We'd met another Westerner, she explained first in Mikan, then to us in English. We were taking a tour of the temple when a man shoved Reece. This George guy—she wasn't sure of his last name: Delano or Delaney—was trying to protect us, for it was very crowded and the Westerners (she gestured to Reece and me) were uncomfortable. The man named Delaney became furious and pushed back. Another was knocked off his feet. This foreigner started talking out of his head and pushing the wheel. She had no idea why. He could have been drunk, though he'd shown no sign of it earlier.

We came out into daylight, squinting like moles. Mei stayed cool and firm. She asked us for our tour passes and passports, and showed them to the guard. We'd be leaving tomorrow, she said, and apologized with deep bows of respect. The guard took a look at her passport, exchanged glances with the soldier at his side. She said, "Haplo D-A. Ainu," and pointed to a page on her passport, then said, "Tourism." They asked questions about Reece and me. Mei kept at it, repeating herself, acting slightly embarrassed at her brief connection to the tall tourist who'd run off. She added solidly that she wouldn't complain to the tourist board, nor to the temple authorities for her friend being so roughly treated. She smiled charmingly, adding that it was important for tour guides like herself to present every culture well, especially one supported by The Edifice.

She gave them the name of the hotel and Tashi's name—after

they demanded both.

At long last the guard returned our passports and ordered us back to the hotel. When they left, Mei said, "It's all right, I think."

Which was a good thing. If I'd had to give my Identity Answer right then, it would have been a red-faced blither of blather. "Anybody see…where the other guys…went?" I asked, my heart still thumping.

Mei said, "Let's go. The police may search our rooms." She turned to Reece. "It's all right. It's over."

Reece was flushed, but smiling mysteriously. "We don't know if it's over or not."

A block from the hotel, Marcus stepped out from an alley and joined us. Turns out he had plowed through the crowd, thinking we'd follow. "When I saw you were surrounded," he said, "I dropped behind a post, then followed in case they arrested you. Mei, the way you stood your ground…impressive! If anyone knew I was one of the troublemakers, no one gave me away. The regular folks don't want to throw anyone into the clutches of The Edifice, even us rude tourists."

Marcus and I stayed in our room all afternoon, the girls in theirs. He and I packed our clothes, drank water, talked trivia, and checked on the girls every little while. The always-steady Mei busied herself journaling and rearranging her daypack, the strain now clear on her face. She'd saved our hides by a skill and a bravado she'd learned in recent years. But one more surprise, one more threat, and she might just crack like a thrown teacup. She offered to bring in dinner, being the most likely to blend in to the crowd out there. We reluctantly agreed. An hour later she was at our door, her wide brimmed hat pulled down as far as it would go. "Here are your sandwiches. If everything is okay, we will get souvenirs in the morning. Be ready to leave at any moment."

"But our train leaves tomorrow afternoon—" I started.

"Be ready! If separated, we meet at Diamond Lake Restaurant. Or at the big square near the fountain. Yes, that would be better. Keep tickets with you. Watch out the window for him. He may signal us."

I hardly slept that night, socks and jeans on, bags zipped, ears perked for footsteps in the hall, keeping watch at the window, trading off with Marcus every little while. If Elijah showed up, we'd try hiding him under our luggage. But if The Edifice came, we'd have no way out—four floors up with no fire escape. I offered to hang out in the lobby all night and take the stairs to warn them, but Mei said no.

I mentally replayed her conversation with the guards as best as I could. Man, she'd had her spiel locked and loaded—working every angle, swaying the guards with her protected status and her polite deference to their authority, her stand-up courage, and her gentle threat: "Let us go and I'll not complain." With just enough facts to satisfy them, enough guts to garner their respect, and by throwing them off Elijah's trail by mispronouncing his alias as George Delaney instead of Geo Telanoo, she covered every base I could think of.

She'd been through this before. We hadn't. She'd been ready. I wasn't.

CHAPTER 23

*I am hurt but I am not slain. I'll lay me down and bleed awhile,
then I'll rise and fight again.*
—FROM AN ENGLISH FOLK SONG

Leaving YangDi. Thank God. Sunny and breezy. We were driven
to the train station, a fresh, big-windowed facility built by The
Edifice to improve tourism. Reassuring and composed, Mei had
a final conversation with Tashi, who was asking distressed questions out of earshot of the driver. Mei and Reece gave her hugs,
squeezing huge prayers of blessing into her. We officially said
good-bye with envelopes containing big tips, as per the written
instructions from the tour agency. Marcus and I shook hands
with the driver, whoever he was. Friend or foe, we'd never know.

Itching to get back to Kim's Kozy where Elijah had said to
meet (I figured that his yelling "Kim's!" before he ran out of the
temple meant he'd meet us there), we hauled ourselves into the
sunny train station and up the escalator into a sea of people. The
waiting area was huge. People filled the rows of chairs. Others
sat on their luggage or stood in clumps. A few stretched out on
the floor to nap wherever they could find a spot.

Mei led us through the crowd to a window overlooking the
tracks. "Wait here. We need snacks. There is a shop downstairs."
She took off.

As far as I could tell, we were the only foreigners. Hopefully Elijah was curled up under a chair somewhere, or in the mob still pouring up the escalator.

"Is he coming?" I wondered out loud.

"Beats me," Marcus said grimly.

Last night while we were packing he'd asked if I knew what those two words meant, adding, "Since you're the brain, Wingate."

"Well, I think he translated as he said it—drought and emptiness—so Tufanis and pilgrims and Westerners alike would get it."

Marcus had tossed his shaving kit into the duffel, saying, "It sounded like...I don't know...like an edict. You know, like a curse....I think the people in the temple believed him." My swarthy friend had flung himself under his bedcovers and stared at the ceiling in the dark until—like the rest of us, no doubt—he had drifted off, wary of every footfall outside our door, fearful of strange dreams and of sleeping too soundly.

Jarring me back to the present, a uniformed train official barked a call across the waiting area. The masses rumbled to their feet. He walked over to us directly and held out his hand to see our tickets. He looked at them, at us, then pointed crisply toward double doors on the other side of the room.

When we hesitated he nodded curtly, pointing again.

Reece asked, "Are we getting on?"

He nodded again.

Reece shook her head and pointed toward the escalator. She showed four fingers. "We are four! There's another one. She's coming!"

He met her plea with a stony expression.

"Very sorry," Marcus said to the official and held up a hand to wait a moment, explaining to us, "They're wanting to let us *gaijins* go first, and we're holding up one heck of a line."

A thousand dark eyes veered in our direction.

Reece craned her neck anxiously toward the escalator. "Should I go get her?"

"I will," I offered. "You guys go on."

"No," Marcus said, and repeated to the official, "One moment please?"

The official returned our tickets, dropped his hands to his side, and stood.

For a minute—which seemed like a week—we watched people on the escalators drifting up as if rising from the floor. Then she came. Her dark hair and gold skin mingled with the crowd's, but she stood out, not just because she was pretty and wearing yellow, but with an inner glow that required no smile. If not for getting to know Mei those years ago, I probably wouldn't have fallen so hard for my own Asian love, Lydia. Funny how things work out.

"That's her!" Reece chirped at the officer and motioned for Mei to hurry.

Doggone it, life was tense here. A fellow was always feeling like he could be singled out, hauled in, worked over, or shot up for the least infraction.

We were escorted like celebrities (or firing squad victims) out to the pavement ahead of everyone else. It was a sleek train, not as streamlined as Japan's bullet train but more like the Orient Express, maroon with gold trim. Perfectly groomed hostesses stood by each door with looks of mass-produced confidence pasted on, stiff as soldiers. I heaved a lung-full of relief when we actually boarded the train without bullets in our backs. Not home free, but homebound. We worked our way down the narrow hallway and into our "soft sleeper" cabin. Which meant it had beds: two sets of bunks with fluffed pillows and perfectly folded blankets, a table in front of a huge window, and reading lights over each bed. And vents. Lots of vents, which I—unflinchingly paranoid by now—hoped would be pumping oxygen-rich air and not some death gas into our cabin.

The highest, most inaccessible train on earth. Two days of nothing but hanging around in spanking clean comfort with my best friends. We guys took the top bunks because girls always have to go to the bathroom. Reece hugged Mei and thanked her for arranging a soft sleeper cabin.

Marcus added his two cents: "Sweet deal. Aizawa, you outdid yourself. Suh…weet!"

Mei humbly accepted the praise. "A wise man, Sensei Maxey, once gave advice: 'Only the best for the servants of the Lord.' So I must give you the best. The hard seat is an open car with uncomfortable seats. Very crowded. Most Tufanis have to ride in those cars. The Edifice," she whispered, "must impress tourists."

I was on my bunk and settling in when Mei looked up at me coyly. "Rob…do you remember many years ago…the overnight bus we took to Shimabara?"

"Sure. I remember every day in Japan. The bus was super nice but not so good for sleeping. This is luxury! *Domo.*"

Slyly she smiled. "And remember what you reeeeally liked?"

"You mean…" I raised an expectant eyebrow. "They have…?"

She giggled. "Yes. They have—"

I burst out giddily, "An itsy bitsy, eensie weensie kitchen?!"

"At the end of the hall. A tea station! You can get all the hot water we need!" She dug into the bag of snacks she'd bought and presented a box of tea bags and packets of instant soup. "You can cook for us. But wait until we get going."

"Soup!" I cheered. "Glorious soup!"

Stretched out on his bunk, sleek as a panther, Marcus chuckled at me. "Wingate, you are a true nut. Here we are in a cozy bunk room with two gorgeous babes, and all you can think about is making soup from packets of powder."

"Hey, man, I got a living doll waiting back home." I didn't mean it as a personal jab, but he didn't respond with another witty comeback.

A friendly sort of rhythm took over, each of us taking turns glancing out the window for a certain tall trekker to show up, until the train pulled out with a *chug*. I pressed my face to the glass, watched the station disappear, and with an obvious lack of confidence said, "He said Kim's as he ran out of the temple, so…"

There was a tap at the door. Reece stifled a gasp.

"Come in," Mei called cheerfully.

A uniformed hostess with perfect posture checked our tickets, comparing our faces to the passports with the same hard, suspicious air that I'd gotten used to by now, sad to say. Mei thanked her. She gave a curt nod and left.

Marcus flopped on his back in the upper bunk, tucked his hands under his head, and muttered, "Robot."

Mei set our little table with cups and a box of tea bags. She stashed the toilet paper in the top shelf of the closet. "The toilets will run out in the first day and will not be restocked." She held up a packet of table napkins and said, "Use these to wipe your shoes off after the toilet, and please leave shoes beside the door—inside the cabin or they will be taken." She wiped down the floor with a napkin and sighed with satisfaction. "I think we should eat in the diner first to see if the food is good, then use our snacks until they run out."

We reached cruising speed. I went to the tea station, passing a half dozen sleeper cabins. All were closed except for one carrying two *gaijins*. I said hello and asked about them, Australian archaeologists returning from a quest. Like the couple we'd met at Kim's, they were searching for ancient sacred texts hidden in caves. So there *were* other foreigners on the train. Why hadn't we seen *them* singled out like us and escorted to the head of the line?

I brought back cups of hot water. We moved the pillows around to make the girls' bunks into couches, then kicked back, staring out the window. The train was comfortable, the *click-ety-clack* of wheels on tracks soothing, and nothing for us to do but lounge around and ruminate on what had happened. We'd found him. And lost him. But he was alive. Mission accomplished. I guess. In a way it was like our search for The Armor. We'd found it and lost it and had taken a couple of years to put it back together again. Maybe the same was true for Elijah. He had to be put back together again. I hoped we still had all the pieces.

The dining car was laid out just like you see in old movies: linen tablecloths and wide windows with velvet curtains, water goblets and silverware. Mei had a long conversation with the waitress about the menu, then informed us: "We'll share a rice dish and a noodle dish with vegetables. The prices are okay, but…"

A young boy came in and curled up under the counter at the other end of the dining car. He was small and grimy and underdressed. Reece asked Mei, "Should we help him?"

Mei said, "They may have given him a free ride, or he belongs to an employee."

"Shouldn't we give him something to eat?" Reece asked. While we thought about it, his eyes began to droop. We waited to see whether he'd be kicked out of the car or someone would claim him.

"He's probably from the hard seat car," Marcus suggested.

We all felt guilty eating on white linen while that kid slept under the counter like a stray pup. Mei suggested we not draw attention to ourselves. We agreed, but I was struck with how people will generally compromise their better instincts under pressure. In the States I'd buy him a sandwich and not care who saw. But here—and it was sinking in how much a culture can affect the whole way you see the world—your bad luck is karma from your past lives. You get what you deserve. That's how misfortune is rationalized, even if you're just a kid.

The paling light of day's end nudged us back to our soft sleeper car.

Reece sat by the window, hardly noticing the wide plain and meandering river, a solitary nomad tent every few miles. "We've missed Sunday meetings," she said, meaning worship. "We should have one, sing a song or two. You wonder how many millions around the world sing in secret."

"Many millions," said Marcus with authority.

"Should we?"

"We're heading out of the region, back toward Jinsha," he said. "Train's public transportation."

Leaving the disputed region of Tufan made us a little more free, in theory. But it was naive to assume we'd be less monitored on a train. The soldiers at the temple could have posted our names on a blacklist, flagging us for future reference. The Edifice apparently did that kind of thing. I had assumed the station officials had held up the mob of passengers for us because we were foreigners. But the Australians down the hall hadn't been escorted, not that I could see. I could have missed it though. There was a lot going on.

"Go ahead," I told Reece.

"Okay. I want to praise Y for our five lives. Then I want to study more on what E said there." Meaning those phrases Elijah had chanted. She chose a song and we joined in, quiet and cautious.

A mellow mood of security settled in, and Tufan disappeared under a smoky sky the color of wine. Insanely, I kept checking the window, hoping to see Elijah running alongside.

Mei sang peacefully, eyes closed, allowing herself a tear or two. Marcus joined in, soulful and deep. Singing worship songs together makes you sort of let go. Reece began another one.

"Don't know that one," Marcus interrupted.

She sang a few bars, and we joined in when we could.

Marcus grabbed a packet of soup and shook it in rhythm, adding gospel-y embellishments like "Oh yeah," and "Lawd, please."

There was another tap at the door. We stopped singing. I wheezed, "Identity Answers," nodding at Mei to be the spokesperson.

"Come in," Mei called nicely.

The door slid open and Elijah eased in. He'd rid himself of the red yarn. His hair was still long and shaggy, but all other traces of a Gampa nomad were gone. He slung a rucksack in front of him and closed the door.

He glanced up at Marcus's bunk. "May I?"

"Sure, okay," we all said, "that's fine."

He took his shoes off, climbed up, stretched out.

"Glad you made it," I said in a stupid, ordinary way. "Did you get into any trouble?"

"Not really."

"Do they know you're here?"

"Who's they?"

I had no good answer.

Mei asked, "Can I get you some tea? Or soup?"

"I'm good. Thanks," he said, rejecting her hospitality.

Mei's brow wrinkled. "Do you have a ticket?"

"Hard seat."

Reece smiled up at him and whispered, "We were having… *koinonia*. Okay with you if we go on?"

"I heard you," came the noncommittal voice from the top bunk.

Marcus and Mei were sitting under his bunk and figured I could see him. They watched for my reaction. But he'd flattened himself out. The tip of a nose, an elbow, a knee—gave me nothing.

Reece said to him, "After that we were going to have a lesson. I was thinking I'd look up those words you said at the palace and temple. From the Quella. And the other two words."

"The other words aren't in there," came the glum voice. "It's pretty straightforward. Empty emptiness. Drought."

Cheerfully undeterred, she said, "Okay. We'll praise first."

We three joined in, whisper-singing psalms: "You, O Lord, are a shield about me, my glory and the lifter of my head."

He peered down from the shadowy upper bunk. My mind wasn't on the words. Annoyance nudged out the sweet spirit Reece was working so hard to bring. Fine with me for my cousin not to grace us with a morsel of a clue—about anything—until he felt so inclined.

Mei, who'd been flipping through her Bible, began to read very softly: "For who is God, but the Lord." She actually said the word *God* after telling us not to. And halfway into it, I realized she was exchanging *my* and *I* for *him* and *his*, applying the verses to Elijah.

"And who is a rock, except his God?—
> the God who equipped him with strength
> and made his way blameless.

He made his feet like the feet of a deer and
> set him secure on the heights.

He trains his hands for war, so that his
> arms can bend a bow of bronze.

You have given him the shield of your salvation,
> and your right hand supported him,
> and your gentleness made him great.

You gave a wide place for his steps under
> him, and his feet did not slip.

He pursued his enemies and overtook them, and
did not turn back till they were consumed.”

No one moved. Reece began another song: “The Lord is my
light and my salvation, The Lord is the strength of my life. And
I will not be afraid, no I will not be afraid.”

Marcus, Mei, and I didn't sing the first time around, hesitant
to drown out that dewy little voice filling the space. But her voice
started to shake, and she motioned for us to join in.

Elijah's shoulder had turned toward the wall. I thought he'd
fallen asleep and was snoring. But no. Suppressed sob-like sounds,
guttural and awful, grew and spilled from the top bunk. One
by one we stopped singing. Reece quietly stood and touched
his shoulder. He flinched, but didn't pull away completely. Mei
followed suit, laying her hand on his arm. Marcus seemed shaken
to hear one of his own kind—an alpha male—falling to pieces
over his head, but he rose and wrapped his long fingers around
Elijah's ankle.

The eerie, pulsing moan of his sobs embarrassed and frightened me. I'd never heard a grown man spend himself so shame-
lessly. Reece pleaded at me with her eyes until I joined them,
the four of us shoulder-to-shoulder, touching Elijah.

I was a few seconds from saying something trite and normal
to break the gloom when Reece whispered, “Father, *omen*…
Father, *gi*…Father, *langundowagan*….”

She was praying the armor of God on Elijah, using the words
only we five knew, words inscribed on the old suit of armor
we'd found years ago: *omen*, Hebrew for “truth;” *gi*, Japanese
for “righteousness;” *langundowagan*, “peace” in the language of
the Delaware Indians.

We joined her: “Father, *creidim*…Father, *soterion*.”

Faith and salvation. The words were full of power and meaning,

Reece reminding Elijah of the supernatural strength built into him, surrounding him. Not his own strength.

The entire length of Elijah's frame convulsed with emotion.

Reece whispered, "The sword." We joined in when we understood what she was saying. "*Ee...ah...oh...uu...eh.*"

The word grew in the cabin with each syllable: "*Eeahohuueh.*" The flashing sword of the Lord had spoken that word one afternoon in a park in southern Japan seven years before. When Elijah had assembled the sword and brandished it for the first time in centuries, it sang—sang the very name of God: Yahweh.

It might have been risky saying the name on a train in Tufan, but few would have understood what we were doing, even a believer. And to an Edifice ear on the other end of a bugging device, our drone could have been any of the mystical chants from the new religions. But of all the things that could have been said to Elijah that night, of all the words of comfort and strength, Reece had nailed it. The name of his Lord and master: Yahweh. The name of the sword from *the* Sword himself echoing out of our past.

Power was there in our soft sleeper cabin. How can I describe it? Strong and protective. Big and tender. Overwhelming. We all felt it. Marcus wrapped his free arm over his face and leaned weakly on the mattress of the upper bunk, weeping. I was crying. So was Reece. Mei smiled.

"You're covered," Reece assured Elijah, patting his shoulder in a tender, motherly way, like I'd seen her comfort her little Olivet. "You're safe."

His breathing slowed, and his body went limp so quickly that I thought he was dead. Then I thought crazily that he was possessed like the shaman, and had fainted. Which would explain his dark looks and that awful moan. I braced for him to erupt, an inhuman face overtaking his, a face like one of those

gruesome gods from the windows of YangDi. He could kill us
easily, quickly, quietly…trapped as we were in a tiny room.

Bracing for the horrors I'd tried to protect Reece from and
shocked at my own rampant thoughts—fears that my cousin had
been emptied of his soul; sudden visions of ghouls pursuing the
train, raising skull bowls of blood in celebration; corpses with
winged shawls of human flesh flying above, keeping pace—and
wondering if it were truly happening, I stood beside my friends,
not daring to ask what was in *their* heads.

The trail of my thoughts faded into the *clickety-clack* of the
train until only one truth was left: we were speeding through
a darkening plain as high as planes fly, the only track in and
out of Tufan, and no one but The Edifice knew where we were.

Elijah didn't move. The suspense was awful, the silence vast—
bigger than the cabin that contained it. At long last his ribs began
to rise and fall, rise and fall.

Mei whispered with relief, "He's asleep."

I pushed the nightmares-in-residence from my mind, and
it seemed as if a big presence was in the cabin. We removed
our hands from Elijah's body one by one. Marcus was the last
to let go, the last to sit down. I'd have thought he was playing
it for melodrama if I hadn't seen his stricken face. For several
minutes we sat.

The strangest kind of peace came, silent but musical, as if the
echoes of our singing still lingered. A relief and joy that had no
business being there, was there.

Those moments are hard to describe without sounding wacky,
but here goes. It was like the time I was at home watching real-
time coverage of the fourth tsunami in recent years. The clothes
dryer buzzer went off. I retrieved an armload of towels and folded
them on the coffee table while waves rolled in on the other side
of the planet, drowning thousands of people. As I watched. In

real time. While folding towels. Rational. Detached. Calm.

I'd noticed a similar detachment worming its way into our culture. I'm speaking of a way for the mind to manage the incomprehensible. Or a way to make the incomprehensible entertaining, like when early Christians were thrown to the lions as amusement. Turn on the tube, pop a cold one, get a bag of chips. Watch people die.

Whether my watching the tsunami with such detachment meant I was in horrified denial of the tragedy or in callous appreciation of the thrill, I still didn't know. Or whether there was a third reason: a deep faith that God was in the midst of a horror that I could do nothing about and working things out in his own way. If it was faith, I probably should have been praying for all those folks drowning. But I just calmly folded towels and recalled the Scripture: "Distress of nations in perplexity because of the roaring of the sea and the waves." *We've been forewarned.*

Here in oxygen-controlled comfort, I sat at the table, nothing to see in the window but my own reflection. Not a single light out there on the plain. No houses or street lights or campfires, no moon or stars. A country abandoned to darkness, engulfed in emptiness. My cousin was a wreck, and me the last one to reach out to him. But horror and guilt were gone and, in their place, a great—if detached—calm.

Mei joined me at the window and whispered dismally toward the world outside, "*Nanni mo nai…*"

"What?"

"There is nothing at all."

"I'd have gone stark raving mad out there."

Reece curled up with the Quella. Mei broke out the tea bags. I went to get a pot of hot water. When I got back Marcus was standing by the window in the hallway. He didn't seem to know what to do with himself.

"You okay?" I asked, wiping my shoes on the hall carpet.

"Yeah," he sighed. "What happened to him, I wonder?"

"I dunno, but look out there."

We cupped our hands around our eyes, like kids, and pressed our faces to the glass, toward that featureless night. I said, "Mei calls it *nanni mo nai*: nothing at all."

Mei and I fixed tea. After a while, Marcus came in from the hall and sat next to her. "Can you show me to the hard seat car?"

"Why?"

"Not enough room for all of us. I'll take his seat...if he actually has one."

"Reece and I can fit in one bunk," she answered. "It's okay. The steward may ask questions if someone else—"

"Or more questions if the seat is empty," he snipped softly. "Which do you think?"

She considered the options. "We could wake him."

Marcus stood and got a blanket from the closet. "I'll need your help to find it."

She said, "Leave your wallet and anything of value here. Wear your passport and tour pass inside your clothes. Do you have your red gem?"

"Not on me."

"Good." She unzipped the pockets of Elijah's rucksack until she found his ticket. "Here. If anyone asks, tell them a friend is sick and sleeping in your bunk. Don't argue. If they question why your friend booked a hard seat instead of staying with you, tell them that you met a few days ago and you don't think he has much money. We can wake him if there's trouble. Let's go."

Minutes later Mei returned by herself. "Marcus is in the first car beyond the diner, fifth row, on the aisle. It will be the long night for him."

The girls made a curtain with a blanket hung over Reece's

bunk and took turns getting ready for the night. We turned the lights down. I kept checking on Elijah's breathing, fighting off thoughts of waking up with a re-animated corpse in our cabin… and us four thrown off the train in the middle of *nanni mo nai.* Fear was having a holiday in my head. *Stop thinking morbid thoughts. What's wrong with you?*

I lay there a long time, watching Elijah's back, monitoring his breathing rhythms. On the bunk below him, Mei was writing in her journal, using her head lamp like a cute cave explorer. Reece was in the bunk below me, still into the Quella.

Mei reached a laminated card up to me. "Rob, you will like this."

I read "The Train Rules," which were funkily translated into English. I chuckled and snorted. I'd read these to the gang tomorrow.

The big presence was still in the room, but not so obvious as before. And I had the silliest image in my mind as I drifted off: of a huge guardian angel crammed into the corner in the dark, his wings smooshed to fit the space, watching over us and folding towels.

CHAPTER 24

The rest of his journey was both monotonous and uneventful.
—Agatha Christie, "The Girl in the Train"

My ear registered a *clickety-clack,* my body was gently rocked awake by the train. Eyes opened to early light. Elijah was in the opposite bunk, staring down at Reece in the bunk below me. She must have been asleep, for his was a private stare. Whether sad or ominous, I couldn't exactly tell. I closed my eyes undetected and turned to the wall. I made mouth noises, then regulated my breathing to mimic going back to sleep, mulling over what should happen next.

We had one more full day of crossing the plains of Tufan in comfort and elegance. I'd keep the mood light. We'd retrieve Marcus from the hard seat car and have breakfast from Mei's stash. *Love that girl. Thinks of everything.* For everyone's amusement I would read the "Train Rules" card. Then we'd cocoon in our cabin all day and I'd go spend the night in a hard seat.

I stretched and turned and made a show of rubbing my eyes, but Elijah had turned his face to the wall. Maybe he'd gone back to sleep, or maybe he was faking too. Mei, quiet as a mouse and already dressed, had made her bed. I whispered in her language, *"Ohayo gozaimasu."*

She whispered back in mine, "Good morning."

The browns and greens of northern Tufan's terraced farms and rustic villages passed the window like a smeared watercolor. Low hills opened up to more lonely plains. I checked my weather clip and made a tea run. Reece heard me stirring and got up.

Elijah sat up looking drained, his eyes swollen and empty.

"Mornin', all," I said, then to Elijah, "Marcus tackled the hard seat car. You want me to go get him? Or since you know where your seat is, you could go. Both of you come back and we'll have breakfast."

No one mentioned last night's crying jag. As Reece set out packaged pastries and fruit cups, Mei said to Elijah, "I think it's okay for all of us to stay in the cabin today. Passengers in the hard seat car will like the empty seat. They'll have more room to rest. Last night I met a steward in the hall and explained that you were a new friend with altitude sickness and that we traded a space with you. When I offered to clean up your vomit, he said okay. Today you are not well." It wasn't an observation but an assignment: play sick.

He climbed down from the bunk, slid open the door, and looked both ways down the hall. He slipped on his shoes. "I'll see. Thanks."

Soon all five of us were sitting together on the girls' bunks and eating breakfast. We'd managed to arrange ourselves so Reece wouldn't be next to Elijah. Mei neither. After the foot-doctoring, she'd kept her distance, not wanting to give Reece a wrong impression. Marcus didn't sit next to Mei, probably so I wouldn't suspect that he liked her. I was the only one with open seating. At such close quarters and with heavy emotions still oozing, we were like five people trying to dance in a closet without any body parts touching. Elijah tucked himself in the corner of Mei's bunk, close to the window and facing the door. I sat next to him, then Mei. Across from her was Reece, then Marcus, looking beat from his night in a hard seat.

No doubt we each had theories about Elijah, but nobody wanted to ask deep questions, especially since the cabin might be bugged. Reece handed Marcus some coffee—his preference—and cheerfully observed, "Like the old days hanging out in the Camp Mudj lodge."

Not wanting nostalgia added to the emotional ooze, I pulled out the laminated card and gave my wrist a snap. "Okay then, campers, here are the rules for the Mudjokivi Express. Pay attention now. First, the tea station rule." I cleared my throat. "'Walk steadily and slowly to the boiled water and pour it not too full as this can be scalding you or the other passengers when the train is shaking and braking to get back to your seat.'"

They grinned.

"Secondly, the pubfic rules: 'Please stand to the pubfic rules. Please not to buy foods from those peddlers along the railway line in case of possible food poisonings.'" In a teacherly way I added, "Are we all clear on the pubfic rules? All righty, on to fire safety. 'In case of fires while the train is in motion don't be scared. After the train is stopped completely, the passengers would be evacuated. Take a wet towel to cover your mouth and noses and run quickly bowing.'" I had their full attention now. "And here's the ever-popular clothes hook rule: 'Please don't hang the heavy articles on the clothes hook for it is easy to break off with its bad endurance.'"

Light hysterics went around the cabin.

Mei seemed glad to lighten the mood. "We have sayings like this in Japan. You Americans call it Japlish. You make fun of us. In Tufan I saw on a menu 'ham and cheese pickpockets' and 'food pizza.' It's funny to me, too."

Reece laughed. "I remember the 'Dly Creaning' sign for Dry Cleaning in Tokyo. The Japanese only make mistakes because everyone tries so hard to speak our language. We're cowards about trying yours! We'd be much, much worse! What are some more, guys? Just for fun, let's think of more."

"Ahem!" I cleared my throat officially. "Not before I deliver the dangerous goods rule: 'Dangerous goods are forbidden on the train. Once anything dangerous goods are found with you or the other passengers, please get to the train staff for help and they would make a handle of them. The train police would hand over the dangerous goods to the security organs in the station. For the sake of safety, they would destroy forthwith on the spot those are necessary.'"

More cackles. Mei's face lit up. "Oh Reece, did you see the sign in the restroom at Jinsha airport when we arrived? It said, 'Deformed Man End Place.'"

Reece pitched forward, laughing. "Deformed Man End Place? What does that even *mean*?!"

"I think it was the restroom for handicapped people," Mei said.

Elijah laughed out loud. He put a foot up on the bunk and hung his arm over his knee, all relaxation and ease. Again for a brief, shining moment we were the Magdeline Five. A lump lodged in my throat, an ache for what used to be. I realized fully again—Elijah and Reece laughing, Marcus sipping coffee, Mei's quiet dignity—that it had been the best. *We* had been the best, the five of us. Time slipped away with the rhythm and rocking of the train.

The problem with living your glory days so young is, what comes afterwards?

The train slowed. Elijah got up quickly, slipped on his shoes, and slid open the cabin door. "We're making a stop. I need to be in my seat."

Early afternoon he came back. We were lying around listening to Reece read Agatha Christie's "The Girl in the Train," a story that my troupe had produced at the Little Theatre. I'd brought a copy along to make travel time pass. Elijah climbed up on my bunk and listened for a while, then fell into another deep sleep.

Keeping it low key, the four of us played cards and took pictures out the window or went out in the hallway to watch the other side of the world go by. Elijah woke after a long nap and we had dinner together in the cabin: cups of soup and canned meat sandwiches. All cozy and friendly. We didn't press him. Small talk came easier now, because it had more purpose. To help Elijah make his way back. Occasionally my heart would swell again. *He's alive! We found him!* Then I'd realize, *It was God, not Elijah nor myself, who'd orchestrated this. Too many loose ends from too far away for me to take credit.* Then I'd catch a hollow expression, a dark look, and I'd settle back into the incongruities: an elegant train through the state of *nanni mo nai*, Edifice tracking, long lost friends, a miles-high tea party, an unhinged cousin.

The landscape changed. I took a few shots of dark clouds over rolling hills, explaining to the others, "See those vertical streaks coming down? That's called virga, rain that doesn't reach the ground. The dryness of the atmosphere dissipates it."

Elijah moved to the window and stared out, concerned.

"What's up?" I asked.

"Is that typical in this region?"

"I'm not sure where we are." I checked my clip. "Northern hill region. Um…says here they sometimes have 'tears of the gods' in this region, snowflakes that disappear before they touch down. Supposed to be auspicious. It follows that virga would occur."

Reece told Elijah, "Rob is studying end-times weather. He calls it escha-meteorology."

He chuckled sourly. "Think you can predict the end of days by the weather?"

"No, not predict. That's not it," I said, my tone defensive, "I'm just studying the current weather in light of—"

"It's been predicted," he cut me off and turned attention to Marcus. "What I said at the temple—*than pa* and *stong pa nyid*—means emptiness and drought. Wasn't I clear?"

Marcus stopped rearranging his wallet. "You put a curse on the whole country?"

"It's already cursed." Elijah stayed at the window and said nary a word until the sun went down.

I stewed in my bunk.

Reece and Mei cheerfully offered to sleep in one bunk so I wouldn't have to endure the hard seat car, but Elijah insisted he was fine and thanked us for the rest and the food. "I may not see you in the morning. But..." he lowered his voice to a whisper, "Kim's."

．　．　．　．　．

Cool as the train ride had been, I was relieved to grab our luggage, de-board, and hail a taxi in an early afternoon downpour. Little did we know that our driver was on his last run of a long shift.

Mei and Reece, in the back seat with Marcus, were talking low like you do in an empty church. In the front and paying little attention to the bridge up ahead which arched high over a muddy river, I was anticipating a stroll in the gardens and a cheap, delicious dinner on the veranda, when I noticed our taxi drifting to the right. There was no curb or guardrail on the bridge approach, just a bank dropping steeply toward the swollen current. I shot a glance at the driver. His eyes were closed, his head bobbing, his hand lax on the wheel. Not wanting to embarrass the guy and not wanting to plunge to a watery grave either, I threw my arm over the back of the seat and yelled to the others the first thing that came to mind: "LONDON SURE IS FOGGY THIS TIME OF YEAR!"

I made "jokes" for the next mile, guffawing and slapping the dashboard to keep ol' sleepy eyes from going beddy-bye merrily down the stream.

Kim's Kozy Tropic Inn. I was never so glad to see a foreign place in my life. No Edifice troops. No ghouls, gods, or other unsavory manifestations. And there was air to breathe. Nice, thick jungle air smack in the center of a smoggy Asian city. Nothing like home, it still felt like home—better, in a way. Here at Kim's there was no work, no schedule, no pressure. A room cheaper than any place I'd ever stayed, interesting strangers from every corner of the globe, and all the time in the world.

As much as I wanted to, I couldn't fly my fiancée over to join us, but I'd sure look into booking for the honeymoon. Not a bunk room, of course. Wouldn't want to carry my bride over the threshold into a room of snoring gypsies. But one of those bungalows half-hidden at the back of the gardens. Little jungle paths. Trickling water. Breakfast on the terrace. Daypacks and maps to new places. Just the ticket—Asia, her homeland. I could afford a month stay here, not a few days in one of those shmancy places in Paris or Hawaii. Sure Jinsha was smoggy and crowded, but from our little fenced-in paradise we could take trains and buses to a hundred cool places. I'd check with the girls at the desk before leaving. Lydia would love it. Asian adventures, just the two of us. My life was okay again, my future bright.

The four of us checked in, got our valuables, freshened up, and met one of our random roomies, a wiry, spectacled guy named Valentin from Germany who was biking to God-knows-where. Another guy was snoring away in a curtained top bunk.

I went out to the open hall window to take a gander at the gardens, and here came Elijah breezing down the hall. He had changed clothes and his long hair was wet. "Where are the others?" he asked nonchalantly, stopping to look out the window with me.

"Getting cleaned up. You got a room?"

"Not yet."

"How'd you get a shower?"

He rested an arm on my shoulder, like old times. "See, you lurk by a door until someone comes out, then pretend like you're fiddling for your key. They always let you in."

I thumbed toward our room. "You coulda just…oh, never mind. Dinner later?"

"Get one of those bamboo rooms off the veranda."

"Sure. Right after I check in with Lydia at the com station."

"Mum's the word," he cautioned me.

"Got it."

But when we five gathered in the bamboo room, he borrowed my sat phone first thing and sent a message. Within a minute it beeped. He read the message, sent another, and handed it back, exhaling as if a load had been lifted.

Well, how about that. Mum's our *word, but not* yours? I made no bones about reading the message and saw two phone numbers which he'd already coded K1 and S1. His message was "Pleiades is bound." The return message said, "Orion is loosed!!!!" Elijah had responded with "GII. IUI."

"Pleiades is bound?" I asked.

"I'll tell you later under a clear night sky. A scientist like yourself…it'll blow your mind."

Elijah and I used to hide in the trees at Camp Mudj and squirt watery glue on the campers who believed they'd been pooped on by birds. They'd squeal; we'd snicker. I saw that same conspiratorial twinkle in his eye now and seized the moment: "It's good to have you back, cuz. For a while there I thought your brain had been infiltrated with alien spores."

"Almost," he said without explanation.

We lit candles in the bamboo room and closed the glass doors after our meals were delivered. Elijah dug in, taking particular pleasure in the first mouthful of salmon fried rice and the first gulp of the house specialty, jasmine tea. If Kim's was a favorite mish stopover, his first meal must have tasted like home cooking.

He said, "The Tufanis have a saying: With tea, one can buy a horse, and when one has a horse, one is free."

"Sounds like small talk," Marcus said with reserve, referring to Elijah's difficulty with light conversation.

Elijah had positioned himself with his face toward the comers and goers on the veranda. The rain diminished to a drizzle, then ended at twilight. The waitress wiped down the seats out there and the number of customers—mostly ragtag trekkers—picked up. The place never entirely emptied, which seemed to keep Elijah on edge. But I'm getting ahead of myself.

My first question to him was, "How'd you find us out there— some Native American tracking method?"

"I intercepted an unsecured radio communiqué as if from Parabolani, posting one last search for me."

I was stunned. "You knew Dom had searched for you?"

"I knew there'd been a search."

And you didn't trust him enough or care about us enough to report in?

He interrupted my thought. "The post gave your travel details, which was against protocol. I didn't trust the source as reliable."

Irritated, Marcus said, "Dad thought you'd been disappeared. You knew that and didn't contact him?"

Thanks, Marcus.

Reece was upset too, for a different reason. "Wait. Someone sent out *our* travel details to Parabolani, and they posted them for the whole world to see?" Her unspoken question: *You mean Greg could have tracked me?*

Elijah went on matter-of-factly, "Your info was bait. I was being baited."

"Baited? By whom?" I asked.

"Wasn't sure. Someone provided your itinerary details for my possible benefit."

"How'd you get the message?"

"I made a radio."

Marcus's eyebrows raised. "Did what?"

"An old World War II trick: razor blade, safety pin, coil of wire…"

Marcus went off like a siren. "Whaaaaa—?"

"It's not reliable, but sometimes you get a signal."

"You didn't have a com device?" I asked in disbelief, hoping it didn't sound like the third degree.

"They all have built-in tracers now. It's back to smoke signals and Pony Express."

I said, "You were reported MIA and presumed dead. We were told…"

He wasn't listening, but was watching a couple take a seat on the veranda. He moved the candle away, casting himself into shadow.

I continued quietly, "Dom reported you as MIA and presumed dead. We thought you'd been eaten by wild dogs."

"Why did you come," he asked me, "if you thought I was dead?"

Awkward silence. "Cairo."

He made a gruff sound of acknowledgment, then continued, "I tracked you—"

"To the monastery."

"Tufani guides will change the tours based on political uprisings and road conditions. I wasn't sure. But when a mystical ritual is scheduled, they make every effort to get tourists there." He let his gaze rest on Reece for a good while. "I spotted you first."

She smiled self-consciously. "The hair."

"Stuck out like a sore thumb."

Mei affirmed Reece. "And you spotted *him*, didn't you?"

"I felt like I was being watched."

"Why didn't you make yourself known, there at the monastery?" Marcus asked him curtly.

"I didn't know why you'd come."

"A final search, man," I stated obviously. "Why else?"

Marcus sniped, "Or Reece was an unwitting pawn in an evil plot to capture you? Come on. When did you know we weren't sent to entrap you?"

"I still don't, exactly." He wasn't joking.

"You don't trust us?" I asked.

He stirred his rice. "I don't trust myself. It's been years…'Brother will betray brother to death'…None of us is immune. We can't be naive."

My jaw dropped. Marcus's eyebrows went up. Reece scowled. Mei waited tolerantly. We'd spent thousands of dollars and risked jobs and left loved ones to track him down. Entrapment?! Well. It did explain his standoffishness.

One hour stretched into two. We ordered more food and made runs to the hot water machines. I can't begin to remember all we talked about, meandering from old times to weird weather to travel nightmares, from nostalgia all warm and cozy to suspicion all edgy and stiff. I tried to think how an Edifice spy would interrogate a person and tried not ask Elijah those types of questions. He could shut down any minute.

It was feeling pretty fake when Reece asked out of the blue, "Where's The Armor of God?"

Elijah did another rare eye lock with her. "I hope you're wearing it."

"I am. We all are. We've all been praying." She glanced uncertainly at me.

Elijah took his good ole time to answer, and again I was irritated. The Armor belonged to all of us, not just him, whether we were spies or not. He had no right—

"Telanoo." he said at last. "It's in Telanoo."

"You're kidding," I said.

"Gilead," Marcus guessed.

"You know the rock."

"The one you almost died under," Marcus added. "Karinna told me."

I exploded at Elijah. "You told Karinna where The Armor is!?"

He shushed me. "Only Dr. Eloise knows. I told Karinna that in the event of my death, she was to tell my old friends a key word: Gilead's Rock. I didn't give your names. She already knew you. Only you would know the rock."

"Steven," Reece said quietly. "He found me." In the embarrassed pause, she blushed. "I…I got it."

A forgotten memory flashed across Elijah's face.

"Thank you," she said.

"It's nothing."

It was approaching ten on that balmy night in our bamboo room off the tiki-lit veranda. We'd taken stabs at old times. I was spent and ready to cut out of the I-am-not a-spy-and-you-can-trust-me marathon. A curtained bunk was calling my name.

Then Marcus uncorked like a bottle. "All right, enough of this! Come on, people, who do you think you're fooling? Wingate!" he barked my name. "You're waiting for Elijah to apologize for making fun of your end-times weather hobby and to fall all over himself in gratitude for this rescue trip you organized." He turned to Mei. "And you, the proper peacekeeper: all politeness and restraint and agreement, as if that solves everything. And brave Reece!" He snapped so sharply that she gasped. A few customers on the veranda turned, but he went right on. "You're just flat out lying. Always the brave one. Living a lie." He turned to Elijah. "And you're still in love with her. People. Time for some honesty."

CHAPTER 25

Better is open rebuke than hidden love.
Faithful are the wounds of a friend.
—Proverbs 27:6

Jaw tight, hand shaking, Marcus managed to pour himself another cup of tea. "I'll start with me. Here it is. I didn't want to come, okay? Backstory. I'm a big disappointment to my parents. My older brother is well established and they expected the same from me. Everyone did. I wanted to go into the military like Dad, but I'd always be Dom's son, you know what I'm saying? He's sort of a legend, and who can compete with that?"

He directed the next comment to Elijah without making eye contact. "And he had you. So I went a total other way. I tried modeling—go ahead and laugh. I did pretty good. Talent agencies love us ethnic mixes. I even did a couple of bit parts in movies. But it got weird. I tried sales and was good at that too, but my heart wasn't in it. Partly I blame you." He was still talking to Elijah, jaw tight. "From the night you tracked those camp counselors into Council Cliffs Park, then survived Gilead in an ice storm…Dad totally respects that. So when you disappeared from Qolo, Dad broke agency rules and a couple of international laws. He issued the statement that you were presumed dead, but I didn't think he believed it. He thought you were invincible. If Dad had died out there trying to find you or been disappeared and his body parts sold on the black market, I'd have cursed you for the rest of my life. It's my issue, I know that. I'll deal with it. All I'm saying, I can't do what you do, stay on the run. It's not normal." He grabbed the back of his neck, kneading the tension with long fingers.

I—for one—felt Marcus's pain. To be upstaged in your own dad's eyes by another guy? Ouch.

Marcus wasn't done. "For a while, I bummed on the beach. Played volleyball, waited for the talent agency to call, hung out with girls. It was cool. It was worthless. I'm working odd jobs now," he said nonchalantly. "To be expendable is good. Part-timing your life, it's good. The security job, I got it on Dad's reputation and clearance. On looks and charm too, but in Los Angeles that and six bucks will get you a cup of coffee. I like my work okay. It's all right." He shrugged out of his confession as if it were an itchy sweater. "Okay, who's next?"

Mei said politely, "You are right, Marcus. I am a peacekeeper. It's our tradition that everyone in the family group should agree before we move ahead. Remember our saying in Japan, 'The nail that sticks up will get hammered down?' No one should stick out and be different. We do what the group wants, not what the individual wants. You Americans are extreme individualists. My politeness, as you call it, is not as false as you think. It's only part of who I am. After finding God, I'm changed. I don't always wait for family agreement."

With as piercing a look as I'd ever seen from Mei, she told him, "I find underground gatherings and help them. One time I posed as a prostitute to save kidnap victims from slavery. I use my status as endangered people group to deliver Bibles in the dangerous places. What you see on the outside is a mask we wear. This is true. The polite Japanese businessman wears a fine suit to work and obeys his boss's every order. This same man flies to Thailand, takes a young girl for the night, and terrorizes her. It is the same man—the company man and the brutal man. Which one is the mask?"

She delicately wiped a shimmer of sweat from her upper lip. "Some women wear masks of weakness, and they are stronger than their husbands. Children obey parents, then commit suicide when they don't get expensive toys they ask for." She looked down at her bowl, then around to us so that we'd know she was addressing us all. "I think you underestimate me." She closed her eyes and made a small, formal bow. "Thank you for the opportunity to be honest."

Ouch again.

The side of Marcus's mouth curved ever so slightly. Alternately deflated and impressed, he gazed at the candle in the center of the table, made a little huff, and sat back, eyebrows raising in resignation. "I stand corrected."

Reece reached a hand towards Mei's arm, but pulled back guiltily. "You're right, Mei. I didn't know…You have so much courage!"

I nodded for Reece to go next. She balked. If she was going to bare her soul, she'd need to muster some nerve, not to mention how Marcus had painted her and Elijah into a corner with his comment.

"My turn," I said. "I got no secrets except for my end-times weather thing, and who the heck cares about it but me? (Not the whole truth, but I wasn't about to unearth the ION Task until I had it figured out.) The scientific community would laugh me to scorn, 2,000-year-old prophecies about future weather anomalies? Ha ha. I'd never get funded. Theoretical research has to be approved by the National Institute, and who in that bunch gives a rip about the Bible anymore." I was rambling. "Never mind."

I addressed Elijah. "I know it's petty, but I would have liked a kudo or two, a simple thanks. You always led the group. For the first time it was me, and leading is not my happy place. I initiated this trip because…because of Cairo, as I said. You were afraid and suspicious. You hinted at an internal affairs thing, so I didn't trust Dom's so-called final word." I added, "Sorry, Marcus," before continuing with my cousin. "It was typical of you to withdraw when you couldn't handle things. Like when you ran away and got trapped in your woods, in Gilead. You survived that, so call me naive, but I couldn't believe you'd gone into some man cave in Tufan and gotten yourself eaten by dogs, that not a trace of you was left. That didn't wash. And remember that day at Devil's Cranium when you nailed ol' Salem between the eyes with your bow and arrow? I kept thinking you'd never go unequipped, that out there you'd have some kind of long-range and short-range weapons."

"I had a crossbow, but it didn't help." Elijah huffed. "Different predator. Our battle is not against flesh and blood."

"Okay." I took deep breath. "If we're getting all this honesty out in the open…I had another reason for coming."

Marcus whispered, "I knew it."

"What do you mean by that?" I asked.

"I got a com from Dad: 'Keep an eye on Wingate.' That's all he said."

"Not surprised," I jabbed back. "Let me finish. A verse in Revelation says that at the end of days when the second angel blows his trumpet, something like a huge mountain, all ablaze, will be thrown in to the sea. A third of the sea will turn into blood, a third of the living creatures in the sea would die. I had just read that statistic in an *Eco-Science Today* article about coral reefs, warning that a third of the sea life could die. A coincidence, these predictions 2,000 years apart? And in the book of Luke, Jesus said there'd be signs in the sun, moon, and stars, and nations would be in anguish and perplexity at the roaring and tossing of the sea. What could cause that? An asteroid? An underwater super-volcano? Then three tsunamis hit, a few years apart. I started looking in the Bible for other weather-related prophesies and was knocked off my feet."

Marcus leaned in. "This is an honesty session, Wingate, not the daily forecast."

"Hear me out, beach-comber. The whole world is watching the sky and the sea. Something may be going down climate-wise, but the models are complex and not always in line with the data. Meteorologists are studying the effects the Qolo mountain range on upper-level currents...but also the effects of newly discovered high-level biological matter—a microbial ecosystem set aloft from deserts in Africa and Asia—which may be affecting not only the weather but world health. It's controversial, sure. But I was primed to go do some research on my own. I'd hoped to get started at Mt. McKinley."

This was all true. I was going to investigate the ION fields, with the upper eco-system study as my cover. "Then you disappeared near Qolo. It came like a sign from God. Go to Qolo. Get the whole story. I was killing two birds with one stone."

Reese asked, "Are you saying...you had me learn those weather terms to actually cover your tracks about some secret research? Were you using me?"

"No! No, Reece. I didn't mean that at all. It was an extra cover. If we were questioned, we had reasons for being in Tufan beyond a tourist reason. I'm just telling him about it."

"But thousands of tourists go every year."

"Just having a Plan A and Plan B. That's all." I forced myself to make eye contact with the cousin right next to me. "What would you have done in Tufan if we hadn't come? Were you going to keep us thinking you were dead? For months or years or forever? I assumed you were a wanted man for breaking protocols. But you breezed through Edifice checkpoints, then disappeared at dinner time, a phantom who left us hanging, over and over. Why? Weeks ago, you could've sent a code message like 'Great Oak' or 'Bloody MacMerrit' or 'Mum's the word'—any secret word from the old days. I would've known it was you. I would have kept quiet. I don't know what's gonna happen with the Mag Five. But one thing I do know—you owe us. Reece, you're next, and I'm not covering for you." Still steaming at Elijah, I blurted, "She'll probably sit here and *not* tell you how her whole life is falling apart. And how she dropped everything and drove by herself all night to meet up with me so we could find Marcus so we could try last-ditch to find—you. She left her baby girl and a husband behind and big problems. Maybe I'm blowing her whole story, but are you even getting that?"

I'd said too much. To derail a possible emotional meltdown between the two of them I inserted, "And Marcus probably has no money. He lives in a dive. And Mei probably used up all her vacation time…"

"Guys…" Elijah began helplessly.

Reece broke in as if to cover for him, a little too eagerly. "Let me talk, while I can. It's my turn. I love Greg. He's my husband and the father of my child. But…he has a girlfriend. I found out a week before coming. It's not the first time. I thought when my surgery worked that things would get better. But he—it's like he resents my freedom now. It took this distance from my situation to see it. He resented my handicap before, he resents my freedom now. That's the only explanation I can think of for his unfaithfulness."

Mei took her hand. I studied my knuckles and glanced at the others. Marcus looked sympathetic. Elijah was stricken.

Reece said, "He would deny that, he *did* deny it. I thought that his love for Olivet or his love for me, or God, would be enough to stop him from doing this—again. I didn't have the courage to tell him where I was going. Like a coward I left a note on the kitchen table at midnight." She heaved a couple of hard, panicked breaths and jumped up to leave. "I can't do this."

Marcus leaned across the table and grabbed her wrist almost violently. "Don't run. Don't." He softened with each word. "Don't run. Reece…sit down…stay with us."

It was then I knew what he'd said to her so fiercely in the breakfast room when she tried to bail and go home. And I understood why. He'd been running, too.

Reece took her seat, struggling to continue. "I didn't want Greg following me. I lied *about* him, I lied *for* him, and I lied *to* him." Once out on the table, her confession seemed as much of a revelation to her as it was to us. Both hands went to her mouth, then raked through her hair at the sides of her head. "What has happened to me? I believe in *truth!*"

Mei said comfortingly, "You had a very hard time. You were trying to keep your marriage together."

Marcus asked if she felt in danger. She said reluctantly, "No. Not until this happened."

We gave her time.

"When you have a child," Reece explained defensively, "you become more careful, but not for yourself. I was afraid of having the operation. What if I died and left her? What if another woman raised Olivet and my own baby girl didn't remember me? What if Greg married someone who wasn't a good mother? Or what if the surgery didn't work and I'd be in a wheelchair? I kept thinking he'd change, that his love for Olivet would be enough. That she'd be happier if everything stayed the same."

She made a motion with her hands like an umpire yelling "Safe!" over home plate. "No one owes anyone an apology or thanks. It was right that we came. We all have our own reasons."

Marcus to Elijah: "Your turn."

Our long-lost leader took his time. "I owe all of you apologies. And I thank you all for coming. He turned to me. "Out there you evaluate things on another scale. Mission is first. Life and comforts have different value. I'm sorry for the consequences of my actions on your lives."

He began his story. "I went down out there. Lost consciousness. Nomads took me in, and I was down for days, until days ran together and time wasn't important. It took a while to get back to a city. I picked up a radio signal and heard about the searches for me. But see, there shouldn't have been a search. It's against policy. And who sent that message out? I didn't know. Did Edifice pick up on the signal that there was a rogue mish on the heights? Had they somehow enlisted your help, using you to get to me, after which we'd all be disposed of?"

I was slightly offended. "We wouldn't cavort with The Edifice."

"Westerners are naive," he stated bluntly. "I didn't know what the nomads might have done to me in those lost days, while I was unconscious. Chants and spells—you don't have to believe in them. They may work simply because you're arrogant and ignorant. The power is very strong, very ancient. No one can know when and how it works. I didn't want you infested by touching me until I got it figured out. I only let Mei touch me because I've kept track of her." He smiled at her. "If anyone was braced against the darkness it was you. The upside of growing up in a pagan culture is, you *get* it about the cosmic danger. You get it."

Mei smiled back. "Tufan is full of his glory, but no one knows that glory, no one praises him. Our ancient shrines and temples—places the five of us have seen—are the same. Full of his beauty, empty of knowing him."

Elijah turned to Marcus, "And you're getting it now, or should

I say it's getting you. There's a darkness in you that wasn't there before."

The smallest turn of Marcus's head conveyed that Elijah had struck a chord.

One of the candles went out. Mei relit it.

"I can't say what I would have done if you hadn't come." He addressed Marcus. "Your dad and me, yeah, we have a bond. But he's not my dad. I'm not his son—you are. I wasn't sure I could trust him, didn't trust anyone but Karinna and Steven, and hardly them. I don't trust myself."

Fear altered his face.

Marcus refilled our cups. The air got tense again. Elijah had put off addressing Reece. The two of them had to know that the three of us were waiting. There was struggle in his demeanor, and a few uncharacteristically nervous gestures: cracking of knuckles, shifting in his seat. He bucked up, took a breath, and said, "Reece." He leaned toward her as if to exclude us, and in a deeply private way said, "Reece. I've known a lot of strong women in my life, but none stronger than you." He paused, swallowed. "I've known pretty women, but none prettier. I've known wise women, but none wiser. Good women, but none better than you."

Her eyes glistened with tears.

He reached across the table and took her hand. "Someone—or something—has been chipping off pieces of your armor. Pieces of you. That's gotta stop. You have to stop it."

She nodded in mute obedience. A look passed between them so gracious and deep it made my heart hurt. Mei bowed her head, Marcus wantonly stared.

Then Elijah sat back, letting go of her hand.

"Okay, people," Marcus moderated, "we're done. Truth's out. Water over the dam." His voice thickened and dropped. "We're still the Mag Five."

We gathered up dishes.

Down on the garden path wet palm leaves dripped, bejeweled by strung lights. A lullaby of trickling water quieted the comings and goings, all balmy, dreamy. Elijah had gone ahead by himself, Marcus trailed behind him, Reece and Mei next, with me bringing up the rear.

Reece left Mei's side and called out to Marcus. He slowed. She caught up with him, wrapped her arm around his waist. He cradled her head against him, and they walked on—our effortlessly cool but humbled Marcus, and fierce, broken little Reece. Not sure who was shoring up whom, or if their mutual weakness—I don't know how this works unless God's in the mix—combined to equal strength. A verse came to mind like a whisper. I murmured it out loud, "When I am weak, then I am strong."

I kept thinking about us in metaphors. We were a tea set in an earthquake, rattled to the very edge of the shelf. The slightest aftershock might just rock one of us over or shake us back into place. We were a cord of five strands, frayed in different places, still holding.

We prepped for bed in our bunks, headlamps glowing through the orange curtains. Valentin had moved on and Elijah's rucksack was piled in his place, under me, across from Reece; Mei above her, Marcus next to her. One by one our lights around Reece went out. I drifted off to sleep, exhausted. Hours of hard truth is like being held under a pounding waterfall. You come out beat up but refreshed. Bruised but better. Maybe this was another reason we'd been drawn back together: to fix what was broken in each of us.

CHAPTER 26

He loads the thick cloud with moisture;
The clouds scatter his lightning.
They turn around and around by his guidance,
To accomplish all that he commands them
On the face of the habitable world.
Whether for correction or for his land or for love,
He causes it to happen.
—Job 37:11-13

How well the others slept I don't know, but I was a log. The gritty feeling I'd had about the ION Task didn't keep me up like I thought it might. I'd process data first chance I got and keep watching to see if Elijah showed worsening signs of mental distress. I still wondered if his brain had been blasted with waves. But it was time to build trust, not throw another wrench in the works.

I messaged Lydia that I'd be home soon, pending another typhoon delay—the worst chain of them since '64. Coffee by myself on the veranda with my Bible, my weather clip, and a manga seemed like a good way to start the day. Later I went downstairs to the lobby, took a left across the carport, another left up the flight of wooden steps to the laundry porch. I bought some detergent from a dispenser, put the coins in the machine and dumped a load in that I grabbed from our open window. It was okay to leave it in the washer or on the line, Mei had said. People steal toilet paper but not your clothes.

Something else I liked about Kim's: you could be alone, but not lonely. The clothes hanging on the line—hiking socks and jeans, little blouses and big flannel shirts—belonged to one big family of global gypsies. *Hello, world. Your boxers are almost dry.*

We of the Mag Five tribe were looser that day, strolling the gardens, watching giant goldfish make figure eights in the pond, drifting off to check on laundry, having devo time alone, chatting with the ragtags of the world who were doing all the same things.

Elijah had planned to tell us a bunch more stuff, I sensed, but had gotten derailed by the honesty session. It was just what we needed, though, and I told Marcus as much when we crossed paths. He was reading in the lobby. I plopped down on the worn couch beside him.

"Thanks. We needed that," I told him.

"We need a few more."

"Maybe. Reece is still pretty fragile. That husband of hers is a piece of work. You're right, though. We're still the Mag Five."

With a curl at the corner of his mouth and a nod to our little patch of jungle, he said, "S'good to be here. I guess we follow his lead about leaving."

"Yeah. Flights out are pretty much all standby, with the storms lined up like the planes on a runway, waiting their turn."

"Where is he, by the way?"

"Where's who? Oh, you mean that barking lunatic from the Temple of Doom?"

He rolled away from me on the couch and doubled up. His shoulders shook, but he didn't make a sound. Didn't want to give me that, I guess. I finished him off with a bit of Shakespearian brogue: "Methinks he ambles about in yon leafy thickets."

He came up for air, wiping a corner of his eye. "We're different than we were, you and me." It was a compliment.

I messed through the magazines on the coffee table. "In a way. But what we are—the potentials for good or bad—have always been there. Like Mei. She was such a nice little wallflower in high school. But when you get to know her, she's a rock. How does a person come to a strange, new culture as a kid—not knowing the language that well—and rise to the top of the class? She's tenacious. All that's surfacing now."

"And look at you," Marcus said. "Scaredy-cat turned storm chaser."

"Acting is scarier than chasing."

"How so?"

"A thousand people aren't watching you screw up when you're chasing tornados."

"But if you screw up on a chase, you die."

"Better than flubbing your lines," I insisted. "Different write-up in the papers, too: 'Tragic Hero Lost in EF-5' or 'Rancid Performance by Local Yokel.' How would *you* want to be immortalized?"

"You're funnier than I remember."

"Well, I always liked how you could do those off-the-cuff running travelogues when we were on the road. So I've been practicing spontaneous humor."

He was flattered but couldn't bring himself to say thanks, remarking instead, "I *thought* your creative genius sounded familiar." He made this gesture—a head-shake and an apologetic shrug. He couldn't help getting the last word in.

"Yep, yep," I conceded. "I was a crashing, insufferable bore before I met you."

We were both grasping at that new thing: not the old Mag Five, but a mending of bonds for whatever lay ahead.

He had a faraway look.

I ventured in. "Speaking of honesty…you like her?"

"Who?"

"Mei."

He ignored me, put his nose back in the magazine.

"Get your act together, buddy," I said, dropping a friendly fist on his knee. "You're a class act, you know. Voted 'Most Likely to Be Spiffy.' You just needed a little fire lit under you."

. . . . . .

I can't say it enough: I loved the floaty pace at Kim's, time gauged more by the need to sleep than sun and moon, more by the movement of weather fronts, and by the opening and closing of the giant gate that kept Kim's Kozy Tropic Inn secure after hours. (Although any thug could stroll in from the street by day and hide in the jungle or in one of a hundred nooks and crannies, could even worm his way into a bunk room like Elijah had, could pull the curtain and lie in wait. Safety and security are relative terms.)

Elijah was conspicuously absent until mid-afternoon when we drifted back together for a communal meal, cautiously more comfortable with each other, if that makes sense. At lease he hadn't slipped away again, our flesh-and-blood revenant with his different personas and a passport for each, no doubt. And with the two names we still hesitated to say out loud.

"Whatcha been doing all day?" I asked in a sing-songy, non-spy kind of tone. "I want to hear more of your story."

He chose a round table at the wide section of veranda over-looking the very back of the property. Strategic. Like at the Diamond Lake Restaurant. If troops or police came storming in he could catapult himself over the fence, I figured, and dash down a back alley. Maybe he'd been checking out escape routes all day. I spotted a palm tree within leaping range for myself, if the need should arise. My plan would be: shimmy down and hide in the darkest corner of the com station under a desk.

It was Florida-style afternoon. We sat under the shade of a big umbrella, perched above a jungle, and in the path of a breeze. We had a teapot and a pitcher of ice water. We spooned samples from each others' plates. The girls looked rested and beautiful, Marcus was mellow, Elijah was with us, and all of us as far from home as we could be. (To be accurate, the exact opposite of Tulsa is about 2,000 miles west of Australia in the Indian Ocean. But who cares.)

I got the small talk going in order to lead to the large talk. "Say cuz, what do you eat out there in the vast unknown?"

"Anything."

Marcus grimaced. "Ewww…"

"Sacred fish if you get desperate. But don't get caught doing that. Just about anything tastes good if it's seasoned with starvation." He changed the subject abruptly. "I was arrogant. I shouldn't have gone alone. The agency was showing less and less resolve for difficult missions. The hatches are closing every day, there was that explosion that killed dozens of the last tribe. And I was tired of hiding."

"Sometimes it is necessary to hide," Mei said, sprinkling fish flakes over her rice, jumping right into the large talk.

"We're getting a rep for being liars," he objected.

I assumed he meant the mishes.

Mei stiffened. "The underground people work regular jobs and speak truly about it. They will say they are believers, if asked. A few have lied because of threat of work camp or prison, but many thousands are new believers. Shouldn't we give them a chance to grow in faith? Do they have to sacrifice their lives so soon? How many of your people in the States are risking their lives?"

Elijah wasn't bothered by her objection, giving her another one of those looks (which I now understood as big brotherly and nothing more, nothing like how he'd looked at Reece.) "Few," he admitted. "I was four or five days into the trek when I came under full attack. I'd ignored the method of going on mission two by two, but others in history have gone alone…."

"Attack?" Reece asked.

"Spiritual."

"How did you know?"

"I sort of felt them—like the flutter of dry wings, wind whispering up from the valleys. I got disoriented, lost. I went down in a stream bed and couldn't move.

I interjected, "I've never known anyone who was *literally* dry-gulched."

"I heard strange noises like the snort of a pig then the hiss of a reptile, a rippling horrible sound." His eyelids drooped for a second, as if he were fighting sleep. "I lost consciousness. Sheepherders found me. They got me back to their camp. I don't remember it. Why they didn't rob me and leave me for mastiffs and vultures, I don't know.

"Maybe you cast seven shadows," Reece offered.

"What?"

"We were here at Kim's before and met a couple who'd heard about a foreign hiker near Qolo. He supposedly cast seven shadows."

I added, "We were excited to hear about a lone *gaijin* living with nomads. On the other hand, these shadow casters are apparently such good luck that they're often—" I made air quotes, "'encouraged to sacrifice themselves,'—like with a nudge over a cliff or a kosh on the head, whereupon they are ground into fairy dust and consumed."

"Holy communion from Hell," Marcus muttered.

Strangely unaffected by Marcus' comment, Elijah said, "They did consider me good luck. They hid me from The Edifice. Most outlanders distrust them, even though the new regime is bringing back the ancient gods." He put his chopsticks down and leaned back, curious. "Seven shadows…"

"Did they give you flowers?" I asked.

Elijah struggled to remember. "I think so…yes."

"Yikes," I said. "They may have been setting you up for sacrifice."

"But *Someone* already sacrificed himself," Marcus added powerfully. "You told them about him, *ne?* No need for new blood."

"I did tell them. But while I was still recovering," he recalled, "they kept me hidden from the shaman who'd threatened death to any believer. He was the reason the area was off-limits to Peregrini. And he was the one at the temple."

Reece's blue eyes went wide. "Wait. Wait a minute. That shaman—the one you yelled at in the temple—was the very one you defied by going into the Qolo Mountains? And the one the nomads hid you from…that was *all the same person?*"

"The very one. What a coincidence, huh? Holy men make rounds at the settlements to rid homes of evil spirits. He knew a stranger was inside the nomads' tent and wanted to come in—but they hid me. They lied to him. I got the idea that they respected his power less when I was with them." He added, as if to himself, "This is starting to make sense. I was walking around in the sunshine…then he got the flowers…"

I was still trying to filter it through my Western brain. "So black magic and human sacrifice really exist on this planet. For real."

Elijah warned me, "No need to look into it any further."

"Okay."

"I mean it."

Mei suggested, "Maybe they saw spiritual things around you. Our Father can use their strange beliefs as a starting point to know him. He uses what they have. It may be a strange work, like in Isaiah 28. What if the nomads saw seven shadows and protected you? I used to believe in many ghosts and demons and gods. My belief about them was wrong, but I knew the spirit world is real. After I saw the Father in your life, I could believe in him, too. In our ancient sacred story, *Kojiki,* there is a creator, but we don't read the old books, so I didn't know about him. It is a hard thing to accept one God who asks me to give up all others. My family cannot believe in him yet."

The ice in my glass melted, the cubes broke and bobbed. A lull in the conversation allowed us time to grasp the sadness Mei lived with every day.

I said, "Lydia's grandparents. Same thing. They can't believe yet."

"My family too," Elijah sympathized. "And Grandma Creek."

I couldn't bear to tell him she'd died a few weeks ago.

He went on. "There was a man who spoke a little English. I had the only Quella in their dialect." His smile widened. "We brought the gospel to the last Tufani clan, and they accepted the book eagerly, which is unheard of."

"How long were you with the tribe?" I asked. "'Cause I've read up on them. Other Tufanis are afraid of them. And why again did you wear their colors?"

"The tribe lives in unforgiving terrain inhabited by malevolent beings. Life is little more than survival, often days from starvation, with no hope after death but absorption into the void."

All of which completely did *not* answer my questions. I wondered if he'd even heard me.

"The void," Reece said with a twinge of concern. "We have a new book at home about that…"

"Any lie can seem true," Elijah said, "if it's all you've ever known. People came down from the heights to the main temple on the Day of Appearances to summon spirits they believe the shamans can control. They were all there…" A haunted gleam came into his eye. "All there. Oh…" Thoughts were firing. "All there…" He chuckled privately, whispering a prayer, "Brilliant. You brought them all down. On one day. So they would see…"

He kept smiling. When someone came around to light the tiki torches, Elijah took no note of it this time, being intent on the story. "We call it superstition, we laugh at their mountain ghouls and toilet demons. But do the shaman's tricks really open doors? Do they see things humans are not supposed to see, kept from us for our own protection? Is it forbidden by Yah because it's useless or because it's dangerous?"

"Or both," Marcus offered.

"Exactly. I was brought down by dark spirits. I didn't think it could happen."

Marcus attempted to diagnose the damage. "And you don't know how deep it goes."

"It goes deep and wide. A total regime change, not just here but everywhere. Not just Edifice, but every authority. Our own friends and families fall into lockstep." His hand flew up as if swatting a fly, that gesture of frustration. "How do good people become part of the regime? They don't believe in resistance."

"*You* resisted," Marcus said, "and they still took you down."

"I confronted," Elijah corrected him. "I examined and re-searched, went in head first. Resisting didn't occur to me. I thought I was immune. I flirted with it."

I was hearing a different level of person than the scrawny cousin I grew up with. The same quiet, introspective camp kid with a good heart, sure. But more—a resolute, burned-out guy who'd gotten in too deep. A guy as in tune with the unseen as the seen.

Elijah shifted the subject. "Okay. About my not trusting

you…I'm not sure I trust myself. Like I said. If an occult curse or blessing—either one—was done over me while I was in and out of consciousness for those days, could it transfer to another person? I don't know. You can't figure the evil one's every specific scheme. He has billions."

Marcus quoted, "It would be supremely naive to think we can one-up the evil one."

I kept feeling that he was running a parallel track on Elijah's conversation, but about his own life.

"It's not personal, this lack of trust," Elijah said, "I'm viewing my *own* thoughts with suspicion, because some of my thoughts are not my own. These parasites lie low and attack when the advantage is theirs."

Mei whispered, "We should intervene for you."

She meant pray.

He kept teaching. "Fallen beings corrupt one's imagination first, then they work on the will. When the mind is invaded, when you open the door yourself…"

Again I wasn't following. "Explain yourself."

"For example, you might imagine things that aren't there, planted in your mind. Like when you watch a scary movie, then think a monster is under your bed. You're fearful. Your behavior changes. You accommodate your will based on false imaginings."

Mei persisted. "We will renounce any curse put upon you."

Elijah resisted. "I don't know that anything was done to me."

"The nomads gave you flowers," I reminded him.

Elijah changed the subject again, obviously processing several streams of thought at once and—just as obviously—feeling safer to confide in us. "That sound that came from the shaman in the temple, it was the sound I heard when I went down in the stream bed."

Reece's eyes went to saucers again. "He was there, too?! The shaman who said to stay out of his region, who knew you were in the nomad's tent—and the one in the temple—he had tracked you down in the mountains, too?!"

"It," Elijah clarified. "It was there. Let's be clear. In the temple I wasn't addressing the shaman. The man is a tool. Oracles don't live long. They're used up by the spirits and cast aside. And they're not always willing vessels, but it's a high calling to have a so-called ancient war god invade your body and shut down your mind and share secrets of the future."

I whispered a reminder, "Not supposed to say the G word…"

Reece asked, "It followed you there? How?"

He said aside to himself, "I don't know…there was a sand fox…on the third or fourth day. The look in his eyes…" He shook it off.

Reece surveyed the sunny, crowded veranda. "Is it safe to intervene here?"

Marcus smiled wryly. "If we make it look like a séance."

She snipped at him. "We don't want to present that as acceptable."

"Right," he relented.

She took my hand and dropped it to her side, took Mei's and did the same. "We keep it like a conversation. Eyes open, smiling." We followed suit around the circle. Reece began, "Father, if there is something here that is not of your kingdom, by the name Y'shuah we say to it, 'You go where he sends you.'"

Elijah stopped her. "Maybe this is not the place."

But Mei continued, saying the forbidden name. "By the blood of Jesus and the word of our testimony, leave."

He was flustered. "What if it manifests?"

"Who is in control?" she scolded. "Who is *present* with us and in us?"

Marcus took over. "Where two or more are gathered you are

here. Send anything bothering Elijah away. Our words don't save. The Word made flesh, he saves."

Elijah whispered worriedly to Mei, "I've seen it happen—manifestations."

"So have I. Didn't *you* open the door?" she gently accused.

It was my turn. I prayed generically, "Send away anything from the dark force."

Elijah gave me a look. Reece snickered.

Marcus muttered, "Oh man…"

I blundered, "Okay, that was a line from a movie. Sorry, God. Oops, I mean Y. Not *why* but *Y*. But you know what I mean." Pathetic prayer. "Okay, Big Guy in the sky, you get my drift. Amen."

While I was ruining the mood, Marcus snuck in a request. "And if I have invited something into my life…I want to get rid of it now, too."

We had another infected patient?

Mei said, "By the name of the one who gave his life, you must leave."

We all whispered, "Leave."

I felt silly. Other customers around us were sharing the usual social inanities against a background of clinking silverware, with occasional laughter from the garden and bar below. At our table, worried expectation as the drone, "Leave, leave," died down.

"Did it work?" I asked my cousin.

"We pray. He hears," he said simply, confidently, so different than a minute ago.

Reece said, "We can ask again."

We finished the meal. He shuddered now and then.

CHAPTER 27

In our country we pray that bad things won't happen to us.
In other countries, they pray for faithfulness.
—DAVE EMPSON

The girls went downstairs to buy cookies. Elijah wandered a wide circle around the different tiers of the veranda at Kim's Kozy, glancing over the rail into the gardens on all sides. Casing the place.

I followed. "You looking for someone?"

He came back and sat down across from Marcus, his back to the rear fence, his face toward the building.

"Is someone looking for you?" I pressed.

"Don't know. Let's go for a walk."

The old, cigarette-smoking Asian man—the one who'd watched the four of us arrive at Kim's that first day—was standing in the doorway of the bamboo room and had caught Elijah's eye. He tapped ashes over the rail toward the garden, his head tipping ever-so-slightly in that direction. *Scout.*

Hurriedly, but without panic, we left our dishes and met the girls on their way up the stairs with the box of cookies. We rerouted down a back stairway, through the kitchen, under the laundry porch, and out the giant doors. Elijah led us around pedestrians and parked bikes, past men at small tables playing mah-jongg.

"You going stir-crazy?" I pried innocently, as if I hadn't seen the clear signal from the old man. I was newly annoyed at the cloak-and-dagger stuff. *Testing our blind obedience, Elijah?*

We turned down a side street lined with skinny trees, a few parked cars, and mom-and-pop shops: soup kitchen, bicycle repair, fresh fruit stand. He paused in front of the bike shop. A guy in jeans and white T-shirt was putting new tires on a rusty bike. We gathered in under a tree and passed around cookies. Elijah took up the story without explaining our sudden exit.

"Let me say one more thing about what happened at the temple—"

"—when you ran off and almost got the rest of us arrested?" Marcus joked acidly.

"I had to get distance between us," he said without apology. "I would have incriminated you. And you would have slowed me down, okay? Now. I'd come to believe that my mission was one of judgment, but what was I supposed to do? The nomads had saved my life and protected me, and they had the Quella to teach them the way. In history, judgment was for a nation in rebellion or as ultimatum to a pagan system, not for new brothers. How could I speak against them? Jonah told the people of Nineveh that it was their last chance, and they repented. Gomorrah had no intention of repenting and was destroyed."

Marcus chipped in, "I see what you're saying. The shepherds were like Ninevites not Gomorrans."

"I didn't speak the language well, only knew a few people. I was stuck. I should have had more prep, I see that now. But in YangDi, at the palace when we walked and prayed, then at the temple, the very seat of black magic, everything changed. You girls probably didn't see the way the monk leered at you."

"I saw," Mei said thinly. "He touched me."

Elijah continued. "In one of their rituals to offer warm flesh and blood to demons, a shaman will use a human thigh bone as a trumpet. The bone of a murdered girl is supposedly the most effective instrument. I've seen a monk measuring a girl's skirt with a cord."

Reece whispered, "Are you serious…?"

I said, "That's why you went ballistic when the monk brushed up against Mei."

Elijah glanced at the bike repair guy, who was making a phone call. They nodded hello to each other. *Another scout. Criminy.*

"You have to understand what I *didn't* know," Elijah said. "So let me back up. I *didn't* know for certain that everyone thought I was dead. I *didn't* know if my triskele had been compromised. But if that was the case, who was behind it, and why? I didn't know. My friend Steven was the last to have it, but he couldn't… he wouldn't have sabotaged it…I didn't think. Anyway, it wasn't working right. And I *didn't* know why the Gampas hid me. Were they wanting my possessions? Was Yah using them to protect me? The agency wouldn't search for me since I'd broken the triskele. But then I heard about that one last search. And I didn't know why."

Reece dug in her bag and handed him the triskele. "Dom searched. He found it."

Elijah turned it in his hand, stunned. "There's no way he could have found it…no way. I broke it."

"You put him in extreme danger," Marcus said bluntly.

"He shouldn't have come," Elijah said, puzzled.

"You shouldn't have gone," Marcus countered.

"I broke it!" Elijah shot back, his hand holding the pendant. "He couldn't have tracked it. This is impossible…."

I told them, "Let it go."

But they didn't let it go. Elijah said, "I broke it to be sure no one would come."

"Obviously you didn't!" Marcus pressed, quickly surveying

our surroundings, because he'd raised his voice.

Mei said evenly, "Please go ahead with the story, boys."

The argument screeched to a halt. *Classy put-down, Aizawa.*

Elijah frowned at the broken pendant, muttering, "Dom was that close." He shoved it in his pocket. "It all came together in the temple, the shaman in trance. And I heard that sound...." He propped himself against the tree and seemed very far away, glancing only briefly at the bike guy. "'Do and do, rule on rule'... the endless rules. 'Do not fear what they fear'...the people's dread of The Edifice, the gruesome rituals and things going on in that isolated place for centuries.... A zombie religion alive again, and no one to give them any hope." He chuckled in an odd way. "You know, I had the Tufani words 'empty' and 'drought' in mind only because the Gampas were reminding my translator about a terrible drought in their history. I had the two words I needed."

"The curse will fall on the people you were there to help, not just the shaman," Marcus stated, though not accusingly.

"I know."

"Why couldn't you gather prayer forces and drive the demons out?"

"They won't leave."

"What about the power of the Holy Spirit?" Marcus pressed.

"Nothing's stopping the Spirit except the apathy of his people. The hatch was closing, and no one wanted to go."

"Innocent people will go hungry," Marcus concluded, still scanning the side street, putting his security guard skills to work, adding skeptically, "If a drought does happen..."

"I know." Elijah looked guiltily at the cookie in his hand. "They're the hardiest people I've ever met, living in the harshest conditions. Most are no different than our ancestors, simple farm folks scratching out a living. But here, under the iron fists of spiritualism and atheism, two principalities rule side-by-side.

And I've made things worse for them."

How a person could love a people who didn't know him, didn't want him on their premises, whose high priests would grind his bones to make their bread…

"You did what you were told," Reece jumped in to divert Elijah's mood which, for good or ill, had become our guiding star.

"There are pockets of believers, closely watched," he said. "If they live out their faith in too obvious a way—for instance, taking in abandoned children or teaching the Word outside the few churches—they'll be arrested for perverting the culture." He huffed in frustration. "Bones of murdered children used for ritual, people living hand-to-mouth, then dying in terror. They don't realize the oppression of their own culture, having nothing from the outside to compare it to."

Lightly I said, "In Magdeline, culture was a junior high band recital, or one of those Shakespearian troops who came to the school and danced around in leotards talking weird. Now that was culture! Hey, anyone want a bottled drink? There's a mom-and-pop pop shop." I had enough change for everyone. We gathered under the tree again, with beverages to wash down the cookies.

Reece said, "What happened in the gap of time between leaving the nomads and us finding each other? You were gone for weeks."

"I stayed with the nomads until I could pull away and hike to the closest city. I had no money, so I…took food…and some souvenirs to sell." Shame-faced, he added, "If an American Dhebu-Gampa grips you by the arm and asks, you give. If he presses you to buy—you buy. I didn't do it for long, a couple days. I was messed up."

Marcus couldn't help pressing his point about the triskele one more time. "Are you sure the triskele quit? Out there in the mountains, you could have been hallucinating. Altitude does that."

I was one second from bringing up the ION Task—despite my resolve to do otherwise—to explain a possible reason for the triskele malfunctioning or Elijah's confusion, or both.

But my cuz needed to get through the story. "On a mountainside above the city I heard a sister from the West singing one of our songs. She's been underground for years. Alone. Under all the radars. Mountain Singer…she kept me."

Marcus raised an eyebrow. "You stayed with her?"

"She offered floorspace to sleep," he explained dryly, "and never asked my name. I'm Light Traveler to her. She's Mountain Singer to me. I did chores for food. I didn't want to use her com to contact the agency or anyone stateside. It could put her in more danger. So I made the radio and picked up the intel about your coming. It was very detailed with dates and time. I was sure I was being baited, drawn out of hiding. Two places you'd be on the itinerary for sure: the dance ceremony and Qolo. People on tours are taken to the holiest pilgrimage sites."

Mei added, "To show tourists the sacred culture, and to earn merit for the tour guides."

"And to fund the religion," Marcus added sourly. "If we tried this kind of thing back in the States, choking off people's choices…"

"What else is there in Tufan but mountains and temples, all homes to the gods? So. I found you, and watched."

"But you were still stuck," Reece clarified, "because you had a vow to fulfill."

"Right. Until we walked the palace together, then went to the temple. Everything blew wide open."

Reece asked, "How did that shaman know you if he'd never seen you? I saw recognition in his eyes."

"Those weren't his eyes."

Mei explained, "It was the spirit inside him."

"Right again," said Elijah. "The pieces fell into place: the shaman's curse on any believer to stay out of his region, the judgment given to me at Qolo to pay it back into their laps and the encouragement from the Spirit, 'Do not fear what they fear.'"

"Here's a problem, though," Marcus said. "Who are the people going to believe—their holy men or the crazed Gampa-styled foreigner defiling their temple? Hard call." The sarcastic tinge to his comment wasn't lost on us.

"Not my job," Elijah answered, then turned to Reece. "I would never have seen the shaman if you hadn't been pushed by the worshipper. We'd have walked right past the shrine room."

She added, "And at Pajuu monastery, if you hadn't spotted me in the crowd, we would have missed each other by seconds."

Marcus nudged her. "See, lady? You came for a reason."

"Mm-hm." She looked frail and tired.

"If the people couldn't understand what you were saying, that *tsav la tsav* thing or the English," Marcus asked Elijah, "what good will it do?"

"I was addressing the spirit…" he corrected himself, "the spirits. They were there in droves. Listen, I'm not sure we should even do that. I don't advise that—addressing a spirit. They're powerful, hateful beings and they'll engage you anyway they can. They'll set you up. There may be a price to pay yet. But the crowd did understand the words for emptiness and drought. And the monks are educated. They know some English. We pray they connect the two: empty skies as a symbol of the emptiness of the shaman's power."

I hesitated to say, but went ahead. "You seemed just a tad possessed yourself, there in the temple, if I may be so bold."

He smiled mysteriously. "I am."

Off my shocked expression he explained, "We all are, aren't we, possessed by the one Spirit? Owned by one who comes only by invitation, gentle as a dove?"

"Oh…never thought of it that way. I'm possessed…okay…"

Mei handed the last cookie to Reece, who offered it to Elijah. He declined, insisted she take it, crumpled the box, and handed it to Marcus, who looked in vain for a trash can. Noticing litter scattered about, he dropped it in the gutter, and in a kind of security guard posture, once more scanned up and down the street. He had a final word on Elijah's story, "The good news for humans is gonna be bad news for ancient war gods."

I asked, "And while we're into the heavy theology, what's this so-called covenant with death you mentioned at the palace?"

Elijah explained, "At the time the book of Isaiah was written, Israel was making agreements with foreign kings they thought would protect them, instead of keeping covenant with God."

Marcus nodded. "A deal with the devil."

"Exactly." Elijah and Marcus shared a fleeting glimpse of their commonalities.

Now, if Marcus can balance his insecurities with his phenomenally cool presence, and if Elijah can find another honcho to replace Dom, we'll be on solid ground.

The bike guy was on the phone for a second. He stood the bike up, tested it, and drove it off for delivery, with one wave back to us.

All clear.

"Anyone need supplies?" Elijah asked. We started back.

Optimism rushed through me and I raised a fist to the heavens. "Though this be madness, yet there is method in it. Cry, 'havoc!' kings. Back to the stain-ed field!"

Marcus gave me an approving wink. "That just about says it, Wingate."

CHAPTER 28

Beyond the horizon, something I long for,
Just beyond the night, something I need.
—Andrea Summer, "Seeker, Finder"

Making a triumphal entry into Jinsha, the wing of small typhoon tore through the palms at Kim's Kozy, swirling their big fronds, throwing a few to the ground. Flights into and out of the city: cancelled. We'd have to layover at the hostel another day. Fine by me.

The bamboo room was creaking in the wind, so we tucked ourselves into an under-the-stairs hippie pad near the upper dining area. We chilled, had tea, relaxed on big pillows and bean bags. We'd aired our dirty laundry, thanks to Marcus. The honesty session had to have been harder for him than anyone, maybe more than Reece. Sad to say, but Marcus was living a loser life right now. I'd always assumed that his massive confidence sprang from his natural coolness. But the bigger the ego to maintain, the bigger the cover-up when things don't go as planned. I guess.

I was making a name for myself as assistant to the head meteorologist in Tulsa, and as a storm chaser of some note. I'd bought a little house in the suburbs and was engaged to a great girl. I occasionally made the papers—the community one, anyway— from my roles in the theatre. But I still admired Marcus Skidmore, not as a part-time beach bum or for his suave sophistication, but for his raw honesty. Elijah, I noticed, was deferring to whatever Marcus wanted, staying in the background and not making eye contact, probably for the same reason I did: to give him space. We all seemed to be on the same level, finally. Except for Mei, of course, who'd been in the driver's seat the whole trip, despite her quiet ways.

Reece still worried me. Away from Tufan's thin air and demon-encrusted architecture she was still fragile. The Mag Five hadn't regained its fancy-free childhood status. Dark, exotic Tufan was miles away, but something of it still hovered in the air, like stale smoke in your clothes. I wasn't going to bring it up, though. Some guy in the dining area half a flight up to our right strummed his guitar. The weather raged, but we were as snug as bugs in rugs.

Elijah was taking it all in when—in the stairwell on our left—came the sound of fast footsteps. Urgent or playful? I couldn't tell. Elijah's back stiffened. He leaned out to listen. Light spilling down from the dining area painted a strip of gold across his otherwise shadowed face. He was a wax figure with a chilly glass eye gleaming with urgency and threat and protection, a mouth half open, ready to grunt an order. Funny how half a face can tell the whole story.

Four kids, rain-drenched and laughing, thundered up the steps toward the dining area.

How often had Elijah disappeared into the woodwork or hidden in the underbrush of some wilderness, one searchlight of an eye peering out from between banana leaves or tent flaps? I was startled when he finally did move. My phone buzzed. He jumped.

I read, "It's from S1 and says, 'We're here.'"

Elijah grabbed it, read the message, ducked out of the nook, and scanned the surroundings. The drenched veranda was empty;

the indoor dining area almost empty, the guitarist practicing his licks, a waitress bringing a tray of silverware up the stairs.

"It's Karinna and Steven." Elijah punched in a message.

No sooner had he sent the message than hurried footfalls could be heard again coming up the stairwell. Karinna, in a jeans jacket, long wet skirt, and hiking boots took one look at Elijah and burst into a big smile, mouthing, "Geo."

Steven came up behind her wearing khakis and navy T-shirt with a plastic poncho wadded in his hand. He went kind of limp and his face collapsed into quivering relief. They approached Elijah calmly, holding back from making a scene, though no one but the guitarist could have seen us. They melted into a group hug, Karinna whispering something into his shoulder, Steven's eyes squeezed shut as Elijah encircled both of them with his arms.

We crawled out of our nook to greet them and watched the reunion that had never happened with us: the smiles and hugs and thanks and all that. *We were the ones who found him,* I brooded. *You guys let him go off and get lost. Why were they invited to our—What am I thinking, resenting Elijah's piddling few friends in the whole world? And as for them stopping him, who's going to stop Elijah Creek once he made up his mind?*

Exchanging introductions with Steven Lockhart where needed, everyone skirted around whether to call the star of the show Elijah or Geo. Steven called him Geo a time or two with a kind of innocent openness. I figured he didn't know Elijah's real name. As we settled back in to our hippie pad and I made a run to the hot water machine, it hit me how history was repeating itself. We, the Magdeline Five, had lived secret lives those years ago: discovering The Armor of God after a twilight break-in at Old Pilgrim Church; hiding the truth about the relic for years. We'd been recruited and trained by the Stallards in the art of spiritual subterfuge. As long as we—seven of us now—hung together, a few secrets between us wouldn't hurt. By the time the tea had steeped, I'd adopted a whole different attitude.

Karinna and Steven told how they'd flown in ahead of the typhoon and were stranded for hours in the airport getting through customs and finding a cab. Reece exchanged a few quiet words with Steven who was glazed over with relief, and starstruck by her for some reason. Karinna and Elijah—or Geo, as we were apparently calling him—sat close and comfortable. Forget the Middle Eastern babe he'd brought along to Cairo. How did Karinna fit into his life? While the others chatted I leaned over to Karinna and apologized for my earlier suspicions. Not that I wasn't still suspicious. But lying around on pillows like a hippie, with guitar licks playing backup to an Asian typhoon had a strangely narcotic effect. "Sorry about the other day, Karinna. I was on pins and needles."

"You had every right to be."

For the next hour the Mag Four took a back seat to Karinna and Steven. They updated Elijah about missions goings-on. They didn't exactly exclude us, but the names of people being fired, recruited, and re-assigned, and new partnerships forming were mostly unfamiliar. Their news annoyed my cousin to no end. He kept shaking his head, especially when Steven said things like, "After you were gone…" and, "With you not there…" Did Elijah really have all that much pull? He was only in his twenties and seven years into the work. *Idol worship's not an exclusive Tufani problem.*

A stranger came through with news to anyone in earshot that the laundry wasn't drying on the covered porch, that gale-force winds were blowing things off the lines. *Hey, world, there go your boxers.* We split up to tend to housekeeping duties while Karinna and Steven got settled in their room. Elijah said we'd meet in one of the bamboo rooms for dinner in a few hours.

Steven volunteered to go early and claim it.

I checked my weather clip and told him, "Hold off until the winds die down, or you might be swimmin' with the koi."

We hung shirts and socks and jeans over the sink and shower rod. We strung up personal items in our bunks, and cranked up the fans. The silky, orange curtains flowed even more, putting the room in constant motion. In a teacherly voice, Elijah said, "Always be ready to go. Know where your essentials are. Rob, keep that weather clip handy. Let us know."

The eye of the storm approached Jinsha with winds upwards of eighty miles per hour, and four inches of rain already, while Tufan—two days' distance by slow train—was bone dry.

We journaled, repacked, took naps, then gathered in the bamboo room as the first swipe of the typhoon passed. A sunny hole opened up in the sky. The other side of the eyewall was due to hit in less than an hour. I took particular pleasure sipping tea there in the eye. Elijah took center stage. We called him Geo.

When we'd been served our meals, he initiated what felt like a secret board meeting. "Certain members of the *Parabolani, Peregrini,* and *Seraphim*—the three branches of the mission network—are wandering from truth. It started with a shift in worldview from some of the leaders. I wouldn't have been aware myself if I hadn't been doing the backstory on Lotus. I brought it up and was dismissed by a staff theologian as 'uninformed.' A couple of them painted me as unstable. Maybe I was. But some of our most respected leaders are buying the lie. We've been warned, haven't we, that a day would come when many followers could fall away?"

No one answered.

"This stuff is hard to grasp…" he paused a long time. "Someday soon, I believe, when an army of empty warriors"—he tapped his head—"has been programmed, the systematic annihilation of the seed of Abraham will escalate. This comes from both Christian and occult sources. Both sides are aware of the plan."

Marcus sat up. "Seed of Abraham?"

"All people who believe in one God. They're the target."

Marcus was perplexed. "All the seed of Abraham? That would be…three belief systems, not just ours."

"Looks that way, from occult sources."

"What are we supposed to do?" Reece asked him.

"Get as many into the target group as soon as possible."

"The group to be set up for annihilation," I said grimly.

"Exactly. Review Revelation."

Chills went through me.

"Whoa…" Marcus sat back. "You're saying it's happening?"

"It's always happening, but not on such a grand scale."

I asked, "Why would people become 'empty' warriors? What's that mean? How's that happen?"

"Altered states. Deliberate rejection of truth. The first causes the second and vice versa," Elijah answered almost casually. He spoke of the war in Asia in the last century when soldiers trained in dark zen invaded and ravaged 100,000 people in one fell swoop.

Mei backed him up, shame-facedly. "My people did this. It is the power of *muga-mushin*. No self and no mind."

Elijah explained. "Meditation training until there is no concept of self, not one hair's breadth of personal will between the leader's command and the soldier's deed. Delivering the wishes of the leader with no assessment of them." Elijah always said he wasn't a man of words, but he was doing a pretty fine job. Reece, pale and preoccupied, didn't appear to be getting any of it.

I didn't like keeping my secrets from the others. But the enormity of those secrets did connect to Elijah's dilemma. And the ION Task was hard to grasp, too. What my cousin viewed in spiritual terms I was seeing in atmospheric ones. An increasingly hostile, global plot. Mine was, "He Who Controls the Weather Controls the World." His was, "He Who Controls the Minds of Men Controls the World." Control of minds and weather meant control of...everything. Food supplies, homes, families—everything.

What if—I sat listening with one ear—what if those plots were two wings of the same creature? The same end game? What other wings might be sprouting? I lost the conversation entirely to compile a list of potentials: control the weather, control people's minds...their food, property. Water supplies and health care in times of war and disaster. Air quality. Education. And *ba-da-bing,* control the *information* about all those things so that no one knows what's happening until it's too late. News media. My field.

A few years back I had asked myself, *Doesn't God control the weather? Sure. He can. But if we mess it up, would he fix it? Not forever.* Somewhere in Revelation 11 I'd read that his wrath would come to destroy the destroyers of the earth. I'd found that verse at the time the ION Task caught my attention, which was around the time of the third tsunami along the Pacific Rim, now called the Great Third. More were expected, coastlines sinking, sea beds rumbling.

"You're wrong!" Reece's agitated voice shook my thoughts back to the present. Mei was frowning with concern, Marcus's expression one of surprise and amusement, Karinna was tight-lipped, Steven stunned.

"I'm tired of it!" Elijah actually snapped at Reece.

I was embarrassed to ask for a catch-up.

He quoted a verse, "For whoever is ashamed of me and of my words, of him will the Son of Man be ashamed when he comes in his glory and the glory of the Father and of the holy angels.' The hatch is closing on these last opportunities. The agency is backing down. No one would have gone with me but Steven." He smiled at Karinna. "And you perhaps."

"Not me!" she said with a laugh. "I thought it was foolish and irresponsible. But I didn't want your last memory of me to be standing outside the tent calling you an idiot. Were you successful?" she asked, then aside, "We may never know in this life."

"I was," he said firmly. Then to Reece who was sitting right across from him, "You're wrong."

"No, I'm not!" she shot back. "Look at what *he* did." she pointed up. "When he was on earth, he kept *his* work and *his* real identity a secret at first. He spoke in parables and riddles that his closest friends couldn't decipher. Those riddles pushed people to think for themselves, until he explained himself later. You weren't doing what he did. He gathered leaders and trained them. He didn't go off—"

The subject, I deduced, was secret missions.

Elijah opened his mouth to object, but she cut him off.

"He built a reputation, he built a team!"

Elijah flinched ever so slightly. It hit me. He'd lost a team member before. Maybe he didn't want to risk another life, other than his own. Maybe he didn't want a team.

Reece was on a roll, still pointing upward, "He proved his message with miracles. They knew he had authority and kindness and miracles. But they didn't know his true identity at first."

Karinna sided with Reece. "Geo, going to more countries right now isn't—"

His voice lowered to a wheeze. "Call them what they are: police states."

Reece pressed on. "And *he* spoke openly little by little. He had an objective and planned it out and accomplished it. Even then he was eventually killed."

"Did I not follow the pattern set before us—all of us—to go

and teach?"

Marcus jumped in. "It's like you're trying to make the rest of us feel like slugs because we can't pull up roots and live out of a rucksack."

"When did I say anything like that?" Elijah asked.

Karinna stepped in. "I don't think he's intending that, Marcus. He didn't make *us* feel guilty for not going."

"You wouldn't let me! I wanted to!" Steven said.

Karinna went on. "Some go to new places as teachers or farmers or doctors to help improve lives for a greater purpose down the road. They are our *seraphs*, the burning ones.' They stay and take the heat." She smiled sympathetically at Reece. "Sometimes it's hardest to stay put."

Reece addressed her coolly. "I understand that. But to go out into hostile territory all alone is suicide." She practically glared at Elijah. "You're not him, you know. You're not supposed to take on the whole world by yourself."

His eyes blazed at her for a moment, then fell. Shaken or angry, with only enough wind left in him for one last defense, his jaw clenched. "I wasn't doing that."

Steven said gently, "Don't go there, Geo. It's not the same, not at all."

Karinna patted the table firmly. "He's right. It's not the same thing. It's not coming from the same place."

Steven said supportively, "Some work fast, others slow, some go, some stay. It's all good, isn't it? We're here, aren't we? We all made it."

Marcus said, "Amen, Stephano. Amen."

Reece persisted but with less steam, seeing she'd touched a tender nerve. "From the beginning they were sent out two by two. You went alone."

Elijah wasn't giving up either. "Hudson Taylor went alone.

Gladys Aylward went alone. And pioneers like Rjinhart, Loftis, Dittemore."

Karinna corrected him, "Not exactly the same. They had people on site to meet them, or people back home sending them."

Both girls were stealing his thunder at the moment, but Reece's comments obviously stung the most. He'd made a mistake which cost us a ton in grief and airfare. Maybe he was just now realizing it.

Marcus' hands went out airily to Elijah. "Don't beat yourself up, bro. You sealed the deal. Got in and got out in one piece. Mission accomplished, *ne*. We got a great vacation out of it. Never thought I'd see Qolo in person. But most importantly"— he gently shook Reece's shoulder—"You woke the lady up. The fight's back in her."

Elijah frowned at his plate good-naturedly. "She started it."

Reece relaxed, smiled. "Did not."

"Did too."

"Did not."

Marcus had a way—I was to realize more and more—to say the vaguest or most obtuse thing, and it becoming a tripwire to open up people's relationships. It was a gift.

To everyone's total shock, Elijah reached across the table and took Reece's hands in his. "You're right. You win." She blushed and shook her head and started to object. He tightened the grip on her hands, and with another drilling gaze whispered, "You. Win. That's an order."

We went back to eating. At the first opportunity Karinna said quietly to Elijah, "Two people can say the identical thing and it mean something entirely different. It's all about motive."

He kept digging into his rice. My guess: Reece's comment must have touched the same nerve as that chick in Cairo.

Our pretty blond friend suddenly dropped her chopsticks.

"The drought. Okay. Yes! I see now. When a drought comes, what happens?"

Elijah glumly stated the obvious. "Crops fail. Animals and people starve."

"And what will the people do?"

He shrugged. "They have to sell what they can, try to get work."

"Where?"

"In the cities."

"Right. And where are the mountain singers and the good news bringers?

He locked eyes with her. "In…the cities."

Reece beamed. "Do you see? They'll come down from the mountains and they'll hear. Nothing else would bring them into the cities. Except that holy day. What you did was a shocking way to get their attention."

Steven asked, "What are you talking about?"

I quickly summed up Elijah's crazy-man exhibition in the House of Mysteries.

Steven grinned. "Way to break all the rules, Geo. But she's right. Drought. A severe sort of mercy, but a mercy nonetheless." He added in a tone of awe, "You…pronounced a curse?"

"It all makes perfect sense!" exclaimed Reece. "And with the improvements The Edifice has made—roads and trains and airports—people can get in. And out. They tried to control the people, but actually opened the door! Now people from the outside can settle in those cities and bring the good news and do underground work, like Mei does!"

"Yes they can," Elijah agreed. "But it must be done first *in secret*."

Marcus commented, "He gotcha, Reece."

She didn't seem to mind.

I said to Karinna and Steven, "YangDi will be talking about

it for weeks, how a grumpy Gampa *gaijin* disturbed the peace in the House of Mysteries. How he spun the wheel backwards and called down drought and shouted down that possessed shaman-demon guy and suffered no ill effects. Hey," I addressed Elijah, "you know, if you could show yourself to the people at some point, so they could see that you're okay—"

"He can't go back," Reece said protectively.

"Agreed," said Karinna, equally protective.

Mei had been stone-silent to this point. The clear eye of the storm passed and the wind resumed, but we stayed put, as if our good friendship vibes could keep walls in place. She said to Elijah, "His strange work. Isaiah 28 tells about it. Because you gave them the Quella, people will hear in the mountain villages. A few will come down talking about it. This will be unusual. News usually comes from the city and moves up into the mountains. Our Father used their own strange belief about a man casting seven shadows to show them the truth. He works with what they have. When we pray, he will honor our prayers for them. The Lord will rise up to do his strange deed, his alien work."

That night, strolling the rain-soaked gardens along thatch-roofed pathways, I ruminated over Karinna and Steven. Were we moving forward together as the Mag Seven? Was Elijah coming home or going back with them, or into hiding? I caught him coming down from the laundry porch, wringing the typhoon out of a pair of socks he'd forgotten. "Why didn't you tell Steven your real name?" I asked.

"I did tell him. I just didn't tell anyone that I did."

"Why not?"

"You know how long I lied to him? Two years. I didn't want to…not in front of everyone."

So, dinner conversation had been laced with subtle deception. Steven knew Elijah was Elijah, but kept calling him Geo so we'd think he didn't know.

Later still, I found him sitting on a park bench under dripping palms, his face raised to the rain.

"What now?" I asked simply.

Elijah had one of those thousand mile stares. "No idea."

"You going home?"

"Not sure."

"You have to tell them you're alive. Your dad's crushed, your mom's a mess."

"As soon as possible," he whispered resignedly. "I can't call. They might not handle it, they might tell…I have to talk to them in person." One hand wrung the other, a short, conflicted gesture. "They'll be angry."

"Well," said a voice behind, "you could proceed with your life of loneliness, isolation, guilt, and misery." Marcus came around the path and took a seat on the rock opposite us. "You're in a whale of a fix, Geo Telanoo."

Clear-faced, Elijah agreed.

Knees spread, elbows resting on his thighs, Marcus asked, "You got something going with Karinna?"

"Friends."

I said to Marcus, "You're sure not wasting any time."

"How much time do we have?" he asked cryptically.

Elijah nodded toward the big entry gate, open to the street. "She went out to get some bottled water. To the right. Half a block. Gate closes at eleven. If you get locked out…" he grinned, "she can take care of you."

Marcus stood.

"And don't be scared," I told him sing-songily, quoting the Train Rules. "'Cover your mouth and noses and run quickly bowing. And please stand to the pubfic rules.'"

So Elijah had granted a go-ahead for Marcus to make a move

on Karinna, who was possibly more approachable than Mei at this point. Elijah's deference to Marcus shifted. My cousin was again the unquestioned alpha. Marcus fell in line, asking permission to approach the available female. Two more had joined the pack: Steven and Karinna.

I was a year older than Elijah, and smarter book-wise. But he was tall and had mystique. And he hardly ever panicked. Maybe the reason I chase storms and take roles in Little Theatre is to learn the things that come naturally to him. Holmes and Watson.

Marcus left for the street. Elijah wandered the path. I made my way to the com stations. It sunk in how hugely important this trip had been for everyone. Pride swept over me…until I realized again that the hand of the Almighty—not my own—had moved us four across the waters for this hunt. He'd used my love for my cousin and the Mag Five, and my dicey curiosity about the ION Task. But even those two powerful forces weren't enough to have pushed me to attempt what *Parabolani* had failed to do. Even these new revelations about our relationships might never have shown up if the storm hadn't forced us to lay low at Kim's, the perfect place to kick back and think new thoughts.

That night I prayed out of the blue a prayer that would *never* have occurred to my natural mind: that the Tufani shamans would turn to God and become evangelists.

CHAPTER 29

He holds the lightnings fast in chains, though all creation reel;
And those whom He will deign to keep
May lay them down in peace to sleep.
—James Edmeston, "The Thunderstorm"

The typhoon had made a strange, right-angled turn and stalled,
not unlike deadly Hurricane Xavier a few years back. The city
of Jinsha was wedged between a deluge on the plains and wind-
sheers in the highlands. Kim's was overbooked, so Steven and
Karinna offered to bow out and stay with friends across town.
The Mag Five slept in and took turns going to the com center,
which was especially crowded, with everybody having to change
their flights. We needed to contact our workplaces and families
so they wouldn't worry. Reece went last.

I was on my top bunk listening to the pounding torrent above
our heads, with Mei and Elijah on their bunks and Marcus at
the little table gazing out the one window, which was open but
protected from the weather by the laundry porch roof. Reece
came back to the room, her back stiff, her face ashen, and went
right to her bunk, closing the orange curtains around her. Writing
in her journal on the top bunk, Mei didn't notice. I caught her
eye and nodded to the bunk below her, shook my head, frowned,
pointed—every gesture I knew to signal her that something
was afoot.

She hung over the bunk, "*Daijobu?*"

A small, choked whisper said, "No."

Mei was down the ladder in a heartbeat. They talked behind closed curtains, drowned out by the racket of rain on the fiberglass laundry roof until "It's not true!" rang out.

Mei opened the curtain to fill us in. Long story short: according to Reece's mom, Greg had hired a lawyer to get custody of Olivet on abandonment charges. He claimed that Reece had disappeared without a word.

"I left a note!" she seethed, her cheeks purple with rage, her eyes flashing and panicked. "He knew I was coming back! Mom knew I was coming back."

With studied expression and an elbow resting on the table, Marcus asked, "Did anyone else see the note?"

Reece faltered. "Well, no. I left it where he'd find it, on the dining room table."

"There you go," he said. "Your word against his. He could say you tricked your Mom so she'd take the kid, then left him high and dry. Always have a witness, Reece. Did you tell him—verbally—that you were leaving?"

"No, I just left the note."

"Then technically he's telling the truth. You left 'without a word', get it? Without a spoken word? In his warped mind that makes sense, and he nails you on a technicality. Oh, he's a slick one."

Elijah, in the bottom bunk across from hers, was staring at the roof of his bed, his hands under his head, foot propped on his knee, saying nary a word.

"We'll be home soon," I reassured her. "You'll get it straightened out."

Mei motioned us to join her. "Let's pray."

We five crammed into Reece's bunk, complaining

good-naturedly as we wedged ourselves into the space. Anyone could sit next to anyone now.

"Thanks, guys," she said brokenly.

"Mei, you start," I suggested.

There ensued a deep, quiet, fearless time in which we pretty much called down fire on anyone who'd keep Reece from her baby girl, but with blessings that the marriage would find a way to heal, because God made families to stick together. It was awkward and intense. We were safe from the outside world, drowned out by the fans, hidden by waves of orange silk.

We said our amens and opened our eyes—all but Elijah whose eyes were already open, his hand pulling back the curtain a few inches. The curtain on the other side of his bunk, near the door, was moving differently, as if from a puff of breeze. The door had been opened. A huge, shadowy shape quivered on the curtain. Someone had crept in during our prayer, cat-quiet, and was standing not ten feet away, listening in.

Moving like a curl of smoke, Elijah left Reece's bunk, eyes fixed on the shadow. He slipped his hand under his pillow, pulled out a mean-looking knife, and padded around the end of his bunk, coming face to face with the shape, shifting against the light of the window. Elijah's silhouette spoke: "Boo hag."

A deep rumble of a chuckle came from the shadow.

I looked at Marcus in disbelief. "Your dad?"

Dom came around the corner of the bunk, as big and dark as his shadow. He grabbed Elijah in a fierce hug. Even in khakis and oxford shirt, he oozed military training, all posture and muscles and composed expression while his eyes ranged the room, assessing the situation, resting finally on his son.

Marcus climbed out of the bunk. Dom let go of Elijah and wrapped his son in a deep embrace. The rest of us took turns hugging Dom without saying much. I was wondering, though, what the blazes he was here for and how he got through the typhoon with all flights grounded.

"Let's talk," he commanded.

There was no good place. The terrace and gardens were drenched, the downstairs bar and lobby packed. The closest restaurant was blocks away. We pulled the one table and three chairs between our bunks. Mei sat with Reece on her bed, I sat on Elijah's bunk, with Dom and Marcus and Elijah at the table. I didn't know what to expect: a storm of correction, a big whopping thanks, an explanation of his visit, or a one-man firing squad. I reminded myself to please stop thinking such thoughts.

"How is everyone?" he rumbled above the rain.

I answered for all, "We're good. How's the weather?"

His large, dark eyes twinkled at me knowingly. "The trains are still running, Wingate."

It was like he'd read my mind, like he'd already pegged me as the suspicious one trying to figure how he made it through what we in the West call a Category One.

After a few pleasantries, his focus drilled in on Elijah. "You did it."

"I did," Elijah said simply.

"You're in big trouble," he said pleasantly.

"I know," Elijah replied, as pleasantly.

Another long pause. Dom made a few slight movements— adjusting his foot, moving his hand a quarter inch on the table. Something unsavory was coming next. At long last he came out with it. "I apologize."

"For what?"

"I threw you in too soon. I thought you were ready, and you weren't."

Elijah looked hurt.

His superior said, "You *don't* go alone."

"*You* did." Whether he was referring to Dom's solo search for him, or some other secret mission was impossible to tell.

"I'm experienced."

Elijah defended himself. "I was *there*." Meaning Dom wasn't there, no one was there to take the message to the Dhebu-Gampas.

"Results?" he asked officially.

"They have the Quella. One believed the message, I think. They trusted me and protected me—for no reason."

Dom whispered a guffaw. "Oh there was a reason." Then his countenance changed, his mouth tightened. With the speed of a martial artist he punched Elijah in the shoulder. "You don't go alone! Do you know why? Not because you might die out there. Because you can be taken. Taken!" He violently tapped all ten fingers to his temples. "Not talking about Edifice or Gampas or scavengers. It takes your mind, kid! You know that! We had you in mental overhaul once already."

Elijah's face flamed, embarrassed, affronted.

Dom wasn't done. "You 'bout gave Dr. Stallard a coronary."

"The hatch is closing, sir."

"We don't *know* that." He stuck a mean finger heavenward. "We're not the one *in charge*! And he says two-by-two! Even Our Man on the Right Hand didn't go into the desert alone. He had the Spirit."

"I have the Spirit," Elijah said.

Dom continued, perturbed but with a whiff of restraint. "The situation is not static. Borders are shifting. Nomads are moving. It could improve at any moment."

"Or slam shut."

"It was a bad plan, Creek. You couldn't return to base camp. Your team—your only cover—had bugged out. Your permits were shaky, but you wouldn't wait for the red tape to clear. You had no solid proof the tribe ahead would be there, or anywhere.

You were walking toward oblivion."

"We had intelligence that they were—"

Dom cut him off. "And you know where that intel came from?"

"The agency…" he said tentatively.

"Who in the agency?"

Elijah didn't know.

This dressing down in front of us, what was the point, other than to humiliate Elijah?

My cousin cowered, but only slightly. "You mean someone in the agency gave me faulty info, hoping I'd go out on my own?"

Dom let Elijah stew over those implications.

"Did Edifice track me?"

"No one tracked you. Because I disabled your instrument." Dead silence. "Suzanne reported you as rogue. I disabled your instrument."

Deader silence still.

Dom cocked his head then thrust it forward, chuckling. "She didn't know I could do that. Neither did you. Now you know. She doesn't. Secret's out to the one who needs to hear it." He tapped Elijah on the chest with a big blunt index finger. "I can control your instrument remotely." He sat back, satisfied.

"Who else can do that?" Elijah asked.

"Nobody."

I knew what Elijah was thinking. Had Dom gotten him lost on purpose for going rogue?

"Who knows you can do that?" Elijah asked.

"Nobody."

"Then *you're* acting alone."

Touché! I thought. Not that I was rooting for one side or the other. We're all on the same team. But my cousin was pretty beat up from whatever he went through, and Dom is just scary, and I was sympathetic.

The unflappable top gun of the Parabolani explained, "I was protecting you. I enabled your triskele a few minutes each day to chart your trajectory, but not long enough for you to be tracked. When it no longer moved, that worried me. I gave it a couple days in case you'd dropped it accidentally or was holed up in a cave. I was sweating bullets, boy, praying like nobody's business. When there was no movement, I traced it to the dry creek, stripped the info. Best I could do. I made it look like a scene, just in case—had a T-shirt with your DNA, left it there in shreds and prayed for rain so it would look like you'd been eaten, and the blood had washed away. It was weak, but my only option. I'd brought some Tufani urine from a toilet to confuse the scene, in case The Edifice brought in their CSI."

Grappling with this scenario, Elijah restated what he'd obviously been told many a time, "Once broken, the triskele is inactivated."

Dom shrugged. "So?"

"That's what we're taught."

"I know."

"You've been lying to the teams?"

Dom leaned in, as if to share a secret. Unconsciously, we all leaned in. "Listen," he whispered. "We gotta beat 'em at their own game. Got that? They try to track you. We turn you off. Understand?"

I whispered, "Who's 'they'?"

"Who indeed," Dom answered.

Dom asked Elijah, "I assumed you wanted to be found?"

Reece interrupted, "No he didn't. He broke his triskele."

Dom said, "Incorrect. I broke the triskele."

Elijah shook his head. "No. I did. I got sick, couldn't breathe… thought I was dying…"

"I found it intact, broke it, and returned saying I'd found it broken."

Off Elijah's dumbfounded expression, Dom added, "How did you think I found it out there in that monstrous solitude?"

Elijah strained to think back. "I had it in my hand, to break it…"

"I know you would have taken your last strength to secure the scene. But you obviously didn't. It was an active signal and it didn't move. Bad sign. Often means you took a bullet."

Marcus said to his father, "But you told me–"

"I know what I told you—that he disappeared, that I risked my life and went blindly searching. I know what I said."

"My brain hurts," I muttered to myself. And why was Dom sharing deep intel with us?

"Let's review," Dom said instructively to me, then turned back to Elijah. "One, you went solo. Two, Suzanne ratted. Three, I told the agency that I'd track you. Four, I turned your instrument off and on, hoping you'd not be traced by any other agent or The Edifice. Five, I also activated a new echo feature, testing it, not sure if it was working, because my rogue here"—he gestured to Elijah—"had no knowledge of said new feature. To further complicate the event, there seemed to be some additional interference. Six, your homer stopped moving. You thought you broke it, but you didn't. I gave you some days. When you didn't return, I kept activating it a few seconds at a time until I reached it. The Edifice is stealing our new technology hand over fist. If they had picked up a stationary signal, they'd have had the device *and* our man. That would be the end. But. If such had been the case—if they had our man—the thing would have kept moving. They'd have taken it back to their headquarters. I could have tracked you there. Seven, I concluded that a) either your carcass was dragged off for God-knows-what purpose, with only the active triskele left behind, which made little sense or," he concluded in a really unfriendly tone, "b) you dumped the triskele deliberately to throw me off your trail. But if that were the case, if you were throwing me off, why not just break it?"

Worriedly Elijah said, "Honest, I went down, thought I was dying, thought I broke it. My compass malfunctioned, too."

"Not my doing." Dom said. "You have it on you?"

He retrieved it from his pocket. Dom popped the back off, said, "It's clean. I don't know why it quit working. Hells bells, what are they doing up there in those tractless, terrible mountains?"

Messed-up atmospheric disturbances? I thought. *Should I say anything?*

Dom was still talking. "I gave you the few weeks you wanted. If you were alive—which I assumed—I didn't want to compromise your situation, since there was no trace of your body."

"So you did think he was alive," Reece stated.

"I didn't know."

"But you thought he'd been kidnapped?" I asked.

"Didn't fit. I already explained that. If the Gampas had him…" Dom shook his head gloomily at me. His persistent, steely glare scared me less than it might have five minutes before. "Recall, Wingate. I tried to dissuade you from going to Tufan. It would be dangerous for you, and perhaps unnecessary. Our Mr. Creek might have disappeared himself deliberately. When you insisted on going as a group, I dispersed your travel plans within the agency. If Elijah was viable and getting updates," Dom turned to Elijah, derailing the conversation again. "You haven't reported in—" He punched Elijah in the shoulder once more. Reece flinched, Mei didn't.

It was then I noticed Mei's undisturbed calm. A lightbulb went on. Was this confrontation as much a training session as it was a reprimand for the rogue missionary? Was Elijah even playing along as the fall guy, so we'd get Lesson One of whatever they had planned for us? Whatever the current situation, Mei had been through a lot with her underground church and rescue missions, and wasn't easily fazed.

Almost apologetically, Dom said, "I delayed the news release as long as I could, Creek. I kept thinking you'd show yourself. We don't keep news of an MIA to ourselves for weeks. Families go ballistic, and rightly so. Another bad spot you put me in. We have protocols for a reason."

I joked lightly, "He never could color inside the lines when we were kids, either." That one floated like a lead balloon.

Dom said to us all, "You'll like this new tracking device—that echo feature we're testing. It says you're not there but you really are. Or it says you're here, but you're over there." He pointed behind him out the window. "I'm here, but my signal can emanate from a mile that way. We send out an echo, we shut 'em down and boot 'em back up in another location." Dom grinned. "Operation Lambchop." He waited for acknowledgement, as if we'd understand. He coached, "The puppet…Lambchop? Shari Lewis, the ventriloquist? Old TV show? Okay. Before your time. Forget it. This is new, it's prototypical, and we're managing it carefully."

"Who's we?" Elijah asked. "A minute ago you said it was only you."

"Let's clear this up. It's two-by-two, as the Man says. I went to find you, believing you were possibly alive. One-plus-one out there would have been two, me and you. I counted on it." He sat back. "There are more of us now."

"Yeah, yeah," I inserted myself into the conversation again, "and you could tell me who they were, but then I'd have to kill myself…that's how it goes, right?" It did occur to me to ask why he was sharing all this classified info with us. A shifting of loyalties? Testing the waters for a new team? Fact was, though, I didn't know if any of this was true.

He punched my shoulder, too, but it was a gentler, friendlier punch than when he'd popped Elijah, who for sure was going to have a bruise. Dom shook his head at Elijah. "We can't have a man sending signals and showing up miles apart within seconds. They'd catch on. You came close to screwing up a decade of work on this technology. The skin of our teeth, boy."

This conversation was half over my head, but Elijah's wheels were spinning. "Did it work, the echo?"

"Not sure."

Elijah asked Dom almost shyly, "I...was your prototype?"

"That was the plan, especially since you run like a jack rabbit. Quick getaways. But we weren't ready. And neither were you."

Several strands of conversation were left hanging for the moment. Dom changed the subject. "You caused a stir at the temple."

Elijah nodded. "How'd you know?"

"We had people in town that day. You are never to affront the culture or those in control. Another protocol shot to pieces."

Elijah asked, "How do you confront a demon without upsetting its host, and the culture it controls?"

Dom answered, "That's a high-level question."

Reece mentioned kindly, "Remember the Gadarene? When Jesus sent the demon away, the whole town got mad and told him to never come back."

Cautiously I agreed. "Can't argue with biblical precedent, I guess..."

Dom turned to me. "How's the weather on Qolo?

"Cold."

"In YangDi?"

"Dry." I followed suit with Elijah. If my cousin wanted to defend his disappearing or calling down curses on evil-eyed temple shamans—or if he didn't—that was his business. And weather was my business.

I was still considering whether or not Dom could control a triskele from a thousand miles away when he said to me, "You know what makes easy tracking? When you carry a sophisticated suite of instruments"—he pointed his finger like the barrel of a gun across his chest, aimed at my bunk where my rucksack lay, the device stashed inside—"and when you activate it on the heights. That's a little bit stupid."

He knew. He wanted me to know that he knew. But there was more in his look. Concern. The Edifice—or my own colleagues at the weather station—had been tracking me?

"Do they know?" I whimpered, hoping he'd fill in the gap of who *they* were.

"Of course they do."

The others didn't grasp the gist.

This could cost me my job, my career. Could have gotten us killed. "What do they know?" I asked, sick to my stomach.

"We don't know what they know…yet."

Puzzled looks around the room. The storm howled at Kim's Kozy, its monstrous shoulder shoving the side of the building, my mind blowing fuses left and right.

Apparently picking up the vibes among us five kids in the brief quiet, Dom eased into a look of satisfaction, mulling over what I myself wouldn't fully grasp for a while: that we'd already re-established a firm allegiance among ourselves, and to Elijah.

Dom to Elijah: "I have to report you as found."

"Right."

Unnaturally still, Elijah obviously didn't trust his superior a hundred percent. Vice versa, too, now that Elijah had showed himself to be prime renegade material. Dom had an appetite for complete obedience. But after another drilling gaze, the ex-special forces leader sat back—maybe an inch—and said, "All right." The speck of concession in his otherwise brick-hard demeanor suggested that he just might be acknowledging Elijah's mistrust of him as partly legitimate. Or his headstrong mission as valid.

Dom switched gears once more. "You still dabbling in the old brimstone, boy?

Elijah paused. "I can't un-see what I've seen, can't un-know it. But, no. Never again."

Dom put it in neutral. "Did everyone enjoy the trip?"

We all said we did.

Dom to Elijah: "You could have endangered the others. Can't hide intel."

"*You* did."

"Someone has to have the big picture."

"God does." Elijah was stinkin' not going to back down, plus saying the G word again.

Dom's eyes fixed on the floor, and I braced for Elijah getting surprise-punched again. But Dom calmly stated, "Deferring to the Almighty to end the argument is playing dirty. You play dirty."

"I had a good teacher."

Nailed him.

Dom snorted confidently.

"Not you," Elijah added coolly, glancing upward. "Him."

Nailed him again. Wow…wait…what? I frowned at my cousin. "God plays dirty?"

His smile was inscrutable. "He lets people die of love."

Dom pointed that gun-barrel finger at Elijah for one last bit of threat or instruction.

But Elijah cut him off. "Sir…" he said, nodding at Dom's hand, "that no longer works on me."

CHAPTER 30

Si vis pacum para bellum.
(If you want peace, prepare for war)
—RENATUS IN *DE RE MILITARI*

Thinking back on that last moment—Dom's unflappable composure, how his big hand settled on the table in our bunkroom, how the corner of his eye got a teeny bit watery—I concluded that Elijah responded just like Dom had trained him to, exactly what the head of Parabolani would have expected from his star pupil: fearlessness, respect, and focus, even if it meant severing ties. If the whole third degree was a test and a toughening, equipping Elijah to strike out in a new direction, my cousin now had friends in tow who knew he could hold his own under pressure.

People with perfect composure bother me, and I told Elijah as much when we caught a moment at that hallway window overlooking the gardens. "I'm an actor. I know how to act composed. But it's not real. No one is perfectly in control of himself all the time." I was referring to Dom.

"You've never met a Qi master," he answered. "They're hollow shells. If you hit one he'd ring like a bell."

"What do you mean?"

"The core is missing. Suppressed emotion and memory. Placid, empty smiles, but something calculating in the eyes. Ever seen a Tufani sand fox? It's the same smile." He thought a minute. "Dom's not acting. You have to know how to read him. And he was right. A person shouldn't go solo. Long-term deprivation is unhealthy."

"Jesus went to the desert." I'd gotten bold saying the J-word out loud.

"But how long and why?" Before I could answer, he did. "Forty days. To be tempted of the devil. Ascetics forget that. He went to be tested by Satan, not to live there." He tapped his temple like Dom had, indicating danger to the mind. "It's not good for man to be alone."

"Dom has misgivings about the mish network, about defectors or spies."

He nodded. "Yeah."

"Does he suspect anyone?"

"Not sure."

"Besides Suzanne…"

Except for a tinge of sarcasm, Elijah's answer came graciously. "Innocent until proven guilty."

Next issue. "You said your compass malfunctioned."

"I don't think I was hallucinating."

"What day would that have been?"

His gaze went from Kim's Kozy urban jungle to me. "Does escha-mete—escha-weather involve magnetic fields?"

"You know me. Always researching something. What day?"

"Third day after I left, maybe fourth."

"Close enough. I'll check it out. What did Dom mean by, 'You're in trouble?'"

"Getting dropped from the agency."

"I figured you'd leave anyway. What'll you do for income?"

He chuckled. "I'm a marked man."

"No kidding," I said soberly, then joked, "My yard needs

mowing."

"Thanks," he said. Time passed. "I don't have a decent resume or a degree. If my sketchy security problems resurface, the only one who'd hire me is God himself."

· · · · ·

Dom and Marcus went out for a father/son dinner, while we four nabbed the cushiony hippy niche under the stairs and had bowls of late-night noodle soup. Ambient clatter from the dining area up a half flight allowed us to talk about God with some ease. Despite all the undercurrents of love and jealousy and secret government plots and mission defections, it was a nice time. You grab moments when you can get 'em.

A logjam of flights out would delay us one more day. A girl (her clothes were drying in front of the window) was sleeping in our only spare bunk, the one under Marcus. We wondered where Dom was going to sleep, but Marcus didn't get in until after ten.

Elijah snatched a five-minute conversation with Dom out in the hall, then led us all back under the stairs. He paused, got a breath, and asked shyly, "Where do we go from here?"

"Home," I said obviously.

"What I mean is, it's good to...to get...to see everyone. It's been so good. These few days."

We agreed.

"I just wondered if it might be...how we might move forward."

"Move forward? Like what?" I asked.

Had Dom and Elijah batted around strategies involving us five? Did Elijah fully trust us now?

He said, "This is out of the blue. I know. But I'm asking if you'd be willing to, you know, I'm asking what you might... bring to the table."

An awkward quiet. I couldn't believe my ears. Without much thought, I said, "I'm not real sure what table you're talking about, but I think I'm hearing a pretty presumptuous suggestion from a pretty unstable guy. Eleven days ago you were dead forever and we were boarding a bus from Qolo to go back to our real lives."

He nodded resignedly.

"What do you need us to do?" Mei asked.

A revelation came bursting into my head.

Mei. Her heart is less in her career than in rescuing victims of human trafficking. She's under constant pressure from her family. She's gotta be missing the camaraderie of us five. She'd be the backbone of any international trip.

"What might you consider?" Elijah pursued.

"What are your plans?" I persisted.

He said rather helplessly, "I don't know," but with a presence of mind that told me certainty wasn't a priority with him. He was sitting in the same place as before, his face in that strip of light, his expression half-certain but fully unburdened.

"Last time, you left us," Marcus commented, not unkindly, but expressing what I'd felt many a time. Before I could let loose on him, another revelation.

Marcus. A hunk of driftwood washed up on a California beach, dried up by jealousy. But raw and real now, rough edges smoothed by the grit of loneliness. Integral to the health of our group, such as it is, and desperate for purpose. His heart wasn't in part-time work or a spartan studio apartment near the beach.

"Okay," I dove in. "Let's play this out. I'm talking long-range forecast. Not a 10-day or 14-day. Let's think three months out. Or six months, like the almanac."

Elijah agreed. "That's good. That's all I mean."

Elijah. A leader without a team. A prophet without a platform. With more purpose than the rest of us put together and the courage to pull it off. A familiarity with things divine, and a willingness to act on them. His heart was on mission, with or without us. Robin Hood and a splinter group of merry men?

I blurted, "I know weather."

"Good."

"But I have a career. And a fiancée. I bought a house."

"Okay." He seemed to take my answer as a turndown, but no solid question had been asked. Just a what-if.

So I added, "I do good accents, especially Irish, German, British. If in six months we…say we traveled to a foreign land… if I got a handle on the scenario, I could play it."

"There's no script," he cautioned.

"Right. Sure. Take the old improv skills to the next level."

Mei said, "I speak English, Japanese, Mikan, and basic French and Spanish."

I wasn't believing this conversation. Had Dom's five minutes with Elijah included a directive, a plea to lay groundwork for a new team? Was the head honcho's surprise visit to our bunk room a job interview?

"I know Spanish," Marcus broke in casually, "and some Gullah." He went deadpan. "Wingate, are you saying that sometime in the future, my life may depend on your lingual skills?"

"Ach du lederhosen!" I barked.

Grateful for the humor, Elijah said to me, "Middle Eastern languages. A person can memorize a hundred phrases in each of the main ones and get around okay."

"What are the main ones?"

"You're the researcher."

Our noodle bowls sat empty. Tea was cold.

Reece said in a cute, ladylike way, "I can pray."

Reece. Her marriage on the brink, maybe already over the cliff, a baby at home. No way she could be a part of us, not in six months. Not in a year. Her prime directive was caring for her child.

Studying the ceiling instead of looking her way, Elijah said, "Your prayers got me into this mess in the first place, remember? What was it, ten years ago you prayed that I'd believe, that I'd have influence, a wider and wider circle?"

"I know," she said sheepishly. "I've thought about that."

"It's good," he affirmed. "I'm glad."

I said to Mei, "And you understand travel—bookings, exchange rates, international protocol. You have experience in rescue…"

She finished my sentence, "To kidnap women and children from human traffickers."

Me. Making a name in Tulsa. Maybe it would be just those three: Elijah, Marcus, and Mei. Add Karinna and Steven. Subtract Reece and me, too entrenched in life in the States. A new Mag Five? The idea hurt like a hammer to the heart. But cheerily I coached on, "Long-range forecast, you know, 20% chance of anything…Highs might be low. Lows might be high. Lots of turbulence."

"Everything from A to Z," Marcus added. "Altitude to…"

"Zephyr," I finished his comment. "A wind from the west."

He pondered, "A wind from the west…yeah. I know about security. I have a conceal/carry permit, for the time being anyway, until the laws change."

Elijah approved. "I could teach you crossbow, blowgun. Those can be unregistered."

Reece said, "I could learn that, too."

Her comment threw Elijah—all of us guys—for a second before he continued the stipulations with Marcus. "You've dabbled in the occult. If you're out of it now…"

"I was never in."

Elijah gave him an undeserved nod.

Marcus bled the words, "You been talking to Dad."

"Didn't have to."

In a sudden conspiratorial mood, Reece said, "The metal rod in my leg...I might be able to sneak things through airport security. Like we almost accidentally did with The Armor of God. But it can't be too risky. I need to be home with my daughter mostly." She settled back, pressing into her pillow as quickly as she had sprung from it. "I may have to get a full-time job."

"What about Karinna and Steven?" I couldn't bring myself to add, "if there ever would be the Magdeline Five again, but not all of us."

"Karinna's out of the agency," Elijah said. "Steven's still in."

"Okay, but what we're talking about here is apart from the agency, am I right? Anyhoo, they both think you hung the moon, if you're looking to form a team."

"We get home and regroup," he answered solidly. "We go back to life, pray, have some discussions."

"Pow wows," Reece said nostalgically.

Marcus added, "Long distance. With secure communications."

"I need to talk to Lydia," I said. "Thing is, we can't go back— we five—to the way things were. Times have changed. We've changed. I need time to plan."

Elijah agreed, "Sure. The thing is, we're almost out of time to *get* ready. We need to *be* ready." He asked Marcus to pray.

We bowed, eyes open in our dim, under-the-stairs hippy pad. "Help us," Marcus said deeply. "Help us. Amen."

No one would be bursting into songs of bygone days or the future quests of five warriors on white stallions riding into the sunset. The uncertain quiet said it all. The Mag Five was only a morning fog, and whether we'd rise together like a cloud or be burned off by the heat... *Wait and see,* I told myself.

• • • • •

The next morning when I woke up, Elijah was gone. *His fan's turned off. He's getting breakfast.* I pulled back his curtain to find an empty pillow, and no knife underneath. *His rucksack...not there. Storage drawer empty.* Throwing on shorts and T-shirt, I scoured the whole of Kim's Kozy: lobby, gardens, veranda, com stations, laundry porch, bathrooms, back stairs. I hit every hall on every floor of all wings. I'd seen Dom go toward the last room down the hall last night. I listened at the door. I fiddled loudly with my keys, waiting for someone to come out, as Elijah had taught me. A middle-aged woman in jeans and a light jacket opened the door. She blocked the doorway. "Can I help you?"

"Mornin'!" I chirped. "I came to get the big guy. Dominic. Is he up yet?"

Suspiciously, she said, "There's only my team in here. We got in at 4 a.m."

I went back to the room and woke Marcus. "Where's your dad?"

"I dunno," he said sleepily.

"Elijah's gone, and I can't find your dad."

We woke the girls.

Reece asked me, "Did you look—"

"I looked everywhere!" I barked. "His stuff's gone. Dom's not in the other room. Hasn't been there since before four this morning."

I replayed the lobby scene from a few minutes before, the usual bustle...except the girls behind the counter had seemed uneasy. Sachiko and her husband had been behind the counter, too, both on the phone. I saw in hindsight the tense expressions of a few trekkers. Had Elijah run? Had Dom been arrested? *My instruments!* I climbed to my bunk and dug under my pillow. *Gone! Right from under my head!*

We dressed and packed quickly, though we weren't due to leave until evening.

Down in the lobby we tried to look casual, piling our ruck-sacks in a corner and picking up chatter amongst the other ragtags.

Mei made a bee line for Sachiko. They exchanged a few words. She came back solemn-faced. "Police came."

Reece whispered desperately, "Did he…did they get away?"

"What do you say…by the skin of your teeth. Sachiko took our names off the hotel register yesterday. There was an inquiry." She turned to me. "The police were looking for you."

"Me?!"

Angry but steady, Mei asked, "At your work, you do research about Tufan weather? Is it a secret thing? When Dom pointed to your bunk, it was about science equipment, *ne*."

I hemmed and hawed. My neck got hot. "It…No. And yes. And yes, a type of scanner."

"Sachiko thinks local authorities were sent by Edifice. She does not know why. What I think…the path of your scanning instrument across Tufan and the path of the rogue missionary became the same path. They had lost him until they found you."

All eyes fixed hard on me.

I stammered, "Um…we're not doing research on Tufan at my station. And yes, it was a secret thing, but it was just me." I led them to the koi pond and drew them into a tight circle. "Okay. Here it is. A while back I stumbled on this report. It was a few decades old and suggested that governments were competing to find ways to control the weather. I did some digging. It's all conspiracy theory, you know. Media wouldn't touch it. No self-respecting meteorologist would, either…but it made sense with the Scripture. I mean, it could explain some anomalies mentioned in end-times prophecies. One gigantic test facility in Canada was recently dismantled, and I had a hunch they'd moved it to the Qolo Mountains. Sure enough, there's an area blurred out on satellite photos. And where better than Qolo, so high and remote that almost no one can get there. This project, they do experiments by heating the atmosphere."

"Heating the atmosphere?" asked Marcus with a frown. "Why?"

"I'm not entirely sure, but it made sense to take readings since we were so close, to see if the facility was really there. I'd mentioned the ION Task at work a couple times and got blank stares. And a few not so blank, you know what I mean? Which made me wonder. I never imagined I'd be tracked!"

I asked Mei, "Did Sachiko say who tracked me? I mean, did Edifice pick up the signal, or was it my own TV station? I got a few quick readings at Qolo, that's all. And another thing"—one aspect that I hoped would legitimize my secret, because they were looking at me as if I was a war criminal—"there are other possible effects of these experiments, deep-earth effects and…and possible damage to people's mental states if subjected to high levels of these heater beams. When we got the call that Elijah went missing, one possible reason was mental confusion. I was in the thick of the research and the Bible study, snatching bits of info from everywhere," my voice grew more frantic, "conspiracies and prophecies, patching things together to see if they fit."

"And did they fit?" Marcus asked coolly.

"I've hardly formed a hypothesis about it. There's a flood of information to process, from many sources. I'd never want to put any of you in jeopardy! You know I'd never do that!"

"Rob…" Reece put a comforting hand on my arm. "Of course not. And how could you know? I'm realizing how sheltered we've been, us Mid-Westerners."

"Not sheltered, Reece," I said. "Kept in the dark. Deliberately."

Mei's hard expression didn't soften. "The Edifice *would not* like people spying on hidden facilities in Tufan."

I felt like a pork chop in a synagogue. "Guys, I'm so sorry!"

Marcus should have been the most ticked. His dad was off

with Elijah again. This time, though, it was me who'd set Dom on a run for his life.

But Skidmore gave me a good-natured bump on the shoulder. "Hey, no. I get it now. Dad took the risk away from us. See what he did? He disappeared Elijah and your instrument, right? The troops think they're following you. We're just plain tourists again. Sweet deal. They get away, we get home. We'd have slowed them down. But it looks like you got yourself on the World's Most Wanted list, bud. Better get out those fake mustaches and hair dyes you use in the theatre. You'll need 'em."

Reece asked, "Do we know *for sure* they're okay?"

Mei softened. "They must have gone over the wall, because the gates are locked at night. We have places of refuge close by."

"The bike shop?" I whispered.

Mei mellowed. "Marcus is right. If we had tried to escape together, we would be caught. Rob, I hope you recorded your findings, because your instrument will be destroyed." Suddenly impassioned, she whispered loudly, "We must not keep secrets. Never again!"

· · · · ·

Alone I wandered the rain-washed path through the garden and past the koi pond, keeping an ear perked for the clatter of weapons and boots, for voices raised in alarm. We'd formed a quick getaway plan, just in case. Our bags were stashed in separate places. Mei kept hers in the room. She'd say we had already left. If police came, we'd meet up at the bike shop at an appointed time. If any of us didn't show, another would check back with Sachiko. I did think of buying some local traditional garb, shaving my head, penciling in a Fu Manchu.

I played a hundred scenarios of what might have happened if the Mag Five and my instruments had been caught in the same room. We might all be hauled off to a Jinsha prison, Marcus's dad shot trying to protect us. Reece torn from her precious Olivet, and me from my Lydia. Mei might have talked her way out of it as an unwitting guide to American spies, but in a pinch like that she'd never throw us to the lions.

Who had implanted a tracking device into my instruments—someone at my station? How had Dom known? Could The Edifice wrangle local police from any country to do their bidding? Oh, the things that could have happened.

Ahead on the garden path a man was sweeping up storm debris. It was the old cigarette-smoker. I stopped dead. He looked up, made an okay sign with bent fingers and went back to sweeping.

CHAPTER 31

I need to be a sojourner to find my place,
Out in the mystery where the heart beats the way.
—Andrea Summer, "Wanderer"

I'm home. Magdeline, Ohio. I arrived sporting sunglasses, long hair, scruffy beard, and a thrift store sport coat, trying to look as unlike my younger Elijah Creek self as possible. I took off for the city's back parking lots along the tracks, like in the old days when I needed to move around town low-profile.

Cautiously approaching the entry gate of Camp Mudjokivi, I took a minute to overlook paradise: Postcard pretty. Late afternoon. Sunlit lake centered in a well-manicured, bowl-shaped campus. Cabins and tree houses beyond. Woods to the right. Lodge to the left, next to my Cape Cod house with the big porch. Memories and homesickness faded. Unlike a postcard, the real camp moved and lived: ripples on the lake, stirring branches in Owl Woods, birds settling into their nests, a breeze. I felt like a first-timer. *I hope I don't throw up in my bunk or cry myself to sleep the first night.* I cracked jokes with myself, nervous and nauseous about how my parents and sisters would react.

It felt safer to see Dad first. I headed toward the lodge, taking in lungfuls of balmy air, the smells of late summer woods, dry grass, a touch of lake algae. I'd started re-acclimating to the altitude while in Jinsha, but the air here was especially rich. *Camp's empty, no kids. Transition weekend. Dad will probably be in his office, tying up loose ends.*

The door was open, his back to it. He was writing on the wall calendar behind his desk, phone to his ear, his voice a one-way conversation. The sound of it hurt my pounding heart. He said into the phone, "I'll make the call. Thanks," and hung up.

I tapped on the door casing.

"Be right with you."

"Dad…" I said softly.

A jolt coursed across his shoulders.

"It's me," I said reassuringly.

He turned, shock draining the color from his cheeks and mouth. He'd aged. There were new shadows around his eyes. *My fault.* He tried to say my name but it was more a cough.

"I'm okay, Dad. I'm home."

We matched strides to get to each other. His arm went around my shoulders, his hand to my head pulling me in. I'd seen him cry once, when Dom's men had found me half-frozen in Gilead and I was hauled out on a stretcher. But never had he broken into sobs, "Son…my son. Where've you been?"

My reasons came in a rush. "I was lost for a few weeks, Dad, then I didn't know who to trust and had to lay low a long time. I was with some nomads. They hid me. Then a lady in the city."

He pulled me back, looked deeply at my face.

"I had no money and I couldn't use the lady's phone to contact anyone. It could have been dangerous for her. People might have been after me. I didn't know. I made a little radio and heard that Rob and the others were coming. I thought it could be a set-up, but it wasn't. I want to see mom now, and the twins. And Grandma. I wanna go down to Georgia soon. But we gotta keep it quiet. Dad, somehow we gotta keep it quiet for now."

A shadow crossed his face. Relief and joy vanished. "Your

grandma…I'm so sorry, son. I'm so sorry…Grandma had a heart attack…She's gone."

"When?" I asked hollowly.

"A few weeks ago. A neighbor found her."

"When exactly?"

He shifted his weight uneasily, let his hands drop. He pretended to have to recall, "A month."

"She left this earth thinking I was dead."

He pulled me back with one arm, squeezing my shoulder briefly, turning me toward the door. "She had a good long life." He absently lifted his clipboard.

"You need to make that phone call?" I gestured to the calendar behind his desk.

"It can wait." He hung the clipboard on the wall.

"There was a funeral, I guess…" *Dumb thing to say.* "Did my disappearance, did it cause her heart attack?"

"No, no. She was eighty-four. The services were down home. Everyone—" he was going to say that everyone asked about me or something like that. "She had lots of friends. It was good family time." He frowned. "You said Rob came looking for you?"

"Rob and Marcus, Mei and Reece. They all came." Answering his stunned, sort of hurt look, I said, "They had to keep it secret, Dad. In case something went wrong. They couldn't make it public that they were looking for me. Once we met up, we still had to get out quietly. I can explain it all later."

He locked the office door and we headed up the path.

"That's why Rob didn't come to the funeral," Dad said thoughtfully. "He told Grace and Dorian he was doing research and had to be out of the country."

"I'm sorry that you and mom and the twins were left in the dark. I couldn't call, then storms delayed us. As soon as I got out, I came straight home."

"Are the others okay?" he managed to ask. "Did everyone make it back?"

I answered, "We got into a little trouble that last day, but yeah, we're all okay. It's so different over there, Dad." When the time was right we'd talk about The Edifice. But I couldn't discuss trouble in the mission agency. He already held a dim view of people who'd rip a man's son from his family and take him to the other side of the planet. And the possessed shaman and all that? He'd never believe it. It's the kind of subject you have to ease into. "Reece's mom knew about the trip," I went on, "but only because she kept the baby. She didn't know where or how long or any details." My mind was back on Grandma. I sat down on a park bench beside the path. "I can't believe she's gone."

He said gently, "Listen, I have to go back down to settle the estate. She left boxes for each of the grandkids, to be opened by them. The girls didn't want to open theirs without you. How about we go down, walk through the house before the auction. If you want a memento…"

"I don't know…" I glanced around, instinctively surveying the camp for troops. How could I meet the rest of the relatives? If I was too secretive, they'd be suspicious. Too much information could put them in jeopardy. How well did I know my own flesh and blood, anyway, except for holiday get-togethers? Was re-integration even possible?

Dad put a hand on my shoulder a third time, cautiously, as if he still wasn't sure I was for real. "We can talk about it later. Let's go up to the house. Your mom's fixing dinner and the girls are in."

"Okay." I stood hesitantly.

"No one else," he said supportively. "Just us."

"Is Bo around?" I asked.

"He's gone for the day. Oh, will he ever be glad"—he broke off when I shot him a look. Reality quickly set in. Who to tell and who to leave in limbo? "Are you in danger?"

"The rules keep changing, Dad. It's not like here," I joked, "where you still can't eat potato chips in your bunk or sneak into the girls' cabins at night, right?"

He responded with a humorless chuckle. "Let's go see your mom."

We walked to the porch with few words between us and a few incredulous side glances from Dad. "Are you okay, really? You're thin."

"Mom's cooking'll fix that. But I'll earn my keep. You need wood chopped? Trails cleared?"

"Always." He asked me to wait in the entry hall, whispering, "I should prepare her. I need a minute."

The entry had a new coat of paint, kind of a peach color, and the living room furniture had been rearranged. Music drifted over the balcony from the girls' upstairs bedroom. I heard Dad's deep murmur from the kitchen, then a gasp and a rush of foot-steps as Mom appeared at the other end of the hall. Her hands went to her mouth. She came by baby steps, then reached out and squeezed my arms and looking me over in disbelief before giving me a frantic hug. "Girls!" she called. "Girls! Come quick!"

They appeared at the top of the steps, identical younger ver-sions of mom, squealing and thundering down. Tears falling, questions flying. My mind in a fog, my heart in several places.

In minutes we were at the table like old times, passing around baked chicken and potatoes. I asked a lot about them so they wouldn't ask a lot about me. There was no good time to broach the subject. "I'm glad to be back. Camp looks great, dinner's great, the house—it's all great. Listen, this is going to be hard, but for now, I'd like to keep my visit private."

Mom stiffened. "Visit?"

"I hope I can stay. For a while. I hope. Can we keep this

between us for a little while?"

"A while?" Mom asked coolly. "You mean don't tell anyone you're home? Don't tell them you're alive?"

I remembered now why trips home had dwindled to nothing. How could I explain my work to a family of unbelievers? And beyond that, the spreading tentacles of The Edifice. I'd tried before, and had done more harm than good. We Westerners sure were an over-confident and naïve bunch.

After the trip to Ireland, after Mom had seen the damage done to her birth mother in the name of God, a core of anger had grown and hardened. Dad had been more permissive—if not approving—of my decision to leave those years ago. But Mom and the twins had a time with it. And Grandma…I'd never said goodbye. A few postcards, that was it. I answered Mom's question about my next step. "I may know better when I talk to Dom again."

Dad couldn't hide a flicker of resentment. He, like Marcus, probably thought that Dom and I were too much like father and son.

Father…I appealed to the one relation surpassing all others. *Lord God, King of Heaven's armies, help me mend what I've broken here.*

Stacy said delicately, "We have a few weeks before classes start. Can you stay that long?"

"Should be good. I'm sorry to be vague. It's the nature of the beast."

I settled into my room later, energy and emotion spent, accepting towels and hotel-type amenities from Mom who was polite to a tee. I climbed into my old bed and switched off the light. There was a tap at the door. "Come in."

Mom came over crying, knelt by my bed, and kissed me hard on the forehead. "My boy…my sweet boy. You're home."

CHAPTER 32

Love is a minefield, a perfectly fine feeling,
Turns on a dime, sealing the fate of two.
—Mae Klingler, "Minefield"

On her second Sunday back from Asia, Reece went to Audrey's house around two o'clock and asked for a few minutes of her time. They sat on the front steps, Olivet playing at Reece's feet, the other woman disheveled from an afternoon nap, but pretty, with dark hair and eyes. She was taller than Reece, and elegant even though barefoot and wearing shorts and T-shirt.

Reece talked in vague terms so Olivet wouldn't grasp the subject.

Audrey defended the affair. "Our love is pure."

"A liar lies," Reece replied, quietly determined to say her piece. "A person doesn't lie to me and not to you, or to you and not to me. A liar lies. It's what he does. I have pictures of his other girlfriends in church directories if you want to see them. You're making a mistake. And as for being pure, I saw the two of you in his office one night. From the window. I climbed up and saw you."

"Our love is an act of worship," Audrey tranquilly replied.

By two forty-five Reece had returned home and put Olivet down for her nap. Greg pulled in. She made a quick call to her mom. "I need you here. Can you come? Don't make a scene, though. Just come, okay?"

"Are you safe, babe?"

"Yes. He said he'd be at the office all afternoon, so I went to Audrey's to talk to her. She must have called him, 'cause he just pulled up."

"On my way."

Reece locked the screen and opened the pocket knife hidden in her skirt pocket, reeling at how quickly a marriage could deteriorate, and on the other hand, how long it had taken her to wake up.

"I need to get some paperwork," Greg said matter-of-factly, tugging at the screen door.

"This has nothing to do with paperwork."

Fury shot out of his eyes. He yanked on the handle. "You had no business going to her house. What is wrong with you!"

"The neighbors will hear!" she hissed. "And Olivet is asleep."

He collected himself quickly, spoke evenly. "I won't wake Olivet. Unlock the door."

When she hesitated, he said condescendingly, "It's a screen door, Reece."

Across the dining room table she and Greg fought about who did what, and who said what. And when. And why. A buckshot conversation, wounding and accusing.

"Shhhh. You'll wake her."

"I'm not yelling," Greg retorted. "What do you care about Olivet anyway, abandoning her the way you did."

"I didn't abandon her. That's what you're doing."

"There was no note."

"Why do you keep bringing that up? I left it right here," she poked the table. "And I saw it in your hand that night. I drove past." She hobbled out to the front porch, joints stiff, still recovering from the strains of Tufan. He was going to hammer ideas into her head until she believed them herself: there was no note, his affair was innocent, whatever he said was true, and whatever she believed was silly.

He followed her. "You were all broken up over your boyfriend's untimely demise."

All week Greg had deflected guilt, pressuring her at every turn. To do what? To keep quiet like she had the other times, when it was only some back taxes not paid, or just one inappropriate embrace. But every single day of the past ten had brought crushing new heartbreaks: moral, financial, and now mystical—Tufani religion bathed in Christian terms from her husband's own mouth. From the pulpit.

Reece sat in the swing, wanting to escape, feeling Marcus's long fingers grip her wrist as they had in Tufan, his breath skimming across her face. "Don't run!" His deep whisper echoed, every bit as weighty as the counsellor's advice a few days before.

Rachel had made an appointment for her daughter the hour she'd arrived home, saying, "I'll not have you muddle along like I did."

Dr. Patricia Bourne, who preferred to be called just Trish, had sat with her new client on that first Monday, in matching chairs in a sunny office. "Picture yourself in a war zone, Reece. Bombs are dropping all around, unexpected and unexplained. That's what it will be like for a while. That's hard to hear, but if you understand the process of working through marriage issues, and how chaotic it can be, it does help to know that these feelings are not unusual."

"I'm not going crazy?" Reece had asked wearily.

"You're not."

"I can barely function."

"You're doing fine. You're a strong young woman. This is an

especially sensitive situation because you're in the spotlight."

"Should I keep going to church?"

"If that's your support system. Go where you'll be cared for."

"If I'm not at church, people will ask questions. They'll call the house, or drop by."

"No doubt. But that's not your problem. Have one simple statement prepared and stick to it. Don't let people prod you for more. Truth gets easily distorted, Reece, so it's wise to confide only in a few trusted friends or family members."

That would be Mom and Mei. And Darrell. And Marcus. Brooklyn had been cool and perplexed when they met in the church hallway—a quick hug then off to class. *Audrey's cousin, my best friend. She'll think she has to choose sides. Right now I can't tell her anything.*

"And write everything down, Reece," Trish concluded. "Keep good records. We'll meet together with Greg on Wednesday and Thursday to get things rolling quickly. He has agreed. And I'll meet with him privately if he's willing. Are you all right with that?"

"Of course."

He didn't show up for their first session. Leaning against the porch post now, Greg seemed far away and unfamiliar.

We certainly are posed and poised, aren't we? she thought sarcastically. *Passersby will wave to the Molines enjoying the Lord's Day on their porch, and we'll wave back with smiles.* "Good afternoon. Beautiful day, isn't it?"

And it was beautiful—Cedar Ridge's comfortable hills and homes, its trees catching the slant of the sun. It was July, and while time hurtled toward the great unknown, certain moments hovered like ghosts: Greg's hostile stare when she walked in the front door from the airport. Olivet's downturned face, her little shoulder curling away from her momma's outstretched arms, Reece's baby girl refusing hugs and kisses. *What did he tell her about me? I'm a stranger to my own baby.* She shook it off for the hundredth time and turned her attention back to Cedar Ridge. *I'll miss this view,* she thought without emotion. *Except for that.* The Spirit Center's scorched steeple was gone and in it's place was a stylized, glistening silver tree, not unlike a fork with curved tines, symbolizing attunement of earth and heaven.

"Not atonement," Greg had corrected her when she asked about it. "Attunement."

A car passed. Greg waved, nodding a friendly hello as he checked the mail box.

There he is—husband, father, pastor, handler of every detail. In a dress shirt. It's all in a day's work. Reece wobbled between hostility and heartbreak. "I'm trying to help you," she pleaded from the swing, "to help *us* find a way through this. But I won't be left in the dark this time. When you said you might leave the church—"

"Spirit Center," he corrected, flipping through the stack of letters and bills. "You still don't get it."

"No. I don't." During his last two sermons—polished and powerful and half-true—Reece had grabbed a pencil from her purse to take notes, hoping to clear her mental haze.

He had preached, "Our ultimate authority is what I call Divine Voice. It resides in every soul." Pointing earnestly at individuals in the audience, he cried—"In you, and you, and you! Explore nowhere else but in your own heart and you will find God. Is yours a heart of darkness, that eternal soul that God put within you? Of course not! It's often said that the forces of darkness are upon us today. I think not. It's in the dark, that abyss of the soul, where we find truths that heal."

The strangeness of his teaching was all the more obvious after a few weeks of exposure to Tufani religion: trance possessions, journeys to the abyss, the void—the things Elijah mentioned.

Reece desperately wanted a cup of tea, wanted to get her Bible and look things up and sort things out—even things Greg had said months ago that she'd glossed over. But she'd have to walk right past him to get inside, so she stayed put in the swing. *Those sermons on David and Bathsheba, how a man's weakness doesn't uproot God's high calling for him. I let myself be deceived. Eyes wide open now. I have a frame of reference now.*

Reece had been moving essentials to her mom's house the last few days, just in case, keeping half-filled boxes stacked in the basement so Greg would be less likely to notice and come apart at the seams. She wouldn't be sitting here so close to him if her mom wasn't on the way. Still, she hoped…

Suddenly, unexpectedly, confidence welled up. Beauty over-flowed from the sky and from the purple ironweed and blue corn-flower in the lot across the street. The sun warmed her back, the breeze from the valley brushed her cheek. The heavens declared God's glory and the earth showed his handiwork. With great calm Reece said to her husband, "You've been promoting your own sin from the pulpit with not a peep from the congregation. They believe you because you speak so sincerely. You lie so well, they can't hear what you're doing. I couldn't either."

He idly opened envelopes, saying something about her living in the house. He'd get an apartment. She'd pay him rent. He'd take care of the yard.

But after mowing on Thursday, he'd spilled gasoline in the garage and made sure she saw it. Not as a caution, as a threat. *Even if I change the locks, the windows are on ground level.*

A neighbor jogged past. Poised and posed, the Molines waved. "Hi! Great day, isn't it?"

"Yes it is!"

Greg's overly methodical envelope-opening betrayed his rage. Reece and Audrey were the two worlds he wanted to keep apart but in controlled orbits around himself, and Reece had ruined it an hour ago. She said evenly, "If you want to live at the house for the time being, I'm glad to stay at Mom's. I might anyway."

"Someone needs to be here," he said in a practical tone. "It makes sense for you to stay. For Olivet's sake. It's her home."

"Uh-huh."

All you have to do, Reece pleaded with him in her thoughts, *All you have to say is, "Let's stop this. Take a breather. Let me get my footing, figure things out." Anything like that. You're destroying yourself, and us. We can go to another counsellor. You can choose.* She'd already said those things. So she pushed the swing with one foot, the swaying trees and flowers comforting her the way she soothed Olivet. She glanced at her husband. *You're handsome, smart, a gifted speaker, my lover, the father of my child. I won't be the one to file. That'll have to be your call. Only you and Audrey know what you've done in the dark.*

Reece kept an eye on him, fighting the lie she kept telling herself—that she had no reason to feel threatened. *If he starts in my direction, I'll leap over the back of the swing, shove it at him, jump the railing, head into the street, and scream for help. I'll pull the knife and look ridiculous if I have to. Let the town talk.* She kept reviewing how to do it, watching him peripherally, her finger pressing at the knife handle in her pocket so she'd know its exact position.

Marcus's voice returned again from that moment in the breakfast room at the Ascent Hotel when he'd grabbed her. "Where's your backbone, girl?"

"You don't understand," she'd shot back. "Things at home are—"

"Things at home," he sneered. "Big deal. Who cares? You're here, and you don't get to go all forlorn on us. We have a man to find. So don't run. It doesn't work. Now go have a good cry and come back with some of that Reece Elliston moxie."

That moment with Marcus had been oddly calming. And now, as then, like a summer bird in the dead of winter, for no reason and out of season, joy came rushing in. And hope. She breathed, relaxed, pushed the swing. No news had come from Camp Mudj yet, just a two-word message from Rob the day after she'd returned: *All home.* So Elijah was home. Everyone was safe. Nothing was to be said or done until further notice. If at all.

"He's alive, isn't he?" Greg jolted her back to the present.

He'd misread her expression of peace, mistaken it for…but no, he was holding up the credit card bill. "You went there to find him, didn't you? Fast food, fuel all the way to California… You went across the country. That's where you've been, to find him! No hotels, I see. Interesting. Someone else paid for those?" He hurled a foul curse at her.

Reece stopped swinging and thought for a very long moment. "Here's what I'm saying to people who ask: I'm saying, 'Thank you so much for your concern. We're all in good health. Ministering to a growing church is a blessing, but a big responsibility. We're young and without much experience, so we have a lot to learn. I do appreciate your prayers. I've been out of town for a few weeks for R&R, but I'm back.' That's what I'm saying. But you and I both know that the R&R wasn't rest and relaxation. Or romance or recreation or anything of the kind."

His fist clenched.

Strength kept rising from the deeps. "Greg. It's not from an abyss of darkness where you find help, it's from the wellspring of light." She wanted to add, *Can't you see what I've done, with God's help, what I never thought possible? I married a great guy, had a baby, walked unsupported, and jetted off around the world on a rescue mission. Because of a Person, not a belief in my own cosmic power. It's because of prayer and honesty sessions and mission that I'm stronger. Being with the Mag Five. Stronger. Worship. Stronger.*

We tell each other the truth even when it's hard.

She could say none of that.

Officer Taylor pulled up in the cruiser and got out, dressed in police uniform, belted up with weapons. Greg adjusted his spine against the porch post.

Mom called this in as a domestic scuffle!? Oh no. I said no scene, Mom...

Rachel Taylor got out of the passenger side and strolled up the walk wearing black jeans and jacket, like Marcus but tinier and tougher, smiling. "Top of the afternoon! Us girls, we ready for that ice cream date? I've been craving Uncle Leroy's sweet and salty caramel all day. You men can loiter on the porch, we won't be long, it's supposed to cloud up."

CHAPTER 33

For solitude, however some may rave,
Seeming a sanctuary, proves a grave,
A sepulchre in which the living lie,
Where all good qualities grow sick and die.
—WILLIAM COWPER

I hope the drought didn't follow me home.

The sun was setting over Camp Mudj, the shadows of Owl Woods long and lean across the lake path. "Deep calls to deep," I quoted the Scripture. *And dark calls to dark, says me. I gotta get away from the dark. It's calling me.* Summer in Magdeline, Ohio had been dryer than usual, Dad said, which worried me a little. I passed Great Oak and I don't mind saying that I hugged that old tree. Hugged it like a friend. *Back in my cathedral, and it's Sunday.*

It would be night soon. I'm not much for rituals, but the agency had adapted one from an old war tradition to ease the effects of what they still called "shell shock." They named the ritual H'lotz from the Hebrew halatz (חלץ) meaning to remove, to deliver, or to arm for battle, depending on the context. When a man came home from battle back in the day, a community of friends would take his uniform and present him with a new set of clothes. This signified that the horrors and pains of war were removed, and he was re-established back home as a civilian. Dom recommended it for those coming off a really hard stint. A scripture passage would be read by the assembly for the Deliverance/Dispatch/Arming.

No one would be giving me a H'lotz, but I had to make some kind of clean break. Tufan was calling me. I wouldn't go back. It might be my nature to be alone, but the isolation, the demons in my ear had messed me up. God would work things out for good, sure, but I still had shrapnel. I'd spent the last week mostly hiding in the house from the campers and hoping Mom would honor my wish for one week of quiet with no questions. I did tell two people I was back. Bo hugged the stuffing out of me, and Mrs. Horstley at the camp office cried and said I looked unwell. They both agreed to a week of confidentiality before my having to face the public. I only told them because I didn't want them to catch a glimpse of a disturbed-looking phantom on a trail at dusk, and call the cops.

Further, past camp and into Telanoo—the Land No One Owns—stood The Cedars, my cluster of evergreens, their undersides forming a low canopy, a twilit tent. Then I was in a stream bed, with one small pool of water that had survived the dry spell. *Spring-fed. I remember now. Fresh water.* It was the exhale of the day, but the hollow allowed no breeze. Not even the highest leaves trembled. *It's lonelier than I remember. My cathedral. But Lord, don't speak. I can't hear from you, not right now. Not even Scriptures or inklings, okay? I'm no good for you right now and your kindness would only make it worse. I'd break in half. So don't speak. Reece is with Greg, I guess. Rob's with Lydia, Marcus is hanging with his parents. Mei's back at work. Karinna… Steven…who knows. Man, this place is lonely. But don't speak. If you have to, speak in fire or wind, but not gently. It would kill me.*

Addressing him like I used to when I loved the Indian ways and before I knew his name, I whispered, "Master of Breath." He'd been a presence and a voice back then, as real as any person you'd meet face to face. Later I'd learned about him through his armor. Through Reece and Marcus. Through his people and his Word, a thousand ways, in nature a thousand more. I'd sought him and found him everywhere. Aloud I prayed, "I've come for the H'lotz, to shed Tufan's stains and wounds, to shed the knowledge of things I should never have looked into…and to stop the mental harassment." I'd told no one about the scaly one who invaded my thoughts—not Dom, nor the counselors, not Karinna, nor Steven. Only Suzanne. Which I regretted big time.

The nightmare last night, of a huge black dog circling the house, appearing at every window while I ran from room to room, peering into the night for a way to escape…At breakfast I'd watched the family's expressions for any uneasiness or disturbance. They seemed fine.

I would take off the Tufani clothes that I'd brought home, dirt and all, for this very purpose: the ritual. After the final week of camp, with me stuck in the house or haunting the back trails after dark to help out Dad, I still kept an ear for a soldier's boot, a phantom's papery wing, a four-footed predator in the underbrush. I wore a knife, had my bow and arrow. A couple miles to the east lay Council Cliffs State Park. A mile to the north, farms. To the south, camp. And to the west, my secret place, my Gilead, where The Armor of God lay buried. I fought off the old terror. *I'm not in Bardo, the in-between dying place where the only thing worse than staying put is moving forward toward non-existence. I'm in Telanoo. I'm home.* Compared to the infinite isolation of Qolo, Telanoo's crickets and rustling leaves sounded like civilization.

With each piece of clothing I shed, I would also shed oppression, fear, and the things that weren't fear, but became it: chest pressure, heaviness in the pit of my stomach, images that dry your bones. Marcus had told his dad about that night on the train when I fell to pieces. Debriefing at Kim's, Dom suggested a detox. *This should do it,* I lied to myself, knowing it wouldn't. I pulled off my socks, tossed them on the pile of clothes and stood there above the pool in Army issue shorts. *I'm a wineskin in the smoke, Lord, blackened and empty. But don't speak,* I reminded him. *I can take your Word in print, maybe. The solid, universal stuff. I'll get to it. But don't single me out again, not for a while. You're too much for me.*

I threw some dry cedar branches on the clothes, along with my agency contract for good measure. I struck flint, lit the debris, watched it flare. Time passed. Ashes rose, papery and black, like the things that had swept over me in Qolo. But these heavenward ashes were rimmed in fire, clouds with silver linings after a storm. I was heartened by the rims of fire, the fresh water, and a growing strip of deep red sky on the western horizon. A balmy drizzle moved through Telanoo so gently that I didn't notice it until the embers began to sizzle. *You baptizing me again, in water and blood?*

I'd bought a T-shirt and jeans in Chicago, and I stashed them under The Cedars, out of the mist. *I want to complete what the others prayed over me at Kim's. They renounced whatever had been done to me. Now I renounce what I did to myself.*

The drizzle was so fine it seeped through my skin and into my veins, as if great care was being taken not to bruise me. *You know I'm burnt. Even my skin can't take the pressure of your rain. My ears can't take your voice, my eyes your light. I'm pulling away for a while but I'll be back. Don't leave.*

Trickles of ashy water ran from the burned clothes, over rocks and into the pool, traces of Tufan's vampire native soil washed away. "Don't you curse my ground," I threatened the ashes. One tiny stream ran off into the dirt.

The heaviness of the words I'd screamed in the temple lifted. He would use it to bring people down from the heights to hear the good news. *Even your acts of wrath are pleas for lost children to come home, those who need the stern hand. You never give up, but you won't force us. You let us choose. But don't ask me to do that again.*

I renounced the gods, agreeing with the Scripture that says, "Make no mention of the names of other gods, nor let it be heard on your lips." But this one last time, before the court of the Almighty, I named my accusers. "I renounce___! I renounce___! I renounce___! I reject their rituals, their heavens and hells! I reject their soul annihilation. I reject the images in my head. I reject any curse or blessing of the shamans or nomads. But bless those men and their wives and children, Father. Save them and curse the darkness that keeps them from you. Their magic is smoke in your nostrils. You hate it. But you love them."

A person may drive the tricks of demons from his mind, but they linger in the spine. I admitted to Yah that black magic is not without its charms, that I still had a sort of morbid fascination for wandering down one more dark pathway, just to see. *They all lead to the Abyss. No bottom to that bottomless pit.* "I repent of those months when I couldn't seem to get enough of it. I wanted to know, to be smarter than Rob about at least one thing. I was arrogant and needy."

The gruesome posters near the temple came to mind…*Where did your images come from, YangDi? From the warped imaginations of human artists or from Hell's realities? You Tufani gods, are you in fact the gods of Ur and Egypt and Babylon who changed your names and identities to avoid detection, like I myself did?*

At the very moment of my repentance they were trying to draw me back in to speak to them, to know them. Above the sound of crickets I said, "Doesn't matter. Evil is contingent, goodness is eternal. Darkness flees from light. Holy is the Lord God Almighty. Heaven and Earth are full of your glory." In my heart I begged my Yahweh, *You, be You! Make me ready. Send me anywhere. Ruin my life in any way you see fit, but spare the others from harm—spare Reece and Rob, Marcus and Mei—if you will.*

I broke down and bowed, face and belly to the ground.

> King of Heaven's armies,
> Be my best thoughts, by day and night.
> Be my presence, my wisdom, my light,
> Be my shield and sword for the fight
> Be my dignity and my might
> Be my soul shelter, my high tower
> The power of my power.

A breeze dried my skin. I wiped my eyes. A reassuring curtain of darkness and rain approached from the region below the blood-red sky. *We need more rain,* I told him. *It's too dry here.* I took a handful of damp dirt, smelled it, breathed rain-smelling air. I crawled under the shaggy cedar branches and dropped down on the carpet of dry needles, breathing out the last of the renouncements. *I'm done. Done with it. I'm free. Free of it. I'll be human for a while. Home for a while. But Camp Mudj isn't my home. My home is me. Not anymore. My home is You.*

When the evening shower passed I lit a new fire to read by. I could bear it a little now, hearing his voice in print. The H'lotz readings promised deliverance from both foe and friend/betrayer: The Edifice, the shaman, the agency, Suzanne. Any and all. Our battle may be against principalities and unseen things, but I'd learned how well they hide under shawls of skin and bone. I added dry sticks to the fire and pretended to be the voice of an assembly reading on my behalf:

The Despair

Give ear to my prayer, O God, and hide
not yourself from my plea for mercy!

Attend to me, and answer me; I am restless
in my complaint and I moan,

because of the noise of the enemy, because
of the oppression of the wicked.

For they drop trouble upon me, and in
anger they bear a grudge against me.

My heart is in anguish within me; the
terrors of death have fallen upon me.

Fear and trembling come upon me, and
horror overwhelms me.

And I say, "Oh, that I had wings like a
dove! I would fly away and be at rest;

yes, I would wander far away; I would lodge in the wilderness;

I would hurry to find a shelter from
the raging wind and tempest."

The Destruction

Destroy, O Lord, divide their tongues; for I
see violence and strife in the city.

Day and night they go around it on its walls,

and iniquity and trouble are within it; ruin is in its midst;

oppression and fraud do not depart from its marketplace.

The Deception

For it is not an enemy who taunts me—then I could bear it;

it is not an adversary who deals insolently
with me—then I could hide from him.

But it is you, a man, my equal, my
companion, my familiar friend.

We used to take sweet counsel together; within
God's house we walked in the throng.

My companion stretched out his hand against
his friends; he violated his covenant.

His speech was smooth as butter, yet war was in his heart;

his words were softer than oil, yet they were drawn swords.

The Deliverance

But I call to God, and the Lord will save me.

Evening and morning and at noon I utter my
complaint and moan, and he hears my voice.

He redeems my soul in safety from the battle
that I wage, for many are arrayed against me.

God will give ear and humble them, he
who is enthroned from of old,

because they do not change and do not fear God.

Cast your burden on the Lord, and he will sustain you;

he will never permit the righteous to be moved.

The others in the Magdeline Five might need the H'lotz at
some future time. We each had our enemies and friend/betrayers.
Especially Reece. And a person always has his own self-deception
to wrestle with. The H'lotz usually ended with the re-issuing of
the armor of God. *I'll wait for the others on that. If they decide to
come. Okay, ready to face Mom and Dad for the hard talk?*

I dressed in the fresh clothes and headed home in the dark,
Tufan's power now a few scattered ashes and a smoky skim on
the pool. Whatever my parents' thoughts on the subject of my
future, we had to get to it.

· · · · · ·

We sat in the family room, Mom and Dad, the girls, and me. "I'm
not part of the mission agency anymore." Mom's face lit up. "I
went into Qolo without the proper permits. The Edifice probably
knows it, even though I passed through a few checkpoints with

no problem, switching identities. I'm a risk. How long I stay here may depend on how quickly Edifice governance spreads. I may be on their blacklist for a while."

Mom asked again, "It's been over a week. You're saying we're still not allowed to tell our friends that my son is alive?"

"Dom suggested that I lay low for a while, but not overtly hide the truth, or myself. It looks suspicious. If I'm recognized on the street I'll quote Mark Twain, that the rumors of my death were greatly exaggerated. So here's the simple truth: I got sick in the mountains somewhere in Asia, was taken care of by kind folks, then made my way back to civilization. Don't tell anyone that I couldn't call home because my paperwork had expired, or that I might have endangered those who were helping me. You can say you're angry about the misinformation. I'm sorry, Mom. I hate putting you on the spot. I guess there was a write-up in the paper about my disappearance?"

"Of course there was!" Mom cried. "Everyone knows!"

"Put a correction in, then, like what I said—that I got ill in the remote back country, but made it home and am recovering. And thank everyone for their thoughts and prayers. That I'll be out and about soon. If the paper calls, tell them I'll get in touch with them when I'm better."

Dad asked, "What are the others saying to their friends?"

"Marcus is a loner. He's not accountable to anyone. No problem there."

"Where is he?"

"Still on the west coast, I guess. Reece's situation is complicated. She and Greg were having problems before she left. The less said the better. That's not our business right now. If you get cornered, say that she and Rob went to Asia. All five of us met up, but were delayed in the typhoon with a bunch of other trekkers. And we were always with a group. And we came back separately—if people ask. Mei lives in Japan. If it comes up about her or Marcus, just go simple: it was a last-minute thing. If anyone asks what region in Asia, say, 'Oh, one of those disputed regions whose names change every few years.' Just say that I'm home taking a breather. If they prod you for further information, they may be…" I cleared my throat, "they may be trouble."

Okay, here goes. "Hey, thanks for letting me be a hermit this week. And please forgive me for the pain I've caused you. If I could take it back, I would. Let me say again, my leaving home seven years ago has nothing to do with how I feel about you. It had everything to do with what I believe about God. If I hadn't found him, I might still be here helping run the camp. But maybe not. Who knows, I might have become an Appalachian trail guide or gotten myself shot by a hunter or eaten by a bear, or fallen… off a cliff. Life and death happen." It came back in a rush again, Foster harnessing up for a rappel, me not checking his gear, distracted for a moment. Gone. Two hundred feet. Blink of an eye.

Mom picked up on my distress and made a sound of sympathy. "Dom sent a note about that young man on your team at the time of the accident. He said to give you space if you came home, that you were taking it very hard. I thought you'd come home."

"I couldn't, Mom. I had to deal with it my own way." I cleared my throat. "What I want to say is, my worldview is different. I don't know what you believe about God. And I'd love to talk about that. But you see how it puts us on different paths? I don't want it to be that way. My going or staying—whatever happens—please don't hold that against God. I chose it. And Dad, about my relationship with Dom—he's my boss and a Christian brother. But he's not my dad and never will be. You taught me everything about integrity and hard work and survival. One of the reasons I was able to accept God as my Heavenly Father is because I had you as a model."

CHAPTER 34

Wildness is a necessity.
—John Muir

Fall leaves were in full color. Rob came and we cooked dinner down by the lake. The stars came out in force, the air turning just this side of raw. He asked about the others, if they'd be coming. I wasn't sure, hadn't pressed for a commitment. I'd asked them to pray and think things through. Besides the logistics of making the fire and the meal, then cleanup using a leave-no-trace method, conversation was sparse and deep. Rob called it "stewin' the bones," good for what ails you.

With campfire smoke in our lungs and the gamey richness of venison stew in our bellies, we decided to sleep on the porch. I got a couple of Army cots, a pile of blankets. The only light came from the curtained living room window and a few security lights making pale pools on the Camp Mudj lawn.

Rob asked me, "Hey, what was that 'Pleiades-is-bound, Orion-is-loosed' thing?"

"Oh yeah. This is cool. You know the constellation Orion, the hunter? And the star cluster Pleiades, the seven sisters?"

"Sure."

I stepped out into the yard. Rob followed and we searched the sky. "There, above the horizon. They climb overhead through winter. A few years ago I stumbled on this verse in Job 38 that says, 'Can you bind the chains of the Pleiades or loose the cords of Orion?' God was speaking out of a storm, firing strong questions at Job about how nature works—just to show him who's boss. Questions like, 'Have you commanded the morning since your days began, and caused the dawn to know its place?' This is the same big section of Scripture with the passage about the Lotus. 'Under the lotus plants he lies…the lotuses conceal him in their shadow.' Referring to the mysterious beast. Remember?"

"How could I forget? Those chapters are full of weather stuff, too. Found it in my research."

"Well, I got curious. What does it mean that Pleiades is bound and Orion is loose? I went digging into astronomy and here it is. Only a few of the stars of the Pleiades are visible to the naked eye, but that faint blur in the sky is actually a cluster of 250 stars. Suns. It's unusual because, while most of the universe is spreading out in all directions, the stars in the Pleiades move through space together, at the same speed in the same direction. Pleiades is bound. The stars in Orion, on the other hand, are moving in opposite directions. Orion is loose. In a few thousand years it won't look like the hunter anymore. God made his point to Job with facts about these two constellations that mankind wouldn't grasp for thousands of years. It's one of many places in the Quella where poetry and history and science and theology collide." I laughed. "You probably already knew this."

"I didn't…but why would God give Job a science lesson he couldn't understand?"

"Job understood the basics, that he had no power over the stars. God's asking, 'Can you bind them and loose them like I can?' But yeah, for centuries no one would understand it. And all that time God's biding his time, thinking, 'Wait 'til they get a load of this.' I think God gets a charge out of you scientists. All kinds of truth in the Quella, man—the circle of the earth, foundations of the earth, the sequence of creation—light first, man last. No other creation story comes close. I'm sorry for what I said about your escha-weather research. You're right to be curious." We gazed at the night sky. I got a lump in my throat and went back to my cot on the porch.

Rob followed. "What do you think about the roaring of the sea, giant hailstones falling from the sky…"

"It's the living word, man. It's alive. That's going to happen."

"Literally?"

"Literal or figurative, symbolic or metaphorical—those are man-made constrictions on the Word. God can do it all at the same time if he wants. Take a tornado. Can it blow you away literally and figuratively at the same time? Can it be a metaphor for his judgment and symbolic proof of his powerful protection—if you escape it?"

Rob answered soberly, "Yeah. It can. All at once. That's actually sorta very creepy."

I hunkered into my blankets. "Creepy in the best way. It reaches into your soul and changes you. Dr. Eloise says that the Sword of the Lord is the only weapon that can cut you to ribbons and put you back together again."

· · · · ·

I woke up at dawn, went in to get breakfast, and brought it out in bowls.

Rob had heard the screen shut and was sitting up on his cot, sniffling and stretching. He received the bowl and muttered thanks. "Wasn't bad out here," he commented about sleeping on the porch. "D'you hear the frogs? I heard something rustling under the shrubs. I almost woke you up."

"Raccoons."

"You heard it?"

"Uh-huh." I hadn't slept much, wrestling with images. I'd

renounced the gods, but that's not to say they weren't waiting for me to drift into morbid curiosity again, to step over some invisible line. Images of Foster's death came back, too, my team members watching me scramble down the cliff, frantically calling for a copter even though he was already dead. Unable to keep a Dom-like composure. Lack of attention can kill. If it ever happened with one of the Mag Five, I wouldn't survive.

I sat Indian-style on my cot, inhaling the mist coming off Silver Lake, always and ever keeping watch over the camp, from the entry arch to the treehouses, for any out-of-place movement. If no one but Rob showed up today, I'd keep on helping Dad around camp, staying in the background like a half-hermit, skirting questions in town about what had happened to me. Afraid to date. Who'd be on my wave-length in Magdeline? I didn't fit anywhere. Life as a Camp Mudj firewood go-fer or head of the Mag Five, leading friends into the wild unknown with their lives in my hands—tedium or terror, those were my choices. *I need to find a church where no one knows me. Start over. Should I be Elijah or Geo? Or a third? Dr. E can advise.*

My Qolo team came to mind, waking in our tent in the cold before I'd struck out on my own…the warm fire, pancakes and honey, the friendly mama, Steven's and Karinna's concern, Suzanne's smirk. Dom had already sent out a memo to most of the team that I was alive but laying low. Suzanne could hear it through the grapevine for all I cared.

Crunching granola and scratching himself, Rob said, "I bet I look like sin on a soda cracker. I need a shower."

I laughed but was nervous about the morning. "The others won't be here for a couple hours. If they decide to come…"

"And I smell like a beach at low tide. It'll be good to see 'em," he added optimistically. "This month has flown. Hey, we should watch an old horror movie, like in our olden days, like 'The

Screaming Skull' or—

"No."

"Oh…right. Okay. In any event, I still have questions for you, Geo Telanoo, or whoever you are *really*. Cause you left Kim's Kozy in a bit of a rush."

"Ask away."

Friendly crunching and slurping followed. "So why did you reveal yourself to us at base camp? What convinced you to take the plunge?"

"The awful looks on your faces there, your pain at leaving with no answers. I saw the girls crying at the far end of base camp. I wanted more time, but I sensed that you were going to make a run for the cliff and try to get through. That sealed it. And when Marcus went off by himself behind the bus? He lost it, went down in the dirt and sobbed until I thought he'd hyper-ventilate."

"I didn't see that. You watched us? From where?"

"Various places. So despite my reservations—"

"—that we were there to trap you?"

"Not you, not necessarily. The agency or The Edifice using you. General paranoia. But you never know. Brother will turn against brother. I stayed in the same tent you were in." Responding to Rob's frown of doubt I added, "In that back room."

As lights went on in his head, I explained, "My previous team had stayed in that very tent. When you first arrived, and while your guide negotiated with the tent keepers, I was telling the base camp mama to bid low and get you. That you were secret friends and would be no trouble, but that I had to stay hidden. She loved our team from before and did what I asked. Then, while the others tried to sleep—with the baby having a bad night—I heard you leave. I stood behind the outhouse watching you. Mei came. You had a conversation."

Rob stirred his granola, reliving the scene. "So…that's what the mama meant when she said to me, 'I keep your secret.'"

I chuckled. "Man, I didn't know that. She almost gave me away? She didn't understand why I made myself sick to get on your bus, either."

Rob gathered his fingers to his forehead and made a gesture like he was tightening some loose bolts in his head. "Okay. Next question. The ION Task. What do you know about it?"

"Much less than you, and only after we got back. Dom said that in the past these high-level secret things used to be called *projects,* which means a list of tasks. Or called an *operation,* an ongoing series of procedures. If the name is any clue, the ION *Task* has one goal to accomplish with one big event to do it. That's worrisome to Dom. How are things at the TV station?"

"I'm walking on eggs. Afraid to do more checking."

"We need to get ourselves a trustworthy hacker."

"Elijah, who do you trust…now?"

"Who d'you think?"

"I dunno. Dom? Dr. Eloise? They know everything. What about Karinna and Steven?"

"Those four. That's about it at this point. You know, Dom had his doubts about your motives after he found out you weren't just coming to find me, but also poking into the ION Task." Now I had a question. "Tell me. If I'd been lost in the Australian Outback or the Carpathians, or someplace other than Qolo, would you have come?"

Rob understood the question: his real motive for going into Tufan. He struggled a minute before admitting, "I don't know."

It hurt a little, but I understood. I had to remind myself of the risks he took to bring the others along, knowing nothing of Tufan or my situation.

Rob pulled his blanket around him against the morning

chill. "I honestly don't think I could have let them pronounce you presumed dead and just go on tra-la, tra-la with my life. Especially after you met me in Cairo, so edgy and secretive. Then weather things started lining up in the eeriest way. I had suspected that one of the ION fields was moved to Tufan. You went missing in that very region. Reece's church was struck by lightning. That same week an EF-4 hit Walton, Kansas, and two churches were destroyed. An eyewitness was quoted on the news, saying, 'It looked like the hands of God were pulling it apart brick by brick.' I did some checking and the stats are uncanny—an inordinate amount of church buildings destroyed by weather-related disasters. I know most have steeples. That could account for lightning. I'm getting what you mean about literal and figurative…" he faded off.

"Did you come to a conclusion?" I asked.

He shrugged helplessly. "Is God doing it directly or will the world's troubles come from 'those who destroy the earth' as it says in Revelation? Are they people or spiritual forces? They say the ION Task is scientific tests, but it's an arms race, plain and simple, and the weapon is the weather. Did they orchestrate Hurricane Morgan? Can they guide lightning like God says he does in Job? Are the latest rumblings in the New Madrid fault line their doing? Oh, and get this. Similar, but much smaller ION experiments in the Magdeline Mountains—Magdeline! Now isn't that an eerie coincidence?—caused underground seismic activity years ago. What happens when you multiply the power of those earlier beam experiments by thousands?" He sat his bowl down with precision. For a second I saw a man of science in deep turmoil. "They're treating our planet like a plaything. Beyond the human toll, the second tsunami cut global automobile production, shut down power plants. And you know what else? A sizable percentage of nuclear plants are built near fault lines. Is it coincidence or an evil plot? I know I sound like a marginalized conspiracy crank." He dug into his breakfast.

"Not at all. As you say, he who controls the weather controls the world."

"Yeah, and as I said before, Revelation predicted that a third of all sea life will die, a statistic that marine biologists recently came up with in their models about coral reefs: thirty five percent could die off in the next century. It floored me. Famines and plagues, the churning of the sea—all of that. Is God doing it? Is the earth in some natural new phase? Is it The Edifice, or us polluters? Who exactly is behind it?"

"Does it matter?" My answer startled him. "The point is, he knows. And he shares his secrets with his sons and daughters."

Rob's intellectual rambling on the porch in early light with the smell of lake and woods cleared away more of my mental cobwebs. "I like hearing you brainstorm. It's reassuring." If no one else came it would be okay. It would. We sat back to watch the sun's rays filter through the woods.

"How's it reassuring?" he asked.

"You don't take things at face value. You investigate. Fewer and fewer folks do that. We're sheep. We follow any celebrity leader or news report with hardly a bleat."

The rising sun threw a ribbon of flame across the surface of the lake.

"What's the hardest thing about being back?" Rob asked after a while.

"Stores. Going to stores."

"Why?"

"Everything. Security cameras. Aisles and aisles of stuff. Just stuff. Tufanis starve and we have a whole aisle of cat and canary food. Garish colors and loud music. Sensory overload. You know what, it's similar to an Edifice torture technique: sensory blasting. We're slowing driving ourselves crazy. You know that trend to build tree houses in the woods, or give up city jobs for off-system shacks. Those people aren't the crazy ones. We are."

Rob looked worried.

"Mom thinks it'll help me get back into the swing of things to go into town, see people. But I go early before the crowds. When we do field training and you get a chance to flush your senses, you'll see what I mean."

"I never thought about it," Rob said after a pause. He respected my thoughts, even if they were uncomfortable. "What I observe as natural science, I think you see as a wild God's expression of himself. I was in a vortex once, in our storm chase vehicle. We call it the Peeler—steel framed, half-inch armor of layered rubber, steel, Kevlar; seven tons and top speed of 100 mph. We drive straight into EF-2s. Not a huge deal unless they suddenly grow. Anyway, I'm looking through the roof, debris dancing around hundreds of feet up and for a second I see clear blue. I wanted to stay in that eye, run with it, take the Peeler off-road, surrounded by destruction but unscathed. Time stood still."

I concurred. "Your mind operates so fast that time seems to slow down."

"Three seconds in a vortex is like an hour. Life is pure. You know what I mean? In that moment, it's just you and God and the wind. You'll have to go chasing with me sometime."

"I bet you revisit those moments in your head," I said.

"Oh yeah. It's my war story. Like your weeks with the nomads."

"When I was half-conscious, it felt like a lifetime."

"Did you think they'd kill you? I mean, were you scared?"

I didn't want to talk about it. "If you die, angels come get you. Whatever happens, it's okay. Hey, when you're in a tornado, can you run with it, really? Is that possible?"

"Not once the stabilizing spikes of the Peeler are in the ground.

And twisters change course without warning. You're liable to drive into a bridge abutment or flip into a ditch. We're working on one that will withstand an EF-5, up to 250 mph."

"That's insane."

Rob studied me. "Somewhere along the way in Tufan—maybe on the train—I started to see how you live in the storm's eye, always moving to stay in the sweet spot. In the zone you seem perfectly calm. I saw that a few times. But no one's timing is that perfect."

I smiled. "We're all in a dance with death."

"My storm chasing is not a death wish," he insisted.

"I know. Same here."

Something moved in the trees across the lake. I rose, crouching.

"What is it?" Rob whispered, following my gaze.

The thing came out of the shadows as a shadow itself. "Wow, it's a coywolf, a hybrid wolf/coyote moving down from the Northeast. Real survivors, they are. Dangerous. Remind me to tell Dad." I made mental note to myself: *apex predator, broad diet, flexible behavior, stealthy. Remember that for myself.*

Moments passed.

"The best way to find trouble is to go looking for it," Rob commented mischievously. "Chasers creed. Hey, what did Dom do with my instruments? I figured they're gone, but was afraid to contact him."

"He smashed 'em about a block from Kim's Kozy, and tossed them to an old lady cooking on the street. She threw the wad into her fire and hid us. Right before the police got there, she fished the thing out, wrapped it in foil and pitched it into a passing motorcycle cart."

"No kidding…You have people all over."

Commotion from inside the house. Dad was up making coffee. I asked Rob, "No one authorized you to study weather patterns on Qolo and write up a report, right?"

"Right," he said.

"Unauthorized is the same as non-compliance to The Edifice. You have a few things to learn about covering your tracks."

"Is The Edifice still following us?"

"There's no way to know, but I doubt it. It's a manpower problem. They're tracking millions for as many reasons. They suspect anyone who's gathering data. And they don't appreciate curiosity. But," I quoted Scripture, "'Do not call conspiracy all that this people calls conspiracy, and do not fear what they fear, nor be in dread.'"

"I'm not participating in any government scheme, just to be clear," Rob said strongly.

"I didn't say you were, and neither did Dom. I looked at his report. He noted that there was no steady stream of communication between you and anyone connected to the ION Task, just erratic browsing. Search patterns can reveal things. For a few days you were frantically looking into Qolo, then a couple of all nighters where you didn't let up. It's the regular or rhythmic communication between a person and an organization trying to shut us down, or signs that a person is sweeping up after himself, that's a problem. Dom scratched out a note to himself on the flight back, 'RW: over-researching nerd' and then a smiley face, and the words 'brilliant' and 'asset.' Dom never puts smiley faces on his reports. Never. You rate."

Rob grinned quizzically. "Sometimes I wonder if you and Dom are mishes or spies."

"Not too different, the way things are. We're dealing with spiritual forces who use human agents. But so are the feds, The Edifice, all governments, good and bad. They just don't see it that way."

"This sweeping up—you mean a person covering his tracks."

"Yeah but—"

Rob finished my thought, "—no one can disappear anymore."

I nodded.

"But you stayed gone for weeks."

"Remember when we were kids and we'd pass notes by rolling up a piece of paper and hiding it in a pen, then passing the pen? We're back to that."

"Low-tech com. High-tech cloaking."

"When possible. I had nothing but the Quella, and those were made without tracers until the company was shut down."

"One of these days your Quella will die."

"Yep. We'll be back to paper and leather."

Rob made a mental note. "So…you cut off all connection and traveled light out there in Tufan. That seemed to work. Okay. 'Nother question. What about that blister on your foot?"

"I sort of did what Dom's attempting with the echo feature on the triskele. I thought if I could switch locations quickly enough I'd throw them off my track. But only if I wasn't a passenger on any bus, train, or car. They'd think the guy at Qolo and the guy in YangDi couldn't be the same guy. I had a few passports…It's tricky, how to be two people, or three, and keep all the paper trails going. By the way, be ready not to eat for up to thirty days, and know how to get water."

"How far did you run?"

"I don't know. About forty miles."

"With half oxygen? Criminy." My cousin's expression clouded over, as if considering how much a new mission might cost him.

We finished eating. I took the bowls in. When we'd showered and dressed and turned our cots into couches, he asked gingerly. "You really don't know if Reece is coming?"

I shrugged.

He changed the subject. "Those rituals. The sky burials and

such…"

"Don't be curious. It's foolish. Don't open those doors. Tell everyone to stay in the light!" I sat down quickly. "Sorry."

"That's okay." Rob's brow wrinkled again, but couldn't let it rest. "I just wondered…"

I quoted their own book, "'He will cut out thy heart, pull out thy intestines, lick up thy brain…He will eat thy flesh and gnaw thy bones. But thou wilt be incapable of dying.' That's what their book promises, their lord of death."

Rob put up a hand, repulsed. "Okay," he muttered. "What's that even mean?"

"Whether it's literal or figurative or symbolic or a metaphor, or imagination or revelation…it's real, that's what. It's no fiction. Not a game. It's not a movie or stage play with prosthetics and makeup. It's real, Rob."

"Okay. Okay!"

I went on, enraged at the very thought that he'd bring it up. "'And in those days people will seek death and will not find it. They will long to die, but death will flee from them.' That's what *our* book says."

"Elijah, hey, I won't bring it up again."

Moments passed.

"Got a joke you can crack?" I asked, sorry I'd yelled.

"I can't think of any. Say, um, why was that scripture about every tribe and nation so important to you?"

"Two things. First, it has to be fulfilled. We're responsible for that. All of us. But second, when witnesses from every segment of society gather around the throne on that day, it's proof that all people had access to truth."

"The prophecy is the proof. Interesting." He thought on it a long while. "What's the plan, when the others get here…"

"We'll go into Gilead, check on The Armor."

"Cool."

Cautiously he asked, "Does it…you know, still bother you, about Reece?"

"It is what it is."

"Because if I had come home and Lydia had married someone else, and if he was treating her bad, you know, like what Greg did…"

"It's not my business. He's a pebble in my shoe."

Rob mulled over the phrase. "You mean he's a minor irritation? Or the farther you go, the deeper the wound and the bloodier you get?"

"I have bigger fish to fry. Hey, when I snapped a minute ago, it wasn't about…it's not about her."

"Sure," he said, then added philosophically, "There's a certain line from a play…It's a tragic love scene and the character is sort of in your situation, and he quotes Spurgeon in a soliloquy: 'The mind can descend far lower than the body, for there are bottomless pits. The flesh can bear only so many wounds, but the soul can bleed in a thousand ways and die over and over again each hour.'"

I smiled a little as a wave of darkness brushed past. "I'll live."

"You're a better man than I." He scrutinized me, making us both uncomfortable, then started digging into his rucksack for a razor and went back to a previous subject, a safe one. "You were there…in our very tent."

I nodded. "The readings you took, did they tell you what you wanted to know?"

"They told me what I didn't want to know, that apparently the military is gradually joining forces to manipulate the weather. Not for supremacy, but control."

"Which military?" I asked. Strangely it felt safer talking about global disaster than about a little blond girl who may or may not show up at Camp Mudj.

"I think there's only one military. The nation-against-nation conflicts are staged to keep us on edge, but I think it's becoming one power base, not to defend, but to control us…. You don't seem surprised."

"Jesus told us it would be this way."

Rob went in, got dressed, came back out. "One more question. And don't get angry, okay? One more question and I'll let it rest. Promise."

"All right."

"Well, I bought a lacy umbrella for Lydia. And when the sun shines through it, it throws the shadow of a creepy face on the ground. Those images, those posters on the streets of YangDi, what are they? Did people just make them up, because, yuck."

"The shamans claim to visit the realm of the dead."

"So they're real beings?"

"Yahweh says not to be curious about such things. And you just said it yourself, 'The mind can descend far lower than the body, for there are bottomless pits.'"

· · · · ·

Reece's mom dropped her off and followed her up on the porch to give me a long, strong hug. "It's so good to see you, Elijah. So good! Our prayers were answered in the best way!" Rachel Taylor, blond and beautiful like her daughter, kissed me on the cheek and left.

Rob ran in and brought out a mug of cocoa Mom had made. Reece had on a sweater, long gypsy skirt, and hiking boots, all in the golds and browns of autumn.

"Camouflage," I commented approvingly. My heart was light and too airy. Like a person's lungs on Qolo. A little hard to breathe. Well, I'd adjusted to life without much oxygen before. I could again.

She grinned about wearing camouflage. "I have to start thinking in new ways." She took the mug, thanked Rob, and sat on the rail looking out over the camp. "How are you guys? It's so pleasant on the porch."

Rob said, "We slept out here last night. I can't get my feral cousin indoors. Says he wants to feel the weather coming. I just did get him housebroken again."

I nodded at the sky. "We both like to watch the Creator work," then glanced at Rob. *You getting even for my snapping at you? Go ahead, be snarky. Embarrass me. I deserve it.*

Reece took a small pouch from her bag and handed it me. In the pouch was a red diamond stud and some cash.

"It's not yours. I sold yours. I didn't use all the money, so there's the change. I had one of my earrings altered to make a necklace. This is from the other one. We all should have a gem, to save a life, like you said back then."

"Thanks. How you doing?"

"Okay."

"Olivet?"

"Sweet as ever. My friend Brooklyn is keeping her for the day. Greg will pick her up later." Then she asked me uncertainly, "We're friends?"

"Always."

Rob looked like he wanted to disappear.

She sipped her cocoa. "I don't know what's going to happen…"

I spoke in generalities. "People make amends if they can. Preserving the family is good."

"Un huh," she agreed, taking in the view. "There's a mist rising over the lake."

"It's been lingering there for an hour," Rob said. "Humidity at"—he checked his weather clip—"a whopping 85%."

"Indian Summer," I said.

"I always loved that mist." Uncomfortably she said, "It's not good to hide things from your spouse. I kept the earrings hidden. It was a Mag Five secret, you know, impossible to explain without telling it all. He didn't want to hear about the Mag Five. Maybe I talked about it too much at the beginning. So many times I wanted to share it with him. Did either of you tell another person about the gem?"

Rob and I shook our heads in unison. He said, "Lydia doesn't know."

Recalling how I'd kept other deep secrets from Suzanne after I'd shared the wrong ones, I said, "I understand perfectly. None of this is your fault."

"My surgeries were expensive," she explained. "We struggled. All along I had the earrings. When he found them he was furious. I'd hid them in the base of a lamp." She turned to Rob. "Last night a thought popped in my head. Why was he looking in the hollow base of a lamp? Who'd peel off the bottom of a lamp, unless he was hiding things, too? What do you think?"

Rob, the one who'd been so good at hiding things from the rest of us, flushed guiltily.

Reece's mouth dropped open. "Oh, I didn't mean anything. I need smart friends to help me think it out, that's all." Then she looked at me directly. "It's not that I don't trust Greg. It's that he can't be trusted. You see the difference?"

"I do."

This was Reece as I remembered her, that edge and energy. The wildfire. When she thought we weren't looking, she made a little fist, kneaded the muscles in her thigh, and winced.

Marcus cycled in with a rucksack strapped to his back. He parked at the side of the house. He was bursting to say something, but took a mug from Rob's outstretched hand instead, and propped himself on the porch rail facing Reece. After a few sips he said, "I'm in."

"In?" she asked.

"Parabolani. Just starting. Long way to go. Dad's working his way out of the agency without them knowing. So we're both in, but working our way out. We'll get what we can in the way of data."

Reece beamed. "Marcus, I'm so happy for you!"

He wouldn't make eye contact with me, obviously wanting my reaction without appearing eager. But I already knew. "Excellent," I said. "Once you're both out, then what?"

"It may take a couple of years," he said. "After that, who knows?"

But we did know. All of us knew, and our hopeful faces showed it: a new thing, built on the old.

"Is Mei coming?" Reece asked me.

"I haven't heard from her."

Around ten o'clock a dark blue compact pulled into the camp parking lot close to the lodge. Mei got out. She'd parked there to look like a camp customer, not a visitor to my house. Always thinking ahead. She grabbed her rucksack from the trunk and looked in our direction. We four waved from the porch. She broke into a huge smile and waved back.

Rob announced, "We're all in."

"It never would have happened without you," I said gratefully, trotting down the front steps to greet Mei. A seven-year prayer that I'd never had the courage to pray—only wish—was answered. We were together again. Different, Rob had told me, as if we'd been separated to grow more alike. Mei's strength had emerged, like Reece's, maybe deeper. Rob had grown courage, Marcus had some of Rob's humility. Reece would regain the strength she lost. She would. And me...I didn't know, but I was here in one piece. That was enough.

CHAPTER 35

What is this road I'm on, and who goes with me?
I feel a long-way-off kind of love, and it calls to me gently.
—ANDREA SUMMER, "TRENCHES"

"We'll need these." I handed out the monocles as we sat in the shade of Great Oak, its red leaves overspreading us. "You strap it on to fit over one eye. If we need two lenses we can get them, but we'll make do with these for now. They're flip-downs, like when you go to the eye doctor. But one's for night vision, and you can switch on the infrared illuminator right there on the strap, above your ear. These will give you a 70-foot field at 200 feet, with click-ocular focusing. The others are magnifiers, two long distance and two for close work, in case you have to remove an implant or read micro-print. The lenses are low and medium power separately, and when you use them together, they're high powered. The long-distance one is also heat-sensitive. There are more sophisticated versions, but they have trackers embedded. This is the best we could do. Learn to switch out the lenses in darkness and in silence, and to combine them for the purpose needed. We'll practice in Gilead. It'll be jungle maneuvers, but without the boo hags."

Rob and Marcus were thrilled. The girls looked a little scared. Or maybe I imagined it. I assured them, "First you learn to walk while wearing the lenses. There's no danger except tripping over a rock and getting scabs on your knees. These cannot fall into the wrong hands, are we clear? It's frowned upon for civilians to have this kind of technology, and it's illegal to have ones without trackers built in. Keep them in a safe place."

Rob turned the monocle in his hand excitedly. "This is some crazy kind of missionary technology!"

"You're going to receive mid-level tech training for now: Quella, triskele, glyphs, monocles, and survival. Master those first."

"Why do we need these?" Reece asked.

"Night escapes or searches in total darkness. We don't know what we'll be doing—teaching children in Miami, healing the wounded in the jungles of Myanmar, outrunning troops in Paris. Mei, you could have used these on one of your rescues."

Rob adjusted his monocle and flipped on the infrared light. "The advantages of running in pitch-dark alleys without detection."

Mei's dark eyes sparkled. "This will be useful."

I handed out tiny leather bags, each one smaller than a deck of cards. "Medicine pouches. Here. Keep these oils with you at all times. They help with all kinds of infections and ailments. Instructions are with them."

Rob asked, "Steven and Karinna—are they high level?"

"He's low, she's mid," I answered. "Currently. We're all in flux."

"Who's high?" he asked.

"Hardly matters anymore with the big turnover. Dr. Eloise is top echelon. And Dom. They're the only ones now, in my book."

"Ah." Marcus pulled a letter out of his pocket. "From Dr. Eloise. It says to read it together." He tore it open. *"My dear, dear children! I praise the Almighty, our Author and Sustainer that you are alive and well! Elijah, you gave us a worry. I will come for a visit soon."*

Marcus grinned at me. "You. Big trouble." He read on, *"Marcus, congratulations on your appointment. We three—you, your father, and I—are navigating choppy waters, but for a short time. Use every moment wisely. Rob, you are in an excellent place, but I hope you realize there's little clear journalism anymore, just chatter and minutia, speculation and cleverly devised arguments."*

Rob solemnly agreed. "Exactly."

"Don't be swayed by the industry. I don't see their bias improving. Oh how wonderful is the world of The Edifice! How pathetic are conditions where their benevolent influence has yet to ooze."
Marcus looked up. "She's being sarcastic, if you didn't catch it."
He went back to reading. *"Reece, precious girl, continue to do the right thing. Evil cannot stand in the unswerving presence of good. When this becomes apparent to all parties, things will change quickly. Do not stay by yourself. Dear Mei, you are doing great work, and very quietly. Be wise and guard your privacy. And, sweet girl, when the old gods call you back, go to the one who sits on the throne. Tell him! He understands. All of you, he is your fortress. Regards, Eloise."*

Marcus apologized to Mei. "She grilled me about you. If I said too much, I'm sorry. Hey, by the way, Dad recruited those two special forces men he served with in the military. Peck and Yancy. We guys met them once, on the way to Farr Island. In the new arrangement he's working on, everyone will be in the field, each with his own gifts. No middle management and very little admin. For now we're free agents. Rogue. But I'll pretend that I'm not. Soon as we find a church that understands this and can oversee us, Dad'll feel better about the whole thing. Dr. E, too. It'll probably be an overseas church, one that knows the ins and outs of persecution."

Would the others mind if I took the lead? Rob had earned it, leading the search into Tufan. I caught his eye and nodded toward Gilead. "You want to lead?"

He considered it, then stood and struck a lofty pose: "Come, come, good cousin, be advised. I wonder very much, being a man of such great leading as you are, that you foresee not what impediments drag back our expedition if I shall traipse ahead."

Reece sighed. "Shakespeare. Oh, please."

"Miscreant," he muttered.

"Hold that pose, Wingate," Marcus said. "Forever."

Sappy, hokey kids again, embarrassing ourselves. But when they stood, I couldn't help but gather them in, squeezing them hard. "Thank God. Thank you all. A cord of five strands is not quickly broken."

Rob heaved a sigh. "Finally."

"I might need your help to clear my head some more," I confessed.

Reece chirped, "Then let's get going."

"And guess what, Reece? Shadow Bridge is still there, in Telanoo."

"I know."

Marcus pulled out of the group hug and saluted the sky. "Yes, Lawd. Yes, my people."

Rob looked at his weather clip. "Okay, well, that came out of nowhere—a big patch of red on radar heading right for us. One to two inches of precip. High winds. Half hour at best." He licked his index finger and stuck it up into the air. "My Official First Alert Storm Chaser Wind Digit says we should get cracking."

I slung my rucksack on my shoulder. "I have a stash of dry firewood, tarps, and food under an overhang in Gilead. But training means getting used to discomfort."

"What?" Rob whined, picking up his bag. "No plug-in for my hair dryer? What about my espresso machine…my Grill-Daddy…my Waffle-Mama…"

Thunder rumbled overhead.

We struck out, my mind's eye beyond Gilead. With friends, changeable skies, the wall-less-ness I'd grown accustomed to, and The Armor of God, I just might rid myself of those last stray and nameless demons.

I welcomed the western front—not the gentle mist Yah had sent at The Cedars, but boiling black clouds and earth-vibrating rumbles. Words of Elijah the prophet came, and I spoke them as my own. "'Let us go eat and drink, for there is the sound of heavy rain.'"

END

Burn the ships, we don't need them,
'Cause we aren't goin' back the way we came.
Burn the ships, 'cause where we're going
We've got roads to pave.

—MAE KLINGLER, "DRAGONS"

ABOUT THE AUTHOR

 **"Go far, Go light"** is Lena Wood's mission. She's an author, speaker, adventurer, mom of two, and grammy of seven. Lena's been **going far** her whole life: to Asia (seven times), South Africa, Egypt, and Ireland. She climbed Mt. Fuji, slept at Everest base camp, and recently emptied her bucket list on a 5600-mile drive across the US.

Going light means traveling light, seeking simplicity, and writing books that enlighten. And Lena uses her home, The Ridge, to host friends who share a passion for taking the light of Jesus to the uttermost.

Her *Elijah Creek & The Armor of God* series sprang from a desire to prepare kids—and adults—for the dark stuff. To that end, she became an unwitting expert on occult mysticism. She speaks on the topic around the country.